SPEED DATE WITH DESTINY

AN ASCENSION SOAP OPERA

MOOSLIE WIGGINS
AND
LUVIAJANE SWANSON

A
KUKUI PRODUCTIONS
PUBLICATION

ISBN 978-1-7323358-5-1

The characters and events in this book are fictitious. Any similarity to real persons, living or dead, is coincidental and not intended by the author.

Cover design by LuviaJane Swanson and Bruce Swanson,
    with inspiration from M. Kelley Hunter and Leonardo da Vinci

Drawings by LuviaJane Swanson

Book design by Bruce Swanson

Printed and bound in the United States
First edition

A Kukui Productions Publication

www.soulworksinc.com

Dedications

This book is dedicated to the Terry in us all...the uncomplicated, base and somewhat paranoid aspect of our psyches that often irks us and if we're fortunate, also makes us laugh.

Initiated in affectionate parody of the psycho-spiritual journey, we never considered that this story might traverse squirmy depths and complexities that could possibly resonate with real-life human experience.

Our wish is that if and whenever it does, it might also lead the reader through to the "other side," where Creative Works, Methods Division and all the diverse human subpersonalities mutually recognize and celebrate each other. As above, we say, so below.

—Mooslie Wiggins and
the Creative Works team

To Layla. Always Layla.

—LuviaJane Swanson

"People are going back and forth across the doorsill
where the two worlds touch. The door is round and open."

—Rumi

Acknowledgements

For invaluable editorial assistance and good advice, accolades and cheers go out to Bruce Swanson, John Nelson of Bookworks Literary Services, and Erin Murray.

Many others have also contributed in assorted ways as readers, friends, critics and sources of information and inspiration. You know who you are. To each of you—whether sporting a body or not—go our boundless gratitude and love.

— Mooslie and Luvia

CONTENTS

CAST OF PRINCIPAL CHARACTERS

The Human Lifestreams

Terry's family:

Terry Gillis	the human experiment
Bill Gillis	Terry's older brother
Fran Gillis	Bill's wife

Associates of Terry:

Cara	flute player; Dolores' best friend
Dolores	aka Madam D, director of psychic institute; Cara's best friend

At Ricki's Halfway:

Jim	Terry's roommate
Tull	therapist
Mira	transgender candidate
Wanda	massage therapist

* * *

Terry's Major Subpersonalities:

Aunt Ethel	critic
Chaz	bodyguard
Helen	fearful subdivision of an unnamed personality
Elaine	dominatrix

* * *

At Interdimensional Soul Works, Inc.

Methods Division
Terry's Team:

Snarrow	senior lightworker, team leader
Mabel	behavior specialist
Vormis	Terry's personal field guide
Pryluck	impulsive team member
Bulista	department intern

Others' guides:

Millicent	senior lightworker, leader of Cara's team
Forwyn	Dolores' personal field guide

Creative Works Unit:
Bouffant Head
Diamond Hoops
Mooslie Wiggins

What Came Before

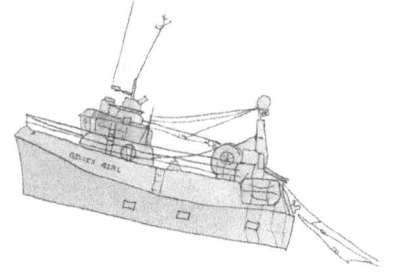

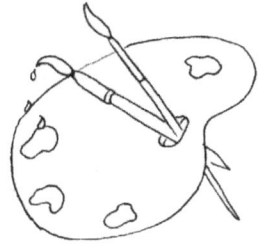

~ 1 ~

1962

Plucked from the warm, sweet fullness in which he had been steeping, Terry feels sharply sundered from the group of souls that was like one soul—like a blissful beehive or a nest of worms.

Unseen hands lift him high enough to view several softly illuminated bassinets arranged in a circle. An ornate, colorful tag adorns the foot of each bed. As one bassinet zooms into focus, Terry understands it will be his. He reads the tag:

Male

Level 1

Fisherman

He hears, "PUSH!" and then everything goes dark, cold and incredibly cramped. He's alone. And really mad. Where the flip is everyone?

Hands place him on his mother's breast—that's not so bad. And then, he smells fish.

A deep, male voice booms in his newly formed ears, "Can't wait to get this little nipper on deck. We could use another good hand."

Terry howls.

***

Beings composed of light—the attendants to incoming

souls—have retired for the day, leaving their ring of etheric bassinets bathed in a field of gentle, rose-colored light. The chamber resonates with the soothing drone of harmonic chords.

A sudden flash of muted light approaches one of the bassinets. The tag at the foot of the bed, which reads:

Male

Level 1

Fisherman

is furtively raised and flipped over. On its back side, chaotic multicolored strokes scrawl out:

Level 5

Artist

Experiment!

The tag is quickly righted. Resounding titters are abruptly shushed.

***

Terry, the incoming soul of the newborn "little nipper," sheds a gauzy fabric made from light, which had cloaked both himself and the prankster he'd just accompanied on their stealth mission to his bassinet.

Still clutching his guilty paintbrush, the spirited attendant claps Terry on the back. "Our little secret, OK?" A bit of electric blue paint drips from the brush, and pools on Terry's foot as the lightworker leans in close. "Go on now, you need to get yourself back into that cuddly new body of yours."

Terry gazes at the sleeping baby body that he supposedly, at some time—was he drunk—agreed to inhabit. Alright then. He cringes...in we go.

~ 2 ~

A small beam of light pauses on the threshold of Interdimensional Soul Works, Inc. The consciousness that calls itself Bulista has been singled out from scads of interviewees to intern in the Methods Division, where all spirit guides get their start. Nervous excitement about her first day on the job makes Bulista's efforts to steady her energy feel like an attempt to skipper a sailboat in gale force winds.

Two luminous forms emerge from a bright sphere that has materialized before her. An aroma of sugar cookies surrounds the first of these, which quickly assumes a round, gray-haired human sort of shape.

"Hello dear, I am called Mabel. And this is Snarrow, our department's senior lightworker."

Bulista admires the second light form, which shimmers close beside Mabel, emanating cool blue tones from a brilliant center, like a spiraling star. The field of light that surrounds the one called Snarrow flares brighter when he addresses the intern.

"Welcome to Methods, Bulista. Mabel and I will show you around the department. Of course, you may freely interact with whomever you'd like, but Mabel will function as your mentor for the duration of your internship."

Bulista is relieved that Mabel, and not Snarrow, will be her mentor. Snarrow is pleasant enough, but something about him—perhaps his official-sounding introduction—puts her on edge.

Snarrow continues, "Our department is composed of several guidance teams that attend to souls who have chosen to incarnate into human bodies." He widens the scope of his mind to illuminate for Bulista a bird's eye view of the Methods Division. Clusters of bright, multicolored light-forms are arranged in radiant, geometric patterns.

"These are our teams," Snarrow explains. "Each team is responsible for overseeing the lifespan of one or more individual ray-projections."

Bulista freezes. Up until now, throughout the rigorous application process—including each of several interviews—she has successfully concealed her phobia about company jargon. Nevertheless, first hour on the job and it's surfaced like a leviathan in her mind-field. She knows she can succeed in the role of spirit guide—after all, didn't she waft to the top of a huge field of candidates? But, technical terms have never been her forte. She prays she won't lose this coveted position at Soul Works before she's even had a chance to prove herself.

Mabel rescues the moment. "Come, dear, I will show you how ray-projections are created. The teams of lightworkers you see here," she explains, gesturing toward the bright, geometrically arranged clusters, "guide a group of linked souls. You could think of these groups as being kind of like soul families. If you look closely, you will notice that each soul group consists of several individual rays of light."

Upon closer inspection, Bulista can see that each team of lightworkers surrounds a colorful network of intertwining strands. These strands must be the light rays that Mabel is referring to. Which would mean that the whole clump together constitutes a single soul group. Her insight is affirmed by a sharp intensification of light within the golden field surrounding Mabel.

"When a soul decides to divide itself, it sends out—or

projects—one of these light rays, which then eventually embodies into 3-D human form. We, at Methods, regulate the life expression of these ray-projections. Is that better, dear?"

Bulista's light-field tinges pink. "What's the difference," she ventures, *"between a ray-projection and a human being?"*

"Why, none at all, dear." Mabel emits a blast of sugar cookie scent, the telltale sign that her curiosity has been piqued. "Although," she reconsiders, "I suppose you could think of 'ray-projection' as what a human lifestream originates from, whereas 'human being' is what the human lifestream perceives itself to be."

"Um...what is a lifestream?"

"It is all the same, Bulista," Mabel sighs. "Lifestream, ray-projection, human being...please do not worry, you will do fine here. Simply listen for the essence of the words; you really must not stumble over terminology."

1968

"Happy birthday to you..."

Without waiting for the birthday song to end, six-year old Terry Gillis blew out the candles on his baby brother's cake. With a quick glance toward his mother, he swiped a finger-full of thick, sea foam frosting and ran.

Maddy Gillis leaned across Terry's empty chair to grasp her husband's arm. "He still hasn't adjusted to having a younger brother. Don't be too hard on him."

Terry's fish-redolent father turned to face his wife. His broad, choleric features, embossed by wind-parched skin, congealed in a scowl. Hands gnarled from years of wrestling briny ropes and nets pushed his long frame away from the table. "That's no excuse. The older boy never had this kind of problem.

This one needs discipline."

Maddy sighed. The older boy, Bill—at not even ten years of age—had already been consigned to work each weekend on the family's fishing vessel. But Bill, she thought, would turn out OK. He neither possessed Terry's sweet, creative nature nor his stubborn sense of independence. She feared how her husband's old-world austerity might impact the younger boy.

Terry reached under the bed after his father had left the room. His bottom ached from where he'd been spanked; his heart ached from the loss of his best crayon box. He confirmed that a small collection of mostly broken crayons was still tucked away under the bed. But the box that Dad had confiscated held the whole rainbow assortment of sixty-four Crayola colors.

What's more, Dad had pronounced that as of Saturday, Terry would have to "man up" and go to work on the fishing boat each weekend, alongside his nine-year old brother Bill. While Terry hardly considered the prospect of spending weekends on the water any punishment at all, it crushed him to see his most detailed, true-to-fantasy version of a blue and green winged giant torn from the wall, crumpled and tossed in the trash.

***

A capricious spirit guide called Pryluck ticks his disappointment. That human child he'd had a little fun with during birth is turning out to be rather a bore. Not that he'd ever really expected that their pranked upgrade of the child's destiny tag would in fact make a difference, or that the rest of the kid's guidance team would even notice the switch. But still, Terry had—at least at the time—shown some spirit. Nevertheless, it has become apparent that the poor soul must remain anchored to the monotonous drudgery of Level I human consciousness after all.

Pryluck summons Terry's personal spirit guide—the one whose job it will now be to comfort the boy in the wake of his father's "discipline."

1987

Shouts of laughter erupted over the incessant din of wind. Clothed in heavy rain pants, suspenders and rugged rubber boots, with his head thrown back and chest full, Terry roared. On the deck of his family's wooden trawler, he'd been swapping fish jokes with a group of fifth graders from a school community outreach program.

"What did the boy octopus say to the girl octopus? I want to hold your hand, hand, hand, hand, hand, hand, hand, hand."

The teacher shepherding the group, a tight-jawed gal who Terry judged could not be more than his own age of twenty-five, shivered and clutched her parka to her sides as if she was more accustomed to Hawaii or someplace equally mild.

"OK everybody, listen up," she insisted. "Does anyone have any final questions for Mr. Gillis about his job or the tour of the boat he just gave you?"

A small boy, all but swamped in rain gear, raised his hand. "How do you make an octopus laugh? With ten-tickles."

Stealing a glance at the fractious teacher, Terry couldn't help himself. "What was the tsar of Russia's favorite dish? Tsardines."

After the last of the school kids had been loaded into their van, Terry turned to the teacher with a wide open smile, and reached for a handshake. His eyes were the same shifting color as the sea.

She shrank a little further into herself in an ill-humored attempt to evade this onslaught of high-spirited vitality.

"Thanks for bringing your class," he said, holding onto her hand a bit longer than necessary, and chafing it with his other broad, fishy paw. "Your hands are cold, you should wear wool gloves or something."

The teacher extracted her hand, puckering as if she'd taken a swig of pickle juice.

Terry grinned at the kids, and returned their waves through the van windows.

***

"Departments here at Interdimensional Soul Works are arranged in a trinity," recites Mabel, with intern Bulista in tow.

Bulista has arrived at Methods Division this morning, fresh and determined to maintain her composure throughout this second orientation session.

"First we have Management, then there is the Creative Works Unit, and finally..." Mabel's light flares wide to encompass the surrounding expanse. "...our very own Methods Division." A sugary fragrance erupts as Mabel marvels, "Why, Methods itself is a trinity! Lightworkers in our department occupy three distinct positions.

The techno-conductors over there," she gestures, "are upper level spirit guides who design operational programming for individual human lifestreams. They pretty much keep to themselves." Mabel's voice drops to a whisper. "Snarrow and I suspect that the technies collaborate quite freely with our Creative Works Unit, although neither party would admit to it. All of them can be exasperating, really."

Bulista notices blotches of canary yellow light, moving in rhythmic patterns in the region that Mabel has indicated. "What are the, uh...technies, doing?"

Mabel tosses her simulated hands. Not only do the hands appear amply wrinkled, they show evidence of brown spotted sun damage. A nice touch, Bulista has to admit, for a guide who has never experienced the ins and outs of life in a human body.

"Who knows, exactly? The technies almost never communicate with us directly. Most often, we receive their data via memos—things like programming updates and such—which help us keep our activities coordinated with the soul goals for each lifestream in our charge."

Mabel's field clouds. "A warning, dear: Creative Works typically attends to matters on a much vaster scale than we here in Methods do, but you never can tell with them. If you find the technies eccentric, you certainly do not want to get too near Creative Works. They will drive you mad, and enjoy doing it. CW Workers do not maintain individual forms or characters, but they do love to pretend. They will imitate or fabricate anyone and anything."

She takes a breath and her field brightens. "Now, the second category of spirit guides within Methods Division includes lightworkers such as Snarrow and myself. We are responsible for executing those programs that the technies—and perhaps Creative Works—design. But since our frequencies, like your own, are too high to interface directly with the human lifestreams, Soul Works also employs a third category of guides."

"Follow me, dear," Mabel urges, ushering Bulista into a narrow corridor. "I will show you how this last third of Methods operates."

They drift single file through the dim lit corridor as Mabel continues her briefing. "The lightworkers you shall see here are *lower-level spirit guides who are able to function within the human energy field. You shall hear them referred to as 'field guides.' Every human lifestream has its own personal field guide who serves as a companion and assistant throughout its lifespan."*

The corridor opens onto an observatory, where the activities of several human beings, the so-called "lifestreams," can be seen. The lifestreams' forms seem to waver, as if viewed through several feet of water from a glass bottom boat.

Bulista draws a sharp breath. Her field scintillates with excitement. "I've never seen a human lifestream before," she gushes. "They're less solid than I expected."

"Well, of course you cannot view them from their own dimension." Mabel squints and tilts her head. "I suppose the dimensional phase shift does distort their appearance." Noting the intern's disappointment she adds, "We can only take the field guides' word about the solidity of 3-D."

"But," Bulista whispers, "that's what I was hoping to do here. I want to work with the lifestreams."

"My dear, no lightworker who has never taken human form can be a field guide. You would simply not be capable of achieving sufficient density to match and blend with a human energy field."

Bulista lingers wistfully, watching as one field guide flits brightly about his lifestream's head, while the lifestream—a female child—cries and fusses. Moving deeper now inside the child's energy field, the guide conjures clouds of butterflies, which distract the girl from her snit. She quiets and sleeps.

A second—adult male—lifestream pauses to contemplate the section of a shark's head that he has been tattooing onto his client's forearm. Within that pause, the tattooist's field guide projects a brief flash of an image, revealing details of the shark's shape and color scheme onto as-yet un-inked skin. In an apparent rush of inspiration, the lifestream then adds color to that very spot.

After observing several similar incidents, Bulista asks, "Why is that lifestream so rude?"

"What do you mean?"

"He totally ignores the guide who is helping him draw!"

"Lifestreams are not normally conscious of their guides' existence, at least not until they have attained the higher levels of frequency that approach our own. The tattoo artist here is only a Level 3 human. By comparison, his field guide would be the equivalent of a Level 8—if the human scale even went that high, which it does not. The rest of us guides might be considered Levels 10 and above.

"But, as you can see, even relatively unconscious lifestreams—such as this Level 3 tattoo artist—derive great comfort and benefit from their guides' presence. Field guides create an invaluable bridge between our light world and the lifestreams' embodied existence. It can be a very rewarding job...as can ours, dear."

1998

"Cut it out! Mom, Alex won't stop hitting me."

Fran Gillis—the new wife of Terry's older brother, Bill—shifted the straw basket she was carrying to her other hand, and called out to her nephew, "Alex, leave your sister alone. And don't bother your mom. She's helping Uncle Bill's mother down the stairs. Why don't you go up and help her? She'd love that."

"Mom says there's nothing wrong with Uncle Bill's mother."

Aunt Fran tried not to laugh. Her mother-in-law—aka

Uncle Bill's mother—was in fact not a bit less robust than any of her seafaring brood, the whole of which was making an en masse assault on Lockside Park for a joint-family picnic.

A Frisbee sailed over Fran's head. The words "Go out long for it!" registered just before the inevitable stampede of long-limbed, brawny men and shrieking kids swirled past her on the rhododendron-lined path.

Fran set down her basket of supplies, and turned back up the path to retrieve another load from the car. "Almost there," she encouraged her mother-in-law who, holding fast to Fran's sister's arm, had made it down the fieldstone steps.

"My knees are acting up today. It affects my balance." Maddy Gillis skewered Fran with arresting blue eyes that dared anyone to doubt the veracity of her story.

"Well, hang in there. Terry has made a nice seat for you under that big magnolia tree."

Maddy Gillis' son Terry had also made a very Terry-esque proposal to modify the horseshoes game that was already in full swing. In his version, adult players would up the ante of the game by tossing a boat anchor in place of a horseshoe. Kids, of course, would be exempt. Terry's younger brother Fred scoffed, tossed his horseshoe and scored a leaner.

"What a bunch of wusses." Terry shoved Fred aside, aimed and threw a twenty-pound plow anchor that he had evidently carried down the stairs from his truck, which was parked in the lot above. The anchor landed nearly halfway across the horseshoe pit.

Bill laughed. "Wusses, huh? You call that a toss?"

To Fran's dismay, Bill retrieved the anchor, and positioned

himself at the throw line. "Bill, don't be stupid," she warned.

He heaved, and the anchor landed just shy of Terry's attempt. Both brothers roared, and neither tried a second time.

~ 3 ~

The Methods Division of Interdimensional Soul Works, Inc reverberates with an incoming message of encoded light. Receiving the memo, Snarrow's personal emanation—normally a modest blue swirl—is suddenly a chaos of shuffling shades and hues.

Hovering close by and fairly reeking of sugar cookies, Mabel extends her own tawny light field, in hopes of perusing the newly arrived message. She sighs. Despite Snarrow's agitation, he is well shielded, as always. Mabel can detect nothing more than that the memo has originated at the very highest level of Management, only to arrive in Methods headquarters after making its way down the chain of command via the company's Creative Works Unit.

Recovering from his initial shock, Snarrow opens his mind, permitting Mabel to view the enigmatic message. Her stunned silence matches his own.

One by one, other lightworkers drift into Mabel and Snarrow's sphere to examine the memo, until an incredulous aura pervades Methods.

Rookie spirit guide, Vormis, bounds in, graceful as a puppy at a funeral. "Hey, you guys…" He reels backwards upon colliding with the thick milieu. As a relatively new lightworker, Vormis' transmit and receive skills are hardly sufficient to identify much more than general impressions. In this case, that is more than enough to stifle his chatter.

Snarrow calls an on the spot emergency strategy meeting of all Methods Division personnel. Two swift lightworkers are sent to round up the field guides. Promptly, luminously, they filter into Methods headquarters.

Snarrow addresses the assemblage. "So this is it," he begins. "We have received a 'not to be contested or reversed' memo. We are to oversee a non-regulation person transfer."

"And what's the big deal?" A veteran lightworker wonders, sending an orange blush throughout the communal field.

A small beam of light flickers at the periphery of the group, where Bulista is struggling to keep up. She gulps and takes a chance. "Excuse me, can you please explain the term 'person transfer?'"

The collective field curdles while everyone waits to see how Snarrow will respond. This latest intern is still quite new to Methods Division, but even so. The basics never seem to stick with this one.

"OK then, once more," Snarrow obliges. "Normal procedure is that a single persona is built and cultivated throughout a ray projection's—otherwise known as a human lifestream's—lifespan. We coordinate several of these ray projections within the same soul group.

"The way it works is that each body/mind complex is programmed to manifest a particular personality type in tandem with all the others in their group. We refer to these concurrent lifestreams as 'parallels,' for obvious reasons." Snarrow peers closely at the intern, making sure that she does in fact find the

reasons obvious, before he continues.

Despite her best effort to assimilate Snarrow's narrative, Bulista's field has begun to fray, as it does whenever he tries to explain anything at all. She doesn't know what it is about Snarrow that makes it seem to her that he speaks in gibberish. The worst of it is that this aberration of hers has escalated in the weeks since her initial orientation at Soul Works.

Mabel notes Snarrow's gray and spiky field, but before he can resume his presentation to the group, she demands, "Vormis, have you finished with the Guide Manual yet? I believe this would be an excellent time to pass it on to Bulista. Just as soon as you can, dear."

"Is that manual still kicking around?" a veteran guide wonders. "Didn't we receive a notice—eons ago—that it was to be eliminated?"

"Well, I kept a copy for the rookies. It made no sense at all to eliminate such a useful reference."

Empathy for a trickling exodus of bored co-Workers grips Snarrow. He adeptly refocuses his own field and doggedly spells out, "The idea is that each human lifestream gains experience, learns pre-chosen lessons and, hopefully, makes strides toward expanding their worldview and self-concept. Finally, when their natural program lives itself out, or at the time of image-destruct— the human lifestreams call it 'death'—any information gleaned from that life is transferred to the other parallels in the group by means of typical download procedures. It is simple, standard methodology from which the whole soul collective benefits."

Mabel has by now discerned that the intern's impediment has more to do with Snarrow's delivery than with what he actually says. She faces Bulista. "'Person transfer,' dear, is simply the information transfer or shift of accumulated experience from one human being's lifespan to all parallel lifestreams within their own soul group. This transfer occurs when the soul drops its body, and the lifestream experiences what it considers death. It is a method of education and growth for the entire soul group."

Snarrow pauses until he is certain that Mabel has finally finished. "However," he underscores with a vermillion flare, "according to this memo, someone within one of our soul collectives is to undergo a person transfer in mid-lifestream. With no body drop. Not even a ray-projection exchange is to occur, as would be the case with a walk-in."

He swells to address the whole group. "This lifestream is to remain conscious throughout the whole process. We peel off and deprogram the former character. It experiences—consciously— the whole of nervous system stripping, mental wind down and emotional deprogramming. In other words, we essentially 'image destruct' the persona while maintaining physical structure intact. Oh, and they ask us please to avoid lapses in his reality perception."

A lemon yellow field guide chokes. "Change people midstream with full awareness, no psychosis please?"

"Exactly," Snarrow sighs. "But that's just phase I. We will need to re-template the entire circuitry to insert and run the new person's data. Without a body drop, we are in for behavioral training hell."

Mabel comes to attention. Behavior is her area. "Self-identification repatterning for someone with conscious memory of their former self? Is it possible?" she considers, loosing another oven fresh waft. "We would have to do something with all of the old thought forms."

Snarrow agrees. "Creative Works has this idea for a thought form and subpersonality reprogramming institute—something like a rehab center for the subs."

A jaded field guide emits the hue and tang of a clogged storm drain. "So, we're to endure the exhaustive rigmarole of reprogramming habit patterns, beliefs, values, postural styles... for what? To satisfy some fart-blowing jerks in Creative Works?"

Mabel steals a glance at Bulista. If the intern's scant, wavering light is any indication, they will all have to endure yet another digression. She marvels at how one so spectacularly gifted in perceptual acuity, as Bulista seems to be, can be so dense when it comes to learning and remembering language and procedural concepts. She is about to attempt another explanation, when Vormis reappears with the guide manual.

He flips to the entry about subpersonalities, and reads aloud. "The personality of an average human lifestream is essentially a composite of several, often conflicting, fragments. Each fragment is like a distinct person within a person. Although a mere sliver of a larger composite being, each subpersonality thinks and operates as if it is the complete individual. Consequently, a sub's sense of reality is quite limited."

Snarrow momentarily quivers out of visible range before coalescing beside Vormis and Mabel. His field settles into a watery, powder blue motif. "I think we would all agree that this project bears the stamp of Creative Works. They must never have thought that Management would actually go along with the idea, but here we are."

Sidling up to Bulista, he adds, "Our department oversees the soul collective that Creative Works, or whomever, has decided to reconfigure. So, as long as Management continues to support

CW—or whomever's—intent for this project, it is our job to design and execute the methods of operation."

"The problem, dear," Mabel adds, "is that the lifestream in question has already been fully programmed to run according to standard protocol, but we are now supposed to create and superimpose a whole new set of programs without so much as a hard drive crash. We have no technology in place to do it, and no leeway for experimentation error. Creative Works is opposed to scientific method. They are 'try it and see' all the way. Management adds the 'no damage' clause."

"I like the idea," murmurs the intern.

A disturbance of light ripples softly through the room.

***

As a boy, Terry Gillis dreamed of superheroes. If, at six years of age, Terry had ever been inclined to dissect his thoughts enough to consider their underlying motives, he would have discovered that a superhero—any superhero would do, he didn't play favorites—would have been the closest thing to a personal role model he could have come up with. Not that he ever would have. Terry's primary objective was to be bigger than life: stronger, faster and morally better.

At age thirty-six, and having gained not a whiff of self-awareness, it had never occurred to Terry to amend his action film inspired values. Like a joke or cliché, the gist of which he would never get, Terry Gillis walks into a bar.

I

The Problem

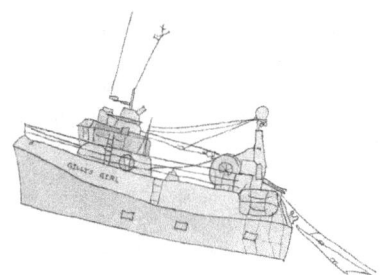

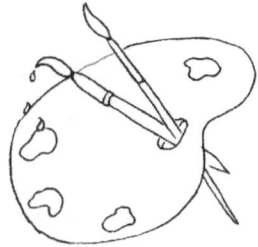

~ 1 ~

A small, but audible, grunt managed to escape as Terry Gillis heaved a crate of ice packed rockfish from the deck of the dockside Gilli's Girl. He pulled himself together in an instant, setting his ruddy face in a smirk and forcing his work-hardened body to assume its habitual taut swagger.

Embellishing a second grunt, Terry winced at the fishy seaside odor—precisely the same marine scent he had breathed with gusto each day of his thirty-six years. "This stuff stinks, I gotta get some fresh air."

Pacing once around the waiting delivery truck, Terry swore under his breath, praying that this charade would mask the fierce spasm that had hijacked his left hip, threatening to bring him to the ground. Another one! These episodes were getting harder to hide.

Before his legs started fizzling on him, Terry could always count on a rush of euphoria from hauling nets and lifting crates on Gilli's Girl, the wooden trawler that had been his family's lifeblood for the last two generations. Lately, though, he'd be sore and tired after a day of fishing. He had begun volunteering more often for delivery runs in lieu of boat trips, but these days even loading and unloading the truck could trigger a crisis.

Parading now around the vehicle, Terry made a silent emergency call to the Lord. "Dear Father," he mouthed.

"Bless my brothers and me with good sales today. And bless our family with good health. And Lord, I'm begging now, You've gotta remove this curse from my legs. I know I haven't always been strong in my commitment to You, but I swear I'll do better. Just help me get this truck loaded. Amen."

Terry's 911 calls to Above were becoming more frequent, as were his stops at The Oyster's Pearl Tavern on the way home from work. These in turn led—aside from a rapidly enlarging paunch—to beery midnight prayers à la "Dear Father, Please forgive my weakness. I promise I'll be true to Your cause and do my best to resist Satan's temptations..."

Terry's favorite of Satan's temptations was, at present, the twenty four year old barmaid at The Oyster's Pearl. Half Aleutian, disarmingly solid and sultry, her smoky voice cut through to his spine and stuck as unrelenting as beach sand in his shorts. That was just when she spoke. Ever since he heard her sing one night at The Oyster's talent show, he was helplessly and unrequitedly hooked. Her name was Suzanne.

By the time Terry made it back to the stack of crates, his older brother Bill had jumped down to the dock to help load. Bill had been surreptitiously watching the change in Terry for some time. Something was clearly troubling him. "Meet me at The Oyster after deliveries?" he asked.

"Yeah, alright."

The Oyster's Pearl was quiet for a Thursday. Terry's stool at the far corner of the bar was vacant. He settled in, his heart jumping at Suzanne's nodded greeting. Damn! That buzzard-faced manager Dave was hovering behind her. Under his stingy watch, Suzanne would be all brisk and business. Left to her own nature, she would be more attentive and personal...sometimes even flirtatious.

Terry ordered his schooner and glanced at the clock. Almost 6:00. He was surprised that Bill would suggest meeting for a beer. Ever since Fran had the baby, she complained if Bill did not come right home after work. Maybe something was up with Fran and him.

Suzanne reached over with a rag to wipe up a spill. Terry's sea-green eyes devoured the sight of her shirt pulled tight across her back, coming untucked a little at the waist. His breath contracted.

"Hey, buddy." The slap of Bill's hand was a rude ride back to reality.

"Hey."

"Refill?"

"Yeah."

"So what happened out on the dock today?" Bill's direct gaze compelled Terry's eyes to meet his.

Terry looked away. "What do you mean?"

"You don't act like you're into work lately. What's up?"

"Nothing's up."

"Well, are you gonna be on the boat tomorrow?"

"I don't know."

Bill silently stood his ground until Terry finally shrugged. "Maybe I will."

A small herd of university students tumbled in the door and clamored past the bar. Shouts of laughter surged in their wake.

Bill's lower lip pressed upward, wrinkling his chin in a gesture as familiar to Terry as his brother's insistent gaze. Bill was clearly bothered about something. "Fran and the kid OK?" Terry wondered.

"Yeah, we're fine. You got someone these days?"

"Nah, not really." His eyes followed Suzanne down the bar.

"Well, what's eating you then?"

Terry met Bill's stare and felt a sudden, hot threat of tears. He blinked and focused on a passing woman's rear. "Who says there's anything wrong?"

Bill's gaze never left Terry's face. "Not me."

The brothers locked eyes: two identically matched sets that seemed to absorb and reflect cool ocean depths. After several seconds, Terry closed his. "I'm not feeling right sometimes, Bill."

Bill's breath exploded. "What's up?" He strained to hear his brother's reply over an ambient mix of conversation, music and assorted barroom clanks and thumps.

"My legs feel sore all the time. Weak some days. And I get tired too fast."

"Yo, Gillis!" Terry and Bill both scanned the room. A stocky, dark-haired man was gesturing with a handful of darts in his upraised hand. "You in?"

As if a switch had been thrown, Terry lurched into form. He pushed back from the bar, draining his beer as he stood.

Bill sat back to watch his little brother's persona inflate to match the power of his stride, his manufactured brand of potent presence certain to draw the eye.

"Who's playing?" Terry hollered. "I'll take you two on one."

Bill smiled, shook his head and headed for the door.

~ 2 ~

The new field guide, Vormis, has been trying in vain to make contact with Terry, his first solo charge. As Terry's personal field guide, Vormis is most likely of the lightworkers to establish and maintain a necessary bridge between Terry's consciousness and theirs. But this lifestream has been freaking over nothing. His body is mobilized for attack, even though all they've done so far is to slightly amp up his frequency.

Vormis' energy field emits a brief, high-pitched hum. "I'm out of ideas," he tells the others. "This guy is defensive even in his sleep. And now his nerves are getting all touchy. When I approach, he awakens having an anxiety attack. I think he believes we're the devil."

"Oh, the Christian myth?" Mabel muses. "Perhaps you could appear in a form he recognizes as friendly...they like angels, don't they?"

* * *

Terry, dreaming: despair like black clouds, like billowing smoke is pressing in, filling his nostrils, oppressing his chest. He tries to breathe. No air comes, only black substance. He clutches his throat, gasps, gags. The body struggles, heart racing, pressure building...

"Pull him out of it, Vormis!" The committee of lightworkers assigned to Terry for round the clock monitoring observes anxiously. None but a field guide can get in close enough to Terry's energy field to exert a direct influence, and rookie Vormis has no experienced backup at the moment.

His field squeaks. "I can't reach him!"

Snarrow appears and takes in the crisis. Terry is beset by night terror, with stabilization Workers on duty apparently unable to infiltrate the dream or to even make a "rescue," which would have involved an abrupt, gross snatch of his mind to a different plane of consciousness—the psychic equivalent of a dope slap. If they could effect such a rescue, the insertion of Terry's awareness into an alternate, manufactured, dream sequence might allow his physical and emotional aspects to re-integrate with the mind. Not orthodox procedure by any means, but effective enough in most emergencies.

Terry, however, is in an odd state. Although he has never before been consciously aware of his guides' presence, he has at least been amenable to comfort, along with a limited measure of guidance. In fact, prior to the initiation of this new project, Vormis and Terry had made a fine team.

Fully aware of his role as liaison between his own light world and the 3-D world of his human charge, Vormis has practiced diligently to become proficient at stablizing channels of communiction between himself and Terry. And, he continues to refine his self-regulation skills. If mastering the squeak in his energy field is proving problematic, well, that's not a major flaw. But ever since the initial stages of Terry's frequency shifts, the entire team of lightworkers is having trouble maintaining even simple contact.

Mabel shakes her head, suffusing Methods with a burst of eau de cookie. "His response should be just the opposite: higher frequency, less density, greater receptivity. I don't get it."

Vormis flickers. "I still can't get in, I think we're losing him."

An ancient guide, just in from field duty accompanying his primary lifestream on a bird watching expedition, wafts over.

"Vormis, you're a field guide. Stop thinking from this dimension and blend with your human. Remember what it's like to panic?"

Vormis titters, realizing that his higher frequency co-Workers have never experienced the actual sensation. With careful focus, he manages to silence the hum in his field, to allow his awareness to drift down far enough into Terry's energy body to touch with a shadowy, half-remembered sense of emotion. Only then does he begin to experience the uniquely human sense of separation, isolation, of feeling enclosed within a physical body... helpless, afraid and defended.

As if from a distance he hears Mabel's thought, "This dear human is suffocating in despair and he is panicking. Imagine what might reassure him."

A shimmer passes among the other lightworkers. What does she think they've been doing? They've already tried inserting every comforting image they can think of into the dream, but Terry's consciousness remains inaccessible—despite the host of angelic thought-forms that now hover all around his bed.

From his deep rapport within Terry's emotional body, Vormis begins to perceive the image of a child curling into itself like a frightened caterpillar. He sees the black, smoky substance moving in to block and seal off each of that child's senses. "Of course, that's it! Terry's program experiences the higher frequencies as an invading force. With no avenue for escape, the body's defenses pull him inward for protection."

Vormis matches and blends his own frequency with Terry's energy field. Thus undetected, he can now head straight into the center of contraction, where pain permeates a vast black emptiness. He reaches out to his co-Workers, drawing their gentle, warm light in to where he rests at the depth of Terry's core. The

Workers all follow suit, sending in a steady, thin stream of light.

Instead of endless darkness, Terry's involution now brings him to this custom designed, toned down frequency of light and love. The lightworkers watch with breaths held as his body's tension begins to drop, its functions slacken and the crisis passes.

~ 3 ~

The Oyster's Pearl was abuzz with Saturday night's crowd. A loud darts game competed with the trio of street musicians that had moved their retro-rock just inside the door. Terry considered their oldies sound a welcome change from the bar's usual jazz CDs. He also thought the blond flute player might be warming up to him.

She was dressed like a gypsy or a flower child, in layers of skirts, toe rings, earrings and bangles. Her breasts, eyes and hair were alive and free. Not his type, but pretty. He watched her move with the beat, feeling the beer take up the magician's seat in his blood and melt the whole world into a warm, flowing river.

Suzanne took his empty, pausing to inquire with her eyes, did he want another? In one hazy, inspired moment...in a perfect mix of perfume, smoke and beer; of bass notes and high harmonies, the drone of talk, bursting peals of cheers and tambourine, and two bottomless dark eyes...Terry laid a light hand on Suzanne's arm. "Come with me after work?"

The arm retracted with her laugh. "Looks like Terry's had enough for tonight."

He pivoted away from the bar feeling the bottom drop out from under him, like in those anxiety dreams he had; like walking on deck in rolling seas. There had been that moment of synthesis when everything was aligned and somehow united. Didn't she know she was part of it?

Terry's psychological nose-dive was arrested by a wink from the dancing blond. Eyes like blue fire saw him and laughed, but not like Suzanne. These eyes appraised and embraced him with utter impartiality and yes, with friendly amusement. In one lightning quick glance, Terry's feet found solid ground. Somewhere in his reeling, drunken self, his heart stilled and he relaxed.

He awoke next morning on a bench at the edge of the pier, about a block and a half from the bar. A large cloth, patterned in navy blue batik, draped him like a blanket. It smelled dimly of some musky, unfamiliar—though not unpleasant—scent. He assumed it, and he, had been left there by the blond musician. He remembered only bits and pieces from after the time they left the bar together.

But that was peculiar. He had not been drunk enough to be having memory lapses, yet he had no recollection of how he— or they—had arrived at the pier. Moreover, he felt no morning-after evidence of having had too much to drink. No sluggishness, no heavy head. In fact, he felt refreshed, better than he had in quite some time. His sleep, though brief, had been peaceful.

Walking back uphill to his own apartment, Terry revisited images of a small table in a kitchen filled with plants and stained glass, the woman at her stove giving him a mug of tea of all things—some herbal mixture that tasted like a barnyard. He remembered looking into blue eyes that sparkled and seemed to mock him. Uncanny as it was, he felt comforted and held like a child by its mother.

He didn't know her name, whether he'd forgotten or had never even heard it. They must have talked, although he couldn't imagine about what. Most curious was that he knew beyond a doubt that their encounter had been entirely chaste. And that worried him more than his amnesia. He paced and tried to pray, but found that his mind was too agitated. Fuck it! He threw the balled up blue cloth against a wall. A spasm gripped his side.

* * *

From her vantage point at Methods headquarters, Mabel studies Terry. She turns to the team of lightworkers that she is to relieve. "What is with the musician?"

Her co-Worker Pryluck, whose appearance and character both tend toward the eccentric, is currently favoring an electric shade of turquoise. "Oh, she's one of those sensitive ones, knows more than she knows she knows. We've been somewhat successful in directing her behavior."

"What?" Mabel gasps. "That is not allowed!"

"No, no, it isn't like that. She kind of knows we're here and doesn't mind. It's all a bit vague and unfocused for her, but she senses us."

"Pryluck, you know we are not permitted to influence their wills. That is basic law."

"Right, and this one's will has said, okie dokie, come on in and steer this canoe. You'll see. She's a real find. Very friendly."

Mabel purses and puckers, but consents to extend a thin, experimental ray in the direction of the woman. It is true. This one seems to be awake. Mabel can feel her immediate response and it is in fact receptive, though somewhat devoid of conscious presence. They shall have to tread carefully here, but it does look promising.

* * *

Father Sulleran was hearing confession. On the plus side, Terry's unholy lust for Suzanne had apparently withered like a dying stalk. While that was well and good as far as God-Church went, it had been arousing in Terry considerable panic about his rapidly eroding masculine self-image. The withering effect had apparently extended to other women as well. Terry feared it might extend to all women. He cringed to think of having spent a whole night with a very attractive, certainly liberated woman and not have even tried...he hadn't tried, had he? His confusion about events then raised the further question about his mind beginning to go. The delicate attempt to reveal all this to Father Sulleran in such a way as to prevent further implication of his undeniably endangered soul was creating a lengthy and thoroughly incoherent confession.

Father Sulleran skillfully interrupted. "The Lord shows mercy on all of his sheep. Even some of our shepherds have been known to, shall we say, hear a different drummer. Perhaps I might help. Come see me and we'll have a talk. Meanwhile, say five Hail Mary's..."

With the baby in bed for the night, Bill Gillis contemplated his wife Fran from across the kitchen table. Maternity had added a rich softness to her thin frame. Lingering over dinner, they took advantage of the quiet moment to share details of the last few days. Eventually, Bill's recitation came around to his brother Terry's brief admission about his health.

Fran was concerned. "Terry should see a doctor. Odd sensations and weakness like that could be something serious. I mean it isn't like we're talking about your mother, where new symptoms are how we know she's alright. Remember that roommate I had when I lived in New Orleans? She started feeling weak and it ended up being Lou Gehrig's disease. He's your brother, Bill. You should get him to go see someone."

Bill snorted. "Mom wasn't always like that, you know. She's lonely without Dad."

"Yeah, I know," Fran conceded. "But it's been almost ten years. She needs to find some other way to ask for attention."

"You're in fine form tonight," Bill growled. "Anyway, Terry thinks his problem has something to do with God. You know the way he's always praying and all that, and how he keeps promising he'll stop drinking and screwing around?"

Fran scoffed. "That's like a politician promising to stop lying."

"Yeah, well he thinks it's some kind of punishment, that God is taking away his manhood or something. He worries that he's turning into a wimp."

Fran laughed. "Your brother Terry a wimp? That'll be the day. First, he'd have to quit making everything into some kind of extreme sports challenge. You remember his anchor toss?"

"Anchor toss?"

"At Lockside Park. That family reunion when he challenged us all to a game of 'sailor's horseshoes'?"

"Oh man," Bill chuckled. "I thought I dislocated something."

"Well, you and Terry were the only ones dumb enough to try it."

"I couldn't let my baby brother out tough me, could I?

Anyway, you ought to pretend you don't notice anything is up with him."

"Give me a break. If he's really sick, ignoring it is the worst thing to do. Terry would wait until he's dead before he admits he needs help. Probably not even then."

"Look, Fran, my brother trusted me enough to confide in me. I want to keep it that way, OK? He doesn't want people feeling sorry or superior. Go easy on him."

"Dear Father, please bless my family and the boat and all the crew and their loved ones. Let the catch be plentiful today...

"Look, Lord, I'm really trying. I know my thoughts were unclean, full of lust and all, but that's not mortal, is it? All I did was ask her out. Other guys are a lot worse, forcing themselves on women and not praying at all...anyway, please Lord, don't mess with my head, too. I accept the penance of my legs being fucked...or, uh, impaired. But please don't take my memory. I don't know what happened the other night, but I know it wasn't the beer. Maybe You could just tell me what I need to do? Amen."

* * *

Snarrow arrives just in time to hear Terry's prayer. "You have your work cut out for you," he warns Mabel, whose latest assignment is to devise a model for Terry's personality destructuring.

"Oh, he pretty much runs on automatic," she argues. "Nothing original. All we really need to do is isolate the programs that run his thoughts. He loops around the same ones over and over. Of course, that does mean they have become quite deeply impressed into his field."

"What was he saying about his memory?" Snarrow

wonders. "I thought our frequency boosts are still confined to physical wavelengths."

"Right," answers Mabel. "But his mind does not encompass a broad enough scope to comprehend anything outside of the programmed loops. The woman's frequency was too high for him to make heads or tails of. His body could register and respond to her at that point, but his mind could not recognize the sensations. The poor dear, now he thinks he is both going mad and losing his touch with women."

An oscillating light, akin to a snicker, wafts over from where Bulista sits overhearing.

Snarrow glances in her direction. "Well," he explains, "it is one of his programs. Self-identification as a man in the late twentieth century."

"That one is set to disintegrate in the mass population anyway as they move through the next decade or two," Mabel declares. "But it may present some challenges for this lifestream during his changeover."

While it is clear to Mabel that Snarrow's presence still discombobulates Bulista, she is optimistic that the intern might finally be acclimating. Not only does Bulista's field freeze up far less often, but she would swear that Bulista and Snarrow might have even managed to communicate directly with one another, at least once.

~ 4 ~

Downtown, across from the wharfside market, the flute-player, Cara, took a long drag on a joint before handing it back to Evan, the rangy guitar player in their trio. She sat on the curb, leaning her back against a pedestrian crossing sign. It was a warm day, with enough haze to obscure any glimpse of the not too distant Cascade Range. Her bare, ringed toes played with the small pile of sand that had collected at the edge of the street. The musicians were taking a break, taking in the afternoon and the human river that flowed by them on the sidewalk.

"So, Cara," asked Evan, "what did you end up doing with that stray pup you picked up at The Oyster the other night?"

Cara exhaled a ribbon of smoke. "Gerry," she said. "Or maybe Terry."

Their bass player, sitting nearby, tapped out the beat on the back of his bass. "Ger-ry, Ter-ry, ver-y mer-ry." Evan joined him, drumming palms on thighs, adding syncopation. What the hell, Cara picked up her tambourine, stood and danced out the rhythm to their chant. A passing tourist dropped some quarters into an open guitar case and the trio's chant changed to laughter.

"I gave him some tea and put him to bed," Cara told them. "He seems like he's about to crack up."

"Who is he?" asked Evan.

She shrugged. "He fishes. It was kind of bizarre, like he was my kid or something. I felt like I was supposed to take care of him. He is pretty...I don't know, limited. Or trapped. But I get the sense that he's on the edge, maybe looking for a way to wake up."

"Stray puppy."

"I guess so. Hey, guys, I'll see you later. I need to be up on the north side this afternoon." She stuffed the flute and tambourine into her sack and headed for the bus stop.

Cara had agreed to meet her oldest and dearest friend,

Dolores, for lunch at a Unitarian church where Dolores ran a psychic institute. Cara arrived just after the morning psychic development class had ended. A small throng of students moved excitedly through the hallway toward the stairs. Cara observed this latest crop with some amusement.

As with just about every sort of student clinic or training facility, the public was enticed here by low fees charged for supervised student services. In this case, those services included psychic readings and energy healings, offered by student and instructor teams. Prodigiously intuitive in her own right, Cara occasionally entertained herself by adopting the guise of a prospective student, and sitting in to observe the proceedings. In fact, she found the readings to be a bit silly and slow, but had fun reading the readers. Few, she insisted, possessed sufficient clarity to objectively and accurately take in the complexity that defines another human being.

Her friend Dolores tended to be cleaner and clearer than most. But still, Cara was not too sure about the whole business of people seeking counsel about things that, in her opinion, were no one's affair but their own. Nevertheless, Dolores did well for herself. People generally seemed pleased and, Cara supposed, no harm done.

They sat in the church kitchen, eating peanut butter sandwiches and drinking elderberry tea. Dolores gave Cara a sharp, quizzical look. "Who's the audience?"

"What audience?"

"Well, there's your usual crew of guides and elementals that are always with you, but you've come in with a whole new group today...oh, not yours, just observing. Wait, that green one is too eager for just observing! Don't let him push you around,

Cara."

"Uh, sure, no problem. Want to hear a new song?" She took the flute from her bag and Dolores settled in to listen.

* * *

At Methods Headquarters, Mabel scolds Pryluck. "You see? Even the lifestreams can tell you are out of line."

"Not out of line, Mabel, all the lady said was eager."

"She said too eager, and you know perfectly well that pulling another lifestream into our project is out of line."

"Well sure, pulling is a no-no. But a little leaning in our man's direction, a little coordination of coincidence..."

"Leaning is NOT permitted," Mabel fumes. "The female is not even our lifestream. None of us has any business monitoring her."

Snarrow speaks up. "Mabel has a point, Pryluck. "Leaning, steering, pulling, it's all the same. If a lifestream other than our own is conscious enough to perceive us, then we may offer our perspective. But each of them must be free to be as dense or rebellious as they choose."

Pryluck sighs. "Our own is too thick. He is not going to make it."

The space dims with agreement. Odds seem slim unless they can enlist some help or come up with another plan.

"Maybe the blond one's guides will work with us?" murmurs Bulista. "Then we wouldn't have to...infiltrate, or was it trespass you were doing?"

Pryluck shoots a jagged dart of light in the intern's direction. Now that Bulista has successfully emerged from the requisite probationary period at Methods, her initial nervousness— exasperating as that was—has devolved to downright cheekiness.

"Very funny. But the idea is a good one. Any objections?"

~ 5 ~

All month long, dockside after days at sea, Bill and Terry had been discussing the upcoming City Arts Festival. It was a big-deal citywide event, held on a weekend before the onset of unrelenting winter rains, when not-too-overcast weather might be expected. The brothers were planning their annual booth, where they sold fried fish sandwiches with help from whatever family members and friends they could lasso into it. Free entrance passes and great music were the draw.

Now, with summer progressing, street fairs abounded up and down the coast. Summer fairs and festivals like these brought out the region's most creative and eccentric talent. For street performers like Cara and her friends, summer was the mainstay of their financial and social survival. Musicians, jugglers and artisans, along with food booth crews were reunited annually, buoyed by crowds and fine weather.

Dolores took her show on the road, reading palms and telling fortunes. In the role of "Madam D," she adorned both herself and her booth with embroidered silk scarves and glitter. A large crystal ball took center stage on her table, although this was just for appearance; Dolores was no scryer.

It had been a brisk morning, with a chilly breeze and sun just beginning to burn through lingering clouds. The City Arts

Festival's opening day attendance had been equally brisk. As noon approached, Dolores was ready for a break. She left her table for a walk around the grounds, visiting with other vendors while she kept an ear out for the sound of familiar flute music.

Dolores found Cara and her trio just inside the main entrance. "Cover my booth for a few?"

Cara laughed. "You would entrust me with Madam D's sterling reputation?"

Dolores rolled her eyes. "Fifteen minutes. I need to wander."

At the back of the fairgrounds, lined up outside the main buildings that would house featured afternoon and evening concerts, was an impressive array of food booths. Vendors represented every imaginable cuisine, from cotton candy to gourmet French pastry, African vegetarian to Italian sausage.

Fried fish sandwiches were a hit, as usual. Terry and Bill had hired and organized shifts of helpers to carry them through the weekend. Bill's wife, Fran, arrived to take inventory and replenish dwindling supplies. She surveyed the line of customers, assessed the crew and then grabbed Terry to accompany her around the fair.

Bill locked eyes with Fran. After several seconds of standoff, he relented. "Go on, take five," he told Terry.

Relieved to move away from the heat and heavy smell of the fryer, Terry noted these additions to his growing list of sensitivities.

Fran linked arms with her brother-in-law, to propel him through the crowd. The quality of his presence at her side came as a shock to Fran. His body had lost none of its powerful brawn, yet he seemed to have somehow hollowed into himself, leaving little of the swaggering confidence that used to dominate.

"Ooh, look!" she exclaimed as they approached Madam D's booth. "Let's get our palms read."

Terry glanced at the booth in question. Sudden, inexplicable panic rendered him incapable of intelligent function. He tried to mutter a protest about all that nonsense, but it was too late. Cara had seen them.

"Hey, it's the fish-man! How ya doing?"

Terry grunted something inarticulate before tossing Cara a perfunctory, "Hiya, sweetheart," while attempting to steer Fran away from Madam D's.

Fran would have none of it. "Terry, don't be rude. I want my fortune told."

Cara smiled. "Sorry, I'm a fake. The real thing, Madam D, will be back soon. I'm just sitting in for her. Come back in maybe ten minutes."

Fran looked from Cara to her peculiarly awkward brother-in-law, who seemed to take up more space than ever, despite his apparent reticence. Decisively, Fran announced to Terry she was going to visit the perfumer's booth. "Wait for me," she demanded.

Slouched, mute and brooding, Terry ignored both women. Very gently, Cara reached up from across the table and took his hand. "Show me your palm," she told him.

* * *

Excited by this fortuitous and unengineered meeting of Terry with Cara, the lightworker Pryluck is stirring up a shower of sparks. It's just too tempting. He sends a quick inquiring mind-link in the direction of Cara's overseeing guides—playing it straight, although the effort to contain his zeal is rousing a kaleidoscope of color. "Affirmative, let's go," he crows.

Snarrow scolds, "Get a hold of yourself, Pryluck. Your field looks like a fireworks display. And by the way, you do NOT have clearance to make decisions regarding our input into either one of these lifestreams. Here, Mabel, you will work with me."

Under Snarrow's direction, the team sends a ray of warm, gentle light into Cara's heart. Her personal guides look on and nod. No harm in that. Terry's field guide, Vormis, hovers within Terry's energy field, monitoring his condition.

* * *

Terry was behaving badly. Cara still had hold of his hand. Stiff and unyielding, he seemed to study his feet, but internally he churned every which way to avoid the contact.

Cara's voice broke through his unease. "Sit down, look at me and for heaven's sake, stop squirming!"

Startled into compliance, he sat—fully aware that his body had, up until that point, neither squirmed nor even moved a bit. Curiosity drew his eyes to meet hers, and something shifted inside his head. The noise and bustle of the fair faded behind a new point of focus.

Cara did not look at his palm, but held his gaze. "Are you afraid?" she asked.

"No." His own voice, emerging small and childlike, astonished him.

"Don't be scared," she told him. "Everything's OK. It's all going to be alright."

"I ain't afraid," he growled. Unable to break their visual communion, Terry wallowed in an oasis of solace, unaware that he did so and oblivious even of his need.

Then Fran was there, chatting about vanilla musk and,

"Oh, Madam D's not back? Well, I'll try again later." And, "Nice to meet you." And so on.

Fran left the booth, with Terry—docile and stupid—trailing in her wake. "Who was that?" Fran asked over her shoulder. "An old lover? You two sure seemed into each other."

"Nah," he muttered.

* * *

Snarrow calls another mandatory meeting of Methods Division lightworkers. Seeking an update on the person-transfer experiment, Management sends a representative to sit in on the meeting. General consensus is that the experiment is failing. Snarrow addresses the Manager. "It can not work with this lifestream. He is simply too full of fear." Heads nod, lights glimmer. "It hardly seems possible, but if anything the fear is increasing despite our attempts to reassure him. How can we proceed any further when he is so stressed out over his first frequency boost?"

Customarily gray in color, the Management rep brightens a tone or two. "Fear? What is that about?"

Snarrow exchanges a look with Mabel before responding. "Increased light erodes the mind programs that constitute the human persona. We shine light on them, and they begin to dissolve. This human lifestream, Terry, is so completely identified with his mind programs that he thinks he is disintegrating...which, from his perspective as the mind-based personality, he is."

"Mm-hmm," rumbles Management. "Can anything be done to override the fear?"

Mabel takes over. "We will have to get his subpersonalities into rehab. We can meet when he is asleep. I say we check it out tonight. We shall see how many of these aspects of his personality are ready to go."

"What do you mean, ready to go?" Vormis wonders.

"We can not force anything, you know, so we shall need to find parts of his persona that are tired of their roles and will welcome a change. We shall start there. As these facets of the mind come around, we should encounter less and less resistance. Without the subs' cooperation we might as well abandon the whole project."

"Yes," agrees Management. "We will organize a committee." Addressing Mabel he adds, "I believe we can count on you to spearhead the sub rehab project. You will be receiving an official memo."

Mabel squarely faces the Management rep, ignoring the subtle titters she feels oozing through her field from behind. "As you say," she replies.

~ 6 ~

Methods' holographically simulated meeting site appears as any standard institutional building circa late 20th century. Lots of concrete on the outside, rotten egg green with curdled milk beige inside, fluorescent lighting and water-stained ceiling tiles. Mabel has insisted on one deviation in the décor. The large, rectangular table at which she now sits is mahogany rather than the Formica top that one might expect. Looking on from an observatory in Methods headquarters sits the core group of Terry's team, including Snarrow, Pryluck and Vormis. Mabel has chosen to assume her holographic, plump and gray-haired humanoid form, on the advice of once-human field guides, who consider a grandmotherly image in keeping with Mabel's sugar cookie quirk.

Earlier recruitment efforts have yielded a small group of Terry's subpersonalities who are willing to give Mabel's rehab program a try. Only, to them it has been described as a sort of occupational training with potential for upward mobility. Most are, understandably, a bit touchy on the idea of change. Any success at roping them in will clearly have to come from the offer of various perks.

Three have joined Mabel for this preliminary meeting. The first is a severe looking, middle-aged woman with dark eyes and brows that slant toward the bridge of her nose. The eyes hold an angry, accusatory gleam. Incongruously, she wears sneakers, along with a nametag that identifies her as "Aunt Ethel."

To Aunt Ethel's right sits a robust looking man whose nametag reads "Chaz." Chaz is muscled like a wrestler, with a body reminiscent of a bulldog.

Finally, appearing to take up as little space as possible, sits a weepy girl of about twelve years of age who bears the nametag, "Helen."

Mabel addresses the group. "Thanks to each of you for volunteering. The way this will work is we shall begin with individual introductions. We would like to get to know you and hear about your personal goals. The program will consist of both individual and group counseling. Some of you may come through the program in just one or two sessions. For others, the process may take quite some time. During that period, I and the other counselors will be here to support and to reinforce the new skills you will be learning. Are there any questions before we begin, dears?"

Wary silence.

"Alright then. Aunt Ethel, can we start with you? Would you give us a brief description of your current job?"

Aunt Ethel's voice emerges throaty and cantankerous. "I keep him in line."

"Very good. You keep him in line. How do you do that, Aunt Ethel?"

"Shame, shame, shame, pick, pick, pick."

"No wonder the guy is such a train wreck!" Pryluck blurts. Snarrow shushes him.

Mabel maintains her encouraging tone. "And what is your reason for keeping Terry in line?"

Aunt Ethel peers at Mabel's holographic face. "Why, to keep him out of trouble."

Mabel's field blooms rosy with understanding. "He is in your charge, you protect him?"

"Yes, without me he would be into all kinds of nonsense. I keep him in line, he stays safe."

"It sounds like you keep a tight rein on him. And I bet you do not miss a thing."

To everyone's surprise, Aunt Ethel cackles. She appears less imposing now, and more relaxed. "Not a thing," she agrees.

"Well," affirms Mabel, "you have evidently done an excellent job of staying on his case, and you do show promising ability in the area of discrimination."

Mabel senses the atmospheric ruffle of her co-Workers' reaction. "Discrimination as in discernment, telling what is what," she spells out, trying not to lose her unflappable demeanor.

Aunt Ethel beams.

"Yes," Mabel continues, "you do seem to merit some kind of

reward for such long-term, devoted service. Would you like to work toward a promotion?"

"I have been conscientious," Ethel croaks hopefully.

"OK," Mabel proposes. "How about as our first goal we define your new role and job description? Maybe it will help to see how Terry's needs might have changed over the years."

Amid a storm of puckering brows and lips, Aunt Ethel gives a tentative nod. "I'll consider it," she says.

"Excellent," answers Mabel with a smile. "Take all the time you need. We shall check back with you about it next time."

Mabel's last few words are interrupted by loud crashing sounds coming from the direction of the front entrance. These are followed by a rapid succession of curses. A buxom redhead, whip in hand, stumbles in on spike heels. Rolls of her apple abdomen protrude between a black leather miniskirt and textured bra-top. Heavy orange make-up cakes coarse skin. She laughs, her voice very much reflecting the appearance of her skin and frizz-fried hair. "Shit, am I late?"

"And you are...?" Mabel begins, offering a hand.

"Elaine."

Resting her hand on the back of an empty chair, Elaine surveys the group. Her eyes settle on the miserable Helen. With a sneer, she abruptly lunges to thrust her breasts close to Helen's face. "What the fuck is she doing here?"

Helen whimpers into her handkerchief, cringing as if she might will herself to disappear.

Elaine's smile splits a mire of crimson lipstick. "I ain't hangin' with a bunch of assholes." And out she staggers, her exit as coordinated as was her entrance.

"Well, she's vile," Vormis breathes.

Snarrow disagrees. "I bet this one turns out to be a pushover."

"What makes you think that?"

"She is in the first roundup of volunteers, which suggests she is not as set in her ways as some of the others might turn out to be."

* * *

As security guards, eager to go home, escorted the last of the weekend's revelers off the fairgrounds, Bill and Terry tossed one last bag of trash into a dumpster and started the truck. Fran had left with the baby just after the dinner rush.

Terry had been sullen, remote and irritable all afternoon. Bill turned to him. "You know, Terry, it might help to go see someone about your legs."

"Fuck off," Terry grumbled.

"Hey, buddy, no offense." They drove in silence for several minutes. "Just, you seem kind of depressed."

"What, you think I need a shrink?"

"That's not what I'm saying, don't be like that."

"What are you saying?"

"Maybe it would help to tell someone and get it checked out. Just that.

"Right. I'll think about it."

Terry had, in fact, been thinking about Father Sulleran's suggestion to see him for a talk. And now, Bill. He wondered if it was so obvious that he was cracking up.

~ 7 ~

Terry found Father Sulleran in the courtyard where they had appointed to meet. They shook hands.

"Come, let's walk." Father Sulleran put a fleshy arm around Terry's shoulders and led him along a path between labeled horticultural plantings. Terry felt agitated at the touch, an entirely different sensation from the squirmy need to pull away he had experienced when Cara took his hand at the fair. This was more like a hot, prickly rush of danger that he felt in the pit of his stomach.

"So then," Father Sulleran began. "You say this crisis of yours started when the barmaid laughed at you?"

Terry stammered. "Uh, no, not really. Or, well, just one part of it."

The priest dipped his head toward Terry. A resultant waft of aftershave rivaled the zestiest of restroom air fresheners. "The part about..." His hand tightened on Terry's shoulder. "...altered sexual urges?"

"Uh, I guess," Terry answered, clearly confused.

Father Sulleran nodded. "Terry, have you ever considered the message God might be communicating by way of your recent affliction? Do you suppose He might have a reason to chastise you in this way?"

Terry's muscles went rigid. He had been over and over this train of thought, trying to think of a wrongdoing dire enough to warrant such a drastic decline in health and vigor. "I guess I don't know," he admitted.

"Terry, if a dog somehow thought it was a cow—you know

what I'm saying—and started doing things against its own nature, say, like eating grass instead of chasing rabbits...don't you think that God in His great mercy, in order to instruct His misguided child, would run some kind of interference? Send a message?"

Terry felt the priest's hand grip his shoulder. Father Sulleran was peering intently into his eyes, and Terry couldn't breathe. His eyes glazed, but Father Sulleran persisted.

"Son, look at the facts. We are each God's Own Creation, and it is unholy to deny our God-given nature. You can be sure that God would eventually see to it that the misguided dog stops grazing in unsuitable pastures, yes? So how can you think He would allow you to continue to chase after women?"

Terry regained his focus. "So what are you suggesting, Father, you think this is about lust?"

"No, Terry," Father Sulleran gently shook his head. "Lust would be the dog chasing too many rabbits. We're talking about a rabbit chaser eating grass."

Terry stared at the priest. "Father?"

Father Sulleran sighed. "If chasing women is against your nature and you persist at it, you can expect to be smitten down."

Flushing, Terry disengaged himself from the priest's grasp.

"Relax, Terry, I'm on your side. Here." He pressed a business card into Terry's hand. "This center might be just what you need. It's a quiet place in the country where you can get away, sort things out. Kind of a retreat for men only."

Terry took a breath. This sounded more like the priestly advice he had expected. Maybe a religious retreat would help clear his mind. He glanced at the white card with bold letters that read, "Ricki's Halfway." "Odd name," he thought, examining the subheading. "Let us design the new you." He pocketed the card, took leave of Father Sulleran, and directed himself toward The Oyster's Pearl feeling not too steady.

* * *

"And I thought our guy was the nutcase," sputters Pryluck. "What is that priest trying to do?" Red and orange spikes of light flicker like an aurora borealis.

Mabel is beside herself. "Must we always let the lifestreams go their own way? Is there no time when it is justified to step in?"

A pallid Snarrow answers, "It is part of their free will that they sometimes get exposed to deception or outright lies, injustice and all of that. They are amazingly resilient. Field guide Vormis here will see to it that this one stays connected to us, and so too, to his 'own nature.' There is no real harm from the priest, just a little more confusion."

Mabel sounds sad. "Confusion for one already so confused."

Vormis insists, "He is guided, you know."

* * *

In a shocked state of inner fog, Terry ran headlong into a woman waiting on the sidewalk for the light to change. Barely registering the collision, he muttered a vague excuse me, when a hand on his arm arrested his progress. He glanced down into clear blue, and increasingly familiar, eyes.

"Hey," Cara wondered. "What's up?"

Terry gazed at her with such an aura of despair that she did not press him. "Come on," she commanded, leading him by the elbow she still held. "I was on my way to the zoo."

He followed, too rattled to resist. Nor did he attempt to extricate himself from her grasp, for he experienced none of the agitation he'd felt at the hand of Father Sulleran. Realizing this contrast led to a dawning, as yet unformed, sense of significance close to the edge of recognition.

He suddenly turned to Cara, interrupting her cheerful patter with a choked sob. "I don't want to have sex with you."

Cara took in his tormented expression. "Wow. And I don't want to have sex with you. Is that a problem?"

Unleashed now, Terry ranted and gesticulated. Cara hardly made sense of his words until she heard, "I don't know what's happening, I thought God hated homos."

"What?" She stiffened. "First of all, the God I know doesn't hate. And not wanting to have sex with me might mean that you have bad taste, but it doesn't make you gay."

He stared vacantly, unable to begin to imagine that it might mean anything else. Equally disturbing to him was the realization that there was no God that he could claim to know. To him, God was all hearsay.

Repelled, Cara was about to turn away when she noticed a strange but quite nice warmth creeping like an oil spill throughout her chest. "Haven't you ever had a woman for a friend?" she wondered.

"Yeah, sure," Terry mumbled.

"And didn't you ever touch them without wanting to have sex?"

Terry looked at her like she was cheese gone bad.

A sound of disgust escaped Cara's throat before she again felt the odd sensation in her chest and with it once more, dispassionate interest. "Have you ever wanted to have sex with a man?"

"NO!" Flushing, he wrenched his arm from hers.

"Then what's given you this idea about homosexuality?"

He clammed up, unable even to form the thought in his mind.

"Look," she told him. "I think you should have a talk with my friend, Dolores. She's awfully good. Do you know how to find her?"

Terry took the number to placate Cara, and made his escape. Another talk with someone else was not about to happen.

* * *

In the simulated meeting room, Mabel turns her attention to the next subpersonality, Chaz, who sits tough and imposing at the mahogany meeting table. "And may we have a brief description of your job, Chaz?"

Chaz rises, towering to his full, impressive height and bulk. The massive head and shoulders jut forward as he announces, "I'm de bounds keeper." He grins, exposing a checkerboard of missing teeth.

"Bounds keeper?"

"His body guard," Chaz spells out slowly. Mabel has the feeling of being toyed with, like a mouse in the paws of a cat.

"He seems a bit of a bully, wouldn't you say?" Pryluck, watching from a dimensional shift, addresses no one in particular.

Mabel hears, but keeps her cool. "Would you say that your strategy includes intimidation, Chaz?"

"Yeh," he answers, not in the least offended. "I gotta keep out de trouble, know what I mean?"

"You hold his territory, his physical space?"

"Yeh."

"Exactly what are you protecting?" she asks.

Chaz regards Mabel as if she is a slow child. "Well, his life."

"Oh, are you are about physical survival then?"

"That's right," he says, and tries a different tack. "Here, check this out." He offers Mabel a flexed bicep to feel. It is, naturally, steel hard.

"Very tough," pronounces Mabel.

Chaz nods, self-satisfied. "'Scuse me for a second," he tells her, and abruptly disappears.

Mabel and the overseeing lightworkers watch as Chaz vacates the virtual reality of the sub rehab session, and drops into Terry's dreaming mind.

"Is that Chaz?" Snarrow wonders, scanning the dream. An enraged ogre of a man has materialized to attack a small wandering dog, whose appearance on the scene had inadvertently startled the dreaming-mind.

"The same, in action," replies Vormis with an uncontrolled squeak.

"Yup, a little short on the trigger," Pryluck agrees.

A moment later, the dream sequence shifts and Chaz is back at Mabel's rehab meeting. The young subpersonality, Helen, is in tears.

Mabel looks from one to the other. "Helen, are you afraid of Chaz?"

Helen sniffles and nods her head.

"Chaz, I am curious," begins Mabel. "You seem like such a nice guy—conscientious, polite, proud—is it your intention to frighten people?"

Chaz's monstrous brow wrinkles. "Naw, I just do my job, I don't care nothin' about hurtin' nobody."

Mabel nods. "Yes, well, thank you Chaz. I think we shall hear from Helen now, and then we can discuss opportunities for *each of you.*"

* * *

Cara and Dolores met over tea, at Cara's request. She felt both shaken and intrigued by her conversation with Terry on her way to the zoo, and was eager to talk. "It was as if there was another person, or another me inside myself, that had somehow hijacked my mind. I was thinking this guy totally freaks me out, but I couldn't walk away because of a really great feeling inside me that, you know, seemed unrelated to him. But at the same time, it made me interested in what makes him tick. Have you ever heard of anything like that?"

Dolores had been half-listening, more than half-watching Cara with an odd expression.

"Alright, what are you seeing?" Cara demanded.

"It looks to me like there *is* another person inside yourself. Or maybe another delegation."

"What's that mean?" asked Cara, chewing on a dried apricot.

"Would you mind if I take some time to look into this? Your field has been awfully crowded lately, and I'm getting the sense you're being fucked with."

Cara laughed. "Should I be scared?" She did not share Dolores' preoccupation with ethereal goings on, and figured that there was enough in the mundane world to worry about. If there was a problem from some other world, she was certain that any effect from it would feel to her like a problem. What she had experienced felt weird for sure, but warm, full, and pleasantly spacious. Still, Dolores was Dolores. She would need to check it all out for fairness. "Do what you gotta do. Keep me in on the scoop."

"I'll want to read you, Cara. Can you come by later, say at seven?"

Cara grinned at her friend's formality. "I'll be here. Want me to bring dinner?"

"Wine."

* * *

At Methods Division headquarters, the core team assigned to Terry's restructuring is gathered for yet another meeting. The tone is somber as they wait for a second team of lightworkers to show. Although it is unusual for teams who oversee different human lifestreams to meet and discuss their cases, all involved have agreed that their current project warrants a departure from protocol. They hope to come to some kind of consensus about ground rules, before the psychic, Dolores, starts probing into the matter of their recent collaborations involving Terry and Cara.

Snarrow's pre-meeting pep talk irritates Pryluck. All that jabber about how even a guide's well-intended actions can so easily trigger fear and misinterpretation on the part of a human lifestream. And, how we lightworkers know throughout the spectrum of our beings, that such a result runs completely counter to our purpose.

"Just look at how agitated our Terry is becoming. They are all made of essentially the same stuff," Snarrow harps.

Before Pryluck can reply, Cara's guides arrive in a lighthearted flurry, infusing the meeting with pale, heart-colored tones. The ambient mood surges in their rosy pink and green wake. Several guides have arrived in forms that resemble children. One is utterly engrossed in blowing very large soap bubbles, which another captures when she can, to don as hats or billowing skirts before they pop. Effervescent chatter, accented by fits of laughter, cascades into the room along with the guests.

The most senior—and staid—members of Terry's team are taken aback by an onslaught of enthusiastic embraces and kisses on both cheeks. It is Pryluck who eventually brings the meeting to order by thanking the visiting guides so much for coming, while thoroughly enjoying his co-Workers' discomfort.

Resonating now with the collective aura, Snarrow recovers his composure. "Yes," he agrees. "And thank you for your willingness to cooperate with our project. May we offer you an update on its progress?"

"Oh, yes!" they gush. "We are curious about the greater goal of your lifestream. Doesn't he appear to have taken on a bit much...like some kind of marathon soul journey?"

"More like a decathlon," Pryluck complains.

Peach sunset tones sweep through the group of visiting guides. One asserts, "Ours is doing just the opposite. Her life is to be a respite, with none of the big sufferings, persecutions or all that of the accelerated path."

"Ours suffers enough for two...or more," mutters Pryluck.

"What is your lifestream's purpose?" Snarrow asks the guests.

A shimmering guide, robed in rainbow iridescence, responds, "Her greater task is simply to know herself as love. Experiences for her are programmed to maximize appreciation and joy. As she appreciates, she grows in compassion and so in the capacity for love.

"The ultimate soul goal, naturally, is for her vibration to be sufficiently elevated as to emanate the pure, impersonal love that embraces all of creation. She is not in a hurry, of course."

Peering at Mabel, one of the smaller, bubble-blowing guides adds, "One can't properly appreciate if one is in a hurry."

Mabel absorbs the obviously targeted advice. "No," she says. "I see your point. But, with this assignment we have had to shove our lifestream onto the fast track. Are you then implying that he cannot appreciate or enjoy his experiences?"

"Well, how is he doing?"

Amusement washes the room. Pryluck projects a holographic image of a violin-playing melodrama.

"Yes, well, I guess that is what this meeting is all about," admits the bubble-blower.

"We need to define bounds and limits in relation to how the two lifestreams may interact, and to what degree we can use the one to help stabilize the other," Snarrow summarizes.

A sugary aroma scents the room as Mabel wonders, "Can it work the other way? Might there be some way that Terry can be used to further Cara's path?"

The robed guide, who seems to wield an elder's leadership role similar to Snarrow's, answers, "Naturally, all things occur in reflection and reciprocity. So far, in each instance that our lifestream's heart frequency has been augmented in service to your lifestream, she has been furthered in compassion in accordance with her soul intent. They, and we, can be a mutually beneficial team.

Snarrow regards the spokeswoman. "In what capacity do you perceive our team's benefit to yours?"

"Oh, serious is not all bad. You each have tremendous endurance. You would have to in order to go the long haul with your lifestream—who, by the way, must be designed like a tank. Management may have its weak points, but you have to admit they made a good choice in assigning the team to carry out their experiment."

~ 8 ~

It is the subpersonality Helen's turn to speak, but she's apparently beyond words and able only to whimper. Mabel shrugs, conscious of the team of lightworkers who both surround and infiltrate the room. "What does one do with this?" She broadcasts the thought.

Lightworkers move in close. Staying just out of phase and frequency from visual perception, they form a circle around Helen, welcoming her into the center of their warm and infinitely loving presence. As Helen begins to calm, Pryluck adjusts his frequency such that he seems to hover at Mabel's ear. "Looks like we've found our terror file."

Mabel grimaces. "Or at least one of them...not the time to chat, hm, Pryluck?"

Reluctantly, Pryluck reassembles himself back into the circle of light that holds Helen in its nearly solid embrace.

A sudden inspiration occurs to Mabel. "Helen, dear, are you feeling a little more comfortable now?"

Helen sniffs, and without raising her bent head, nods imperceptibly.

"I want you to give me your full attention now, Helen," Mabel continues. "Do you feel the presence of the light beings that are helping you to feel safer?"

Helen's head pops up in surprise.

"Well, would you look at that?" Pryluck laughs. "She

thought it was all her own doing."

Sharp enough to catch his comment through the dimensional phase shift separating sub rehab from the circle of Methods Workers, Mabel glowers at him.

She then brightens. "Helen, these beings never leave you. You are loved and safe in their...in our...presence at all times. I want you to look at them now. You need to know that they are with you."

Happy to ride the light waves down a few notches, the support team begins to assemble in congruence with the meeting room's frequency. To Helen, they appear stellate, with soft light radiating outward from intensely brilliant centers. She draws a deep, ragged breath.

"Whenever you get afraid, Helen, I want you to remember how you feel right now, do you understand?" Helen nods once more.

"Now," Mabel continues. "What can you tell us about yourself?"

Helen speaks softly and, at first, rather unintelligibly. Words that come through are of the order of "lost," "pain" and "empty." The air in the room seems thicker, as ambient light dulls.

"Helen," Mabel prompts. "Show us."

Vormis, who alone among on-duty Workers has had any direct experience with human emotion, adjusts his frequency so as to infiltrate Helen's configuration, while Mabel and the other lightworkers join forces in a mind link with Vormis. Together, they all observe the subpersonality's state: lost in a sea of emptiness, the grief and pain of separation is seemingly unbearable.

"What is this about?" Mabel asks.

Unpredictably, Helen says she needs to reunite with her

self.

Pryluck frowns. "Reunite with Terry? Kinky."

But Helen is creating a mind-picture of her self. The scene shifts to a French drawing room, in which a dejected, velvet and lace clad man stoops. An epee dangles from his hand.

"Who is this?" wonders Mabel.

The French nobleman shakes his head. "All is lost," he shrugs, gesturing with the sword. "I have been betrayed."

"Yes?" Mabel prompts, not knowing which way to steer the conversation and hoping he'll continue.

"There is nothing for me now. I defended honor. I fought for it. But now?" He shrugs again and his lips purse. "What is ze point?"

"Whose honor did you defend?" Mabel ventures.

The dispirited Frenchman simply shakes his head.

Mabel tries again. "Well then, what made you stop fighting?"

"I was wrong," he answers. "There is nothing to defend and in ze end no one unites with me. They all turn their back, man and God alike."

"I see," muses Mabel. "And what has this to do with Helen? I do not understand the connection."

At this point, both Helen and the duelist regard Mabel with equal anguish. The lightworkers form their mind link to try to make sense of the situation. All they can glean is that somehow, with the shock of betrayal, came the split of fear-ridden Helen from the dispirited swordsman. First step had better be reunion. Later they could deal with the issue of his lost faith.

"Monsieur," Mabel suggests. "Do you remember Helen? She needs you."

He turns to Helen who, aside from shrinking into herself, is holding steady. His face slackens. "Ma cherie," he murmurs, opening his arms. When they embrace, Helen literally incorporates into the man's heart, and tension drains from the erstwhile twosome. Unfortunately, along with the tension goes much of the enjoined entity's vitality.

"Alright," affirms Mabel. "This is a good beginning. Replenishment shall be the first order of business for the two of you, so let us get you into the light."

The Workers steep the re-united subpersonality in their broth of loving radiance, until they see it infuse into the core of the reunited subpersonality.

Still, Mabel's not finished. "Helen, I want you to remember how to come back to this experience." In a moment of insight, she takes a chance. "When you feel afraid, it is OK to panic. But you do not need to pull away from…this gentleman. That just makes him feel deserted and abandoned. It makes it worse for both, you see. If you panic, you can—both of you—come here together. It is safe. There is comfort, have you got it?"

A contented and very sleepy Helen indicates that she does.

Most of Terry's team is present when Vormis returns from dreamtime field surveillance. His field hums and splutters as he faces the group. "Can someone please tell me what went on at that last 'rehab' meeting?"

"What is the problem, Vormis?" Mabel asks.

"I just don't get it. I was fine until that bit about Helen really being some French guy and all that."

A wave of congruence passes among the co-Workers. "I'm with you, Vormis," says Pryluck. "I don't get it either."

Snarrow demands, "Well, Mabel?"

"Uhh, I cannot say that I completely get it either," she manages, before she and several co-Workers erupt in laughter.

An indignant Vormis spews foul yellow fumes.

Pryluck cackles. "Sakes, Mabel, you sounded like one of their psychologists, only without the training for it."

Mabel ignores him and turns to Vormis. "I shall try to explain what I can, but remember that our goal is integration of the persona. It is less important that we follow all the details than it is that both Helen and her counterpart stopped emitting erratic electrical activity and came into harmony for the time being."

Snarrow nods. "It would seem so. As they say, 'Effectiveness is the measure of truth.'"

"Who says that?" asks Bulista.

"Hush!" Vormis has lost none of the prickliness with which he had arrived.

"OK, Vormis, the closest I can come is that Terry's persona had a subpersonality who was somehow in charge of the ego concern they call honor. Is that a familiar concept to you all?" Mabel surveys the room.

The atmosphere remains somewhat murky, and Vormis— the team member most familiar with the ins and outs of human psycho-dynamics—impatiently endures Mabel's commentary.

"Honor is related to pride, and to their sense of right vs. wrong. What we do not know is the event which caused this French fragment of Terry's persona to experience betrayal." She pauses. "Betrayal is the sense of having one's foundation of support suddenly and unexpectedly revealed as an apparent source of danger."

Vormis interrupts. "Mabel, do these definitions matter?

Everyone can sense the guy's distressed."

Mabel ignores Vormis' outburst. "The recognition of betrayal is often experienced as an intense shock that erodes all sense of trust. Such a lifestream remains in self-imposed isolation, without hope, because it refuses all assistance, you see."

"I do see," muses Snarrow. "Because it never knows whether or not the supposed helping hand will, in reality, lead it to its demise."

"Right," agrees Mabel. "As I was saying, it is less important for us to know the details of this story line—we can always trace the program back if we need to—as it is for us to help clean up the after effects of shock. I gather that Helen and the duelist were a single subpersonality before the betrayal, and that whatever the perceived threat was, led to overwhelming panic. That is where Helen, the one who panics, jumped ship."

"But how in bloody hell did she manage that?" sputters Pryluck.

"Obviously not without dire consequences all around. Helen's exit was a split within the Frenchman's own identity, and only served to intensify his insecurity. I do not know what can be done to bring his faith around, but we need to first work with Helen to get her to stay put in the face of fear."

Vormis's field has smoothed. "So, it seems that these two— or is it one—are key to Terry's receptivity to our input?"

"Fear vs. faith is key for the whole human collective," speculates Snarrow.

"So, how do we break the pattern?" Pryluck wonders.

Mabel bristles. "We don't, they do. We encourage and support. Remember boundaries, Pryluck?"

Snarrow waxes managerial. "I suppose we can best

support the desensitization from fear by continuing to reinforce Helen's ability to accept the fear sensation. By the way, Mabel, excellent job. My recommendation is that we initiate the destructuring of fear programs proportionate to Helen's progress. That will mean that we do it in stages. As for the acquisition of faith," he shot a glance at Pryluck, "we will have to follow the lifestream's lead. I suspect that this is an area in which his association with the female musician and her guides will be of benefit."

In the simulated meeting room, Mabel turns her attention to Chaz, the subpersonality bully. She observes him for a long time. "Chaz," she muses. "I do not know what to say. You are devoted, conscientious, the quintessential bodyguard. Who could fault you for that?

"But the thing is, dear, you are so effective at subduing potential dangers that all the good stuff of life is excluded too. Terry needs reassurance now, but it cannot happen when you feel the need to scare off or attack everything he encounters."

Chaz thrusts out his lower lip. "I gotta do my job."

"Yes, of course," answers Mabel, half to herself. "I just wonder if there might be a way to do your job, and to create a way for Terry to learn about true, inherent safety."

Chaz's mild expression reflects not a whit of comprehension.

Mabel casts about for help. A gradual fade-in of Terry's sleeping form appears to guides and subs alike. The solid, earthly version quickly transforms to a more translucent image. Seeming to originate somewhere in his pelvis, a central column of light blazes, ferocious as a blast furnace or volcano.

Hard at work feeding ingots into this "fire," a wizened man

smiles up at Mabel and the others, just as a great blast of steam travels headward within the core of Terry's body. "Dragon steam," the little man advises. "Best keep out of its path."

Catching on, Mabel returns his smile and then turns to Chaz. "Can you feel the power of that dragon steam?"

Chaz is clearly impressed. From their current perspective, the steam continues to build and radiate before their eyes, engulfing Terry in its powerful stream.

"Do you think that you could help to feed and maintain that fire, Chaz?" Mabel asked.

"Yeh." He grins broadly and Mabel relaxes.

"Do you suppose that if Terry's core fire were really strong, he would need to be defended in the same old way?" She holds her breath, not sure of Chaz's mental capacity.

"Naw," Chaz crows. "When bad stuff comes at him, I put a log on the fire and anything comes near him gets fried!"

"Mm, hmm," says Mabel. "I like that. Only how about anything that is of harmful intent cannot come through the light field?"

"Huh?" Chaz blinks. "Yeh, sure."

Mabel tries again. "Alright then, your new, updated job is that whenever danger threatens, you jump right into the very center and build up that light, that dragon fire, yes?"

"You got it," beams Chaz.

"No more need to attack on the outside, right?"

"Nope, I hold to the center," answers Chaz, surprising everyone present.

* * *

Next morning, Terry felt much better. The Gillis brothers were taking the day off from work. No boats going out, and no deliveries to make. Terry slept in, got up when he felt like it and walked outside to find mountain peaks visible through a clear, cobalt sky. He paused to take in the vista and thought he might try a jog around the park. Lungs were a little flabby, what can you expect after so much downtime, but the body seemed to be back in gear. Good energy, not too much pain. He smiled to himself and suddenly felt like crying. Tears of gratitude, he told himself. No big deal.

"Dear Father, I can't believe it! You actually answered my prayers! Uh, thank You for the miracle, I promise I won't let You down this time. Amen."

Terry showered and headed out once more, making his way to The Oyster's Pearl for a burger. A few hardcore regulars on their barstools looked up and nodded. It was good to be back in his familiar haunt, back in himself. He played a round of darts, an hour passed, and then another. On his way out, Terry opened the door onto Suzanne, who was just arriving. His breath caught in his throat.

"Terry, we haven't seen you around here in a while." She smiled her smoldering, heart-stopping smile that left him feeling faint. Yes! He realized both that he had not seen Suzanne since the night she'd rejected his advances, and that she still caused a meltdown of all his senses. So, he must be on the road to recovery.

He celebrated that night at the bar, went home with a girl friend—emphatically not to be confused with a girlfriend—with whom he liked to share occasional drunken sex. The next morning it was back to business as usual: weak, aching legs, fatigue like oppression, the mind a dark morass and back to work.

"Dear Father..."

~ 9 ~

Dolores was not one to pull punches. She had slipped into a light trance, just enough for her astral body to seek and find Cara's guides. "OK, you guys, what the hell is going on?"

The translucent robed elder from Cara's team, who calls herself Millicent, addresses Dolores. "Now, now, you of all lifestreams should know better than to try to muscle your way about by thy will." For a touch of emphasis, she and the entire light-bodied delegation disappears relative to Dolores' perception. In reality, they hover just beyond her frequency range, bantering with Dolores' own guides.

The illustrious Madam D sighed. This was the problem with trying to read loved ones. Caring had a way of making one try too hard, and just look at where effort gets you in this business. She sighed again, this time to clear her mind and to remove her personality from the picture. Allowing her body to relax, she anchored herself into a higher mind intelligence and slipped off her personal identity.

Once more, she dove into the astral waters, and this time achieved a cleaner transition. She took a moment to revel in the delightful sensation of weightlessness and peace, when a third sigh—this last, the mark of comfortable contentment—overtook her body. Dolores opened her awareness to plumb the great sea of consciousness that pulsed all around her, welcoming and inviting. *Her personal field guide, an elflike old male called*

Forwyn appears, highly amused. "How's that temper?" he teases, exuding such a balmy, delicious essence that she takes no offense, but smiles warmly.

"Forwyn, can you get me a line on Cara? I'm concerned about all the new discarnates in her field."

Forwyn laughs, his voice a deep and quiet rumble. "The only discarnate associated with that bunch is one inexperienced personal guide who rarely makes it into Cara's field. No, what they are is a team of higher frequency lightworkers—guides to another lifestream."

"Then how come they're hanging out with Cara?"

"Observing, checking her out. No guide is an island, you know, we do interact...and gossip." He laughs again.

"They're gossiping about Cara?" Dolores asks, incredulous. "Anything I don't know?"

Forwyn's tone grows serious. "I don't know what they have decided. Her guides and his had a meeting. This really isn't my business."

He's gone. Dolores waits, confident that someone with higher authority will show up. Before long, it is Millicent who reappears. "Are you ready to play nice, then?" she chides.

"Please excuse my rudeness," mumbles Dolores. She wears humility about as easily as a lumberjack dances in spike heels. Knowing that Millicent knows this increases her discomfort.

Millicent is less inclined to cruelty than a human in her position might be. She does not gloat. Splendidly radiant, she becomes a perfect ambassador. "We have allowed, and even encouraged exchange and cooperation with the guides you have seen in your friend's field. It is all for the good, both hers and his. No need for concern. Although she is not the one concerned now, is she?"

"Well, no, but she doesn't really believe in all of you,"
defends Dolores.

"Oh, belief enters not into the picture," Millicent counters.
"She simply has not the fear that disturbs so many of your kind."
Choosing a somewhat more merciful approach, she adds, "This
one, Cara, is not programmed for fear and concern. Such traits are
not within her realm of disposition. You must not judge or compare
yourself with her, or vice versa, though it might do you well to
learn from her example."

Dolores is beginning to falter, but has thus far kept her
pride in check. "But who is he—that one whose guides you say are
cooperating with you?"

"We are not at liberty to tell. If the project goes unclassified,
your friend will, of her own accord, become aware of the role she
and he are playing relative to one another. There is really no more
to say about this. You need not involve yourself, and we caution
you against judging the matter, about which you have insufficient
understanding."

Dolores stifles her pride—again—thanks Millicent and
returns to full physical presence.

"Insufficient understanding!" she fumed. "How can anyone
have sufficient understanding when they're so tight-lipped about
it all!"

Cara regarded her mildly, silently assessing how much
wine to pour into Dolores' glass. "So why don't you bitch directly
to their faces? I mean it's not like they don't hear you now."

Dolores chuckled, surprised by the obvious. "Yeah, well, I
guess that's what your friend Millicent was implying, it's because
I'm a coward."

Cara handed her the half-filled glass and a lit joint. "Here, build some fortitude."

They sat in silence, watching the sky long past moonrise and throughout the bloom of stars.

Sunday morning late September brought the first break from clouds and rain in almost three weeks. People were out in throngs, like worms on the sidewalk after a rain. Fran had gone for a walk, baby in tow, hours after helping Bill shove off at dawn.

She sighed. The boys were headed out to sea again, Sunday notwithstanding. Her husband never seemed to be available anymore as her friend and playmate. She cringed at how cliché the thought sounded, threatening to turn her into one more bored, forsaken housewife. She pushed the stroller down the western pier, deciding all at once to turn off toward the farmers' market, which was unusually lively thanks to the fair weather.

Fran's spirits lifted as she moved from stall to stall, aesthetically pleased by mounds of red apples and orange pumpkins, made more festive by the buzz of voices overlain by a percussion of live music. She wheeled the baby through the crowd.

As the trio of musicians set down their instruments for a break, the cider pressman called out from his nearby booth to come and have a cup on him. Eager to oblige, the three brushed alongside Fran and her stroller on the narrow path.

Fran almost tripped in her abrupt effort to u-turn. "It's you," she addressed Cara. "Aren't you the fortune teller? You know my brother-in-law."

Cara appraised the lanky brunette, overdressed for the

warm morning in a hooded green parka. "Hi," she said, turning her attention to the baby. "Who's your brother-in-law?"

Fran blushed. "Sorry," she began. "We saw you at the Arts Festival last month. You recognized Terry. I assumed…"

Cara held out her tambourine to the baby and very gently tapped the clappers a few times, then glanced thoughtfully back at Fran. "You're Terry the fisherman's sister-in-law?" Her focus returned to the baby, who had reached out and clamped her fingers on the tambourine. "And who is this?" she asked, smiling into the tiny face and giving the tambourine a slight wiggle. The baby cooed.

"This is Tracey. You're good with babies. Do you have any children?" Fran felt strangely uncomfortable around this woman who could not have been that much older than she was, yet seemed infinitely calmer and self-possessed.

"My daughter died with her father in a car accident when she was four. That was more than ten years ago."

"I'm sorry," Fran gasped.

Cara held her gaze reassuringly, as if it had been Fran who had lost a child. "She was a lot of fun." She suddenly grinned, tenderly disengaging Tracey's little hand from the tambourine. Waving to acknowledge her band mates, who were loudly hailing her from the cider booth, she turned once more toward Fran. "Well, see you around."

"What are you saying…you want to what, go somewhere?" Bill sat with Fran at the kitchen table after a late dinner. Her increasing depression had become obvious. He was listening now, trying to understand.

"I need a break," she repeated. "And I want some time

with you. I can't be just a mother all the time. It's making me a lousy mother. Just for a weekend, Bill."

Bill regarded her tired shoulders and teary eyes with some surprise. "What about Tracey?" he asked.

"Babysitter, Bill. It's just a weekend."

He gazed at her with open curiosity. She laughed at his expression and took his hand. "If I find us a babysitter, will you take the time off?"

"Yeah, OK." He tried to smile, still surprised, but relieved to see her laugh.

Terry and Bill hauled a full net onto the deck, and began sorting the catch. Bill thought Terry was acting normal this week. He might still lack his typical bravado, but at least he did not seem so vacant. The two brothers fell into an easy rhythm, forged over a lifetime of working together.

Bill brought up his and Fran's recent conversation. "What do you think has gotten into her?" he asked. "She never minded me going to work before."

Terry shrugged while reaching for a ten-pound octopus. "Take a look at this monster," he chuckled, hefting it overboard. "You know, Mom used to be around to help out. Fran's probably not used to her being gone."

"Yeah, I guess," Bill agreed. "I can't believe Mom actually made it to Arizona."

"I know it. She was always afraid she might mildew here. Now she thinks she'll mummify down there."

Bill laughed.

"I could watch Tracey if you want," Terry offered.

Bill stopped working and stared at Terry, wondering if he

knew anything about anyone in his life anymore. "Thanks," he said after a long pause. "She'd really like that."

Pushing Tracey's stroller, Fran walked the western pier, cruised past the farmers' market grounds and finally stopped to rest on a bench at a small corner park. She was beginning to feel the first signs of despair grip at her throat and belly. She had had such a strong sense of hope, had actually felt directed to return here. Tears welled as she faced the reality of defeat. She got up and aimed the stroller toward home.

An advertisement stapled to a light pole caught her eye. "Madam D," she read. "That's her!" She memorized the address and aimed the stroller, feeling far more agitated, or maybe excited, than her sense of logic could fathom.

Surprised to find a church at her supposed destination, Fran double-checked the address. "Well, it's worth a try," she thought. A janitor, cleaning the sanctuary, directed her around to a side entrance that led to Madam D's Psychic Institute. Once inside, she leaned against the closed door and felt the built-up tension leave as swiftly as it had come. Now all she felt was timid and a little ashamed to be there at all.

She pushed Tracey down the hall to an office where a petite, brown-haired woman sat writing at a desk. "Excuse me," she began. "I'm looking for Madam D."

Dolores met her gaze with a smile. "Hi, what can I do for you?"

Fran's face fell. "Oh. Excuse me, I'm actually looking for someone else. I don't know her name. She was at your booth at the City Arts Festival. She plays the flute, I think."

Dolores laughed. "That's my friend, Cara. She doesn't go

in for the whole psychic bit, but she's awfully good. Isn't nature funny!"

Fran saw that Dolores appeared genuinely amused or even delighted at the thought. Her eyes were brown in color, but seemed backlit by some unseen light that added golden overtones. Just as she had felt in Cara's presence, Fran felt somehow young and unsure of herself as she faced Dolores.

"Have a seat, I'll get us a pot of tea," Dolores called, leaving Fran in the small office. While she waited for Dolores to return with the tea, Fran glanced at Tracey asleep in her stroller, and felt another upwelling of tears.

"Sorry, who did you say this is?" Cara asked, turning down the volume on her stereo.

Fran paused, took a breath and launched into her proposal.

Unseen at Fran's end, Cara held the telephone in front of her face, staring in disbelief. "You want me to babysit your daughter?" she finally asked.

Fran, who had presumed the whole idea to be divinely inspired and thus preordained, never wavered, but offered details, dates and times.

Cara spoke slowly into the phone. "Fran, I have a job. I play music for a living. My band plays gigs on weekends. Even if I wanted to babysit I wouldn't be available for a weekend job, you know?" Sensing Fran's urgency, she spoke gently, despite her astonishment.

Under the crush of disappointment, Fran heard Bill's footsteps approach their front door. She prepared to face him with her news of failure.

"It's a go, girl," he bellowed. "Make your reservations. You won't believe who I got to watch Tracey!"

~ 10 ~

"He seems to have stabilized. Any objections to taking him up another notch?" Snarrow is not about to make any solo decisions regarding the pacing of Terry's amplification.

Mabel senses a vague itch of misgiving. "We shall need to do some intensive work with the subs. Is everyone up for it?"

Vormis dims, flickers and squeaks his evident distress. "What is it?" Mabel asks him.

His field oscillates. "I think I may need some extra backup." The room fills with the peach colored light of compassion. Vormis has been holding his own so well that the more experienced lightworkers tend to forget his considerable inexperience.

"I'm with you, buddy," pledges Pryluck.

"Don't worry, Vormis," offers Snarrow. "We will keep a double on you. And, I suppose, we can alert the female's guides to stand by and maybe check in during the initial increase."

There seems to be unanimous agreement, until someone quietly wonders, "Do you think it might be a good idea to wait until after the babysitting weekend?"

"Why that?" asks Snarrow.

"I don't know, just a thought. He might find it easier to be introduced to one new thing at a time."

"Nonsense," Pryluck dismisses the idea. "The baby is his

niece, his own family, not something new. They're all OK with their families."

Mabel wants to disagree, but cannot find any foundation upon which to base an argument, aside from the fact that it is Pryluck who has expressed the opinion. They let the matter drop, not exactly in agreement with Pryluck, but more out of uncertainty. The whole project is one big unknown, and time will tell in the end.

In sub rehab, Elaine is making progress. She paces in meeting, shunning the table and chairs where Mabel mediates for the group of subpersonalities. They have gotten Elaine to talk about herself, which is a promising departure for the belligerent dominatrix.

For Elaine it all comes down to power. That, along with just a tad of vengeance. And what could be a more effective approach for exerting control than seduction and rejection? She's an expert. Submission of her prey is the goal, and sexual control the means. Elaine is highly successful.

The turning point in rehab comes when Elaine admits to Mabel that her modus operandi keeps her own sense of impotence subdued. She raises a dismissive bare shoulder. "Others drink," she spits through twisted lips.

* * *

All appeared to be in order during the weeks leading up to Bill and Fran's getaway weekend. Terry was consistently showing up for work, displaying more confidence and vitality than he had in months. The guys on his darts team got loud, bragging the tournament was theirs for the taking, now that Gillis was playing again.

On Thursday, Terry hit some kind of peak, awakening

early with a surge of energy and well-being. But, by mid-afternoon he began to crash…big-time. At first, it felt like the after effects of ingesting a large pot of coffee—not quite the shakes, but buzzy. His heart raced, and he could not quite get enough air. Then came panic, and his breathing became harder still. Bill noticed his brother leaning over the rail, white-faced as a seasick tourist.

"Ter, you all right?"

Terry did not turn, but sucked in air with all his attention. His throat felt thick and tight. "Yeah," he replied brusquely.

"What's going on?" asked Bill.

Terry looked over his shoulder with an expression that stopped Bill's own breath. The emotion in Terry's face reminded Bill of the time he had seen a dog hit by a car. The dog lay in the road unable to move, with the same look in its eyes that Bill now saw in his brother's.

Terry looked away. "I don't know," he choked.

"Uh, I'll get in the catch. Maybe you ought to lie down or something."

Terry nodded his head, still looking away and out to sea.

Pulling in the nets, Bill fretted. Mostly he worried about how Fran would react to a cancellation of their big weekend plans. But no way could he see them leaving their baby with his brother.

Dockside, while cleaning the deck, it occurred to Bill that Terry might be seriously ill. "Shit," he thought, "I ought to check on him." He made the short jaunt around the boat and found his brother gone. "Shit," he repeated.

* * *

Mabel fumes her disgust over Pryluck's influence in regard to the timing of Terry's frequency boost. Snarrow tries to mediate.

"Remember, it was a group decision. The lifestream was adjusting well. We had no way to know how the increase would destabilize him."

"Right," Mabel mutters under her breath.

Vormis flickers wildly. "I need some help here, guys. I can't reach him again."

Pryluck sighs. "Remember fear, Vormis. It's the human way. Same story as before."

At their console, two techno conductors in charge of the orchestration of Terry's deprogramming exchange a glance. The two are almost indistinguishable, right down to their penchant for canary colored emanations. The one called Barwin clears his throat. "Um, might we have a word with you, Snarrow?"

Snarrow flares a bit brighter in surprise. The technies rarely interact. "Sure, what is it, uh, Barwin, right?" None of the lightworkers is ever quite sure who is which.

"It's just that, well, we've kind of been noticing, um, a kind of, you know, disharmony around here lately, and uh, you know, maybe it's affecting, might be, you know, the quality of work?"

All attention comes to focus on the stammering technie, his field barely visible in his attempt at unobtrusiveness. Once he has finished, the room remains still and silent for some moments.

Mabel is the first to recover. "I think he is right," she breathes.

There's another moment of silent self-reflection among the group, followed by a vibrant torrent of laughter. "Look at us," chortles Pryluck. "We're behaving like the lifestreams! With us quibbling about, it's no wonder our guy's having such a tough time. Alright, Vormis, what do you need us to do?"

With the atmosphere at Methods some few shades lighter,

Barwin looks to his partner for confirmation, before reporting to Snarrow, "Phase One stripping complete."

~ 11 ~

Four days later, Bill knocked at Terry's apartment, let himself in and recoiled at the stench. Drawn window shades kept out the light of day. Unwashed cups and food containers lay scattered throughout, along with various articles of clothing, including four-day since used work clothes making their fishy presence immediately known.

Getting no response to his initial holler, Bill poked his head into Terry's bedroom. Terry lay on his bed unwashed, unshaven, apparently not asleep or dead. Not talking.

"Jesus, Terry, what the fuck is going on?"

Terry's eyes moved disinterestedly in Bill's direction, not fully focused on him or anything else that Bill could see, before resuming their original position. OK, he was conscious, but not responding. Or he had responded, sort of. Bill was stumped. He should call someone. 911? He thought of movies, TV news stories... Drugs, that had to be it.

"What did you take, Terry?" he yelled, looking around the room for pill bottles. Nothing.

Terry again rolled his eyes toward Bill at the mention of drugs, this time allowing his face to express scorn.

"Well, what am I supposed to do, Ter? I'm calling 911."

"No!" roared Terry, half sitting up. "Mind your fucking

business and leave me the fuck alone!"

So, he could respond if he wanted to. "Ter, you can't keep doing this. You need some kind of help. At least tell me what's going on. Does something hurt?"

"Yeah, something hurts," he answered bitterly.

"What is it?"

"How the hell should I know? Your fucking life falls apart, it hurts."

Bill heard the break in Terry's voice.

"Listen, I can't leave you here like this. Stay with Fran and me for a while. I swear, we'll leave you alone, but I gotta at least know you're being fed and all."

"Fuck off," grumbled Terry.

"Then we'll have to come stay here with you."

"Will you cut it out?" Exasperated, Terry's voice took on the same whine as when they had fought as kids.

Balling up a cast-off sock from the floor, Bill pitched it hard at Terry, then another, and then a tee shirt.

Reflexively, Terry ducked and raised his arms to block the barrage of dirty clothes. He flung a pillow back at Bill, who caught it and laughed.

Still holding the pillow, Bill walked over to the bed and sat down. His eyes focused steadily on his brother. Terry appeared miserable and tormented, but no longer catatonic. Bill laid a firm hand on Terry's shoulder.

"We're here for you, man. Come on home with me."

* * *

The registration table is inundated, and chaos prevails. Mabel, with intern Bulista assisting, is trying to attend to all of the subs who have flooded into their rehab center immediately following the first level of Terry's personality stripping. The subs are for the most part confused, frightened and combative. Each is on his or her worst behavior. Even Helen—who has been the special focus for lightworker support and encouragement—is back to crouching, hiding, and crying, and utterly unresponsive to contact. Chaz has retreated to a far corner, holding his space in the form of a large, snarling jaguar. Elaine stands nearby, like Chaz's comrade in arms, snapping her whip and taunting all who would approach.

And still, a steady stream of new desperate and disoriented subs flow through the door. Clearly, more staff will be needed to manage this mess. However, crisis brews at Methods headquarters as well. The technies are getting a recurrent error message each time they attempt to introduce Terry's new baseline stabilization program. They suspect impending hard drive failure, and the whole room glowers in storm-gray waves.

Snarrow addresses the longtime field guide of an aging socialite. "Can you stick close to Vormis for a while? I hate to do this, but I am going to bring in Creative Works. We have got to get some outside perspective on all this."

"I'm good to go," answers the guide. "My gal is at the opera. It's La Traviata, she's seen it before."

"Excellent. Thank you," Snarrow breathes.

* * *

Two agents from Creative Works are sent to brainstorm with Methods Division. They seem to have been suddenly called away from some other Creative Project—or so the Methods Workers hope. One arrives in a holographic overlay that lends his field a distinct resemblance to a thick, human form. The form is decked out in a scarlet bouffant wig over a layering of blue and red striped robes. The image ends there. No hands, feet or footwear complete the picture.

The second agent appears more diminutive, although likewise holographically attired in a stunningly tall top hat that easily matches the height of the entire "body." The rest of this one's costume consists of a rotating, silver hued configuration, something like a diamond-shaped hoop skirt. The garment tapers to a point at both top and bottom. Around the neck hangs a flashing fringe of crimson Christmas lights.

Snarrow is so irritated by their appearance and behavior that, try as he might, he is unable to control the spiking chaos of his field.

"Smashing do, Dude," compliments the diamond-hooped agent, mistaking Snarrow's discomfort for fashion. "This ought to be fun. We hear the changing changeling is just brindling at the seams."

Snarrow gazes helplessly at the peculiar agent.

The bouffant-headed partner intervenes. "Ugh, you're mixing your metaphors. It's bridling is what you mean to say."

The amendment changes not a thing for Snarrow, so he carefully states, "It looks like we might be experiencing a system failure. The lifestream has not accepted any new overlays since completion of Phase I Stripping."

He gestures toward the chaos at Mabel's rehab center. "Defragmentation programs won't run. It looks like we have lost our interim patches, so the personality is trying to run default to the original program. Which, of course, is no longer an option."

"Oh, look!" cries Bouffant Head. "Isn't it grand?" He has already jumped phases to materialize himself in the rehab scene, face to face with dominatrix Elaine, at whom he beams with un-

bridled *joy and admiration.*

"My lady." He bows, taking her spiked, leather clad hand to lead her in an enthusiastic tango.

Snarrow's jaw drops, Pryluck grins, and the scent of sugar cookies fills the air. Elaine has instantly responded, drawn into of all things, Creative Works' sense of fun.

"That's it," Mabel mutters to herself. *"Elaine's thing is the dramatic..."*

Meanwhile, Diamond Hoops has joined the chaos. He and Bouffant Head greet each subpersonality with wholehearted admiration. In their demeanors, the character of each is joyfully mirrored. The troubled, disconnected mass begins to gravitate toward a common center, and the mood is increasingly heady. Before long, a party atmosphere surrounds the two ridiculous figures, who clearly seem to be having the time of their lives.

Back in Methods Dept, the technie, Barwin, exults to Snarrow, "Looks like de-frag's up and running!"

Snarrow sits in silence, pondering the stretch that he—that they all—will have to make if they are going to successfully bring this lifestream through his own expansion.

The two CW agents briefly reappear at his side. Bouffant Head swirls his robes before he and Diamond Hoops blip out of sight. "You see us as buffoons." His whisper lingers. "They see us as hope for salvation from their personal hell. Think about it."

Snarrow's field remains pebbly as he brings his next meeting to order. Along with Terry's team, Cara's guides have also been asked to attend. As the group assembles, many are surprised to find two members of Creative Works in attendance. The air simmers with curiosity.

"I want to thank you all for being here, and to especially welcome our guests." Snarrow's *gesture acknowledges both Cara's team and CW agents alike.*

* * *

Leaving for the day, Dolores encountered Fran—this time minus baby—outside on the street. "Hi, did you get a hold of Cara?" Dolores asked carefully, noting Fran's fragile demeanor.

Fran blinked back tears before blurting, "Nothing's working out. Terry is useless, and now he's in our house, and I'm still stuck at home and I need help."

Dolores gave Fran a probing look. "Did you come here to see me?"

Fran's surprise was visible. "Yes. I guess. I didn't know who else..."

"How can I help you?" Dolores inquired.

"I thought maybe...you know everything, right?"

Dolores laughed. "I don't know everything. In fact, I don't know much at all. That's not what psychic means. But if you're looking for a reading, I might be able to help you get a handle on, well, the forces underlying the events of your life. You know, help you put some meaning to it. Does that make sense to you?"

Fran nodded. "OK."

"OK," Dolores repeated. "Listen, I need to get home now. Can you come by tomorrow at about 12:30?"

I will...but is it OK if I have to bring my baby?"

"No problem," said Dolores. "See you then."

* * *

Camouflaged in shadow, scrambled and shielded like a federal agent, Pryluck does his best to ensure that his whispered consultation with Barwin is not detected by any of his Methods

Division co-Workers. "Are you absolutely sure?" he repeats for at least the third time. "No chance at all?"

Barwin nods vigorously. "There can be no correlation whatsoever between the prank you pulled at the time of the lifestream, Terry's, birth and the mandate we received to implement frequency acceleration of his person. The destiny tag you altered plays no causal role at all. In fact, those tags are mere identifiers."

Maintaining such a lengthy exchange is as radical a feat for Barwin as broaching this sensitive subject is for Pryluck. "When we create a new lifestream's programs," reassures Barwin, "any and all Initiation and Destiny files associated with that lifestream consist of encoded data, which is inputted before the bassinet then gets assigned and tagged. There is simply no mechanism for information to stream backwards from the tags into the system. It just does not work that way.

~ 12 ~

Terry remained sequestered in his room and—in Fran's word—useless, for about a week. She and Bill, as promised, allowed him his self-imposed exile within their house. They did, however, stew over the situation during dinner and in bed at night. Fran was all for giving Terry an ultimatum. After some specified time period, he would have to see a doctor or a priest or someone—anyone. Maybe he should see Madam D, she thought, but did not say.

Bill listened, non-committal. Terry was there with them

out of trust alone, and Bill would do what he could to maintain that trust. But how far would it be right for them to let this thing go? "And if he refuses?" he asked Fran. "Say X amount of time goes by and he doesn't see a doctor. What are you threatening to do?"

"I don't know, Bill, maybe we should commit him. If it turns out he isn't crazy, at least they'll have examined him, and maybe have found something out. Or know where to send him."

"For God's sake, Fran."

As it happened, they never had to resolve the matter. One evening Terry showed up at dinner, dressed and fundamentally lucid. "I'm going out to Preston for a couple of weeks," he announced.

Both Bill and Fran scrutinized him, equally concerned and relieved.

"What's in Preston?" asked Bill.

"I don't know, some kind of church retreat. Might as well," he added under his breath.

Bill eyed him hard, as furtively as he could manage. Terry was functional. That was good, but he could sense desperation below the surface. "So what is the retreat about?" he asked.

"A retreat place, not an event. It's a place to get away."

"How did you hear about it?" Fran wanted to know. "There's like nothing out there in Preston."

"A priest gave me this card." Terry pushed the business card from Father Sulleran across the table to Fran. She picked it up and read, "Ricki's Halfway." Her forehead wrinkled. "That doesn't sound very religious to me."

Bill reached over to take the card from her. "Let us design the new you? It sure doesn't. Terry, what do you know about this place?"

Terry shrugged. "It's a place. What's the big deal?"

Fran and Bill exchanged a glance. "Well, how much are they going to charge you? I mean the name sounds kind of weird. How do you know it's not some kind of racket?" Fran persisted.

"Give me a break," Terry growled, pushing away from the table.

Bill scowled at Fran.

"All right, I'm sorry," she said. "When are you leaving?"

Terry gazed witheringly at her, said nothing and retreated back to his room.

An excited phone call from Dolores jangled Cara. "I've got to see you. Can you come over?"

Cara hesitated. Dolores excited was unusual. "I have to be downtown for a gig. I don't have a lot of time."

"Then can you meet me at Canal Park for maybe half an hour?"

Dolores was early, waiting on a bench when Cara arrived. That, too, was unusual. Cara aimed for the bench, but Dolores stood up to walk. They followed the canal, with Dolores setting a brisk pace. "This is starting to feel really creepy, like I'm watching a stalker or something."

Cara placidly met her gaze, waiting for details.

"You know those—I don't know, snoops—you had in your field that, according to your guide Millicent, belong to some guy who she says is none of my business?"

Cara tried not to crack a smile. Dolores would not let it drop.

"Well, that same woman who asked if you would babysit came to me for a reading. Guess who she turns out to be connected with?"

"Who?" Cara played along.

"Well, she asked something about her brother-in-law, so I tuned in and found him..."

"What do you mean, you found him?"

"I found the astral essence of this woman's brother-in-law in her energy field, and from there I was able to focus in on him. It turns out that the green busybody in your field is one of her brother-in-law's guides!"

Cara stared at Dolores, briefly puzzled. "Her brother-in-law?" she repeated, mentally reviewing the image of meeting Fran at the farmers' market. "No!" she burst out laughing. "Terry's some kind of psychic snoop?" She was consumed by a fit of giggles.

Impatient, Dolores insisted, "Cara, you don't get it. There is something strange going on with that guy, Terry, and whether you believe it or not, your guides are in cahoots with his. They tell me it's some kind of classified project—whatever that means— and now his sister-in-law is on the scene. Don't you feel at all invaded?"

Cara was still not quite over the giggles, and tried to control the grin that her face was determined to maintain. "No. They're an odd family for sure, but I don't feel like they're after me or anything." She inadvertently let another small explosion of laughter escape through taut lips.

Dolores snorted.

"Sorry," Cara offered. "It's just if you ever met the guy..." She stifled another, smaller laugh. "He's really not very threatening. More like a cartoon that's crumbling."

"Well, maybe he—his guides and all—wants to keep himself from crumbling. What if they want to take your life force or something?"

Cara was still smiling, "Like a vampire?"

Dolores also smiled at that. "You're right, it sounds ridiculous, but what do you think he is doing with you?"

"I don't know, D. The few times I've run into him it just seems like he is desperate for support or consolation. Maybe that's all it is."

"Damn, I hate not knowing," Dolores admitted.

Cara opened her arms for a hug. "I love you, D."

* * *

Mabel collapses in an amorphous puddle. It is less the prevailing chaos, and more the complexity of the challenge that overwhelms her. The subpersonalities are tractable enough as individuals. Aside from the few original luminaries—including Ethel, Chaz and depending on her mood, Elaine—when it comes to interacting with each other, the subpersonalities' behavior suggest a combination of severe autism and short-term memory loss.

Time after time, they are introduced and even participate in group-process together, only to forget the entire episode an hour later. At that point, they might pass one another or sit face to face without the slightest recognition of the other's presence. More frustrating still is that new subs are continuing to show up, with no end in sight. The lightworkers have begun to suspect that the existing subpersonalities are actually subdividing in response to increased light.

"It's a defensive tactic," Barwin confirms, speaking for the technies, "to keep the new frequencies at bay. We can, if you

would like, create a file for each thematically similar group."

"Do you mean, for instance, all the rage-related subs would be grouped together?" Mabel asks.

"Exactly. Although there will be overlap between groups. Ultimately, you will probably find that the underlying species-specific program ties them all together. We are working to create a program that will enable self-recognition at that level."

"Please do," Mabel urges.

II

Making Contact

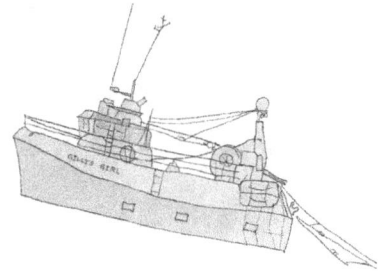

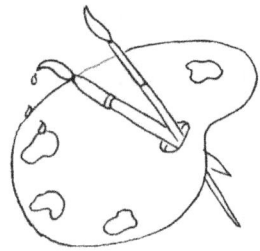

~ 13 ~

Terry drove north and east, relieved to get beyond city traffic as he approached the mountains. He was aware of a sense of emptiness that had been with him now for weeks. At this moment, the sensation was less devastating than when he was in the company of others. Still, it felt oppressive, a pain that he could neither name nor escape.

Tentatively, he tried prayer. "Dear Father, You may think I've turned away from You. I guess I might have. I don't know." His voice broke. "I don't know anything, just You gotta help me." Tears flowed freely down his face and onto his shirt. "Or maybe You don't have to. I don't know that either. But I need help. So if there's someone, anyone out there, please do something!"

Terry could no longer see well enough to drive. He managed to pull the truck over to the shoulder of the highway and wailed like a baby. Afterwards, he felt much better. It was as if some invisible something had held and soothed him as he cried. The recognition startled Terry back to normal alertness.

"Son of a bitch," he muttered. "Was that You, God?"

* * *

Euphoria and high-fives prevail at Methods. "Whoo, you did it, Vormis." Gleeful lightworkers congratulate themselves and each other as showers of brilliant sparks illuminate the air. They have achieved their first conscious contact, proof-positive that the lifestream Terry's personality has successfully come through its first transition.

"With him responsive to us, the rest of the project ought to go like clockwork, hardly more than a matter of programming," crows Pryluck.

Vormis stares at him. A field guide to another lifestream, overhearing this, guffaws. "You've never been one of them, that's for sure! Every lightworker should have to do a turn as a human lifestream, or even spend one day in the field. It would give you all a dose of common sense." He shakes his head, and winks at Vormis. "You tell 'em how it is."

Vormis hesitates. "Well, he's probably a lot more distressed than we maybe realize. We consider our breakthrough a milestone of success, but he's beyond the scope of his reality."

"Well naturally, his original reality template has been removed," insists Pryluck.

"Look," maintains the veteran guide, "with these lifestreams you're always up against hardware. Are you doing anything with that? Is altering hardware part of Management's proposal?"

"What is your point?" asks Pryluck.

"They are hard wired for fear. I mean we're talking every time their circuitry detects anything the least bit unfamiliar. If you've got your man outside his box with no template of experiences to make sense out of the new—for example, Vormis' presence—he's going to do one of two things: misinterpret it to fit what he thinks he knows, or break from sanity."

"That's what I'm worried about," admits Vormis. "We're not supposed to let him go insane."

Snarrow speaks up. "I think we are all thoroughly aware of the fear issue. That is pretty much what we have been up against all along. And we have indeed been asked and authorized to ultimately reconfigure the hard structure. But that process must be undertaken gradually, in order to allow the physiology to change in accordance."

The field guide is impressed. "Big works," he exhales.

Mabel flashes impatiently. "OK," she says. "First, I agree, insanity is not an option. As to the second possibility that you have mentioned, we have already encountered the lifestream's misinterpretation of events. It is indeed inevitable, but not so bad a choice at that. Misunderstanding and subsequently learning to find one's way clear of mistakes is no different from the way any of them learn anything.

* * *

Leaving behind pavement for dusty dirt roads, Terry drove for some time through pine and cedar forest. He edged his truck around a curved lane, following the river until it widened into a small lake, thanks to the industry of local beavers. He double-checked the directions. There should be a white wooden building, #137, just a quarter mile past the beaver dam.

The building itself was unmarked, although a mailbox beside the driveway clearly read 137. The house appeared deserted. Terry guessed that if one wanted to retreat, the remote, nondescript nature of the place was fitting. He tentatively rang the doorbell and was relieved to hear approaching footsteps.

A bulky, overdressed woman opened the door. "Welcome to Ricki's," she effused. Her alarming smile revealed large, stained teeth within thick, heavily lipsticked lips. The glossy gold cap on a lower incisor had to have been recently installed. "The girls are out for a picnic. You'll have some time to get yourself settled."

Terry's forehead creased. "Umm, I thought this was some

kind of all men's retreat."

The woman regarded him from under heavy brows, and rolled her eyes. "Well, of course. Now, I'm Sally. Come along and I'll show you to your room."

She took his sleeve, propelling him along a short hallway to the last door on the right. "I've put you in with Jim." She lowered her voice to gossip tones. "He's a big, tough coal miner, come all the way from West Virginia. I thought you two would be a good match."

Terry backed away. "Whoa, hang on, I ain't sharing no room."

Sally carefully examined Terry, as if seeing him for the first time. "Now, what's the problem, honey? You're among friends here. You'll see, maybe for the first time in your life. Relax, unpack and take a walk if you want. There'll be an orientation before dinner."

"Look," he began. "I never agreed to no roommate..."

To his horror, Sally leaned in close to his cheek and kissed the air, effectively impeding any further grievance. Before he could resurrect his protest about the room, she made a fast get-away down the hall. A chemtrail of mildew and tobacco odor lingered.

Left alone in the room, Terry collapsed onto the one apparently unclaimed bed. He didn't feel up to turning around and driving all the way home, at least not tonight. And just as Fran had said, there was nothing out in Preston—certainly no nearby hotel. Besides, if he returned home he would be in exactly the same predicament he was in before reserving his place at Ricki's. He would just have to hunt down that nasty looking bitch with the gold tooth and insist that she straighten out the rooming situation.

Terry slept through orientation, and would have remained in bed through dinner but for the entrance of Jim, the roommate. As Sally had implied, Jim was burly. Permanent dirt stains were evident in his well-scrubbed skin creases and fingernails. Although Jim's manner was as guarded as Terry's own, his gaze through pale blue eyes was gentle bordering on meek. They shook hands.

"We're encouraged to dress for dinner," Jim confessed with a self-conscious smile. "I'm still new here, I don't know if I can be comfortable with that."

Terry eyed Jim's jeans and cotton shirt. He shrugged. "I don't see any problem with what you got on."

Jim gave him a quick, odd glance, and nodded sheepishly. "Yeah, I guess it's all at our own pace here."

"This guy's in worse shape than me," Terry thought. "What a shame, big guy like that such a wuss." The feeling inclined him toward generosity. Together, he and Jim entered the dining hall.

Meals turned out to be served buffet style in a modest sized common room filled with wooden tables and camp-style chairs. Approaching the buffet line, a waft of perfume alerted Terry to the presence of women. He stopped to scan the room, as a waving Sally caught his eye and hurried over.

"Terry, we missed you at orientation."

He held up his tray and pivoted to evade a repeat of her earlier Latin greeting.

"Good, good, you've met Jim." She laid a hand on Jim's thick forearm, smiled briefly at him, and returned her attention to Terry. "Didn't I tell you he was a bruiser?" she winked.

Discomfited, Terry glanced at Jim, who merely blushed.

With a sickening sensation in the pit of his stomach, he suddenly recalled his last conversation with Father Sulleran in the church garden. He remembered the lingering haze of confusion, and how he had immediately run headlong into Cara. The thought of Cara now brought a sense of longing.

Still playing the hostess, Sally guided Jim and Terry to a table, already occupied by two women and a young man. Like Sally, the women appeared overdressed for the rustic setting in their makeup, evening clothes and high heels. All three at the table seemed unnaturally keen to be introduced, like baby birds straining to be fed. One woman—or girl, Terry could not tell her age—giggled shyly. Her name was Martha. The young man, whom Terry judged to be in his late twenties, introduced himself as Raoul, while grinning as if at some joke. The third, a heavyset middle-aged gal, solemnly shook Jim and Terry's hands and pronounced her name, Mira, in a hoarse voice. She immediately flushed and dropped her eyes.

"I'll leave you all to get acquainted," Sally chirped. "Jim, will you show Terry the schedule board?"

Disinclined to raise the roommate issue in front of Jim, Terry rose in pursuit of Sally when she turned from the table. Her quick dismissal at full volume preempted any further exchange. "We'll get you an orientation packet in the morning, dear."

While Jim and the others tentatively initiated getting-to-know-you conversation, Terry remained still and quiet. His heart pounded. Something was glaringly wrong. He felt a different sort of panic from what he had come to think of as normal. This place. These people.

He brought his attention back to the table where Raoul was relating something about his parents.

Then, Mira spoke softly into her plate. "I've been married thirteen years. My wife thinks I'm on a fishing trip."

It took Terry a minute for this to register. He looked again at each of the women, looked carefully at Jim and Raoul, and remembered Sally's comment, "Of course" it's an all-men's retreat. He began to shake. He thought again of Father Sulleran with his convoluted talk about dogs and rabbits, and a deep blush spread across his face. Unsteadily, he picked up his still-full tray and retreated to his room.

Jim returned after 8:00 to find Terry in bed. He hovered about, shy and concerned. "Are you alright?" he finally asked.

Terry gazed up at Jim from beneath the covers. "I need someone to tell me what this place is," he said, voice tight.

Jim frowned. "This place? You mean Ricki's?"

Terry nodded. "Yeah."

"I guess I don't know what you mean. It's a retreat house."

"For who?" Terry persisted. "What kind of retreat is this?"

Jim reached into his pocket and handed Terry a printed schedule of events. A brief glance showed Terry an assortment of activities: picnics, hikes and swims, along with various support groups and meetings. He looked back at Jim, the question still burning in his face.

"I guess it's a retreat place where guys like us can be ourselves and feel OK with who we are," Jim explained.

Terry's eyes filled as he asked, "Guys like what, Jim? What kind of guys feel OK here?"

Jim looked steadily at Terry. "I like to cross dress, like Martha and Mira..."

Terry closed his eyes and exhaled heavily. "And Sally," he added under his breath.

Jim agreed, "And Sally. A lot of guys who come through here are in some stage of sex change procedures. I think I'm basically straight, but most of the others here are gay, only more or less still in the closet. The retreats can help if someone is trying to become less secretive and more honest. At the least, they can help us to accept ourselves more." He studied Terry, who had not moved. "Why are you here, Terry?"

Terry shook his head. "Christ, I have no idea." He turned his head into the pillow to hide his tears.

* * *

"This is quite a shock for Terry," Mabel clucks and sighs. "How is Vormis holding up?"

Mabel has just returned to Methods observatory after a sub rehab session. In her opinion, the subs are shaping up marvelously. For the most part, they recognize one another at least sometimes, and some have even begun to interact. Mabel considers these changes quite positive. She figures that each one's ability to see and relate to "others" indicates movement away from his or her rigidly subjective viewpoint.

Snarrow expands his field to include Mabel. "Vormis has a backup with him. I would say that everyone has been holding up as well as can be expected. The field guides have not lost contact with the lifestream, and Terry seems to be accepting his disintegration quite well." Mabel and Snarrow survey and reflect in a glow of sunset tones while Terry again lapses into sleep.

With intern Bulista in tow, Mabel and Snarrow meet with two agents from Creative Works, to assess current circumstances and to plan strategy. Creative Works personnel possess neither individual names nor fixed forms, but in the interest of Methods

Workers' convenience, and their own entertainment, these two agents have retained the identities of Bouffant Head and Diamond Hoops.

"Hah! A perfect turn of events, won't Elaine just love this place?" Bouffant Head exclaims, referring to Ricki's Halfway.

Bulista wonders, "Elaine? But she's a subpersonality. She never even surfaces in the lifestream's waking world."

Mabel explains, "At some point the subs will have to become integrated into Terry's conscious experience, just as we will. Do you suppose," she asks Bouffant Head, "we could somehow rework our rehab meeting format to coincide with Ricki's retreat meetings?"

He beams a veritable sunrise. Those Creative Works guys sure can smile. "Rock and roll," he shouts. "Thumbs up."

Before he can catch himself, Snarrow's spiky field resembles a stegosaurus.

~ 14 ~

Someone was knocking on the door. Terry stirred, but didn't answer. He craned his neck to see the time, peering through gaps in the pile of dishes from breakfast and lunch that Jim had left for him on the bedside table. 2:56. There was a second knock, which he ignored.

Finally the door opened—a tentative crack at first, and then wide—admitting a rather short, round woman toting a heavy-looking, large square object. She lurched her awkward load into the room, set it down with a small grunt, and fixed her intent gaze upon Terry's face.

The eyes were warm and concerned, her expression soft. As Terry returned her scrutiny, he noticed that softness was a theme that this woman carried head to toe, from long brown silky hair framing a round, sweet face, down to a pleasingly well-padded bottom and legs.

"Terry?" she asked. "I'm really sorry to barge in on you. My name is Wanda. They told me you haven't been out of your room yet, and could use a massage. Is that OK with you?"

Terry's expression went from annoyed-but-curious to panicked at the mention of massage. Supported on one forearm, he raised his torso. "Listen," he began with obvious agitation, and stopped. He studied Wanda more closely. She remained...well, soft. "Are you, uh, I need, uh..." He gave her one more careful glance. "Are you real?" he finally blurted.

Wanda looked surprised, but allowed a glimmer of a smile. "Am I real? How do you mean that?"

"Are you really...a...Wanda?"

She sat on the edge of Jim's bed, facing Terry from across the narrow aisle. "Born and raised," she answered. "Why, do you know some other Wanda?"

Terry realized what he had said and how she had taken it. He visibly relaxed. "Sorry, that's not what I meant. Are you really a woman? By birth, I mean."

The slight smile again. "Uh-oh, I am. Is that going to be a problem for you?"

Terry closed his eyes and slowly shook his head. "This is the most fucked up place," he whispered.

Seeing Wanda struggling to pull the bulky massage

table—the large square object—from its canvas carrying bag, Terry emerged from the bed, still wearing the same tee shirt and jeans he had arrived in approximately twenty-four hours ago. As he reached to help her with the table, he realized this fact.

"I think I ought to take a shower."

"Good idea," she nodded.

The sensation amazed him. It had taken all of five minutes for Terry to drop his initial nervousness and marvel at how good his foot, then calf, could feel. He was utterly incapable of tensing, flexing, or showing off as he would under a lover's touch. His mind feebly tried to stir up self-expectations that might goad him to make an acceptable impression. His body overrode all such avenue of thought.

After turning over for side two, he became chatty. "Do you work here full time?"

"No." She paused in her stroke. "Just when they call me down. I live a couple miles up the road. I usually work out of my home."

"So why come here?" he asked.

She shrugged and kneaded his shoulders. "I can always use the work. And I kind of like the guys here."

He shuddered. "Man, I'm completely creeped out. I can't believe that joke of a priest who sent me."

Her hands stopped. "What are you talking about?"

"I was, um, having some problems I didn't understand. Talked with my priest who gave me Ricki's card. He made it sound like some church retreat for men. I needed to go someplace so my family wouldn't be making a fuss over me."

Wanda continued to stand motionless. "Terry, do you

mean that you came here not knowing what Ricki's is?"

He exhaled a not-quite laugh, devoid of humor. "I still don't think I know."

"Whew," breathed Wanda, "do the guys here know you're not...?"

He shook his head, then, "Well maybe Jim, my roommate, does."

She stared at him for a few incredulous seconds. Slowly, she began to laugh, unsuccessfully trying to suppress the first snort, but eventually letting it take her.

Terry propped himself up on the table to watch Wanda— beside herself now, with her head thrown back and tears streaming. He felt an initial stab of anger, but before he could stop himself, he had succumbed to her condition. She perched on the edge of the table beside him and together, they roared.

By the time Wanda packed up her gear it was almost 5:30. Terry insisted on carrying the table out to her car. In the hall they passed Mira, the unknowing instrument of Terry's rude revelation the previous evening. "Hi, Terry," she said shyly. "Are you coming in to dinner?"

He and Wanda exchanged a glance, hers full of encouragement. He was still feeling giddy, freer and more confident than he had felt in months. "Yeah, I'll be right in."

Mira cleared her throat and hesitated, clearly caught between gender roles. "Can I give you a hand with that?" she asked in a decidedly masculine voice.

"Thanks, I'm good," Terry grinned. "See you inside."

At the car, Terry lingered. "Thank you," he said, holding Wanda's eyes with his. He shook his head, "Really."

She smiled back at him. "They're good people here, Terry. Don't worry."

He raised his eyebrows. "Yah," he clipped.

"Really, give them a chance. Go to one of their meetings and 'fess up. You'll never find a more accepting bunch."

His eyes began to take on the anxious vacancy she had noted earlier.

"Look, you can always give me a call if you need to." With a gleam she added, "You can report to me how it goes."

* * *

The technie Barwin's partner has been doing some historical research. Lightworkers gather around him. Seems the project they've undertaken—a transfer of personae within a living lifestream—is not a new idea. The technie has come up with example after example of previous attempts, none of which was very successful.

"See, this one here." He indicates the relevant database. "This lifestream is most similar to ours in terms of ethnic, social and temporal factors. He came close, but his blood vessels could not handle the load. Massive stroke."

Snarrow scrolls down the list of lifestreams. "Strokes, aneurysms, heart attacks...these are common side effects?"

The technie nods, pointing out another section of data. "Check out the instances of psychotic break—even more common." He scrolls again. "Here is the nervous system section. Impressive, huh?" The cases cited under nervous system disorders seem to go on forever. "I think our current technology is sophisticated enough that we ought to be OK in the wiring department."

Snarrow's ruffled field transmits confusion.

"Nervous system wiring," Barwin clarifies. "I think Terry'll

pull through on that account. There might be some sensory dys-
function, possibly minor transient motor dysfunctions, but nothing
major. These others—he again indicated the screen of failed exper-
iments—were dealing with seizures, demyelination, various forms
of paralysis..."

"Hah!" Pryluck guffaws. "Doesn't that just sum up 90% of
all human lifestreams: various forms of paralysis?"

The technie doesn't get it. Others extend affectionate
tendrils in Pryluck's direction.

Mabel addresses the technie. "I don't understand your
reasoning. I thought that all body systems are regulated via
the nervous system, and that this experiment involves sending
potentially lethal levels of higher frequency charge directly
through that same system. How can Terry's wiring, as you say,
come through intact? And, if it does, why would other systems be
at risk?"

In his element once more, the technie explains. "This
one's nervous systems—including the brain, spinal cord and all
peripheral circuitry—have already been altered and augmented to
withstand a much greater than normal charge. Incidentally, it is
the initial surges that strain the system. Once he accommodates
to them, it is no big deal to run the current, but contrary to your
premise, the nerves are not the only system that manages frequency
variables. Nor are they the sole carriers of current. Charge is also
carried and maintained by the blood."

"By way of hormones?" someone wonders.

"Yes, with their influence on electrolyte balance. The
nerves receive our initial transmission and carry it through the
bloodstream via endocrine function. The nerves, of course, need
to power up the glands so they can keep up with the demand. It

is all terribly interconnected. My earlier point was that we believe we have got the nervous system sufficiently fortified. From the physiologic perspective, he is a bit more vulnerable at the glandular and vascular end of things."

"Is there anything we can do?" asks Snarrow.

"Well, his cells generally run a bit dry. That does tend to short out the nerves somewhat, and increases his physical reactivity."

"It's probably good they don't serve beer at that retreat center," Pryluck quips.

"True enough," the technie continues. "Maybe you could keep caffeine out as well. And get him to drink water."

"They have a saying," smiles Vormis, "about leading a horse to water, that you can't make him drink."

"Horse, you say?"

"Never mind," says Vormis. "We'll do what we can."

* * *

The Creative Works agent, Bouffant Head, peers over Terry's shoulder to read the activities schedule from the flier that he's perusing. This evening offers a choice of meetings:

1. Who Am I—Questions about self-identity
2. Old Relationships, New Identity—How to adjust as others adjust to a new you
3. Elements of Style—Practical fashion tips

"Ooh, I hope he picks the one on style." Bouffant Head closes his eyes and focuses. "Please, please…"

Mabel is getting used to the CW reps' predilections. She laughs. "Sorry to disappoint, but that one is not even a choice. It shall be the 'Who Am I' or back to his bed."

The other CW agent, Diamond Hoops, speaks up. "Well

then, maybe we can hold the sub rehab meeting at 'Styles' while he does his 'Who Am I' thing."

"Not a chance!" Mabel huffs.

The CW rep merrily ruffles her field. "Gotcha! Lighten up, Mabel. We've got serious play to attend to."

* * *

Terry loitered outside the door to the meeting room. A handful of men were already settled at a round conference table, which was, to Mabel's amusement, mahogany. Terry wanted to bolt. Several times, he began walking away from the room but paced back again, drawn by a variety of impulses.

His morale had been buoyed by Wanda's visit. He also knew that he had long surpassed the scope of his own resources and needed help. In addition, thanks in large part to his recent drop in tension, there loomed a growing curiosity about who and what he had stumbled upon here at Ricki's Halfway. Yet each time he neared the door, fear obliterated curiosity, which then triggered another retreat down the hallway. The appearance of Jim finally interrupted the pattern.

"Terry, it's great to see you." Genuine surprise and pleasure illuminated Jim's shy and usually closed expression.

"Yeah, well..." Terry shrugged.

"You're coming in, aren't you?" Jim asked. Seeing Terry's indecision he added, "You know you don't have to do anything or say anything in there. It'll help everyone just to have you listen to them."

Terry stared at Jim. He had never considered helping them. The notion ground his mind to a bemused halt. He followed Jim to the table and took a seat.

Eventually, Terry noticed that of the nine people present

in the room, only one was wearing women's things. It was Raoul, the young man from dinner the evening before. Their eyes met and they exchanged a nod.

There was a man who seemed to be some kind of moderator. He had a lively face, with intensely deep brown eyes and a full head of slightly graying hair. Terry felt relieved to see that it was not Sally running the meeting.

"For those of you who are new," the moderator began, "I'm Tull. We always begin with an icebreaker activity. This one will be done in pairs, so turn and face your neighbor."

Jim turned to Terry and whispered, "You don't have to participate, but if you want to I'll be your partner." Terry nodded.

Tull continued. "OK, our theme tonight is self identity, so you each have five minutes to talk about how you identify yourself—to other people and to yourself."

Someone interrupted, "Do you mean like how we introduce ourselves to someone?"

"In a way," answered Tull. "I'm talking about the non-verbal cues as well, identifying roles or behaviors that carry a message about who you are, or who you want people to think you are. For example, I'm a therapist—that's one identifying marker. I have gray hair—another. I wear a certain style of clothing." He gestured toward his jeans and embroidered Indian shirt, the leather vest and turquoise earring. "I come from a mixed ethnic background: Cherokee and Scottish. I could go on in terms of social preferences, where I go for recreation, food, drink, what I drive, etc. Things that say something about you to the world, and ways that you derive your own sense of identity. OK, first partner, five minutes."

"Do you want me to go first?" Jim asked.

Terry's sardonic smirk passed for acquiescence.

"I don't guess I have a lot of identity," Jim began. "I'm from Arkansas, but I moved a lot for work. Did a couple of years in Oklahoma and now West Virginia. Been mining, coal mostly. I'm divorced, 43. I don't know, what else?"

Terry sat mute, astounded that Jim would fail to mention the obvious.

"Let's see," Jim went on. "I drive a Chevy half ton pickup." He gave an awkward laugh. A long pause followed in which Terry remained silent.

"I had a daughter," Jim resumed in a quiet voice. But my ex won't let me see her. She'd be nine now. So I guess I'm not much of a father." He shrugged. "Nobody knows about me and this place, so I don't guess it's an identity."

They sat quietly for some time. After a while, Jim spoke again. "I don't really have hobbies. I like the woods...a lot. Sometimes I go fishing just to be outside."

Unmasked sadness pressed on Terry like a hand at his throat. For him, witnessing Jim's stripped down sense of self was a terrible, mirroring experience.

"Time's up," Tull interrupted. "Second partner, your five minutes begins now."

Terry could not look away from the pale blue eyes that continued to hold his gaze, despite the obvious pain therein. Thus he and Jim sat, locked in some dreadful, silent meeting.

Finally, Jim spoke. "Who are you, Terry?"

Terry shifted in his seat and shook his head. "You got me there."

Jim waited.

"I don't know, I was having trouble at home. I can't believe

I ended up here. It all keeps getting worse. I can't believe I didn't check it out first or something."

"So how come you're still here?"

"I have nowhere to go," Terry answered quietly. "No one knows what's wrong. I can't work much, family's on my case. Can you believe it? My goddamn priest sent me here. What was he thinking? That's what I can't figure."

Jim bit his lower lip. "What kind of work?"

"Fishing business." Terry raised his eyes and they shared a smile.

Terry sat quietly through the remainder of the meeting. He felt raw and exhausted. Returning to their room, Jim faced him. "Terry, I gotta say something, don't be offended, OK?"

Terry shrugged.

"Look, I take it you're straight and...don't know much about other choices, right?"

Terry's eyebrows lifted.

"It's just, uh, not easy for me thinking you're maybe scared of me or that you hate us here. I know I'm a little paranoid, so it's probably me, but you don't say much...I can understand it's different for you, upsetting I guess. But we come here so we can learn to relax and be ourselves. I don't know how to do that in front of you."

He had been looking down as he spoke and now turned away. "Look, I don't want to put this on you, but it could make it easier for us all if you would maybe just say whatever it is you're thinking, or ask questions or something." He turned back to Terry to smile his kind, apologetic smile.

Terry forced himself to breathe amid the storm that seemed to encompass his abdomen. He nodded, lips taut, and stared at the floor. "Yeah, OK," he muttered, barely audible.

~ 15 ~

Wanda's phone rang at 8:00 the next morning. "You didn't waste any time," she said, recognizing Terry's voice. "How's it going?"

"I gotta get out of here. Can I see you today?"

"What's up, Terry?"

"I just need a break."

"Did you go to the meeting last night?"

"Yeah." After a long pause, he said, "Look, I thought you would maybe come out for a beer. What, should I not have called?" He was starting to feel foolish and a little angry.

She hesitated. "No, calling's OK. I gave you my number. But I don't want to be an escape, you know? For whatever reason, you got yourself into a pretty strange situation, but that's where you are. Why not just do the retreat time that you committed yourself to do? However it looks, and whatever you think about the place and the guys, they'll always treat you with acceptance and respect. You can't say that about a lot of places."

"Right, I know, I got that. But it's fucking intense. You don't have to be with them all the time...I can't do it," he muttered.

"I can understand that," she relented. "How about if I come down tomorrow and bring you up to the house for lunch? But forget about a beer date."

"Yeah, alright."

* * *

Mabel and Snarrow sit companionably, their edges blurred. "This is almost like being with a regular lifestream," Mabel effuses. "There is hardly more to attend to with Terry than the usual. Do you think that we are really past the crisis stage?"

Snarrow wavers, all blues and grays. "I have no idea," he answers. "You know, Mabel, this project has been…I've been learning something with this project, somehow changing how I see things…"

A golden blush passes through Mabel's field. "What have you learned?"

"I cannot define it, exactly," Snarrow muses. "But haven't you noticed that the whole operation at Methods has undergone some kind of shift since this all began? I feel as if our structure has had to become more fluid as Terry's has broken down. I wonder if Management was really targeting us the whole time."

Mabel's shock is aromatic. "Do you think so? Management seems so stodgy. If anyone is behind a shake up, I would put it on Creative Works."

"Mm," Snarrow speculates. "They are fond of agitation, aren't they? And they have always gotten under our skin…always. It's funny that I never even suspected they might be conscious of how they affect us. Or that it could be intentional. It makes me wonder if they might be working with us in the same way we work with the lifestreams."

"You think!" Mabel exclaims, again sweetening the atmosphere.

"They would never say so upfront if it's true," Snarrow adds. "But it is pretty clear we cannot complete the project without them, and that is because of their ability to move in ways we have

not had to before."

*"Well, that just makes sense. Intradepartmental colla-
boration is nothing new, we are already working like that with the
female lifestream's guides. Yet it sounds as if you are suggesting
that Creative Works is somehow on another level than we are, and
that they are working to raise us up."*

*"But that's just it, Mabel. I am wondering if, bottom line, we
have had it all wrong. Maybe it is all a big mutual collaboration...
between us, and also with the lifestreams...maybe there aren't any
levels, just a lot of different perspectives. As we allow ourselves to
be influenced, we all benefit."*

*Mabel takes some time to absorb the idea, which appears
as a ribbon of color that gradually diffuses through her field, like
cream swirling into coffee.*

*Later, returning to Methods headquarters from a meeting
with Management, Snarrow finds Mabel adorned in a flowing
ribbon candy costume, topped by a wide-brimmed blue velvet hat
and a jumble of feathers. She sits chatting with Millicent, the robed
member of the female musician's team.*

*Mabel winks at Snarrow's double take. "I have contemplated
our last discussion and decided to allow myself to be influenced,"
she announces.*

*Sub rehab has been reworked, from the sequestered
dreamtime setting, to an overlap with Terry's waking reality. When
possible, lightworkers coordinate the rehab meetings in coincidence
with group meetings at Ricki's. A phasic shift remains in place,
which serves to prevent bleed-through of one scene to the other.
Consequently, the only significant gain from the overlap is that*

now the lightworkers are simultaneously privy to both meetings. Their theory is that resonance will eventually increase between the two realities, bringing with it the beginnings of conscious cross-communication.

In the recent ostensible respite from crises, the Methods intern, Bulista, has her first go at mediating a sub rehab session. She and Mabel meet afterwards for debriefing. "I think there might be trouble with Aunt Ethel," Bulista confesses.

"Aunt Ethel? But has she not been cooperative lately? She has successfully refrained from criticizing the lifestream, hasn't she?"

"So it's seemed, but now she is back in her gym teacher outfit, all tight-lipped and sulky."

"Did she talk today?" Mabel asks.

"No. When I asked how she was doing and if she had anything to share, she just gave one of her sounds—you know, the hmmff—and did that knitting thing with her eyebrows. I didn't press it. I really did not know how to approach her."

"You probably did just the right thing," Mabel assures her. "You know how stubborn she is. I wonder what she is up to in real-time," she adds. "Did you get a look at the retreat meeting?"

The intern's field ripples pink. "I couldn't really split my attention enough to monitor both. I did notice Snarrow looking in on us at rehab a few times, though. Maybe he will have an impression of Ethel's state."

Later, a small group of lightworkers sits companionably in Methods headquarters. Pryluck yawns. "I'd say we are having a downright lull in the action. It's nice to kick back and enjoy some R and R."

Mabel flashes. "You all probably ought to know that Aunt

Ethel is looking testy, like she might revert to outmoded behavior. We should not let ourselves become too complacent."

"Ethel?" frowns Pryluck. "We haven't upped the lifestream's frequency in a while, why would she want to revert?"

Mabel sighs. "Look at what the lifestream has gone through in the last few days—with no system failure I might add." She glows and the others join her in visual self-congratulations.

"There have been a lot of new experiences, thought impressions and behavioral changes for the subs to integrate and accept. They have been holding up beautifully, but they are bound to be experiencing stress. If we watch them carefully, maybe we can avert potential trouble."

* * *

Wanda's Jeep turned down a gravel driveway that wound its way past a cornfield, vegetable garden and flowerbeds, before sloping sharply uphill. As she downshifted, a rough wood and fieldstone house came into view. Chickens ran freely through the yard. A nondescript, mid-size dog came trotting up to the driver's side door. Terry noticed a woodpile in varying stages of splitting and stacking next to an ancient-looking pickup.

"Home-sweet. Come on up to the house and meet the crew," Wanda told him.

He froze. "The crew?"

She smiled. "My kids, their friends, and from the looks of the woodpile, my man, Jack."

Terry was, as per usual of late, not at his best. "You didn't tell me there'd be other people," he complained roughly.

She fixed him with a measuring stare. "What is the problem, Terry? I can understand you feeling awkward with the guys at Ricki's, but my family?" She squinted at him, puckering her chin. "You weren't still holding out for a date, were you?"

"No, it's not that," he muttered. "I just...what did you tell them about me?"

"I told them we're having company for lunch and asked them to pick some veggies. Is that too personal?"

"I mean," he faltered, "do they have to know where you know me from?"

"I knew it was too soon to invite you out, you damn bigot." Her tone was milder than her language. "Before I let you step foot in my house, I need to hear from you a promise that you will not display one iota of disrespect to anyone, including yourself, in words or attitude. If you can do that, then I bid you a warm welcome to my home. If not, we're leaving now." Her gaze was challenging and intensely direct, although a kind smile played about her eyes.

He took a breath. "I'll do my best."

Sally again greeted Terry at the front entrance of Ricki's. "Hello dear," she sang. "Did you have a nice outing?"

Terry faced her, pausing for a moment to take in the entire coarse, outlandish picture of Sally, and smiled broadly. "I did, thank you."

When he entered their room, Jim was ending a conversation. "Hi," he greeted Terry as he set down the phone, and then did a double take. "Wow, what happened?"

"What do you mean?" asked Terry.

"You're different. Where were you?"

"I went to Wanda's. Met her family. I'm taking her two boys on that fishing hike tomorrow. You going?"

Jim grinned shyly. "Well, I'll be damned."

~ 16 ~

Aunt Ethel is on a rampage, looming large and severe. Mabel has, by chance, looked in on Terry during sleep, only to find Vormis grappling with an Ethel-induced nightmare. A gravel-voiced Aunt Ethel crabs and harangues as in the days before rehab. Attempts to reason with her have proven futile. Terry's consciousness is in a stranglehold of self-judgment, and the body has responded accordingly with rapid heartbeat, rigid muscles and the struggle for breath. A gray-brown fear-emitting fog obscures sensory perceptions.

"You capture and calm Terry," Mabel tells Vormis. "I am going after Ethel."

"Bulista," she calls to the intern. "Job for you."

Bulista and Mabel face Aunt Ethel and, at first, simply witness her snit. "She's upset...traumatized, poor thing," Bulista observes. She goes to Aunt Ethel and gently takes her hand. Sobs begin to choke Ethel's tirade. Bulista holds her until she calms and quiets.

Mabel begins her part. "Feeling better, Ethel dear?"

Exhausted, Ethel nods.

"What happened here? Last I remember, you had been promoted from judge to chief informer and were doing a splendid job of offering excellent insights with no judgment at all."

Ethel mutely nods. Bulista continues to soothe and rock her. Ethel, in turn, imbibes the TLC in great gulps.

"Didn't pay attention," she finally says, somewhat sheepishly.

"You thought your advice and observations were being ignored?" Mabel rephrases.

Ethel nods once more, with closed eyes.

"Poor thing, how frustrating that must have been."

As Ethel relaxes during the conversation, she has become more and more translucent. At this point she seems to dissolve entirely, and in her place appears the trunk of a great tree whose roots extend downward from its central position within Terry's body.

Mabel and Bulista exchange a pursed-lipped glance. Both are impressed. "She certainly has got the idea," Mabel declares, "and has chosen her role as a strong anchor. Well done, Ethel!" she tells the tree.

* * *

Terry slept through breakfast and was still in bed when Jim checked in on him late morning.

"Are you OK, Terry?"

"Yeah," he answered. "I had a rotten night. Didn't sleep for shit."

Jim hesitated. "Are you still coming fishing today?"

"Oh, man!" Terry bolted upright in bed. "The kids. I forgot. What time is it?"

Jim smiled. "Don't worry, you still got about two hours. Or are you supposed to pick them up?"

"No, Wanda said she'd drop them off. I guess we meet at the front entrance?"

"Right," answered Jim.

"What about gear?" Terry wondered.

"Oh, that's all set. They'll have everything we need."

Terry raised an eyebrow, but made no comment. Instead, he cleared his throat before venturing, "Hey, Jim, can I ask you something?"

"Yeah, sure."

Terry hedged. "Look, I don't want to offend you or nothing, but you said I should ask...these kids of Wanda's, they're like, what—7, 10 years old?

Jim shrugged. "About that, I guess."

"How can she let them hang around this place? Won't it screw them up?" To his credit, Terry was visibly embarrassed and had the grace to blush.

Jim went taut just for a moment before he gave a wry laugh. "You mean isn't she afraid they'll catch some kind of deviance from us?"

Terry held his gaze innocently enough, evidently wondering exactly that.

Jim sighed. "Personal inclinations aren't contagious, Terry."

Terry blushed again. "Alright, but aren't these kids too young to be exposed to this stuff? Isn't it a corrupt kind of role-model for them?"

Jim colored. "Do we seem corrupt to you? What is it, all the sleazy orgies you see going on here? You think you're all moral because you fit in with some narrow minded code of normal?"

"Look," Terry muttered. "I'm sorry I brought it up."

Jim relented. "No, I'm defensive. You don't know shit. Let's try again." His smile was contrite. "OK, it hurts to be targeted and labeled, all that. It's like we all get put into a big deviant box wherever we go. But that bullshit has almost nothing to do with real people who are, most of us, the same as anybody else. Only mostly, we're more honest than your moral majority."

Terry snorted. "I'll give you that."

"Maybe you ought to talk to Wanda if you're worried. Or talk to the kids."

Terry looked appalled.

"They'll surprise you if you don't talk down to them," Jim insisted.

To his credit, Terry was unfailingly polite about the "everything we need" fishing gear, which had probably come from a local convenience store.

The terrain was gorgeous. Their trail to the river followed a streambed that wound a path through massive evergreen stands, intermingled with hillside meadows awash in wildflower bloom. Jim was delighted by his first introduction to marmots, which seemed to him more exotic than their groundhog cousins.

The group—eight in all—ambled haphazardly, stopping from time to time to listen to a thrush call or, to Terry's annoyance, to pick flowers. Two of the beskirted men wove their blossoms into impressive articles of apparel, which they distributed to the others. Terry was alarmed to see the youngest of Wanda's boys accept a golden circlet, which he placed on his head prior to strutting about declaring, "I'm king of the forest. You will obey ME!"

"You're king of the faeries," his brother retorted, to a chorus of laughter.

Jim caught Terry's eye and winked, but Terry stood immobile, his face a display of horror. When he did not move on with the rest, Jim feared he might bolt. "Terry, they're OK. They understand the joke."

Terry flushed. "I don't get it. That stuff you said to me before—it didn't sound like you were joking."

"There was no judgment in the kid's comment. The point is, both of them know who and what we are, they know how the world sees us and they can laugh about it with us."

At the next flower stop, the boys noticed Terry picking up bits of seedpod fluff and pulling downy bits off a feather. "What's that for?" asked one.

"I thought I'd make a bug."

"What do you mean?" Both crowded closer to see.

"Fish like to eat bugs. So, if you watch to see what kind of bugs are flying around and which ones the fish are eating, you can make something that looks like the right kind of bug—it's called a fly—you can use it for bait."

"But won't they know it's not real when they taste it?"

"Sure, but if they taste it it's too late, because there'll be a hook attached to the fly."

"Why don't we use real bugs?" The younger one asked.

"You could do it that way, too. You want to collect some real bugs and see who catches more fish?"

He did. The older boy opted for both methods, catching a variety of bugs as well as gathering items that resembled bug parts. It turned out the only ones to catch any fish that afternoon were Terry, with his fake bugs tied to a makeshift line, and Wanda's older boy, with the real thing. Terry released his. The older boy, Gregory, hesitated.

"He wants to show it off to his girlfriend," his brother teased.

Gregory blushed deeply and swatted at his brother. "She's not my girlfriend!" Terry was relieved. They seemed normal enough for their ages.

On the walk back, the younger boy slipped a hand into Terry's. Terry was surprised, but moved.

"You're straight, right?" The child asked.

Shocked, Terry looked sharply down at him.

"I can tell. My dad is, too. He used to say bad things about Ricki's, but my mom said it was because he's insecure and made him stop. You don't have to be scared of Ricki's." He looked up at Terry with a quick smile and ran on ahead.

~ 17 ~

Terry was gathering courage and determination to "out" himself to Ricki's populace-at-large. Five days into his two-week retreat, he told himself it was time. Tonight. At meeting.

The evening's theme was "How Am I—Further explorations of identity." Terry was glad to see that Tull would again be presiding, although he felt intimidated by tonight's larger group.

He sat nervously through the first half hour, barely registering what people were saying. Only when the group prepared to enact a psychodrama did Terry rouse out of his self-preoccupation.

The cross-dressing Raoul had been selected to be the protagonist in the group's psychodrama. Raoul stood at one end of the room, recounting reluctance since early childhood to expose his artistic nature to his parents, particularly to his strict father.

Tull interjected. "Raoul, why don't we start by portraying some time in your childhood? Is there some incident that stands out as significant to your pattern of withholding?

Raoul reflected for a moment. "I guess so." Tull waited for him to elaborate. "My father's friends would come over sometimes to play cards. They'd smoke, drink whiskey and get loud. We had a small house. I was playing in the next room with my sister one time, when one of them called me in to offer me a cigar. When I refused, he told me I'd better learn to smoke cee-gars and to stop acting like such a sissy if I was ever gonna convince anyone I was a man. They all thought that was hilarious. I was seven years old, for Christ's sake."

"Alright," Tull said. "So let's set the first scene in your house. Where are you and your sister?"

"At the kitchen table. We're playing with her crafts set. I'm gluing glitter on a shirt for her doll."

"Good. How about choosing someone from the group to play your sister, and let's get some chairs up here in the kitchen."

Raoul made his choice, along with a choice for the father's offending friend. He then looked carefully around the room, taking considerable time and care in selecting someone to play his father. Eventually his attention rested on Terry.

Terry, who had not yet spoken a word to anyone but Jim during this or the previous meeting, now froze unable to respond. The group waited quietly until Tull intervened.

"Terry, are you willing to play Raoul's father? We come from truth here. How do you feel about being asked to do that?"

Hot with embarrassment, he finally managed, "I, uh, don't know how."

"Of course not. This will be Raoul's drama. He'll direct

each character in terms of their appropriate behavior and lines. Most important is for the whole group to unite as a single entity, supporting and enacting our protagonist's drama. So you need to ask yourself, Terry, if it feels true for you to be part of it. And to let Raoul know where you stand."

* * *

The meeting of Terry's subpersonalities is in full swing and lively. Elaine and Aunt Ethel are in open confrontation, with Elaine up and pacing, flaunting her flesh, and Ethel vocally running a disapproving critique.

Chaz happily maintains his light-holding role. The French swordsman—with Helen weakly connected, though poorly integrated—sprawls apathetically on the floor. A small group of subs who've signed onto the rehab project at the conclusion of personality stripping observe the proceedings, as do Mabel, Bulista and Bouffant Head.

To Mabel's slight annoyance, Bouffant Head keeps flitting back and forth between the two meetings. Her attention follows him into the psychodrama event at Ricki's, where she notices that Vormis and Snarrow are already in attendance. Mabel lets her field relax and expand. "Alright," she decides. "Why fight it? We shall try an experiment."

"Elaine," she suggests. "How would you like the whole group to help you portray...umm, express...the way you experience yourself? You can choose anyone here to act out, under your direction, any aspect of your existence as you perceive it. And next time, of course, Aunt Ethel will get a turn." She pauses to observe the group. "Are there any objections to putting on such a play?"

Aunt Ethel contracts and contorts her face, but otherwise puts up no resistance. Elaine puffs and gloats at the thought of the whole group revolving around herself. A few subs, including the Helen composite, remain non-responsive on the floor. Others perk up at the prospect of participating in a play.

* * *

Terry finally rallied enough focus to answer Tull's question. "Yeah, alright, I'll try."

Bouffant Head claps his hands in delight before popping back into the sub's session. "Oh, sweet synchronicity," he sings, gliding across the room and waving his arms as if conducting an orchestra.

So far so good, Terry mused as he observed the other players who were, thank God, apparently not required to demonstrate any great originality or dramatic talent. Under Tull's direction, Raoul was apparently undergoing some sort of therapy and in effect playing all the parts himself. A minor release of Terry's tension preceded a growing interest in Raoul's drama.

Scene shift. Now Raoul was to confront his father about colluding with the taunting friend. Terry—in the role of Raoul's father—and Raoul sat in opposing chairs across the "card table," which was being played by Jim, who'd assumed a table-shaped posture on all fours between them.

Raoul began by expressing his seven-year-old feelings of hurt and anger. To Terry's tremendous relief, he was spared the need to come up with a response, for Tull had interrupted with the command, "Role reverse!"

Raoul and Terry each stood, walked to the opposite side of Jim, the table, and took each other's seat. Now Terry was to play Raoul, while Raoul responded in the role of his own father.

* * *

Mabel observes Tull's methods and, inwardly reciting her

earlier resolution to be open to influence, follows suit. She finds herself far less successful at fostering support and unity within the group of subpersonalities.

The whole idea of being in charge has gone to Elaine's head. Seeing the play as a major S&M opportunity, she turns insufferably tyrannical. Some of the more feisty subs have mobilized their own personal defenses. The more docile are slinking to move out of range of Elaine's aggression.

Mabel surveys the ensuing bedlam, and sighs before turning to her amused co-Workers for support. A team effort establishes enough order for Mabel to try again. "Let me explain the rules," she begins.

* * *

Terry's initial amusement at the concept of role reversal was short-lived. In his current role of Raoul, he heard Raoul's father saying, "What do you expect me to say? You are a sissy, and you're proving it right now with your talk about hurt feelings. What kind of son am I raising? Go on, get out of here, I don't want to look at you."

Before Terry could settle the shifting in his belly, there came Tull's command, "Role reverse!"

Again, they switched chairs along with characters. "OK," Tull instructed. "Let's replay that scene. Raoul, you tell your father how you felt about his failure to defend you, and Terry, you respond as the father."

They replayed the scene, ad-libbing the previous dialogue, with Terry finding himself inexplicably drawn into the father's role. Thus cast, the words of Terry's own homophobia came pouring forth.

Once again came the command to role reverse. For the second time, Terry sat in the role of boy-child accused of unmanliness. And miraculous as it seemed to him, he now found himself responding with the genuine tears of a child's shame and rage.

The hour passed gruelingly for Terry, who not only had been exposed to a far greater share of emotional expression than ever before, but who had also played an active part in Raoul's resolution of the charged dynamics with his father. As the meeting ended and the others left the room, Terry stood slowly—pale, shaken and deeply withdrawn.

Tull intercepted his exit. "Terry, do you want to talk about it?"

Terry shrugged apathetically, but did not leave.

"You just gave a lot of yourself in there for Raoul—and for the group. But we haven't heard from you about yourself at all. We won't know how to give you support if you don't let us see who you are. How come you're hiding it, Terry?"

Terry turned anguished, exhausted eyes to Tull and leaned both hands on the table. "Look," he said, "I don't know much about who I am these days."

"Shit, man, you know enough to know you're in an unusual situation. That must feel pretty strange."

Terry's face opened in surprise. "You know?"

Tull laughed, wrinkling his brow as if the answer were so obvious as to be irrelevant. "I mean, come on, a red-blooded, redneck straight guy in a house of queers? Isn't it the ultimate role reversal for someone like you to be the queer one in the crowd?"

Terry recoiled as if chastised, and studied his feet.

Tull took him by the arm. "Here, sit. Tell me. What's going on? What are you doing here, man?"

Terry haltingly filled Tull in on his recent history.

Tull whistled. "That's pretty heavy. Who's the priest?"

Terry answered with considerable reluctance.

"No," Tull insisted. "This is not cool. Not at all. We're glad to have you and all, and my guess is you'll be none the worse for wear after all this, but that Danny Sulleran sounds to me like a real menace. You may feel messed up, guy, but let me tell you, from what I've seen and from what you tell me you've been through, I think you're made of some kind of tough stuff. Just imagine if you were someone with less fiber...no, that Sulleran guy needs to be confronted.

"Now," Tull continued, "tell me about Raoul's drama. How did you relate to his story?"

Terry looked blank. "I don't know what you mean."

"But you did feel what I mean, didn't you?"

"I don't know," Terry replied. "I feel pretty out of it. Sorry, but I've got to get some sleep."

Tull was not ready to release him. "Sure man, but I want you to understand the process so you don't just freak out about the feelings. That's your pattern, isn't it?"

Terry shrugged.

"Do you know the term, resonance?" Tull asked.

Terry frowned and shook his head.

"Alright, look. Human beings share a common life drama. One person's story is everybody's story. When we witness the enactment of someone's story—we call that person the protagonist—we're witnessing a part of ourselves. We come into resonance with whatever issues are brought up. If those issues have not already been consciously dealt with and integrated, the resonance triggers our own unresolved stuff. Intense, isn't it?"

"What do you mean about someone's story being everyone's story?" Terry asked.

"That the details and characters may vary, but the essence behind it all is the same. I don't know squat about you or your childhood, but I do know that you related both to Raoul's experience of being ridiculed, and to his father's disappointment and rejection for not meeting the masculine cultural ideal. Am I right?" he pressed.

"Yeah, I guess so."

"That's resonance," Tull explained. "It doesn't matter what the specific storyline is. We all know the feeling of being made fun of and diminished in value by another's judgment. And we know what it's like to feel that we need to judge others to defend our own self-critique. The point of it all is that as we relate to one another's stories, we get to see how universal our own deep dark secrets actually are. Then, they become not so secret and we become less imprisoned by shame. And, to boot, it opens the capacity for compassion for each other and ourselves. Not so bad, huh?"

Terry's face had settled into a more subdued arrangement. He remained thoughtfully silent.

Tull stood and offered a handshake. "Get some sleep, man. You did real good."

* * *

Mabel lingers in an atmosphere of shimmering turquoise, reflecting on—in Bouffant Head's words—"sweet synchronicity." She addresses Snarrow, who drifts nearby. "The subs were all so much more responsive working this way," she tells him.

The intern, Bulista, joins them. "How does it work that we can run sub rehab while the lifestream is awake? Isn't the lifestream's behavior determined by his subpersonalities' reactions?"

Snarrow answers, and Mabel marvels that Bulista doesn't even flinch.

"Initially, a lifestream's subpersonalities, and therefore that one's overall personality, are exclusively determined by programing within the mental body. Once an individual's circuitry is established, the personality runs on its own, but in predictable, characteristic patterns. In that sense, the subpersonalities do influence the lifestream's behavior. But influencing behavior is not the same as determining it."

"What does determine their behavior?" wonders Bulista.

Both Snarrow and Mabel glow. "A divine marriage of personal and collective programming and soul intent, together with that mysterious element of will and who knows what else?"

Bulista is not satisfied.

Mabel elaborates. "Sub reactions, which are based on automatic programs, will seem to determine lifestream behavior so long as the lifestream has no awareness of the fact that he or she is programmed. Once the dawning of consciousness occurs, the lifestream becomes capable of observing the patterns that the subs display. That is the level Terry has thus far been boosted to. We are accelerating his capacity for self-awareness by shifting his frequency. And we are accelerating both his grasp of, and his ability to alter the subs' patterns, by working directly with the subs. The subs also need to become conscious of themselves in relation to him and to each other in order to make the shift."

"But if the subs are somewhere else—say with us, enacting their own psychodrama—how can they function within his mind at the same time?" persists Bulista.

"Well, yes," Mabel acknowledges. "That was the original perspective, but we have received clearance to deviate from linearity."

Bulista feels as if she's back in orientation. "Excuse me, Mabel, what is linearity?"

Mabel examines Bulista for some time, which makes the intern's field wobble between several shades of pink. "Linearity, as in the concept that one thing follows another in prescribed sequence. Point A to point B, they say.

"You will have noticed the concurrence of themes in both dramas? While Ethel and Elaine played their critic/rebel scenario, Terry experienced lower body emotional responses to same, albeit in relation to another lifestream's program—Raoul's. It is as if we are all tunneling toward each other from different angles, but the work is all one."

"Like the lifestream, Tull, was saying?"

"Yes, I suppose it is something like that. Only it seems to apply between worlds as well. More like you were suggesting," she says to Snarrow. "It appears that their efforts on the gross human level are affecting, and are actually assisting, ours."

~ 18 ~

"I have been thinking," Snarrow tells Vormis. "It may be

time for you to attempt a more direct, conscious contact with your lifestream. He has already proven capable of perceiving your presence. Do you think he is ready for an introduction?"

Vormis wavers. "What do you have in mind? He barely registered my last contact, and wildly misinterpreted it."

"Maybe not so wildly," Snarrow says. "He thought you were God. What else could he think? But the files that house his belief structures now have sufficient space in which to imprint some new data. You could present yourself to him in dreamtime. The data will register subliminally, with minimal interference. What he retains consciously...we'll see." A wave of light ripples through Snarrow's field. "That is not so important. The underlying template will have been set."

The lightworkers find a dreaming Terry rummaging in the attic of his childhood home. "Perfect setting!" exclaims Vormis' backup guide. "We'll keep an eye out for unclaimed subs, but even so, it is possible you may encounter one of them before we do. You'll be fine," he tells Vormis.

The coast appears clear. Vormis waves a greeting to the imposing Chaz, whom he spies guarding the attic door. Chaz's behavior is just splendid. In his new role—keeping Terry's sense of core-self nice and strong—he presents no challenge. On the contrary, Chaz cheerfully returns Vormis' wave.

The immediate question for Vormis is how to attract Terry's attention. He looks at a large trunk that Terry has opened, and watches him lift out various artifacts. Within moments, the dream scene shifts, with Terry now packing clothing and personal items in preparation for a journey.

The woman of the household in which he is a guest

is preparing to depart with her family. She offers last minute farewells, and holds out a long silver key to Terry: the key to the house. He tries it in the lock to be sure it works before the woman turns to leave, saying something about the keys to the Subaru.

Vormis steps in to fill the space where the dream-conjured woman has vacated. Terry gives no indication that he sees him, so Vormis brightens and expands his field, while extending a ray into Terry's heart in the way he has done before. That, he thinks, will at least feel familiar.

Terry pauses in his selection of the right shoes to pack, rejecting one pair for being too coarse and casual.

Vormis flits from place to place, staying within Terry's line of vision in a futile attempt to draw his attention. He feels his backup's amused presence. "Steady, pal," he hears. "You guide him. You don't need to run around chasing after him. Try going for the forebrain."

Vormis colors crimson. He roots deeper into Terry's core, and this time projects himself inside his head, just above and behind the eyes. Terry continues to evaluate clothing, beginning to become agitated that he seems to be missing key items.

"Terry," Vormis calls.

The tones of Vormis's voice held a deep, resonant, bell-like quality that Terry found extremely pleasant. His attention turned from the clothing to the source of the voice. He listened intently and was rewarded with another summons.

"Terry," Vormis repeats.

Vormis now has Terry's full attention. "Hello, Terry," he continues. He projects some light, attempting to go for a visual as well as auditory association.

Terry experienced a flood of peace and serenity which,

thanks to the dream state, he felt no impulse to evaluate or name.

"I'm Vormis," Vormis proceeds awkwardly. *"Your guide... ever at your service,"* he adds, *gleaning what he can remember of relevant modern language.*

Terry simply continued to receive the sensually pleasant infusion of light and sound.

"Well then," Vormis falters, *not knowing how, or if, to initiate a more active dialog.*

Again, the backup's mind-link intrudes. *"Fine, you've established recognition. Just bless him and leave him to his dream."*

* * *

In mid-afternoon, Terry was paged to the phone.

"Hi, how's it going?"

Terry was surprised and flattered to hear Wanda's voice. "Not bad," he answered. "What's up?"

"I need to pick up some chicken feed. Thought you might like to get out on the town."

"Praise God! I never thought I'd see the day. When do we leave?"

"I'm out front right now."

Terry bolted for the door.

On the way back from town, they parked the feed-filled truck and walked to a nearby iron bridge spanning a rocky section of river. Two men in hip waders stood below, casting in the fast current. Wanda turned to Terry, "My boys tell me you know a lot about bugs. That's quite a compliment."

He laughed. "They're good kids."

Wanda examined him more closely. "They had a nice time

on the hike. Thanks for watching them."

He shrugged and reddened. "What are they up to today?"

"They're helping Jack stack wood. He bribed them. They have a choice of a dollar each for an afternoon's work, or they can trade in their dollar for an hour of TV. Tell me, Terry, how is life at Ricki's? You seem more relaxed now."

He braced his forearms on the railing. "I don't know. I've been here what, eight days now?" Grinning, he added, "Just over half my sentence. It feels like a completely different life—not a different kind of life, but it's like my whole life before Ricki's..." He paused and shook his head. "No, my whole life before meeting you, belonged to someone else. It makes me feel piss-all psychotic. I don't know how to live with—or in—myself. It sounds stupid, but I don't know who I am." He paused again, looking down at the water. "See, that's something I would never even think to care about. Something incredibly weird is happening, Wanda."

They stood silently for some time. "You know," she sighed, "I'm sure that the old you seemed normal and well-adjusted and all that..."

"Exactly!" he interrupted. "I was totally normal, then all this shit started. What do you think could have caused it?"

She hesitated. "What I was saying is that what we think of as normal is just what we're used to and familiar with, really. I mean, normal is relative to, for one thing, your environment. If you live in a nuthouse, then nuttiness is normal until you expand your world. You know what I'm saying?"

He listened without comment.

"I think you should think less in terms of normal and familiar, and just accept a wider point of view." She chuckled, "You're getting a crash course in that."

He looked at her with a pained, but amused expression. "Yeah, sounds good, but in about one week I'm headed back to the city, to my work and family. So what is my 'wider' self supposed to do in a 'relatively' normal environment? I mean, here everybody wants to talk about how you're feeling, what you're thinking, but in real life? No one gives a shit about all that. The more I stay, the more of a freak I'm becoming."

"Well," asked Wanda, "How does it feel?"

He shook his head and scoffed. "It feels better than it did a week ago."

On the ride home, Wanda ventured, "Where would you rate me and my family on your scale of normalcy?"

Terry was tiring. "Wanda, you all are not normal. You're great, some of the best, but you are not normal."

She persisted. "Well in your normal world, would you think us any less great? Would you shun us loonies?" He rolled his eyes, but she wouldn't give up. "I'm not kidding. What would you do if we showed up for a visit? Would we be too weird for you to associate with?"

He looked sharply at her. "Of course not. I'd be totally stoked to have you visit."

She slowed the truck and patted his knee. "Terry, what makes you think anyone is going to be any less willing to welcome the not-so-normal you?"

Sudden onsets of contented fullness had, of late, been added to Terry's repertoire of emerging physiological oddities. Of his assorted pains, pressures and disturbances, this was the first sensation he could identify as pleasurable. Powerfully so.

An abrupt wash of well being would unexpectedly arrive, leaving in its wake all-inclusive relaxation, as if pleasure receptors had suddenly awakened throughout both his body and mind.

At first, he found the blissful episodes to be every bit as disturbing as those of pain or weakness. In fact, Terry considered the new sensations to be variations on the same old theme, as if some single, unknown stimulus was inducing responses that his body received and interpreted in different ways at different times. But to his anguish and frustration, he could not in any way direct or affect the nature of the ensuing experience.

The first of these blissful moments occurred during a second fishing hike. He and Jim had returned to a promising looking stretch of river that Terry noticed on their original expedition with the group. The day was brisk, the sun a welcome warmth in the cloudless sky. They walked in silence most of the way enjoying communion with nature, along with a growing ease in each other's company.

They stopped to watch a heron's lift-off: spindly legs trailed like airplane wheels prior to retraction, until the powerful flapping finally gained enough altitude as to afford a more graceful image. In the moment of the bird's apparent transformation from engine to glider, Jim turned to Terry with a smile of pure delight, and Terry's legs gave way beneath him. He sat spread eagle on the bank, illumined by a stoned out grin and utterly overcome by the sense of ecstasy.

His bluster was reflexive. "Geez, I'm telling you, my legs are all for shit lately."

Later, lingering close beside the remnants of a small cooking fire, Jim pulled a small flask of peach brandy from his jacket, drank deeply and passed the bottle with a conspiratorial smile. Terry grabbed it like a lizard's tongue darts for a moth. They sat for a long time without speaking, viscerally sensing as much as seeing the sun's descent alter hues in the landscape. Jim used one foot to push a fish skeleton into the coals, and asked in his soft, shy voice, "What do you think about pleasure?"

Terry's brow creased. "What?"

"Pleasure. How is it with you?"

Terry could sense Jim's sincerity, but sprang to his feet just barely able to hold himself in check.

"Look, I don't know what you mean. You talking about sex?"

A characteristic, introverted smile was Jim's initial response. After a pause he said, "No, I didn't mean sex. I just wondered about growing up and all. Some people show it easier than others when something feels good. Like maybe it's weak or wrong or something. That's how I was brought up, to not show whether anything felt good or bad. I guess that kind of thing got trained out of me, only I didn't know it until it wrecked my marriage. At least that's what I think did it."

Terry gave him a sideways glance. "Jim, what about your, uh, tendency..."

Jim's eyes sparkled. "Wife didn't know about the cross-dressing...you can't say the word, can you?"

"Sorry."

"No, it's alright. Terry, back there on the bank after we saw the heron? You were feeling pretty good, weren't you?"

Terry shrugged and sat back down. "Yeah, I guess."

Jim observed him for a while in a way that was beginning to feel familiar. Wanda did the same thing, he realized.

Jim mused, "What made me ask about pleasure is,

back then you acted like you were almost caught stealing or something."

"Stolen pleasure?"

"Right. Like pleasure, the way a kid feels it, is something bad or embarrassing. Is that what it's like for you?"

Terry hesitated, feeling his muscles contract as his whole person again mobilized for attack. He fought the sensation enough to answer, "Well, yeah, I felt stupid. I don't know what came over me. It was like I was drunk."

Jim grinned. "Damn, people pay a lot of money for drugs to feel like that."

Terry conceded, "Yeah, it was pretty amazing. But intense. I mean all this weird stuff's been happening…"

Jim cut short the now familiar litany. "Next time it happens? You ought to make it into something, give it a name and make it last. Something like, I'm having a bliss break."

"Bliss break," Terry laughed. "I like that."

~ 19 ~

"Here we go again," Pryluck sighs.

Once again, Terry has crashed in the wake of a frequency increase. Bedridden with fatigue and shortness of breath, he's steeped in—as per usual—fear, along with a generous helping of shame.

Vormis is disappointed at Terry's failure to recognize and be soothed by his presence.

"That's why we're a team," Snarrow offers. *"Mabel, is there some kind of conflict up with the subs?"*

Mabel appears in soft, iridescent tones of jade. "It must be one we have not met yet. Our regulars are holding their own, although Helen and her counterpart—you would think those 'two' could come up with a single name for when they are united—anyway, they do seem a bit despondent. But they are not the problem. Bulista and I will go find the culprit. Really, Terry ought to begin doing this for himself," she mutters as she changes phase.

Pryluck chuckles. "Would you agree, Snarrow, that Mabel sounded particularly snippy just then?"

Snarrow flickers. "What is it between the two of you? Come on and fortify Vormis with me."

* * *

By Wednesday, the third of October and Terry's twelfth day into his two week retreat at Ricki's, a lot had changed. If anything, his body's quirks and sensitivities were continuing to increase in intensity and frequency of occurrence. But amply evident to all—both human and non—was an overall abatement of some kind of tension or resistance, as if something inside him had gone belly up. And with it, a sort of steely outer coating had become more malleable.

When Terry finally made the long overdue and anxiety-ridden disclosure about his misplacement at Ricki's, it stirred not a ripple among the participants. Rumor, observation and speculation had long preceded his announcement. No one reacted with hostility and really, no one reacted much at all.

Next morning, Mira made it a point to sit with Terry at breakfast. Afterwards, they walked to the neighboring lake. "I have to admire you for sticking it out," she began. "I can understand your coming here by mistake, but I really can't imagine what made you stay."

Terry studied her patiently before responding. Another thing that had changed was that he no longer saw the large, awkward man under dress and wig, nor did he flinch in the face of that question he had been asked several times in the last two weeks. "I was a little desperate and needed some place to chill. I couldn't go home yet."

"And how about now?" Mira asked.

He shrugged. "Not much has changed, except for having met an interesting bunch of guys." He raised an eyebrow and they both laughed. "What about you? What did you get from being here?"

Mira wrinkled her chin enough that her lower lip protruded. "I guess more confidence. And I think I wear my clothes better, don't you think?"

"Absolutely."

"But you know," she continued, "dressing up isn't enough."

"No?" he wondered.

"I'd like to get dressed and then go do something, you know, some kind of activity."

"Like what?"

"Gee, I don't know. Something...maybe bowling?"

Terry repressed a smile. "You want to go bowling in high heels?"

"Mmm..." she furrowed her brow, then sighed in frustration. "Oh, I don't know, what do girls do when they get dressed up? Shop?"

* * *

Terry took his time driving back to the city. He stopped just shy of the mountain pass to linger at a rest area where, reminiscent of a same-language movie subtitle, a sign informed passersby of the "scenic view." A golden ring of wildflowers that crowned a small knoll aroused an uneasy turbulence beneath Terry's skin. He felt lost and melancholy, and reluctant to drive on into whatever lay ahead.

"Terry!" From some distant place, he imagined he heard a voice calling to him. The sound that was not quite sound almost, but not quite fully, penetrated his thoughts.

"That's it, go on," Mabel encourages Vormis. "You have got his attention."

Vormis presses forward, taking full advantage of the open focus of Terry's mind.

"Terry!" he calls again.

Terry sat on a rock beside a large tree, and listened hard. Wind in pine trees, car tires passing on the highway, the brief call of a western jay. And then a phrase. Heard? Imagined?

"Don't be afraid."

The words were clear in his mind. The realization of having heard them shocked him into everyday consciousness. "What? Who's there?" he asked, addressing his own mind.

It was as frustrating as losing radio reception just as his team was about to score. Nothing but the wind, the jay. He got back in the truck and drove fast, his mind racing.

Vormis sighs. "It doesn't do any good. I finally reach him and he ignores the message."

*A warm glow suffuses the room at Methods. "Vormis,"
Snarrow assures him. "It is an extraordinary breakthrough. A consciously received transmission! Let him first be amazed. You*

can be sure the message made an impression. And now that you both know it is possible, communication can be repeated as needed."

~ 20 ~

As the truck pulls up beside the curb, Aunt Ethel paces, tight-lipped and muttering aloud. She tells herself to practice the new link-up that the subs have adopted in a recent meeting: a joining of hands—metaphorically speaking—in a circle of light. The point is to reinforce their new, inner core of strength as an alternative to previously established patterns of defensive behavior.

Since Chaz seems to be doing so nicely with this strategy and, because all the subs are in some manner or another exhibiting behaviors aimed at keeping Terry safe and out of "trouble," Mabel and her cohorts reason that this link-up might stimulate a reorientation of the subpersonalities' thought patterns: from separatist and often conflict based thinking, to the common intention to maintain Terry's wellbeing.

Nevertheless, Ethel is fretting. The stakes are too high to simply stick with the new program. "My job is information," she reminds herself. "He's got to know that people here must not see him in his present condition. Not OK. Too relaxed. Too exposed. Tough and tight is better." She begins her recitation.

Bulista, on sub surveillance, drifts near. "Aunt Ethel?" she interrupts after a while.

"Huh? Oh...what is it?"

"Could you maybe deliver the same info, minus judgment?"

Ethel stares at the intern. "I was."

Bulista nods thoughtfully. "How many times do you think you might have told him he's not OK?"

"Ohhh," Ethel finally answers. "I guess that seems judgmental?"

Bulista nods. "How about something like: we need fortification to face family and work, we need to build up the inner core?" she suggests.

Ethel presses her lips, ever pondering. "Alright, yes, I see. But I'm not sure that the circle's strong enough. I want to be sure."

"I know," Bulista offers. "But this way you'll have reinforcement. It's less effort on your part, and Terry will be boosted up to a higher level of resilience instead of falling into more self-doubt. It suits everyone."

Ethel nods, and her usual serious expression is suddenly pierced by a rare gleam of fun. "Win-win," she cackles.

* * *

Terry sat in the truck for a few minutes, reluctant to step outside and confront his life. He was even less disposed to see his apartment. Leaving his bags on the back seat, he got out and meandered on foot downhill toward the canal.

Settling onto the same park bench where he woke some months earlier on the morning after meeting Cara, he sat for a long time consumed by the absurdity of himself and his life. Clouds swirled rosy gold, then violet-gray, before the light faded and a chilly drizzle arrived.

After two weeks of intense and often unwanted companionship, solitude now felt empty. Nothing more than longstanding habit aimed him toward The Oyster's Pearl. From the sidewalk, he peered through a window at what remained of the happy hour crowd, recognized many, and walked on. His mind-vacant body carried him up another hill and past the zoo, retracing an imperfect memory of solace.

Terry stared at the wooden door with lavender trim, and wind chimes hanging from the eaves. He knocked softly, and was surprised to hear movement from within the house.

When Cara opened the door, they both momentarily frooze. "Hi," he eventually said, meeting her eyes with a sheepish smile. "I didn't know you'd be in."

She grinned. "Well, that explains the knock."

He brought his cheek near hers, kissing the air in the same sort of Latino greeting that he had so pointedly evaded at Ricki's. Realizing this, he laughed to himself. "Are you busy?" he asked. "I wanted to see you."

Cara studied him for a moment, plainly curious. "I guess I'm not. Do you want to come in?"

"Would you mind going for a walk? We could go to the zoo."

She gave him another inquisitive glance, as much for the fact that the zoo would certainly be closed as for the remarkable difference in his manner. "You know, Terry, I'm hardly recognizing you," she told him, but caught the flicker of fear that crossed his face. She held his eyes with hers. "Hang on a sec, I'll grab a coat."

They ambled west until they smelled the ocean. The silence between them was uncommon, but easy. "So," she finally said, "is this a social visit or was there something you wanted to talk about?"

He glanced down at her, registering the small form wrapped in Peruvian wool, in context of the October drizzle.

"Sorry, my mind was somewhere. Are you cold? You want to stop in here for a while?" He gestured toward a coffeehouse.

"I'm not cold, I'm used to the weather and this is your gig, so how about you decide?"

He placed a light hand on her arm. "Cara, I never thanked you for being so good with me. When I was...well, you know. I went away, and when I was there, I thought of you. I'm sure you saved me from...something." Suddenly self-conscious, he laughed at himself. "I don't know why you bothered, but it meant a lot to me that you did."

Dumbfounded, Cara looked at his face and unsuccessfully willed herself to be kind. Finally she exploded, "Wow, I can't believe it's the same guy. What happened?"

He turned abruptly, but she caught his wrists and held him. "No, please, I like it. You're like a new, improved model." She linked arms with him and prodded gently with her shoulder to resume their walk. "Come on, tell me about it."

He didn't tell much, but they walked along the shore and swung on wet swings—one more unforeseen point scored in Terry's favor—before finally opting for the coffeehouse on the return trip.

"Will you laugh again if I thank you for coming out tonight?" he asked.

She nodded, and then shrugged dismissively. "I might. But thank you. It's been fun."

He stared unfocused at the far wall. "God, I can't even remember anything being fun before this. It feels like forever."

"What happened? Did you just go and get cured of something?"

"No, not cured. Maybe I'm just getting used to being this

way." He studied her, his mouth awry and finally added, "And...I met some people. I'm nervous about being back home. I don't know how to be with the people who used to know me."

"You're doing OK so far," she smiled.

"But you don't really know me, remember? And your greeting wasn't exactly warm."

"Nuts! I was beside myself...in a good way."

* * *

Pryluck yawns. "Isn't it about time to turn him up a notch? Even he agrees that he's acclimating."

"He said he's getting used to it. But you're probably right. We might pull this off yet," proclaims Vormis.

Barwin unpredictably pipes up from the technies' corner. "He is scheduled for the next increase in about a week."

"Scheduled!" exclaims Pryluck. "He's on a schedule?"

"Well, yes, there is a timing to it. No different than with any of the others."

"What are you talking about?" asks Vormis. "Isn't this lifestream a unique project? Are you saying there are others?"

"Not the same project, no, but frequency shifts and periodic influxes of light are basic planetary maintenance. All lifestreams of every kind are continually affected. And, of course it is timed. We have to stay coordinated with the rest of the galaxy."

Pryluck ripples. "I never knew about that end of things. Matter of fact, we've never known much about what you guys are up to, Barwin. How come you've never talked before?"

Barwin's field resumes its customary yellow translucence, so subtle as to hardly be detectable. Vormis and Pryluck exchange a glance. "So much for that," grumbles Pryluck.

~ 21 ~

Someone was banging at the door. Terry sighed and reached to set his beer can on the floor. He remained supine. Another series of knocks accompanied faint auditory clues that signaled he had more than one visitor. "Yeah!" he yelled, still welded to the couch.

"Terry?" came a muffled voice. "Are you home?"

"No," he muttered to himself. "It's the ghost." He heaved himself onto an elbow, swung his legs heavily to one side and grunted as he stood. Limbs, head and mind felt heavy and thick. "Hang on," he called flatly in the direction of the door.

"Holy shit!" he exclaimed. "What are you guys doing here?"

"What the hell kind of a greeting is that?" asked Mira, sweeping through the open door into Terry's hallway. "We're going down to San Francisco for Halloween and thought you might like to come along. Geez, are you alright, Ter? You look like some kind of crap."

Terry smiled weakly and held out his arms to embrace first Mira, and then Jim, who had initially hung back. "Yeah, sorry about that, I feel like some kind of crap. Come on in."

He aimed the remote to turn down the TV. "There's beer in the fridge." He gazed lethargically toward the kitchen. "I guess it's a mess here, huh? I haven't been feeling too good."

"Go on and sit down," Jim said softly. "What can we get for you?" Their eyes met and held. Jim's showed concern.

Terry relaxed, giving in to his exhaustion. "I'm glad to see you," he said. "I wish the timing was different."

Jim's smile was like a trout behind a rock. Most would miss it. "Timing's perfect," he said, barely audible. "What's going on?"

Terry shook his head. "I can't help it. It's like someone pulls the plug on me. It'll pass in a couple of days."

"Beer is fine, but don't you have any food in this place?" Mira bustled out of the kitchen holding out a couple of cans.

"Nope, I guess I don't."

"Well, no wonder you look like hell. Where's your phone? I'm going to order us a pizza."

Terry extended a listless arm in the direction of the hall. "Bujoe's delivers. They're not bad."

"Do you know what's wrong with you?" Jim asked.

"No, that's just it. After it passes I'll feel alright for a while. Sometimes I feel real good you know, like normal, but then every time I do, wham! It's like this sudden jolt and I'm completely trashed."

Jim silently contemplated his feet for a minute. "You know, I have a cousin who's manic-depressive. You sound kind of like that."

"Shit, no. You think I'm nuts?"

Jim flushed. "It's not nuts, it's sick. You've got something wrong, don't you?"

"Yeah, but I mean this feels more like something with my body. Like too much adrenalin or maybe none. Manic-depressive, isn't that like big time mood swings? I never get real happy or nothing like that."

Jim's left foot traced windshield wiper patterns beneath the edge of the couch. "I don't know, Terry, even if it is a body thing. You should at least have someone check you out."

"So," Mira flounced back into the room, "You gonna come with us to San Fran?" Terry looked wanly in her direction.

"Oh, don't go being so sensitive all over again. I thought you started out like this at Ricki's because you were shocked by us girls."

Jim growled, "He's sick, would you give him a break?"

Mira walked over to the couch and took one of Terry's hands between hers. "He just needs someone to get him fed and to get this pigsty into some kind of order." She felt his forehead. "I'd make a good nurse. Maybe I'll go to nursing school after the operation. They make good money, you know."

Terry looked speculatively at his two friends. "What's up with you two?" He gestured from one to the other.

Mira's mouth dropped open in mock affront. A reticent smile lit Jim's eyes. He shrugged.

"Alright, you gotta set me straight here...no pun intended...I thought you were both basically straight. I mean, you have a wife, right?" he asked, addressing Mira. Turning to Jim, "And you were married, kid and all."

Jim and Mira exchanged a glance. She turned back to Terry, lips protruded, and answered, "Yeah, so?"

"So then you're not...?" Again, the hand gesture.

They smiled, relishing his discomfort. "Or maybe we are," replied Mira. "But you still see me as a man," she pouted. "You don't get it."

Terry shook his head. "Damn right I don't. You have a wife who doesn't even know you cross dress, you've started taking hormones and planning for a sex change, and now you're...uh, whatever...with a supposedly straight boyfriend who also likes to dress up as a girl. So what, are you two gonna end up as lesbians?"

"Fuck you!" Jim breathed. "What difference can it possibly make to you how Mira and I call ourselves or what we do?"

Terry shook his head again. "No difference. I just don't get it."

"Why bother?" perked up Mira. "I say, take it if it feels good. Anyway, you ought to play more and lose your hostility. Come down and get dressed up with us for Halloween. You can go as an ogre."

Terry sighed. "I don't believe this. Alright, maybe. But I ain't going nowhere just yet. Where are you guys staying?"

Mira faltered only for a second. "With you is what we figured. We'll take care of you."

"Jesus."

The thought of being seen in public with Mira in drag gave Terry diarrhea. Still, a day's rest, together with the cheery company, had done wonders for his overall state. The least he could do was to take his friends out for breakfast. Terry guessed that a downtown café would afford the least likelihood of being recognized by anyone he knew.

It was not crowded, but far from empty. He began to relax over coffee, and felt preliminary whispers of a pleasure rush begin to flood his feet, legs and belly. Then, like a stretched spring suddenly retracted, he lurched back to his more familiar state of panic.

Cara and another—unfamiliar—woman were approaching. "Hey, look who's here!" Cara exclaimed. "Dolores, this is Terry. The fisherman."

Dolores stared in some surprise before she smiled warmly and extended a hand. "So, you're the one I've heard so much about."

He blushed, but gamely stood to take her hand. "Dolores. Nice to meet you." Briefly holding her eyes, he hesitated. "Um, these are my friends," he finally mumbled. "Mira and Jim. They're visiting."

Cara responded to the introduction with one of her incandescent smiles. Terry tried to caution Mira with a glance, but she had already reverted to gentlemanly form. "Enchanted," she began in a baritone. "Would you ladies like to join us?"

"Love to," Cara answered, pulling up two more chairs from a neighboring table.

* * *

Methods Division gleams as lightworkers assemble. Creative Works radiates broad contentment. Cara and Terry's guides mingle companionably, and a general aura of optimism prevails. Even Dolores' Forwyn makes a brief appearance.

Vormis, however, is all sparks and spikes. Snarrow addresses him. "Rebound from Terry's last increase was the fastest yet, Vormis. We are making progress. What's the problem?"

Vormis dims, brightens and hums his agitation. "His nervous system can't withstand all these fluctuations. He's strained to capacity. I am too," he adds.

A more experienced field guide overhears. "Vormis, have you become caught in your memories of life in human form?" he asks. Startled by the realization, Vormis admits that he has.

"It's only natural. Remind yourself you are on the other side of that dynamic now. It is tricky business, holding both realities at once. The others have no way to know," he gestures widely,

encompassing the gathering of lightworkers.

"What is it you are saying?" Snarrow asks.

The field guide laughs. "What did I tell you?" he nudges Vormis. To Snarrow, he explains, "If you've never experienced physical form, it's hard to imagine the sensation of identification with the body and its chemical processes. It is inherent in a field guide's job that we operate from the full and intimate understanding of embodied experience. To do that without any lapse in awareness of the higher dimensions takes a fair bit of mastery. In fact, it is the ultimate evolutionary challenge for the whole species."

"Yes, yes." Snarrow is more than aware of this concept, theoretical as it may be to him and his peers.

"A novice field guide will either sit too far in the light to effectively reach their lifestream in a pinch—Vormis got over that real quick early on—or, they will resonate too far along the line of empathy and start identifying with the human template. I am impressed with how fast Vormis is progressing."

Snarrow fans in peacock tones. "I agree. And, I think all of us have been speeded up by this project." He turns to Vormis. "I have kept tabs on Terry's body levels. The technies have been delivering updates throughout this phase. Would it help for you to see them?"

Together they approach the technies' corner, dodging a clutter of shimmering holograms. "Look here how Terry's hormone levels correlate with fluctuations in light. Watch how each hormone flood creates a spike in central nervous system output that signals his heart, lungs and so forth that he is under some kind of attack. This is where we can map his episodes of high stress behavior. Notice that each time we have introduced a new frequency, the threshold level of reaction has become higher, and the duration *of the spike has become shorter. This represents successful adaptation, Vormis. His body is accepting the process."*

Vormis studies the holograms. "Does this mean that his nervous system is actually getting stronger?"

"More resilient, yes. You are doing a great job, Vormis. And he is pulling through.

* * *

Conversationally speaking, Cara and Mira were a perfect fit. They chatted amiably to the thorough satisfaction of Cara's curiosity about the ins and outs of sex change. Terry noted that he learned more about his friends at this breakfast than he had in all the time they'd spent together at Ricki's Halfway.

Dolores remained uncharacteristically quiet until she and Cara were alone back at her apartment. "My God, I was expecting some twerpy clod. You didn't tell me he was gorgeous."

Cara turned to face her. "Who? You mean Terry?" Then, after a pause, "Oh. No, D. Don't. He's too messed up, even for you."

Dolores tried to look offended, but failed. "Even for me! He's not gay, is he? It doesn't feel like he is."

"He talks like he's a total homophobe. I can't imagine how he ever hooked up with those two. Unless...I don't know. Maybe." Cara giggled. "Remember that time I told you about, when he confessed he didn't want to have sex with me?"

Dolores' gaze became unfocused, in the manner she assumed when looking between worlds. "Well no, you and he aren't permitted. But Forwyn doesn't think there's any such restriction on me."

"So how does it work, if you didn't like his looks, would I then be granted permission?"

"Cara, it isn't me who decided that. Besides, I thought you weren't interested." She studied her friend's face. "You don't really think I make it all up, do you?"

Cara sighed. "I don't know what I think. Make it up? No. Just be careful, D. You don't need all that baggage."

"I'm just looking!" Dolores protested. They sat in silence for a while. "Let's go with them to San Francisco," she suggested. "It would be fun."

Cara squinted. "Do you really want to go? Even if Terry doesn't go?"

"Oh, quit. I love San Francisco. And on Halloween, I'll bet Madam D can make some money."

~ 22 ~

Jim was alone in the apartment when Terry returned from helping his brother, Bill, with an engine repair. "Where is Mira?" he asked.

Jim shrugged and mumbled, "Out shopping." He seemed more subdued, and even quieter than usual.

A second examination of Jim's face confirmed Terry's initial detection of makeup. He felt his solar plexus give out, as if he had been punched. He turned away, face flushed and lips tight. Forcing himself to breathe, he noted that whereas he had grown accustomed to Mira's full-fledged drag, he still thought of Jim as a regular guy, despite all information to the contrary. He walked to the kitchen and took a beer from the fridge. The situation sucked. He felt trapped in his own place. "Hey Jim," he called. "When are you guys taking off?"

Hearing no response, he ambled back into the other room. Jim, it appeared, was not only prettied up, but sulking. Not his typical style. "Uh, Jim, something up?" he asked.

Closed-faced and decidedly flushed, Jim shook his head without looking up.

"Well, what the fuck!" said Terry. "Look, you want a beer?"

Jim finally brought his head up to meet Terry's glance. Terry recognized overt pain in his friend's face. A storm of anxiety roiled in his belly, constricting his throat. "Shit," he muttered, willing himself not to run. "Hey look, Jim, I don't know what I'm supposed to do here."

"For Christ's sake, Terry, will you just shut up and sit down." Jim's tone of voice, gentle and patient as ever, belied his message and quelled Terry's agitation considerably.

"I'm not used to seeing you in make-up," he confessed.

Jim's eyes moved, but the preoccupied sadness in his face didn't change. "No, I guess not."

"You seem unhappy," Terry tried.

This brought a direct, appraising glance. "Yeah, I guess so."

"So what's up?"

Jim shrugged again and looked down. They had come full circle.

Terry changed the subject. "Hey, listen, my brother needs me on the boat tomorrow. You might like to see our operation. Gilli's Girl is a Scottish wooden trawler, built in the '30's. You could help out if you want, or just come for the ride, but you stay warmer if you work. If you guys are still around."

Jim's expression lost its vacancy. "Sure, that'd be great."

Terry hesitated. "Um, Mira..."

"You don't need to worry. It's not her style. Anyway, she has plans with your girlfriends tomorrow." Jim's gaze returned to his lap, as did the cloud to his face.

Terry's brow furrowed. "My girlfriends?"

"First she's doing something with Cara, and then having some kind of fortune telling session with Dolores. They're coming to San Francisco with us."

Terry felt a jolt of alarm without knowing why. "Whoa, when did all this happen?"

Jim, on the verge of tears, shrugged again and shook his head. "She just really hit it off with them. They're out together now."

Finally, Terry caught on. "You're not jealous, are you?" He took some time to let the realization sink in. "This is too screwed up. The whole thing." He shook his head. "I know I'm out of the loop here, but I don't think those two are interested in anything, if you know what I mean."

Jim attempted a smile. "No, that's not it. I'm just not like them. I'm dull. Why would she want to hang around with me?"

"Lord." Terry looked heavenward. "You're not a flaming..." He caught himself and rephrased. "You're not effeminate, if that's what you mean. But I don't think that's what Mira is looking for in a, um...relationship, Jim. Geez, it would be so much simpler if you all had the anatomy to match your roles."

Jim sighed. "Give me that beer, would you?"

* * *

After the last crate was loaded, Fred—the youngest of the three Gillis brothers—pulled the truck away from the dock. Jim joined Bill and Terry on deck. "It was great to have you on board," Bill told Jim. "Appreciate the help. Why don't you guys come up to the house for a beer?" Turning to Terry he added, "Fran'll be pissed if you don't. She's stewed that you haven't been by since you got home."

Terry glanced at Jim. "That O.K. with you?"

"Sure," Jim agreed.

They were, naturally, invited for dinner and naturally had to decline on account of Mira's absence. Fran was full of questions about Jim and Mira, and how they and Terry had met, and finally about Ricki's. "Oh, that's the place you went to in Preston, with the odd business card?"

She addressed Jim. "So, the place is legit. Bill and I were kind of suspicious."

Jim's forehead creased. "You knew Terry was going to Ricki's?"

Terry intervened. "To a men's retreat place. That's what it is, right?"

Jim didn't laugh, but his face tightened. "Men's retreat. That's right."

"Well then," Fran wondered. "How do you know Mira?"

"What is this, third degree?" Terry growled.

But Jim had already begun his soft, direct reply. "We all met at Ricki's. Mira is still part man. She's undergoing a sex change."

Fran's eyes widened, but she had no more questions for the moment. Seeing them off at the door she asked Jim, "You didn't mean now? She's not undergoing a sex change here, right now, is she?"

Jim muted his smile. "No, it's a pretty long process. She's

out with Terry's friends, Cara and Dolores now, but they'll be back soon and wondering where we are."

Fran's eyes widened again and she retreated to the hallway.

Fran and Bill sat on the living room couch. She was not communicating, but each time Bill attempted to get up, she pulled him back down with a little whine. "What's going on, Fran?" he asked.

She looked at him imploringly, clearly troubled, yet evidently speechless.

"This is not about Terry, is it?"

She barely nodded.

"What, you don't like his friend?"

He almost missed the slight shake of her head. "Why not? Jim's alright. You shoulda seen, he was a natural on the boat today. Did a good day's work."

Shaking her head once more, she murmured something unintelligible.

"What?"

"Not him."

"Who, the transsexual? That's what you call those sex change guys, right?"

"What is wrong with you?" She finally managed. "Terry isn't open-minded about those kinds of things. You know that. And do you have any idea who that Dolores is that Jim mentioned? Bill, she's a psychic. Since when is Terry hanging out with psychics and transsexuals?"

Bill's face was expressionless. "Geez, Fran, the only one I saw him hanging out with is this guy, Jim, who's a miner from out East. He seems real nice and regular. I don't know anything about psychics or transsexuals."

"Well, I do!" she blurted. "I went to see Dolores one time for a reading."

Bill tried not to smile. "And what did she tell you?"

"That's not the point!" she complained, beginning to cry.

He put his arm around her. "Honey, what is this all about?"

"I don't understand any of it," Fran whimpered as she snuggled against him.

They reconvened back at Terry's apartment. Mira's manner was decidedly more feminine after having spent the day with Dolores and Cara. To Jim's relief, she greeted him effusively, eager to report on her afternoon.

"Look at the costumes we bought," she crowed, pulling out beads, wigs and gaudy fabrics. Cara and I will go as *grandes dames* and Madam D will just be Madam D."

Cara walked over to Terry, and held a lavender colored wig up to his head. "This one would look great on you," she winked.

Red-faced, he stormed out of the room.

Mira caught Cara's eye. "He's still not comfortable with the whole idea of gender flexibility. He feels threatened."

Cara found Terry in the kitchen. "Sorry," she said. "I didn't mean to offend you."

He faced her. "I'm not a fag, for God's sake. Why don't you all just leave me alone?"

She gazed at him until he finally met her eyes—the blue fires that had always pierced and calmed him. "Terry, no one thinks you're gay. It isn't about that anyway. It's Halloween.

Don't you like to get dressed up?"

"Not since I was about ten."

"How sad is that!" she teased. "You're gonna grow all up before you're even old."

He shrugged his irritation. "You're telling me I shouldn't have grown up?"

She flashed one of her smiles. "Oops, too late. Come on, old man." She took his arm and led him back to the others.

After dinner downtown, Cara once again took Terry's arm as they all walked back to the apartment. "You still haven't said if you're coming to San Francisco."

He bristled. "I was never considering it. Anyway, it's a whole day's drive just one way. I can't take that much time off from work.

She leaned toward him and whispered, "You know, Dolores is really hoping you will."

He studied her face. "What?"

"Shh," she laughed. "She'll kill me if she knew I said anything. She was huffy that I never told her you were—in her words—gorgeous."

He blushed to feel his eyes fill, and said nothing. He did, however, tenderly place his free hand over the small one that held his arm.

* * *

"I'm confused," Bulista confides to Mabel. "I thought that all of Terry's subs showed up when the technies completed his personality stripping. The one over there fussing about Elaine's S&M outfit is not part of the new program, is he?"

Mabel colors brightly. "Heavens, no! No, the personal subs have already been accounted for, and are all rehabilitating nicely. Terry is in phase two of personality stripping now. Phase one dealt with the individual lifestream's persona. What we are now encountering are archetypal entities. Such as the one harassing Elaine. He simply represents Terry's portion of the collective personality that invokes shame in association with sexuality."

"I never really understood what the collective personality encompasses," Bulista confesses.

"Well," Mabel explains. "Of course, there are different levels. There is the personal collective—that is like the soul group: different lifestreams from the same ray projection living their own unique programs while sharing the higher goal and intentions of a single, common soul. Our department oversees one soul group or collective, of which Terry is merely a portion.

"Then, there is the collective personality of the whole human species, encompassing all soul group personalities. It really just goes on and on. I don't know how far Management plans to go with Terry's reconfiguration."

* * *

Terry set down the phone receiver and slumped against the kitchen counter. Pigfuck timing! Gilli's Girl was out of commission again. She was an old boat. The chronically malfunctioning reduction gear had been refurbished enough times that it was high time for replacement. And none was in stock at any of the local marine supply places. Bill was able to locate a supplier in Oakland, California, who could ship one overnight...but not before tomorrow morning. Which meant a frustrating minimum of three days waiting for delivery and repair. He might as well make the ridiculously long drive down and pick the damn thing up himself. After all, everyone else was hell-bent on driving to the

Bay area.

Mira appeared at the kitchen door. "Who was that you were cussing at? Lord, honey, you've got a real sailor's mouth on you."

Terry's face tightened. "Yeah, my brother Bill called."

"Is everything OK between you two?"

Terry waved a dismissive hand. "Yeah, yeah, it's just the boat's broke. It'll be faster for me to drive down to Oakland for the part than to have them ship it." His face looked as if he'd swallowed vinegar.

*   *   *

Exuding a jagged shower of irregular shapes, Mabel bursts in to where Pryluck cavorts with two Creative Works reps. "Did you have anything to do with this?" she demands.

They observe her emanation with some surprise. "What this is that?" asks Bouffant Head.

Mabel regards the three, while gradually assuming a more coherent field. "Are you—she addresses Pryluck—in any way responsible for forcing our lifestream's decision making process?"

Pryluck flares. "I have never forced any one of our lifestreams!"

"Alright," Mabel counters, "then did you have any influence on the events in this one's latest experience?"

Diamond Hoops intervenes. "Mabel, dear, Pryluck and we have not been on duty, nor have we even looked in on the dimension of the lifestream's current day. We have been taking our recreation just as you found us. But I would love to know what has so ruffled your pin-feathers."

Mabel shrinks back to her usual size. Pryluck maintains his expanded form for just a moment longer. "Excuse me," she concedes. *"It just seems so extraordinary...engineered...that I assumed..."*

Bouffant Head, who currently resembles a royal blue, sequin-encrusted bowling ball, presses between them. "What has happened, Mabel?"

"Oh, it is just that now he is going to San Francisco with the others."

"Whee hee!" exclaims Diamond Hoops. "Party time!" He takes Mabel by both hands and dances her about. "Such divine news you've brung!"

Still at odds, Mabel breaks out in wavy striations. "Brought," she corrects.

"I thought it was brang," declares Bouffant Head.

~ 23 ~

The hous
e in which they stayed belonged to friends of Jim and his ex-wife. They invited Jim to visit when they heard he would be making a trip out west. The house was a sprawling Victorian, less than three blocks from Golden Gate Park. Plenty of space, comfortably furnished. Ben and Elizabeth had money.

Jim called ahead to let them know there would be extras. "Oh, Jim, I'm so glad you called," began Elizabeth. "Jerry—you remember our son, Jerry? He got himself arrested for drugs. We're going up to Sacramento for the hearing. God, this is such a nightmare. Anyway, we need to leave early tomorrow to meet with our lawyer. We'll be up there for a few days to try to get things settled.

"Of course, you'll still stay in the house," she continued. "You remember where the key is? And you'll stay until we get back, we'd hate to miss you."

OK, Jim thought, no awkward revelations yet.

Turned out at the last minute, Cara asked her two band partners to go along. Jim's pick-up would be too crowded anyway; Terry decided to drive his own truck, retrieve the part for the boat and return home with neither delay nor detour.

Their caravan arrived well after dark on hell night, and dispersed at once. Mira and Jim were off to catch a costume party at a nearby gay bar. The others declined the invitation to join them. The musical trio gathered their instruments and hit the streets.

In the wake of the exodus, Dolores found a nearly full bottle of white wine in the refrigerator. She offered Terry a glass.

He grunted. "Have they got any beer?"

"You could look around. I don't see any."

"You wanna go somewhere for a beer?"

She appraised him, the situation and her feelings. Cara was right. The person was far less appealing than the package. She thought, "galoot" and heard the words, *"heavy energy."* The response, of course, was Forwyn's.

"What do you think?" she silently addressed her guide.

He laughs, "Since when do you base your decisions on what I think?" At her obvious inner struggle, he relents. "You are free to choose, Dolores, and will face and handle any choice that you make. We, as always, support you in love and blessings."

She sighed. If nothing else could break her pride, the

experience of being at the mercy of her own flesh offered a distinct dose of humility.

"Respect yourself, Dolores. It is the force of life itself. You will not tame it."

She digested Forwyn's compassion before finally answering Terry. "Yeah, OK. Do you know the city, or do we wander?"

Fran answered the bedside phone. "Hey, Ter, are you home?" she mumbled sleepily and then, "You're what? Terry, everyone up here is waiting for you and that goddamn part!"

She turned to Bill. "He's still in California."

Bill grabbed the phone. "Hey, what's up?"

"Look, I got delayed a day. I'll be back tomorrow night."

Bill heard it in his voice. "A woman?"

"Yeah."

"Jesus, Terry, your timing sucks eggs."

"Yeah, I know. Sorry."

Each brother heard the smile in the other's voice. Fran buried her head under the pillow.

* * *

The number of lightworkers that have begun to routinely observe Terry, among both Methods Department and Creative Works, is continuing to increase. This is quite a departure from normal procedure, wherein each has been concerned solely with the progress of the lifestreams in their charge. Cara's guide, Millicent, now sits with Mabel beneath a row of enormous holographic sunflowers they have conjured.

"What an interesting development for your lifestream," Millicent muses. *"That Dolores will give him a run for his money."*

"Tell me about her," Mabel requests. *"She is not wired up*

in the same way as most lifestreams."

"No," Millicent laughs. "That, she is not. She has an extra circuit programmed into her physical body that allows her to perceive and communicate on a subtler level than most. Although it makes her no less dense in other areas.

Still," Mabel comments, "our lifestream withstood her frequency better than he withstands yours. His mind was not able to grasp the experience, but he never lost consciousness. He seemed to actually enjoy contact with the higher vibrations."

"Yes, well, access through the sexual plane makes it easier and less threatening for him."

"It makes our jobs easier too," Mabel concludes. "I wonder how the union affected the female," she adds thoughtfully.

Millicent's field blurs in a rainbow wash. "It's apparently extra work, but Dolores must enjoy it. Forwyn says she does it all the time."

"Extra work?"

"You would have to ask her guides, but she does seem to go around lowering her frequency to blend with denser beings, and then raising herself back up with the other in tow. She looks a lot like one of their lifeguards or firemen, always carrying others."

"Well," chirps Mabel. "So much the better for us."

* * *

Dolores didn't bother to wonder how the union had affected her. Once she had decided to go with it, she never looked further than her own senses. Which were of late feeling agreeably full and heavy, like a rich winter stew.

Cara's visit interrupted one more lazy morning-after. "I've hardly seen you since Halloween," Cara scolded. "And I can't believe you're not telling me about it!"

Dolores tried feebly to hedge, but they both laughed. "I'm so embarrassed," she confessed. "I couldn't even face Jim and Mira that next morning to tell them goodbye."

Cara settled deeply into the couch, putting her legs across Dolores' lap. "For heaven's sake, they were cool with it. So, is Terry as good as he looks or as bad as he behaves?"

Dolores blushed. "It's so odd. We have nothing in common and nothing to talk about. The worst part is that I feel as if he can't even see maybe ninety percent of me. It's like his reality doesn't register my reality, you know? It kind of sucks. I don't even know who he thinks I am, but I suspect it has nothing to do with me."

Cara took her hand and smiled.

Dolores confessed. "I guess I don't really want to know much about him either. I just want his hands on me." She grimaced. "It sounds awful, but it's like I go all spineless when he touches me. He has really good hands."

"Lucky you, so enjoy it," Cara laughed, and then added, "What's with his hang up about gender ID?"

"I have no idea. I don't think it's about sex. I think it's fear about what people think of him, you know, the macho image. I can't understand why some guys are into that. I hate being out in public with him because of it. But alone, he's better."

"Yeah, I know."

* * *

Elaine's arch nemesis, the shame-filled archetypal sub-personality, does not feel well at all. The indisposition of this entity—who customarily acts out in reaction to Elaine's sexual power plays—is dragging on and on, with no improvement in sight. This depression surpasses mere dispiritedness. He's tired beyond definition of fatigue, almost to the point of collapse. And his color is none too robust. He has become so withdrawn that even Elaine fails to spark a reaction.

"What does it mean?" wonders Bulista.

"I don't know," says Mabel, turning to the others. "Do you think this one's lassitude might be a positive development? With the removal of this archetype's resistance, Terry operates more freely."

"Sure, the man can enjoy guilt-free sex, without archie-the-archetype spoiling the fun," Pryluck affirms.

Snarrow speaks up. "I would agree, but he only operates more freely in relation to how he handles frequency modulations. Isn't Terry's energy pattern now more similar to its appearance before we initiated the transfer project?"

"I think you are right," observes Mabel. "Barwin, can you display Terry's field pattern readouts before the project and at present?"

They examine the images. "Similar," muses Snarrow. "But not the same."

Barwin clears his throat, sending a rapid oscillation through his field. "This would be an example of different octaves of the same pattern. Thus, the lifestream is likely to display seemingly identical behaviors, but at a higher frequency. Higher frequency really just increases the reach of an individual's influence. You won't see radical changes in field output and behavior until the specific codon—the one responsible for fixing that particular spiral of activity—is altered."

Pryluck, Mabel and Bulista look blankly at one another before spewing a rainbow of laughter.

"Eh, Barwin buddy, you lost us there."

"Wait," interjects Snarrow. "Barwin, 'the codon responsible for fixing the spiral,' is that the archetypal sub?"

"Yes."

"Codon?" Bulista ventures.

"It's like a set of instructions," Mabel whispers. "Was the archie depressed like this before we started the project?"

Snarrow speculates, "It is likely that he alternates between over and under activity. Isn't that the way the lifestream's mind typically behaves in regard to his sexual nature?"

Bulista snickers. "Or at least, in regard to self-judgments about his sexual nature." They all laugh, reading in her field the image of Terry's anguished prayers and confessions about his untamable lust.

Mabel considers. "So then, if 'archie-the-archetype' revives, Terry will revert to guilt and remorse. If he does not, Terry will remain disconnected from his sexuality. For him to integrate, to get the heart hooked up with the drive, we shall have to find a way to reach and reshape the archetype."

Pryluck turns to Snarrow. "Now, does that or doesn't that sound like manipulation of the lifestream?"

Mabel flashes mud brown, just long enough to express her sentiment.

"Dear Pryluck." Snarrow drifts over to Pryluck's side. "We so need you on our team."

~ 24 ~

Terry woke himself, screaming in his sleep. The scream also woke Dolores, who had been asleep beside him. He sat up, sweating and gasping.

"Are you alright?" Dolores asked.

He covered his face with his hands, but did not answer.

She put a hand on his back. "You were dreaming. Tell me your dream."

He shook his head, still hiding his face.

She stroked his head, his neck. "OK. It's all OK. It's over now."

He shook his head again, but relaxed his arms and turned to face her. His expression had not yet hardened into wakefulness. "I don't remember. There was something about a boy in an old stone church. It might have been Italy or something."

Dolores was curious. Her extra sense detected something other than a mere symbolic dream. "Did you recognize the boy?" she asked.

"No. I mean he wasn't anybody I knew, but I could feel what he felt." He shrugged. Dreams are weird that way."

"Yeah," she said, eyeing him probingly. "What did he feel?"

"I don't know. I guess pretty freaked out."

She raised her eyebrows. "I'll say. What freaked him out?"

"Something was too much for him to handle. Like if I didn't wake up, he would have exploded or something." Terry smiled at Dolores, his conscious façade congealing back into place. "I guess I woke you up, huh?" he said, gathering her into an embrace.

She sighed, not ready to drop the subject, but sedated by the comfort of big, warm, strong.

"Terry," she murmured, making an attempt. "Would you let me read you sometime? You have a really interesting field."

He kissed her lightly. "A field, huh? Nah, I'm not into that kind of stuff."

She disengaged from him, feeling a hot flare of anger. Pride again, she noted to herself, reaching inward for Forwyn and his different sort of comfort.

She heard Forwyn's voice in her mind. *"It's not about you."*

She breathed slowly, to calm and focus her mind and let the anger pass. "But there is something different about him, isn't there? You even said there's some kind of classified thing going on with his guides. Why is it classified and why shouldn't he know about himself?"

"He should know as much or as little as he—of his own free will—is open to and interested in knowing."

She sighed again and tried, unsuccessfully, to stop sulking.

* * *

Preparations for Christmas seemed to begin earlier each year. "It's not even Thanksgiving yet!" Fran screamed at the Salvation Army worker posted outside the Circle K. The woman—round, solid and iron haired, glanced at Fran with no interest and never a pause in the methodical swing of her bell.

Fran made a dash to her car through a cold drizzle. She sighed. The radio was playing The Little Drummer Boy. Driving south through the miserable weather, she noticed someone walking beside the highway. A woman. Hitchhiking. She slowed and pulled up beside the figure, who approached with a sunny smile.

"Hi, thanks for stopping. I'm soggy," she said, shaking water from her hair before sliding into the passenger seat.

Fran stared. "It's you again. I didn't recognize you. When I saw a woman hitching, I just thought it'd be safer for me to stop than whoever knows who."

Cara smiled. "Thanks. I'm headed downtown. How's your pretty baby?"

The drawbridge took its time. In the pile-up of traffic, Fran glanced over at Cara. "You must be chilly. Would you like to get a cup of something hot?"

"I don't mind the weather," she answered, "but a cup of tea would be nice."

Fran was full of questions. She tried to sound casual. "So, how do you know my brother-in-law Terry?"

"Not well, and by circumstance. Why do you ask?"

Fran blushed. "We were worried that he might be... unwell, you know? He started having some problems a while back, and now in some ways he's acting like a different person. I just thought you might know something."

Cara listened steadily without responding.

Fran shook her head. "And then we met his new friend. My God, I don't know what to think!"

Cara wondered, "Which new friend did you meet?"

"A guy named Jim, who told us he was traveling with a transvestite!"

"No," Cara corrected. "Jim is the transvestite. That means he dresses up in women's clothes. His friend, Mira, is transsexual. She's actually changing her sex. Isn't that incredibly interesting? Imagine how it would feel to relate to the world from the completely opposite perspective—gender-wise—from your whole physical makeup."

Fran looked at her with a mixture of horror and surprise. She said nothing for several moments, and then asked, "Why would Terry make friends with these particular people?"

Cara looked back with equal surprise. "Why not? I liked them both very much."

"But Terry's not like that, is he? Oh God, I couldn't even imagine it."

Cara giggled. "I don't know, you would have to ask him. Or Dolores."

"Dolores? You mean your friend, the psychic?"

Cara smiled. "Well, she's that, too. But I meant in her capacity as Terry's lover."

Fran's jaw dropped. "I, uh, I'm sorry, I didn't know," she stammered. "I guess I've been out of line here."

Cara took her hand. "Oh, nonsense. Gossip makes the world go round. You ought to just ask Terry whatever it is you want to know about him. He comes off awfully prickly, but I think it does him good to talk."

An invitation arrived amidst an unappealing pile of utility bills, credit company solicitations and grocery circulars. The handwritten envelope, return address Preston, caught his eye en route to the trash. "I'll be fucked!" Terry muttered. Suddenly overcome by a wave of emotion, he sat on the kitchen floor with his back against the refrigerator, and read Wanda's note a second time. As if viewing someone else, he marveled at his own body's collapse into sobs.

Curled fetal on the floor, Terry eventually noticed a knock

that, come to think of it, had been persisting for some time. Shit! He rose and moved toward the door. "Yeah, wait a minute," he shouted.

Cara stood in the doorway, holding out a gig publicity flyer that displayed a poor photo of her band. "For you," she began, and then stopped. Terry's expression was direct and startlingly vulnerable.

He hugged her with unusual tenderness. "Hey. I'm glad to see you."

She placed a palm on his chest. "Wow. What's up?"

He laughed. "No, nothing. I'm just glad to see you."

Her smile shone. "Come for a walk," she said, and upon noticing the card in his hand, "What's that?"

He began to choke up again, helplessly raised his hands and smiled. "It's an invitation to a Christmas party." He shrugged and wiped his eyes on a sleeve. "Sorry," he said. "It's just an invitation."

She reached for and examined the homemade card that showed two boys in a classic pose, proudly hefting large, freshly caught fish. Inside was another, out-of-focus, photo of the same boys together with two vibrant, ruggedly dressed adults—presumably the parents.

"Family?" Cara asked.

Terry barely shook his head. "They're a family I met in Preston. "She," he laughed soundlessly while pointing to the indistinct image of Wanda, "reminded me of you. Only tougher." He met her gaze with a mocking smile.

"Let me guess," she answered. "You didn't want to have sex with her either?"

He flushed, but wound an arm around her shoulder. She

slid one of hers around his waist and they stepped out into the rain.

* * *

"Well, Vormis." Pryluck's bolt of light lands like a friendly slap on the back. "Are you getting bored yet?"

Vormis flickers. "Bored?"

"Seems to me you've passed the rookie stage." Pryluck snorts. "You were thrown into the deep end at the start. And now your lifestream's action is trickling along like any other's. Doesn't it seem dull in comparison?"

Vormis regards Pryluck for a long time. "No," he finally responds. "I'm not at all bored. Are you?"

"Well, now you've put the fuse to the rocket! This is supposed to be some kind of fast track, but at the rate we're going, this lifestream will have to live two hundred years if we're going to see the new energies manifest."

Vormis again gazes at Pryluck. "You know," he tells him. "I remember being one of them."

"Naturally. You couldn't be a field guide without empathetic identification."

"Right," Vormis continues. "And so, I know what the life process is like for them. Of course, I also know what it's like for field guides like myself who work between the worlds. But I don't really get, Pryluck, the intention and attitude that your level of spirit guides holds toward the lifestreams that you oversee. What is it you're looking for that makes the pace of human evolution— accelerated human evolution at that—bore you?"

"Ah, ha!" Pryluck blazes bright. "A sharp one, you are. What am I looking for? Variety. Spice, spark, humor…something to break the mold and shatter boundaries. I'm looking for the creative *flame to burst like a fireball through the dimensions and come up with something different. You see I've begun to lose interest, and patience, with the guiding process."*

Vormis dims as he considered Pryluck's statement. "Sounds like you'd be a better fit for Creative Works."

"That's just what I'm beginning to think. Maybe I'll put in for a transfer."

As it evolves, Management has already initiated broad restructuring measures. Methods and Creative Works are no longer to function in a vertical manner, but rather, laterally. "Like spokes of a wheel," states the memo.

Exactly what that means remains a mystery to the Methods lightworkers, but they think it bears Creative Works' stamp. And in no time, Diamond Hoops and Bouffant Head come breezing in with kisses all around, introducing their co-Workers to Methods personnel.

Snarrow takes Bouffant Head aside, to ascertain what will actually change as a result of the restructuring. Bouffant Head is delighted. "Nothing at all, really. But lateral is so much nicer, don't you agree?"

Snarrow dims and flares several times. He will have to think about it, thank you.

In the meantime, lightworkers from other divisions drift in and out of Methods headquarters in a steady stream. One effect of lateralization will apparently be more blending and interaction between departments.

Mabel filters over to join Snarrow. "This change feels good. I think that we shall see more mutual support this way."

Snarrow steadies his still oscillating field. "Perhaps," he finally concedes.

* * *

Bill's head came up, full alert. With his body attuned to the trawler's every hum and vibration, he now sought to identify a new sound. No, not the motor. Not mechanical. He glanced around the deck.

Curious, his youngest brother, Fred, looked up from the other side of the net they were feeding out.

Bill's brow creased. "Nothing. I just thought I heard something."

During a lull in the wind, above the sound of the engine he heard it again, like a high-pitched whistle. A whistle...whistling! He glanced again at Fred, who was quietly absorbed in his labor. A couple of other hands worked in silent tandem at starboard. It had to be Terry. Bill shook his head, incredulous. He had never heard Terry whistle.

"Hey," he signaled Fred, tilting his head in the direction of the sound. "Get a load of that."

Fred looked around, momentarily puzzled. "Terry? Fucking unbelievable."

"Well, he's had the same girlfriend for more than a month now."

"Shit, a girl can't like, morph a guy like that," Fred answered.

Bill laughed. "You wait. It'll happen to you."

"Fuckin' wrong."

Meanwhile, Terry hung over the rail, transformed by the beauty of the water. It began when he paused to observe a pair of porpoises surfing the bow wave. As they dived beneath the boat, he whistled to get their attention, imagining that a whistle might call them back into view.

Drawn into the fancy, it was not long before he became acutely aware of patterns and shapes of water and sky, along with an invigorating sense of euphoria. He relaxed onto the rail with a broad smile, as a tune arose in his mind. The tune seemed somehow linked with the pattern of wave and spray, so he whistled it loudly, feeling that this was his part to play in the concert of water, boat and man.

They sat in The Oyster's Pearl after work. Fred had other plans, so that left Bill and Terry. The brothers drank in companionable silence. They ordered nachos. Terry finally asked, "How come you're not rushing home to dinner with the family?"

Bill snorted. "They're at her mom's for the night. It's not so bad, you know, the whole family thing." He took a swallow of his beer. "Fran says you've got a girlfriend."

Terry looked up in surprise. "What? Who? I don't have a girlfriend."

"She came home all excited that you were going out with some psychic chick."

"You mean Dolores? Shit, we sleep together is all. I'm not going out with nobody."

Bill chuckled. "Most people consider sleeping with the same person on a regular basis some kind of relationship."

"Who's talking about relationship? I just said she's not my girlfriend."

Bill shook his head. "Is this the same woman kept you in San Francisco over Halloween?"

Terry nodded. "How does Fran know about Dolores?"

"She comes home the other day all freaked out. She'd

picked up some girl hitchhiking in the rain..."

Terry interrupted. "Fran picked up a hitchhiker?"

Bill nodded, eyes a twinkle. "They went somewhere for coffee. By this time she recognizes the girl as a friend of yours..."

"Mine?" Terry interrupted again. "How would she know any of my friends?"

Bill went on. "And somehow Fran learns from her that you were seeing—or not seeing—your psychic whatever. Key word for Fran, of course, is psychic." Bill took another drink and laughed. "The best part is she tells me she had a reading with this Dolores...before she knew about the two of you. Can you believe it?"

"I can't. I wonder what D told her? Maybe that's what got her freaked."

Bill shook his head. "No, it's you that freaks her out. She's obsessed with you. I should be jealous."

Terry growled, "What do you mean, obsessed?"

"She thinks you have unusual friends. For some reason she wonders about you a lot."

Bill watched Terry shrink as if scolded.

"What about you?" Terry challenged.

"What?"

Terry studied his beer.

"Look buddy," Bill told him. "I don't give a shit who your friends are. You seem happier than before you went out to Preston. Maybe that's what Fran notices. Maybe *she's* jealous," he said, lightly punching Terry's arm.

Terry smiled, but still did not look up. "Bill, it was a weird scene out there in Preston. In some ways, my worst nightmare. But, it turns out somehow easier, too..." He cut himself off before saying more.

Bill waited. Terry laughed bitterly. "You know that retreat place the priest recommended?"

"Ricki's Halfway," Bill acknowledged.

"Yeah. Well, it was full of a bunch of homos. I couldn't believe it when I found out." He shook his head, and they drank again in silence. "The thing is," he continued, "they were really decent guys. Well, you met Jim. I also met this family that lived nearby. They asked me to come out for Christmas. I don't get it, Bill. Why? I'm not like these people. This girl, Wanda, she does massage and lets her kids hang around at Ricki's... But it somehow works, and..." His voice cracked. He shrugged.

"Look, Ter," Bill began. "Who the hell cares? Get massaged, fuck your psychic lady, hang out with homos if you want to. It's no big deal, OK?"

With neither inclined to go anywhere else, the Gillis brothers lingered through the evening, well past mellow. Suzanne approached to replace their empties. "You boys gonna eat something more than nachos, or am I gonna have to roll the two of you out the door?"

"Lay off it, Suzie, you ain't my wife," Bill slurred.

"Your misfortune," she winked.

Terry sullenly ignored the exchange. Bill prodded him with an elbow, tilting his chin toward the departing Suzanne. "Hey, I thought you had the hots for her," he whispered a little too loud.

Terry blearily met his eyes, and waved a dismissive hand. "Yuh. Hey, Bill, you ever seen the water?"

Bill's brow furrowed. "What water is that?"

"The water. Out working. You ever look at the water?"

"Sure I do, what do you think?"

"No, I mean up close. Not the water like the whole ocean, the water itself. I saw it today. Man, it's a whole different thing." Terry's face brightened, becoming almost animated. "There are these patterns and shapes, like it's made of all these smaller pieces put together. It's fucking beautiful!"

They worked on their beers for a while. Bill spoke. "I can't stand the music they play in this place."

"Yeah," Terry agreed. Then, "I want to make a picture of the water. You think I could draw it?"

Bill frowned. "Don't see why not."

~ 25 ~

"Vormis, darling, it's time," announces Bouffant Head. *"Your presence will please penetrate persistently, positively perpetually."*

On a higher octave, a veteran guide known as Percy Barnett, merges fields with Snarrow to share a private observation. "His English is improving."

Bouffant Head flashes a radiant wink at the two, thereby giving credence to the mounting evidence that the entities in Creative Works have more going on than their maddening presentation leads one to believe.

"What do you mean?" Vormis asks the CW rep.

Bouffant Head softly transfigures his nearly human form into a large floral mandala in gold and russet hues.

"All sensory mechanisms are in place for this lifestream to perceive...pppperceive...Percy...per se—a much wider plentitude of possibilities." A second wink at Percy. "He will positively need prodding."

The guide, Percy, drops his ineffective attempt at shielding himself, to openly ask Snarrow, "What is he talking about?"

Bouffant Head laughs and claps. To the general assemblage, he pronounces, "I'm talking about conscious perrrception of our guiding prrresence!"

Ignoring the others, Vormis asks Bouffant Head, "What kind of prodding do you suggest?"

Snarrow interrupts. "Vormis, I think he is saying that you can attempt active contact at every opportunity." Turning to Bouffant Head, he asks, "Is that right?"

"Every moment!" Bouffant Head blooms. "Make the opportunities!" He turns to Percy. "Perrrfectly plain?"

Vormis has been studying a more experienced field guide, who is lazily viewing his lifestream's afternoon card game. "Did you ever get into playing cards?" the veteran asks Vormis.

Vormis shakes his head. "Never did." They watch the ladies' game for some moments before Vormis asks, "How do you make opportunities for contact with a lifestream?"

The older guide ripples. "Make opportunities? I wouldn't say I ever have, really. When an opportunity presents itself—say, when she's alone, quiet, contemplative—I might attempt contact, but that's not the same, is it?"

"No," answers Vormis. "They want me to make opportunities for continual active contact."

"So they want your guy to wake up. Isn't it a little

premature? Or has he changed that much?"

Vormis' field clouds. "I don't know. He's changed...yes, he's changed considerably..."

"No more nightmares?"

"Well, no, he still has some nightmares, but that's mostly Mabel's doing, with the sub rehab meetings and all. He really is not the least bit conscious." Vormis pauses to reflect. "Then again, maybe he is beginning to wake up," he mumbles more to himself. "He's starting to see a subtler version of his world."

With a grin, the veteran field guide resonates to his lifestream's frequency and subtly illuminates the ten of diamonds in her hand. Visibly delighted, she plays the card to groans from her opponents, when she and her partner take the pot.

Vormis regards his mentor. "Isn't that cheating?"

The field guide chuckles. "Maybe it is...or you could change the spin and say I made an opportunity for contact."

Amused, Vormis flushes vermillion. "OK, I see your point." He reflects for some time. "Then, adherence to ethics in our realm is not all that different from how it is in theirs?"

"You've got to lighten up about definitions and boundaries if you're going to create a new reality. Isn't that what your project is all about?"

"I suppose it is," decides Vormis.

* * *

Dolores listened from the bathtub while Terry, in the next room, released a string of curses. She was therefore not surprised when the door opened and he appeared, red-faced. "It's the damnedest thing," he complained. "I left my jacket right on the chair by the dresser where I always do. I'm sure of it. It's gone. I checked all over."

"Close the door, would you? You're letting in the cold," she objected.

"I don't understand this. Where could it have gone?"

A steamy hand emerged from the bath. "Come here and do my feet," coaxed Dolores. He eyed her, ambivalent. She tried placating. "Look, the jacket is around here someplace. We'll find it. It's not like it could have gone anywhere."

"That's exactly my point!" he ranted. "No one's been in here except you and me." He sat on the edge of the tub, and absentmindedly massaged her right foot. "So how did it get off the chair?"

She murmured and extended her other foot, only to hear the alarm clock buzz in the bedroom. Terry stood, abandoning foot detail. She sighed. "Close the door?"

The alarm was still ringing when he burst back into the bathroom, cursing with renewed vigor, jacket in hand. "It was on the chair like I said. It makes no sense. The damn thing was gone. I looked. I ran my hands over the chair." He began to pace.

Dolores felt a prickle of suspicion and raised an inner eyebrow at Forwyn. Aloud, she just said, "Terry, will you close the goddamn door!"

* * *

Pryluck looses a loud guffaw. "Good show, Vormis! That's one way to get his attention."

Vormis' field distorts. "I feel rather naughty."

Pryluck laughs, "What was that line about effectiveness?"

Vormis colors, embarrassed to be reminded of his earlier ill humor. "The measure of truth," he recites. "Effectiveness is the measure of truth."

* * *

"See you tonight?" A robed Dolores, fresh and scented from the bath, kissed Terry at the door.

He wound a damp curl around his finger and tugged gently. "Yeah, but let's meet at my place. I think your place is haunted."

She did not disagree.

Next morning, thinking to make breakfast before Dolores was up, Terry popped two slices of bread in the toaster. Hearing the phone, he hurried into his bedroom to answer. It was Bill, calling about tomorrow's Coast Guard inspection. "We've got to get that anchor mount fixed," he reminded Terry. "How soon can you get down here?"

"Bill, the job's not a big deal. Take an hour or two at the most."

Bill's anxiety was not about the boat inspection. The Gillis' fishing vessel had been part of the local high school's community resource program that took kids on-site to various work settings throughout the area, with the goal of offering real-life education about assorted occupations. Apparently, brother Fred had failed a random drug test.

"Holy shit," said Terry. "What happens now? Are we out of the kids program?"

"We don't know yet," answered Bill. "But I can't have him on board in the meanwhile. I've got to find someone to crew in his place."

When they finally hung up, Terry got back into bed at Dolores's request. They emerged from the bedroom after twenty minutes, with Terry now legitimately late for work. In the hallway he remembered his earlier intention. "Damn, I was gonna give you breakfast in bed."

"You did," she said sweetly. "Now let's have the second course."

She sat at the kitchen table while he went to retrieve the cold toast. "What the...?" He stared at the toaster before looking helplessly back at Dolores.

"What is it?" she asked.

"I swear I...," he stammered. He pushed the toaster lever down, up again, and began searching the countertop sink. Dolores watched him leave the kitchen, retrace his steps to the bedroom, and return to the toaster. She felt a familiar prickling sensation and silently groaned.

Terry approached the table, eyes like razors. "There's no toast."

"Oh?" she asked lightly. "That's OK, let's have something else."

"Dolores, the toast is gone. I made two slices of toast and left them in the toaster when Bill called. They can't just disappear, right? I mean the toaster is clean. No crumbs, no trace."

Dolores sighed. "Well, I didn't take them. I was in bed the whole time." She grinned. "Which you ought to know."

He would not be distracted. "I know you didn't take them, and I know they were here and now they're not. I also know that my jacket was not on your chair that whole time yesterday morning. And I know this isn't all in my mind." He looked pale, but less agitated. "Tell me what's going on?"

"You're asking me?"

"Don't you know about stuff like this?" He hesitated, reddened, and asked quietly, "I want to know where things go when they disappear."

She met his gaze, feeling strangely uncomfortable. "I

really don't know, Terry. There's a lot in life that goes on where we can't see it."

"What's that supposed to mean?"

"Um, that this reality we're in is just a small *piece* of reality. There's a lot that our bodies' senses aren't able to register."

His mouth twisted. "Yeah, alright," he said. "But that doesn't say anything about stuff—I'm talking about solid objects from this reality—leaving this same reality and then somehow coming back. Or not."

"No," she agreed. "It doesn't."

~ 26 ~

Terry arrived at the jetty that he had recently adopted as his own. Settling himself in among the rocks, immune to spray and drizzle, he had taken to contemplating water in his free time. It was early. Too early for anyone else to be there, yet a small group was gathering on the pier above him. They had luggage: small to medium sized cases, shoulder bags and knapsacks.

The invasion irritated him. He fixed his eyes out to sea and tried to ignore the gathering, but his ears betrayed him. It sounded like a class or a lecture. Phrases jumped out about shades of gray, the first tones of dawn and capturing the texture of light on water. Feeling like a traitor to his bad temper, he turned to see a semi-circle of five individuals, bundled in wool and raingear. Each stood at an umbrella-capped easel. A sixth, presumably the teacher, ambled among the group offering commentary and suggestions.

Terry's blood leapt. Returning his attention to the sea, he sucked air and waited for the agitation to ease, but his heart continued to hyper-react. He approached the instructor. "Excuse me, could I, uh, ask you something?"

"Certainly," the man answered, stepping a few paces from the group. Framed in a deeply hooded raincoat with a full gray beard, little more of him was visible than an inquisitive pair of squinty, dark eyes.

Terry held him with an intense, ocean-hued gaze. "Can you teach me to paint water?"

Surprised by his apparent fervor, the elderly painter smiled. "Yes, water is a challenge. What medium are you using?"

Terry stared back with no sign of comprehension.

"Oh, I see," said the painter. "You would be a beginner, then?"

Terry nodded. "I need to learn to paint water."

The man considered. "I teach an eight week beginner's class, Color and Form, over in the university district. But we don't do water at first. Usually water and light take a more highly trained..." He paused. "...or skilled, eye."

Terry held his focus. "So this color and form—that's where I need to start?"

The painter smiled again. "It might give you a foundation to work from."

"Do you have night classes? See, I'm mostly working earlier."

"There is a six thirty class on Wednesdays. Next session starts in January." He dug a brochure from a satchel and handed it to Terry. "My name is Emilio Garcia. Maybe we'll see you then."

Ten-month-old Tracey sat in a heap of used wrapping paper and bows, enjoying both the color and crinkle. The Gillis family was gathered for an early Christmas dinner and gift exchange at Fran's insistence, seeing how Terry planned to be away for the actual event.

Fran was both relieved and moderately affronted that Dolores was absent, despite her urgent appeals that Terry bring her along. She was more than moderately affronted that Terry was choosing to spend Christmas with someone else's family, while at the same time she fully recognized her own full-clip race to the brink of an emotional sinkhole. The visible result was a sullen, controlled and uptight Fran. Fred would have none of such behavior. He brought out a small hash pipe and goaded her to join him in a smoke.

"You're not still smoking!" she exclaimed. "I can't believe this. You're not even worried about what they'll do to you? You could go to jail!"

Fred scoffed. "You don't go to jail for having pot in your piss."

"You do if they know you're using and they catch you with it."

He lit the pipe and got it going. "Man, you could really use some of this," he taunted, extending the pipe in her direction.

"Fred, there is a baby in this room. I won't have you polluting her mind and ruining our Christmas..." Her voice began to choke.

"Hey babe, ignore him." Bill put an arm around Fran and pulled her against him where she released some of her tension in tears.

Fred turned to Terry with a shrug. "So, I fucked up. You want some?"

Terry, unusually still and serious, nodded slowly.

"For real, man?" Fred smirked. "I thought you never touched it."

"I never have," Terry answered. Fred passed him the pipe.

* * *

"Now, Vormis!" urges Mabel. "Anything at all. He's wide open."

Vormis rides into Terry's field, connected with and well aware of the enthused throng of lightworkers cheering him on. Put on the spot, he feels creatively blocked.

Creative Works reps offer a rapid-fire display of visual images until Vormis complains.

Terry rested on a bench, looking into the night sky. The full moon eventually drew his gaze. A man's face looked back at him. Not the vague, fabled man in the moon, but a perfectly realistic countenance of a man, mid-forties or so, with a wide nose and full lips. Gray eyes reached into the pit of Terry's stomach with a thud. Of recognition? No. He shook his head to break his focus, and the moon again assumed its lunar nature. Terry stood and tremulously resumed his walk toward home.

Mabel sidles up to Vormis. "That was a bit dicey, showing yourself to him. But I'm sure he saw you."

"I know, I felt it," Vormis marvels. "He thinks it's from the drug, though. A hallucination," he adds.

"Sure, but next time you show up he will remember. Well done!"

* * *

A second Christmas dinner come and gone, Terry sat

catching up with Wanda. Jack went in to do kitchen detail while the kids headed outside with new hockey skates.

"Did you ever do any art?" Terry wondered.

"Art?" she asked. "That depends on what you mean. I always lay out my gardens as sculptures. You were here late in the season; I should show you pictures from the summer."

He brightened at the word "pictures." "I've got some pictures. My brother, Bill, got me a camera for Christmas. You want to see?"

They exchanged. Her photos showed wide, geometric patterns of colorful flower and vegetable plantings, which were three dimensionally layered, resulting in a towering fairy's paradise. Chickens and cats peered out from under leafy havens.

His showed water. Photo after photo of nothing but water. No boats, no coastline, no horizon. Just endless perspectives of gray-green and white.

"Why did you take so many shots of the same thing?" she asked.

"They aren't the same." He bent close to examine the photos. "See, look at these round shapes, it's like the water is made out of separate pieces. And here, see how the wake—that's this wave—curves out like that?"

"I see what you mean," she agreed, observing him as he intently flipped through the pictures.

"Here, look at this one," he offered when Jack joined them from the kitchen. "You think of water as one thing, like a solid—well, liquid—unit, but it isn't. It creates all kinds of forms that stand out and then go back into the whole unit again and disappear. Think of the shape of a splash. It's always different."

"You should have mentioned this before. I'd have looked

closer at the dishwater."

Terry was on a roll. "Exactly! Look, I have some shots of toilet water flushing."

Jack's laugh was deep and full. "Let's go down to the stream. You'll want to see where the water's running under the ice."

With sunset, the air turned frigid. Terry lingered alone at the water's edge after everyone else had returned to the house. An early moonrise added intermittent illumination to water and trees. He watched the water, allowing himself to become mesmerized by the play of light on its surface. And then, he saw a face. The image was not clear, but he was absolutely certain that it was the same face he had seen superimposed on the moon. In cold fear, he scrambled up the bank and bolted to the house.

* * *

"Oh pooh, you scared him," Mabel clucks.

Vormis is crestfallen. "I was going to try and say something, but he ran away too soon."

"Whatever happened to subtlety?" Snarrow laments.

Vormis spikes. "What do you mean? You told me to make opportunities for conscious contact. We can write an equation with this lifestream. Conscious equals terror. So what was I supposed to do?"

Snarrow's field clouds. "Vormis, no, it isn't you. It's this whole way of going about our jobs. It is the project itself. I prefer the subtle, old-fashioned love and comfort method of overseeing lifestreams. Our role in Terry's transition looks to me like we are trying to bash him into consciousness—more like a haunting than support."

Mabel agrees. "But, we have our orders."

Vormis turns greenish gray. "I was going to say something reassuring, but I didn't get a chance."

Both Mabel and Snarrow turn to Vormis and say in unison, "Vormis, it is not you."

"You are doing a super—a splendid job," Snarrow adds. "I just wish we did not have to keep accelerating this one. Remember what Cara's team said about it being hard to enjoy an experience when one is hurrying? I wish we could let our lifestream enjoy his process."

A formless rep from Creative Works materializes in their vicinity. "Yes, yes, yes," he mamboes, shuffling a pair of holographic feet. "You are utterly on the right track, you know."

A muddled Vormis asks, "What track is that?"

"The joy track. Your project's goal is to take him from the human drudge state, through the transmutations of light into the open joy of conscious existence. Nothing to lament. Celebrate!"

"Celebrate." Snarrow smiles ruefully at his co-Workers. "Celebrate."

Mabel remains subdued for quite some time. "I think we are going to have to make use of his fear...to somehow celebrate it."

Snarrow opens his field. "What do you mean?"

"I am not sure," Mabel admits. "I shall contemplate."

* * *

Mabel, Millicent and Bulista commune in a simulated garden that winds its aromatic way amongst waterfalls and fountains. Two of Cara's child-formed guides splash and swim in a fountain. The others bathe luxuriously in an ambiance of soothing pastel tones of light. Mabel sighs. "Isn't this the assignment!" Bulista fans out in appreciation.

Mabel turns to Millicent. "We have been wondering what it might mean to celebrate fear?"

Millicent's laugh is a silver, tinkling wind chime. "What an interesting concept. Yes, it makes good sense for you all to go in that direction." She brightens to a sharper point of light. "It makes excellent sense. Indeed, where else can you go with your lifestream?"

"Right," agrees Mabel. "But what does it mean to you?"

Millicent reflects for a while, gazing at her juvenile co-Workers as they revel in their holographic milieu. "Our lifestream's nature is to accept and, I suppose, to celebrate pretty much whatever comes her way. It is her soul's major piece of lifework. Consequently, she does not experience an excessive amount of fear."

She focuses contemplatively on Mabel and Bulista. "It does seem like a conundrum to conceive of fear and celebration—or acceptance, embrace, whatever you want to call it—in the same frame of reality."

"So, to celebrate fear he has to accept it," Bulista states.

"Naturally," Mabel concurs. "That has been our approach thus far in the interest of integrating Helen and the other subpersonalities. But acceptance and embrace of the subs, along with their facets of fear, has a different tone than celebration." She gestures toward the guides cavorting in the fountain. "That is celebration. We need to bring Terry from fear and resistance through acceptance of what is, with all of his subpersonalities and states of being intact, into this state of joyous celebration of life."

"Isn't that just the natural progression?" Bulista asks.

"I should say so," responds Mabel. "The only question, and maybe this is Snarrow's whole point, is how fast can the process

*proceed? How can he arrive at delight when he has no chance to
enjoy the scenery?"*

*Millicent smiles. "Maybe you can help by celebrating for
him, whatever his state, fear included. It might take some pressure
off the lifestream."*

*Mabel erupts in a magnificent rainbow display. "Oh," she
laughs. "Exquisite!" Her laughter becomes riotous. "That has been
Creative Works' technique all along—incredibly effective with the
subs. Oh, we have been so dense!"*

* * *

With the New Year just days away, Terry felt compelled to
track down Cara. In part, he was looking to deliver a Christmas
gift he had found for her on his way back from Preston. He
had already tried her apartment several times since his return.
Dolores would know where the trio was playing these days, but
he wanted a private meeting. He finally left a note.

She phoned. "How mysterious. Or romantic," she teased.
"Are you asking me out?"

"No. I just want to see you."

"How to sweet talk a girl."

"Can I come over some time?"

"Alright. Better make it soon. I'll need to leave by five."

Cara studied him appraisingly. Terry had given her a
cashmere-angora mix sweater, the perfect shade of blue.

"Don't you like it? It goes good with your eyes."

"Of course I like it. But it's a little extravagant."

"Hell, you're worth it."

She laughed and hugged him. "Thanks. Why did you want
to see me? It wasn't just a five-days-after-Christmas present, was

it?"

He shook his head, and his face reverted to its old scared-boy expression. "I don't know how to put this," he said. "I've been having some kind of flashbacks or something and I don't know what to do about it."

"Flashbacks?" She asked. "From acid?"

He shook his head again. "I smoked some pot a little over a week ago. That night, I started seeing things. I feel alright otherwise, but it happened maybe four more times."

Cara's face twisted. "You're having hallucinations from pot you smoked over a week ago?"

He nodded.

She was quiet for a moment. "I didn't think you smoked."

"First time," he told her.

She tried and gave up trying not to smile. "Ter, I don't know what it was you smoked, but either there was something else mixed with it or your hallucinations don't have anything to do with the smoke."

He looked sharply into her face. "You know that? For sure?"

She sighed. "Where'd you get the weed?"

"My brother Fred and I shared a pipe."

"His?"

He nodded.

"Do you trust him?"

"Yeah, I trust him."

"And does he smoke regularly, or was this his first time too?"

"No, he's high a lot of the time."

"So, he'd be likely to know what he actually gave you."

He looked surprised. "You think it wasn't pot?"

She sighed again. "Terry, pot doesn't make you see things for a week and a half. Ask your brother."

"That's the thing. I don't want him to know anything happened."

"Why not?"

He shrugged. "What if what I'm seeing is unrelated?"

"Well, it probably is. So? Then what?"

His face closed. "Maybe I'm nuts. I don't want him to know."

"Tell me what kind of things you've been seeing."

He struggled, visibly embarrassed. "First it was a man's face—first two times. Freaked me out the second time. But then it's other stuff." He blushed. "Once I saw a lady with a whip, like an S&M type. Other times, things just look like something else for a minute before they go back to normal."

"Did you recognize the man you saw?" she wondered.

"No. That's why it was weird to see him twice."

"Where'd you see these people?" she asked, rummaging in her kitchen cupboard.

He hesitated. "The moon. Water. A mirror. It doesn't seem to matter."

Cara filled a kettle and turned on the stove. "You saw something in a mirror that wasn't your reflection?"

"It wasn't a reflection. I was standing off to one side, not in front of the mirror. She appeared, and then when I looked more directly, she disappeared." He trailed off, realizing for the first time that images as well as objects had recently been coming and going.

In keeping with their private tradition, Cara and Dolores reserved New Year's Eve for their own. No music gigs. No parties. They shared a bottle of wine over dinner and wandered down to the beach long after dark.

Cara wedged a few candles between jetty rocks, but the wind found and extinguished them. When they huddled closer to block the wind, the feeble flames still emitted little light. "In Japan," Cara reported, "people climb a mountain on New Year's Eve. They light little campfires all over the mountainsides and wait for sunrise. It seems a lot more hopeful, you know, something like bringing light into the New Year instead of dressing up, getting smashed and making a lot of noise like they do here."

"I don't know," Dolores speculated. "I think that noise-making has some tradition behind it, something like scaring evil spirits away from the coming year."

"You should have been an anthropologist."

Cara leaned her back against Dolores' and they watched sailboat lights and stars. Intermittent sounds of laughter, shouts and electronic bass rhythms reached them like headlights through a fog.

Cara lit a joint. "How's the love life going?"

Dolores gave a short laugh. "He surprises me sometimes. The latest is that things have begun dematerializing on him. I really don't know what the spirit world is up to with him. Well, *you* know," she trailed off.

Cara exhaled slowly and handed the joint over her shoulder. "Terry came to see me the other day for advice about marijuana flashbacks."

"What?" Dolores turned partway, disrupting the backrest arrangement.

Cara laughed. "What is he supposed to think? He started seeing overlay images the same night he tried pot for the first time. You know, I think you were right, back when you said there's something funny going on with him."

Clearly conflicted, Dolores squirmed. "Can you believe it? I feel defensive about him. God! Having sex really screws up your perceptions."

"No pun intended, I take it?" Cara turned so they could sit shoulder to shoulder. She took Dolores' hand. "Don't be defensive. I envy you. A steady lover and your freedom, both. It's strange, don't you think...how he's changed—or is changing—so fast? You used to think his guides were spying on me or something. Do you still think so?"

"I don't know. There's all kinds of interference blocking my access. I've pretty much given up trying to figure it out. He won't let me read him because he says he's not into that stuff."

"You get that a lot."

"Yeah, I do. Well at least his guides aren't crowding around in your field anymore." They were silent while running lights and the distant thrum of a boat engine passed in the channel.

"But how are *you*—the two of you—doing?" Cara persisted.

"It's not much like there is a two of us," Dolores answered.

"Did you know he got me a Christmas present?" Cara asked. "An expensive sweater. I feel strange about it."

"No, I didn't know," Dolores told her. "But I'm not surprised. He is pretty attached to you. You get the heart, I get the sex. He's incredibly loyal to the ones he loves."

"And what about you?" Cara asked again. "How do you feel about the arrangement?"

"I guess I envy you, too—you get love, respect, and freedom

just the same."

Cara laughed softly. "Don't you feel loved and respected?"

Dolores didn't answer for some time. "I don't feel *un*loved or *dis*respected. It's more that those qualities don't come into account in our relationship. It's incredibly fragmented. I suppose that's somewhat sad, but it is easy and in a way, that's nice."

~ 27 ~

The weather was unspeakably foul. Boats were still grounded, three days and counting, as gale force winds continued to batter the harbor. In her office, preparing for an afternoon class, Dolores was startled to find Terry at her door. His presence at the psychic institute suddenly reminded her of the puzzle, "What's Wrong With This Picture?" She laughed. "Hi. How did you get here?"

"I walked. Why?"

"No, I meant what are you doing here? I'm surprised to see you. Come on in." She conducted him to the same seat that his sister-in-law had once occupied. "Are you thirsty?"

"No. I guess maybe I should have called first. I wanted to talk."

Something under her skin went cold. She dropped onto her chair and faced him, bracing her heart to withstand a dismissal.

"You sure you're OK with me being here? I didn't mean to bother you."

Dolores thickly registered his awareness of her feelings.

"It's alright," she said in a small voice. "What did you want to talk about?"

"I'm, uh, you know how stuff has kind of disappeared on me and then reappeared? And it freaked me out. At first I thought it had something to do with you, since you were there the first few times it happened."

She watched him warily, not yet certain where he was headed.

"But then I realized it's all my...uh, this is hard for me to say. I feel embarrassed."

"What?" she urged, hating the anxiety.

"Other stuff happens too. I've wondered for a long time if I have something wrong—you know, mentally—because, see, it keeps getting worse. I didn't want you, or anybody, to know. But I sometimes get the feeling that it could be something else, and that I should ask you. You know, for your expert opinion."

"You came to see me professionally?" she ventured.

He frowned, considering her question, and nodded. "I just thought you could maybe tell me what would make me keep seeing this one face."

She felt a rush of relief that he wasn't there to reject her, felt the pain from the part of herself that had been held taut and afraid and then registered anger that, as always, Terry's concerns were all about himself. She blushed and felt her eyes fill with tears. Closing them, she felt his hand at her face.

"Hey, what's going on?"

She opened her eyes and he was beside her chair, taking her into his arms. She let him hold her. "I'm sorry," she finally said. He stroked her hair.

"I don't know what just happened," he offered awkwardly.

"Did I say something?"

She smiled, sat back and took his hand. "No, you're fine. Thank you. I just had a moment."

He waited, obviously anxious.

"Well, now I'm embarrassed too," she said. "So why don't you tell me about the face?

* * *

"Are the subs aware of Vormis' appearances in and around Terry's energy field?" Snarrow asks Mabel.

"Elaine is. And so is Helen—or her swordsman. But she's— or he's—we really need to ask them what they want to be called. Anyway, they're hanging in there OK."

"The lifestream seems, overall, to be less afraid of his own fear," Snarrow suggests.

"Yes, that is the acceptance phase succeeding. Snarrow, how do you suppose we can celebrate his fearful subs? Should we ask Creative Works to come in and help like they did with Elaine?"

"Mmm, appears to me that what they do is not so different from what you have been doing—you meet, blend with and befriend the subs just as they are, and then gradually offer them new information."

Pryluck overhears and joins them. "True," he says, "but CW is irreverent and gleeful. About everything." He addresses Mabel. "You've just got to lighten up about it all."

She regards him with interest. "Yes, of course you are right. And we are moving in that direction." Her glance takes in the relative bedlam of interesting traffic that was now Methods' milieu. "And what about you, Pryluck? Have you heard back from Management about your request for a transfer to Creative Works?"

"I have. I'm in a preliminary structural retraining program.

It turns out we can't just be admitted into CW all at once. There's an evolution-out-of-form process required." He chuckles. "So now my position is not very unlike that of old 'fraidy pants Gillis."

They laugh with him. "I ought to say it serves you right, but I have to wish you well, Pryluck. You, of all of us, have got what it takes to make it through."

* * *

"OK, we have a plan!"

Methods Workers, along with whatever interested passersby happen to stop, gather for a strategy meeting.

Pryluck arrives late. "Let's hear it," he demands.

The others meet his demand with fond tolerance. Mabel gestures for Bulista to reiterate.

"It's about the archetypes," she begins. "Since we cannot do anything about their programs, we need a plan for," she giggles, "damage control."

Snarrow takes over. "The subpersonalities will be divided into teams according to their...ahem...personalities. Each group will be programmed by an overlay method, to respond in a new and non-limiting way to the archetypal trigger."

"Oh, Snarrow!" One of Cara's child-guides blows a cluster of soap bubbles at him. "Make it simple. You've got the archie who's afraid of sex, and he's part of a whole group of moralizing archies whose bottom line is Good vs. Evil, So Better Be Afraid of Evil, which for him pretty much includes all the sense pleasures. Then you've got all of Terry's subs that react to those kinds of archetypal messages. You team them up, acknowledge their reactions and then give them a basic affirmation of truth."

"This will override the false beliefs that caused the original reaction," Mabel adds.

Pryluck executes a pinwheeling twirl that makes Mabel think he is well on his way in his pre-CW training. "Whee, hee," he hoots. I'm thinking of all those "Dear Father" prayers, how about you?" he asks the others.

* * *

Wednesday night, The Oyster's Pearl was virtually deserted. Terry arrived directly following his first art class. Soaring, euphoric energy pressed at his every nerve. A small cluster of tourists occupied a table facing the TV. The bar itself was empty, save for one regular customer.

Terry gave him a nod of recognition, and took the neighboring seat. Although the guy was as familiar a fixture as the architecture, Terry didn't know his name. He was older—could be anywhere from early fifties to seventies—with the coarse face and questionable hygiene of a lifelong heavy drinker.

Terry gave his order to Suzanne. As she reached to take his money, Terry assessed her with dispassion. Sexy yes, he thought, but without substance, like a cartoon character. He took a long draught of his beer. She had drawn it badly. He licked foam from his lip and glanced at the glass. The foam was visually intriguing. He narrowed his scope of vision to observe the detailed structure of the bubbles, and excitement rose in his chest.

"Suzanne," he called. "Bring me another, would you? But only fill it to here." He indicated with a finger on his glass.

"I can't charge you partial, you know."

"Don't sweat it, I'll pay you for a full one." Again, he noted his own objective appraisal of Suzanne. Not very appealing.

"Hah!" The man to his left barked, and slapped Terry on the thigh. "She's a real bitch," he chortled. "Ain't just you, neither. It's her nature." He raised his brows. "About time you noticed."

Terry considered the crinkled face with its few remaining long and yellow teeth. "Yeah, I guess," he mumbled.

The second schooner arrived, and Terry's attention was diverted to the study of bubbles. Occasionally, he tipped the glass to watch the interchange of color—gold running to white. He held the glass in various positions relative to the nearest lights, to determine which angles cast a reflection of other hues upon the surface.

As from a distance, he was vaguely aware of Suzanne's derisive laughter, so similar to the night he had asked her to leave the bar with him. "You planning to drink that or play with it?" He ignored her and heard his neighbor chuckle.

I need to paint this, Terry thought. Slowly, as if from inside the beer itself, an image formed: a purple and green striped fish within a sea of turquoise. He tipped the glass a bit and lost the picture, then moved it back a bit, playing with the light to try to recreate the scene. No, the image had originated from somewhere outside the play of light.

Nonplussed, Terry raised the glass and drank it down. He pulled a five-dollar bill from his pocket and set it on the bar before the older man. "Hey, have one…or something." Their eyes locked. "On me."

* * *

Bulista's solo debut at leading a subpersonality re-training session is proving tedious. Diamond Hoops, observing with Pryluck in tow, yawns. "Sit in for me a minute, will you?" he asks Pryluck, not waiting for a reply before he disappears.

Concurrently, Bulista's meeting room darkens. A black, vaporous essence infiltrates the space, quickly permeating the nostrils and eyes of the five assembled subpersonalities. They begin to gasp and struggle.

Bulista watches as the black haze shapes itself into an immense and gruesome form. Orbs, like eyes, glow red. The rank, acrid vapor now seems to emanate from beast-like nostrils. A near tangible aura of horror pervades the room.

Despite herself, Bulista recoils from the repulsive presence that has already rendered the subs nonresponsive. Each wanders the room absorbed in his or her personal anguish, apparently oblivious to both surroundings and other entities.

Pulling her field together, Bulista reaches toward her backup lightworkers for support. As she stabilizes, she tries to identify the uninvited archetype. "Death?" she wonders. "Or Hell?"

Abruptly, the black menace seems to pop. In its place stands an ecstatic Diamond Hoops. "Gotcha again!" he bellows.

Bulista is incensed. "How can you?" she sputters. "Teasing me is one thing, but look at them!" Her gesture takes in the room of shocked subs.

Diamond Hoops blows her a cheery kiss and, with remarkable ease and efficiency, he calms and rounds up the subs.

Later, Mabel consoles Bulista. "You are doing fine. Do not let Creative Works get you riled."

"It's frustrating enough," Bulista complains, "that I still react to the archies, without CW rubbing it in."

Mabel laughs. Bulista has such a human sort of tendency to either recoil or giggle when encountering the darker archetypes, it really is no surprise that Creative Works would make a game of it. "Maybe if you just assume it is really CW every time a threatening archie appears, you shall begin to hold your objectivity more readily," she suggests.

"Yes, I know, but in that initial moment of surprise...that's

when they get me."

"It is precisely the same for the subs," Mabel points out. "Your process and theirs are also the same, only you are a much quicker study. Your experience will help us all learn to reprogram them.

* * *

Cara waited on the sidewalk for the light to change. Windy day. She rearranged the scarf at her neck and felt a jolt at the knapsack on her shoulder.

"Sorry," the guy who bumped her mumbled as he passed. Recognizing her, he stopped. "Sorry, my mind was somewhere."

"Terry, we have to stop meeting like this," she smiled. "Do you remember? Last time you nearly bowled me over it was on this same corner."

He glanced around and reconstructed the previous encounter to which she referred. He had been fleeing Father Daniel Sulleran's warped advice then. "That was my church," he gestured, eyeing the winter vestige of the church's landscaped grounds. "I haven't been back since that day."

"Why not?" she asked as they proceeded across the street.

"Nah, never mind. Where you headed?"

"Home. You?"

"I have a class."

"What kind of class?"

"It's called Color and Form. I've got to learn how to paint."

She flung her arms wide and laughed. "That's so cool."

Dolores sprawled, eyes closed, on Cara's floor. Cara and Evan repeated for at least the seventh time, the arrangement they had been working on all evening. Their partner, Boze, had left before this last take.

"Sounding better," Dolores pronounced, sitting up and leaning against the couch. "Break time?"

Evan laughed, lit a joint and passed it. "I think that's a hint," he said to Cara.

Cara sat on the couch and stroked Dolores' hair.

Evan plopped down beside them. "You haven't been around for a while, D, how's the boyfriend?"

"Bad word." Cara mock-whispered to Evan.

Dolores turned halfway around and grimaced. "I've been replaced," she sighed, once more leaning against Cara's knees.

Evan softened his tone. "Replaced? He didn't dump you?" Tenderly he added, "Not the illustrious Madam D?"

"No, he didn't dump me. He probably just forgot about me. He's become completely obsessed with art."

"Art? Wait, I thought you were seeing that guy Cara pulled out of The Oyster that time, the fisherman?"

Cara nodded, enjoying his confusion. "Madam D's influence," she smiled. "Now he sees visions."

"And paints. Constantly," Dolores groaned.

Cara laughed. "And smokes dope."

Evan stared at Dolores. "No shit?"

She tightened one cheek. "I wish I wasn't starting to like him."

* * *

A lively wash of iridescence illuminates Methods headquarters, which scintillates with simultaneous, sundry activity. Creative Works experiments with form, while Mabel and Bulista work with subpersonality groups, and Vormis pops in and out as duty calls.

Millicent, who has been quietly observing the scene, turns to Snarrow. "So, what kind of specs did Management give you for your lifestream's transfer?"

Snarrow focuses his field. "Specs? You mean for the new persona?"

"Mm hmm. Exactly where are you supposed to be taking him?"

"Well, that's just it," explains Snarrow. "They left a lot of room for interpretation. They were clear, though, about an ultimate goal of autonomy."

A shimmering wave traverses Millicent's field. "Autonomy. Any idea what that implies?"

Snarrow blurs. "We have not really gotten that far. The first stage wiring, subpersonality re-orientation and all of that has consumed our attention. Naturally, we realize that autonomy implies mastery on the lifestream's part. We are working toward preliminary integration of consciousness. Vormis is on it all the time, but I have to say, we have not had much success in that area."

Millicent laughs softly. "Has your group ever overseen a lifestream who was working toward autonomy?

"We never have," he answers.

"Think about it," she suggests. "If your lifestream goes autonomous, what kind of role will Methods have in his life?"

Snarrow considers, an oceanic gray-blue shimmer expanding his form. "That is an interesting thought. You know, we have already had to continually restyle ourselves to adapt to his transformation. If he becomes self-regulating, what will be the function of his guides?"

~ 28 ~

Bill slammed a hand onto the rail. "Man, you are really trying my patience! When you're on board to work, I need you working, not fucking around with a camera."

Terry exploded. "For God's sake, would you just chill! I always help when there's work to do. I'd like to know why it bothers you that I'm interested in something besides your fucking fish."

"Christ, Terry, you're not interested, you're obsessed is what you are. It's like nothing and no one else exists except whatever it is you see in the water. And your help? Half-assed, Ter. You haul nets and you sort fish and not a goddamn thing more. I could hire any kid to do the kind of job you're doing."

"Fuck off, Bill. Go hire yourself a kid."

"I guess I lost it," Bill told Fran. His elbows rested on the table, his face in his hands. "God, I need to find someone who can crew." He looked up at her. "I don't know, maybe I should cave."

Fran held his shoulder. "Exactly what happened, did you fire Terry?"

"I didn't fire him. I blew up at him for being a bad worker and he quit."

"Well, if he isn't working, maybe you should find someone else."

Bill looked miserable. "The thing is he does work. And he knows the business as good as I do. He just doesn't act like my partner anymore. I'm jealous of the goddamn water."

They both smiled. "What does that mean? Does he give the water more attention than he gives you?" she asked.

"Fran, it's not just attention. He studies it the whole fucking trip. He photographs the damn stuff so he can go home and paint it. He's no use for anything while he's taking his pictures."

"What is he supposed to be doing during that time?"

Bill gave her a wry look. "Nothing special. Look, I already admitted he does his job. But I'm totally out of the picture. I mean, shit, I used to watch the water with him, but not the way he does now. We would be out there noticing stuff together—weather, whales, birds. Now it's like he's not even there."

She took a seat beside him and put an arm around his back. "You miss your brother."

He laughed silently and nodded.

Fran hesitated, then said, "Bill, remember I told you I had a psychic reading with Terry's girlfriend before she was his girlfriend?"

"Yeah."

"I went when Terry was staying with us because I felt trapped and desperate. I resented him being so useless. Or maybe I was worried. Anyway, she told me stuff about Terry that I didn't really understand."

"Yeah?" Bill encouraged halfheartedly.

"She said something about he needs his independence so he can evolve into some kind of visionary artist. I figured she was telling me to butt out of his life. But don't you think it's kind of spooky that now he's getting so into this painting thing?"

Bill's countenance was an unlikely mixture of indulgence

and exasperation.

* * *

Emilio Garcia's studio was upstairs from a drycleaner's shop. The drycleaner was locking up when Terry arrived. "You just missed him," he told Terry. "I saw him leave not ten minutes ago."

"Thanks," Terry acknowledged. "I'll go on up and see if anyone else is there."

No one was, but Terry let himself in with the key that Emilio left under the mat for students after hours. For twenty minutes, Terry stared at his painting, then finally took up a brush and began to work. The charged excitement that always overtook him when he painted affected him like the buzz of caffeine. His mind shifted likewise, as if high.

He hardly noticed an hour later when the studio door opened. "I saw lights on and figured it would be you," said Emilio. He stood beside Terry to appraise the painting, observed in silence for a while, then nodded his head. "Yeah, I see the effect you're going for. You'll need to soften the edges to make the face look like it's within the water, not superimposed on it. Is that right? That's what you want?"

Terry nodded. "Yeah, he's somehow inside it." He turned to Emilio. "I don't know, maybe like a water spirit or something. But you're right, I can't get it to show the way he looks, like he's inside the water."

"Layered transparency is the effect you're after. Keep the eyes in focus and allow the rest to blend more."

Terry set down his brush. He was still crackling with charged intensity. "Emilio, Wednesday is the last class. I need to sign up again."

"Have you decided what you want to study? You don't need to take 'Color and Form' again."

"I still need to learn how to paint water. It's not just the face. I can't get any of it to look right. The light's not there."

"Water and light, those are tough to master. For less than two months at it, you're doing a pretty remarkable job."

Terry's restlessness was palpable. Emilio continued, "Look, you can continue to come here and paint after your class ends. You just pay a monthly studio fee for supplies. Then, when you decide on a class you want to take, you sign up. Alright?"

Terry nodded, too full to speak.

* * *

"Wake up, wake up, wake up time." Bouffant Head peers beside Snarrow, to observe the simultaneous overlay of Mabel's sub meeting with Vormis' ongoing attempt to break through to Terry's conscious mind while he's painting.

"Shake it up, break it up. You all are in a rut." Bouffant Head delivers this in a chant, accented by a shimmying, undulating dance. Mabel glances up, and then pointedly ignores him. Bouffant Head laughs.

Snarrow challenges, "Why do you say we're in a rut? We are following the pacing of his responses, right?"

"Yeeees, yes, yes. Over and over. Mabel and Bulista are little saints. Sub work would drive a lesser entity utterly insane. Make it a party."

Snarrow's field furrows. "Agreed, you have demonstrated the effectiveness of your approach, and we have been grateful."

"Oh dear," Bouffant Head flounces. "Please do not go all stuffy. Anyway, sub redundancy is a fact. That is not the rut I was talking about. You—all of you—ought to get in there with Vormis.

Make the lifestream notice you."

Snarrow stares. "What are you suggesting? We are not field guides."

"Oh, details," Bouffant Head waves. "Get creative."

*   *   *

"I thought we were being creative," complains Vormis. "And effective."

"Totally effective," agrees Mabel. "You have got him trying to paint your face. That is effective."

Bulista blends the edge of her field up against Vormis'. "He sure noticed when material objects began to shift."

"Precisely. But with some alarm, I might add. The lifestream is just barely accommodating. If we go all dramatic on him it will be no different than a haunting. That is not the goal."

Snarrow ponders. "No, of course not. But I wonder what CW has in mind. They have been spot on so far, whenever we have reached an impasse."

"But there is no impasse!" sparks Mabel. "This communication is no different than what we have constantly had to contend with from Pryluck. These entities get a little bored and they want to manipulate the lifestreams for their own entertainment."

The others glow with amusement. "You can separate those two, but they're still on each other's case," a field guide teases.

Mabel laughs along with the rest. "Well, you have to admit that Pryluck and Creative Works are a perfect fit."

Snarrow, who has remained contemplative, now speaks up. "Bouffant Head was not just haranguing. He told us to get creative. Maybe we should identify exactly what we are to get creative about."

Bulista flickers with characteristic shyness before offering *her perspective. "That is what the lifestream is doing. It's his passion."*

"What, getting creative?" Mabel asks. "You mean his painting?"

A coherent wave encompasses the group. "I'll be blessed!" exclaims Vormis. "It's the two-way street thing, isn't it?"

Bulista repeats the term that Tull, the therapist from Ricci's, used. "Resonance."

Snarrow's field slackens. "Here—we'll match and ride the current of the lifestream's passion. We can apparently best influence his consciousness in synchrony with the creative fire."

He turns to Vormis. "We can reach out to Terry in the manner that you have already successfully implemented, by projecting your image onto the lifestream's visual and auditory sense impressions. On some level, the lifestream has been able to see you and is moved to paint your image. So, how about if we all blend and synchronize our frequencies to the lifestream's own creative process? While he's painting, he ought to be able to receive us as inspiration instead of as a haunting."

* * *

Dolores sat in her office after class, opening mail and sipping tea. For the second time, she was surprised by the appearance of Terry at her door. She stood to embrace him.

Similar to his first visit, Terry seemed awkward, but this time Dolores was determined not to allow her own relationship anxiety to presuppose the reason for him stopping by. "How have you been?" she asked.

He continued to hold onto her while slowly forming his answer.

She fought both impatience and self-doubt while he

mused. "Let me see. I've been...I'm not sure how I've been. I've been interested...and busy. I guess that's good."

She felt ready to scream at his vague and measured response, and was irritated that her reaction was reined in by intense attraction. "Fine," she clipped. "Why are you here?"

He hesitated again, considering the question while holding her gaze, and she, with some dismay, observed her own mounting exasperation. "I wanted to see you," he began.

For some reason this riled her even more.

"And I thought we could talk some more about your expertise."

She felt on the verge of tears again. "Would you be direct already! What do you mean, talk about my expertise?"

He released his grasp and turned. "Sorry, I'll go."

Her frustration felt lethal. "No!" she demanded. "Don't do this!" She closed her eyes and mumbled, "Please."

She followed him to the door and tentatively touched his sleeve. "I didn't mean...I'm sorry," she added. "I'm actually glad to see you." She raised her eyes to meet his and tried unsuccessfully not to laugh.

Cara held Dolores' hand as they sat on the rocks of the western pier. Her eyes sparkled with affection and amusement. "The both of you are like a couple of wary dogs. You need to let yourself be loved, D."

Dolores' eyes filled. "I can't help it. I'm tough and defensive with him."

Cara smiled. "What are you defending?"

The question pulled Dolores into sharp, objective clarity. "What *am* I defending? I guess I need to look at that." She went on, "I can't stop criticizing him in my mind. It's like a mental plague. When it's festering I can't find anything right about him, except his damn maleness, and then I hate myself for wanting that."

"Poor D. Never hate yourself. Wouldn't that be your professional advice?"

Dolores sighed and leaned on Cara's shoulder. "God, what a mess," she laughed. "You're right. Don't hate myself. Listen to myself and find out what feels so threatening..." She paused. "I feel like he doesn't get me. That feels threatening."

Cara watched and listened without comment.

"So, what if he doesn't get me?" Dolores continued. "Somehow I won't be safe. If people misunderstand me, I can be killed!" She looked at Cara. "You think this is some kind of witch-hunt fear?"

Gazing warmly at her friend, Cara shook her head. "Maybe it doesn't matter so much what it is. Just that you know you feel it."

Dolores heard the unspoken whisper in the voice of Cara's guide, Millicent, *"And let that be loved."*

Dolores had been trying for days to humble herself to Terry, but the jerk was never home. And he might as well not own a phone for as often as he turned it on. She finally went to the wharf to meet Gilli's Girl as she docked.

"Hello," she shouted up to the boat, "I'm looking for Terry."

"You too? We haven't seen him for a week." A burly man, wearing suspendered rain pants tucked into hip waders, and with eyes the same variable shade of green as the sea and as her lover's, jumped from the boat's deck to the dock beside her. He dried his right hand on his shirt before holding it out to Dolores. "I'm Terry's brother, Bill."

She saw a slightly rounder, thinner-haired version of Terry. "I'm Dolores. I think I've met your wife, Fran?"

Bill laughed with gusto. "So, you're Dolores? Yes, my wife seems to find you fascinating. Then, I guess, so does my brother."

Dolores smiled thinly. "I don't know. I think he's more fascinated by water and paint."

Bill dropped his head and again, Dolores noted the family resemblance.

"You're right," he told her. "I blew up at him over just that, and haven't seen him since." He winked. "I suppose I ought to go apologize or we'll be short handed for another week."

"That's pretty much what I've come by to do. Poor guy."

Bill looked at his watch. "Used to be he'd be over to The Oyster by this time, if he wasn't out with us. Now, I'd say try the studio."

"Thanks," she said.

"If he's in a good mood," he called after her, "tell him we miss him over here."

"Christ! I didn't hear you. How long have you been there?"

Dolores came to stand beside Terry's easel. "You were engrossed."

He regarded her as if from some deep, internal recess. His eyes shone uncharacteristically bright.

She turned her attention to his painting, and gasped. Her head turned from the painting to Terry and then back again several times. "Do you know what you're doing, Terry?"

"Well, I'm learning," he bristled.

"No, I didn't mean that. Actually, it's pretty good. Amazing, really. I had no idea." She forced herself to pause long enough before proceeding. "I meant, do you know what it is you're painting?"

His long, intense look made her squirm before he answered, "I'm not sure. It's what I wanted to see you about."

"Yeah, well, I'm sorry for the way I acted." She blushed. "That's what I came to see *you* about."

"I'm done here. Want to go home?"

She smiled. "Love to."

~ 29 ~

In bed, she took a chance and lit a joint. She felt him tense before he accepted a tentative toke. "Tell me about your painting," she suggested.

He propped himself on an elbow. "I keep seeing things inside of other things. I might be looking at a cloud or a stream, and then something else will be there. At first, I kept seeing the same face. A lot of times it would show up in water, so I started wondering about some of those people—you know, like Indians—who believe in nature spirits. I want to make that face look like maybe the nature spirit of water. I must have painted that same image fifteen times already, and still can't get it to look like the face is part of the water.

"Then, a couple of weeks ago I started noticing other stuff, like patterns of light and colors that come from somewhere behind the face. It almost looks like a trail that maybe the guy I see follows to come in and out. But I can't really get a good look, because I'll blink or look harder and it's just plain water again. Or whatever. What I see isn't really there, so I can't study it. I have to try to remember and reconstruct it in my mind. And when I *can* remember, I then need to try to learn the technique to paint it. That's the hard part."

He reached for the joint and took another toke, unbidden. "See, Dolores, I wanted to talk to you first, because I realize that seeing things that aren't there isn't good. And if I'm going nuts I ought to do something about it, but I thought maybe you could tell me whether or not I *am* going nuts. I mean, knowing that sort of thing would be along the lines of your work, right?

"The thing is," he continued without pause, "I need to paint what I see. I can't explain the way it feels, but I don't want to give it up. If I'm really nuts and I got cured, I'd have to go back to seeing stuff normally, and there'd be nothing worth painting. So I was hoping you could help me figure out what to do."

His unselfconscious ramble delighted and frightened her. Feeling momentarily speechless, she put out a silent call for help. *Forwyn was there in a flash, chuckling. "Why so nervous, Dolores? He's no different than any of your clients."*

"Then why is there so much blocking and censoring with him?" she wondered. "It makes it so I can't do what I'm supposed to be able to. It's like you're all setting me up to look stupid."

She felt an influx of unfamiliar, rarefied energy, and opened to receive whomever or whatever it was. *"Don't worry, trust us,"* she heard.

No time to argue. Fixing Terry with a penetrating gaze, she heard herself say, *"You are not nuts. Or at least, seeing what you see doesn't have anything to do with that, if you are."*

Dolores appreciated her unseen allies' sense of humor. "You're guided, Terry," she added of her own accord. Exasperatingly, she was censored before she could tell him that the face he had been painting was the same face she saw in his energy field from time to time.

"Guided, what does that mean?"

"Guided. You're not alone. You have help."

"What, you mean you'll help me?"

She smiled. "Trying. We all have guides—entities—beings on other levels that most people can't see, who work with us in our lives." She was surprised to have been permitted to give so direct a clue.

He contemplated the thought for a while. "You're saying there are guides that most people can't see. Does that mean some people can see them?"

She smiled again and nodded. "That's what people pay me to do."

"You see guides," he stated more than asked.

"They're among the things I see that most people don't."

"So you think that's what this face is? Some kind of guide?"

She felt squeezed into her answer. "I don't know. What do you think?"

He shook his head. "I don't know what I think," then muttered, "don't know what to believe. I'll have to think about it."

At sunset, the road to the beach was deserted. Raspberry sundae clouds fringed the bay. Terry parked the truck and walked to the shoreline. A pastel shaft appeared from between two clouds, seeming to lead away, rather than toward the earth. He allowed his gaze to follow, out behind the atmosphere, into a realm of radiance. Something seemed to shift in his head, and subtly, as if from a distance, the same sensation encompassed his whole body.

Bright particles of colored light bathed Terry in stillness. From somewhere came the thought, *"Learn to go between the particles."* Gradually, a buoyant lightness entered and spread throughout his body. While pleasurable at first, the feeling eventually became uncomfortable. Darkness had already fallen, and he turned to leave the beach.

The same wash of rainbow radiance infuses Methods headquarters in peaceful communion. One by one, individual particles of light emerge, separating out into various colors before taking form. Snarrow sighs. "I have missed the old days," he muses.

Mabel solidifies beside him. "Mm, me too. That was nice," she adds. "Maybe there shall be more mergings now that he is beginning to calm down."

Millicent approaches. The delicacy of her field resembles dragonfly wings. "Did your sleeper have a dream of heaven?" she asks.

Mabel beams. "He did. A lucid dream, at that."

Millicent comes into sharper definition. "Really. That is impressive. What do you suppose he will do with it?"

"Are you asking how he will interpret and synthesize the experience?" Snarrow wonders.

"That's right. Has Terry gotten any closer to recognizing his guides or his subpersonalities?"

Mabel dims. "Not in the least bit. Most of the subs do not even recognize him yet. But he has made progress on the higher planes. He is now capable of consciously receiving Vormis' visual tags, and remembering his face between contacts."

Snarrow adds, "He is painting Vormis' image projection."

"And have you thought more about autonomy?"

"I have."

Snarrow's solemnity is so characteristic that Millicent laughs. "And?"

"And the way I see it is that the subpersonalities are the key." He glances at Mabel. "Even if they do have amnesia most of the time, they still ought to achieve gradual behavioral modifications that will enable their faster and less resistant responses. We have seen good progress with some of them. Anyway, once they are more aware and cooperative with one another, the lifestream will be able to make choices from a more Self-centered perspective. You know, what to focus on and what to leave behind."

"Self-centered?" Mabel smiles.

"Well, what would you call it, a higher perspective? That implies some kind of rank."

Millicent and Mabel both gleam. "Self-centered works for me," Millicent says. "So, what about these choices?"

"Well," continues Snarrow. "As he chooses his focus, he will begin to shape his own direction. In effect, he will learn to override reactions from the subs, and thus take over that job from Mabel."

Millicent's glow intensifies. "That is just what I imagined. And have you thought about how that might affect your overall roles with him?"

"I just cannot see it clearly yet. Can you?"

Millicent pulses in peacock iridescence, but remains silent.

III

No Psychosis Please

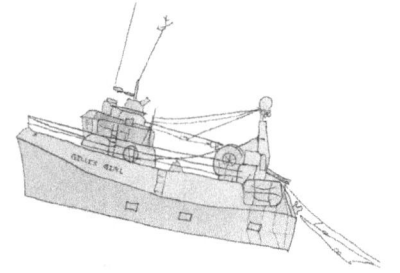

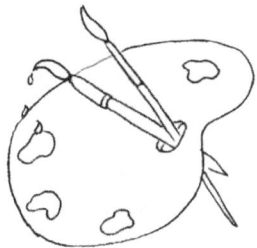

~ 30 ~

Terry's glance froze on the mirror above the bathroom sink. The reflection was not his. He sighed, stood upright and faced it squarely. "Alright. What do you want?"

He heard an eruption of rodent-like sounds, muffled as if from behind a pile of pillows. *The familiar face in the mirror stammers, "I...uh...would like to introduce myself...I'm called Vormis."*

"About goddamn time," muttered Terry.

The face pinkens. "I, uh, we've done our best. Not so easy to make contact."

Terry noticed another flurry of high-pitched background chatter.

"Alright then, who the hell are you and what the hell do you think you're up to, fucking with my mind?" Terry grew increasingly enraged, and as he did, Vormis' image faded from his sight.

Terry awakened moments later from a blackout, with the vague recollection of a word—perhaps a name—Vormis. And a whopper of a headache. The day was lost for any useful activity. At sunset, he ventured out on foot, wandering as if by radar to Cara's door. He didn't knock.

Stepping out after dark, she nearly knocked him off the top step where he sat slumped over, his chin on his chest. "Terry?

What are you doing here? Are you OK?"

He gave no immediate response, yet when she reached out to touch his shoulder, he lifted his head. His eyes were foggy. "Jesus, Terry, what's up?"

"Nothing," he answered dully. "I was just sitting here."

"On my doorstep."

He shrugged.

A smile touched her mouth. "Now why might that be? Did you want to see me, or is this more like some kind of stalker or peeping Tom thing?"

He did not smile back.

"Terry, come on inside. I'll make you some tea, and then you can stay here 'til I get back. I'll be a couple of hours. Will you do that?"

His nod was barely perceptible, but he got up and followed her in.

"Dolores, can you come over? Terry's here. He's kind of flipping out or something."

No response.

"D, I found him on my doorstep like four hours ago. He was asleep when I got home from rehearsal. He's still sleeping, but he's having something like the mother of all nightmares, thrashing and swearing and yelling something about someone putting wires in his brain. I really don't know what to do."

"Shit, Cara, *I* was sleeping. And you call me to tell me that my once and sometimes lover is sleeping at your place and having bad dreams?"

"Oops. I didn't know you two weren't still good. Sorry I woke you up."

"No, that's alright. I'm jealous. He doesn't ever have any time or interest in me, but he goes to your place..."

"To freak out?"

They both laughed. Several moments elapsed in silence before Cara spoke again. "I guess it's how he sees me," she said. "Nursing him through one crisis or another. Your role is a lot more appealing."

They sat together through the telephone line in comfortable silence, before Cara continued. "I really can't handle this, D. Either Terry has suddenly become over-the-top paranoid, or there's something going on with him that is more your territory."

"Yeah, alright. I'll be over."

* * *

Snarrow paces like a first time father unable to tolerate the delivery room. Vormis and a team of more experienced lightworkers, including a rotation from Creative Works, are doing all they can to meet and manage Terry's pain and rage.

Mabel shakes her head sadly. "We never adequately took his personal will into account."

Bulista waits for an explanation.

"This is not a sub reaction, Bulista. Terry has come awake... of sorts. In his sleep, anyway."

They all enjoy a bright wave of amusement. "It is not pretty, but getting all of this up and out will do him a world of good. It is a tremendous achievement, really. The lifestream is willing to own our presence and has begun to voluntarily interact."

"He does like to cuss," Bulista proclaims.

* * *

Dolores sat across from Cara, beside the couch where Terry—quiet at last—seemed to sleep. She could not be sure whether the state he was in was, or was not in fact, sleep. Nevertheless, his consciousness was clearly busy elsewhere. Cara dozed lightly in her chair. Dolores eased her attention toward an expanse between the worlds, where she felt a pleasant relief from the burden of gravity. Widening her scope of perception, she focused on the space within and around Terry. Startled, she popped right back into hard and fast 3-D reality. "My God, his shields are down. I got through."

Cara opened her eyes and smiled. "Well? What did you find out?"

Dolores frowned, tight-lipped. "Nothing. I lost my concentration."

Cara giggled. "Take two."

On her second try, Dolores had sufficiently steadied herself, but could still make no sense of her perceptions. She summoned Forwyn. "I don't know what's going on here," she began. "Why is his field so...it looks to me like a picture on a TV screen that won't come into focus? Too much snow. And the guides...it's all a blur. I can't identify anything or anyone definite. They all keep changing."

Forwyn's loving presence fills her chest. "Yes, well, he is having a storm," he laughs. "A snow storm." She waits through a second chortle, until he adopts a more somber tone to inform her, "Your friend's guidance team is busy and can't talk with you now, but they are ready for you to educate him about how it is between us and you all."

"Human/guide relationships?" she asked.

"More or less. He has apparently been the guinea pig in an evolutionary experiment, and has just gotten to the point of realizing his life is a collaborative venture, not a solo operation.

Pisses him off."

Dolores again waited for another fit of laughter to subside.

"His brain is all a scramble," Forwyn continues. "Some parts are up to frequency, others are in old modes. If he had just found out that his concept of God—the authoritarian, father image—exists and totally controls his destiny, he would have been better equipped to handle it than he is finding out that nobody, particularly not his own conscious mind, is absolutely in charge. It is worse for him that there are those, including other aspects of himself, who have a say and a part to play in cooperatively shaping his existence. You could say he is feeling rather victimized and quite paranoid."

Dolores was silent and thoughtful, trying to grasp and assimilate the gist of what she'd been told.

"Forwyn," she ventured, "you said something about an evolutionary experiment. What does that mean? Whose experiment is it?"

"That is the question, isn't it? Still classified, dear one. Becomes available to you as he gets it. They would appreciate, though, if you would do what you can to smooth out his brain-integration. You know, basic information to help cognitive, uh..." he paused. *"Acceptance of new sensory input is the essence of it."*

She was quiet for another while. "I'm feeling a little pissed off, too," she finally told him. "Why should I take orders from a bunch of entities who have neither the respect nor the courtesy to even greet me, let alone explain anything or say please? If that doesn't strike you as authoritarian, I don't know what would."

Forwyn hoots. "Touché, my girl. I'll convey your sentiments."

Terry awoke, exhausted, just before sunrise. As light slowly suffused the room he suddenly realized he was not in his bed. He bolted upright to find himself wrapped in the same fragrant blue cloth in which he woke once before, on that morning after he first met Cara. He pressed the fabric to his face and breathed deeply.

Next, he noticed that two quilted bundles on the floor near the couch contained the sleeping forms of Cara and Dolores. He lay back again, revisiting a lingering confusion of dream images, wondering how it all fit into his current presence in Cara's apartment. After a while, he disengaged himself from the couch.

With his hand on the front door knob, Terry's exit was arrested.

"Hey, you get back in here! You aren't about to have us sit vigil all night, and then go sneaking off without buying us breakfast!" Cara was already halfway to the door, striding as if she meant it, despite one foot trailing her entangled sleeping bag.

She appraised him as she approached. His arms hung loose, and his face appeared open and undefended, with no visible about-to-crumble vulnerability. As he gathered her close, she felt him speak into the top of her head.

"Thank you, Cara."

She pulled back enough to meet his eyes.

"You OK now?"

"Yeah. When did Dolores get here?"

Cara held his gaze, still assessing him. "Maybe we'll unravel the night over breakfast. Let's let her sleep. You want coffee?"

* * *

Printouts spew like ticker tape, while the resident technies hunch and huddle over their data. Snarrow, together with a Creative Works rep, waits. The guy from CW has not bothered to assume any physical form or take on a name. "He" colors with delight at the scene, and addresses Snarrow. "Nice effect they have created, very dramatic."

"The technies get a kick out of creating props in 3-D form to accompany their activities."

"High art," the CW applauds.

The technies turn from their database and the spokesperson, Barwin, brightens. "Phase three superimposition of moderate range receptivity devices has been successful." He then pauses while his field undergoes an array of proud flashes that belie his modest self-presentation. "Furthermore, the physiology has remained basically intact. Nerve field capacity is up thirty percent. Glandular function continues to fluctuate, but as yet, fluctuations are well outside the range that might be detrimental to circulatory function."

"Are you saying that the heart and its vessels are withstanding the load, and that nervous systems are strengthening?" Snarrow verifies.

"Precisely."

"And the mental body?"

Barwin dims a bit. "We are well outside of psychotic break point, but..." he stammers. "But you had best, perhaps, make the support of mental/emotional functions a top priority. Just our opinion, of course."

Snarrow billows out and in, a gesture reminiscent of a sigh. Mind/emotion was—and had been from the start—their only priority.

* * *

Dolores yawned and looked at Terry's watch. "I have a class, gotta go. See you all later." She gave Terry and Cara each a quick kiss, and left a dollar on the table. "For the tip," she called over her shoulder.

Cara gazed after Dolores' retreating figure before fixing Terry with one of her piercing looks. "I want to talk with you about her," she said.

His open gaze met hers.

She glanced at the table. "Are you done here? Want to go walk?"

They were all the way to the pier before she spoke again. "I guess life has been pretty strange for you. That can't be easy. The thing is, Terry, you don't realize it and it's not something she would tell you, but D is hurting."

"Why, what's wrong?"

She took his arm. "It's different for girls," she sang. "We can't sleep with someone for months and stay emotionally uninvolved. She maybe can't admit it, but it hurts her that you basically ignore her otherwise." She looked at him with that now familiar smile that both mocked and accepted him. "She doesn't feel loved," Cara said gently.

Visibly confused, he tried to clarify. "It's not that kind of thing with us. I mean, we get along OK, but nobody said nothing about love."

"Right. That's what I'm talking about. She is pretty sensitive, you know. Maybe you two aren't in any kind of committed relationship, but ongoing intimacy without any *real* intimacy is kind of damaging for her sense of self, you know?"

He didn't. She changed her tack. "What *do* you feel for Dolores?" she asked.

He shrugged. "I don't know. I like her." He reddened. "I like sleeping with her if that's what you mean."

"It's not at all what I mean. Do you feel close with her? Are you interested to know who she is and what she thinks about? Stuff like that."

He regarded her with a sheepish half-smile. The look, she thought, of a school kid put on the spot by his teacher.

"See, if you did—if you thought of her and for example, went to her house instead of mine when you needed help—she would probably feel more valued. But you don't really care for her in that way. No matter what the agreement is between you two, it's hard for a woman to be a second-thought, good time kind of thing." She smiled sweetly at him. "It may not be my business, but I *do* love her and I think you should be a little more aware of how fragile she is."

He was quiet and clearly troubled. "Do you think I shouldn't see her?"

"No," she began slowly. "That's not what I think. I would like to see you two enjoy yourselves and each other. I also wish you would consider her feelings and maybe talk with her about your relationship."

"We don't have that kind of relationship."

She nodded. "Right. I know." They walked on in silence, arm in arm, pausing to watch gulls scream and flap each other aside over a morsel on the beach.

~ 31 ~

Creative Works is everywhere, and Methods Headquarters

is hardly recognizable for the whirling of sound, color and almost-form. In Mabel's opinion, the CW Workers, rather than bringing cohesion to the department, have contributed hardly more than carnival chaos. She allows her edges to expand and diffuse so as to get an overview. The broader image startles her.

She summons Snarrow, who manifests at her side. "It is all—we are—beautiful!" she gasps. "But I wonder if our department has been eliminated. Do you know what is happening?"

He fades for a brief moment, and returns a bit more translucent than usual. "I, uh," he stammers. "No, I have been told nothing." He pauses for some time. "Mabel, in my broadest scope, I did not see Management anywhere. Did you?"

"Not as such. But then, nothing appears distinct anymore. I have never seen such a blending from one frequency into the next."

"I know," Snarrow agrees. "Do you know what it looks like to me? It is as if we were all stretched out before, into individual units. Even within Methods, various soul divisions occupied distinct linear space, and Creative Works and Management maintained a planar orientation relative to Methods. Now, it seems as if we have been compressed into a layered sphere, only the layers are more like unstable gradations. It is as if we went from being a string of bubbles to concentric bubbles."

"I am going to try to contact Management," he says.

Musical pebbles—laughter?—descend like a mist around them. A gelatinous orb bursts against Snarrow's head. From it, a CW rep begins to take barely enough form to be recognizable as Bouffant Head. "How do you like the new look?" he crows.

As is typical for when he's feeling flustered, Snarrow emits menacing barbs of irritation. Bouffant Head backs off enough to allow him some space.

"Oh, come now. Admit it, it's brilliant. Look here, I'll show you Management."

As they expand to observe the new territory, Bouffant Head points out a uniform and ubiquitous distribution of minute gray speckles. "Micro-management," he declares, collapsing in a fit of laughter.

Snarrow examines the now obvious graininess of the image as he waits for Bouffant Head to collect himself. "Do you mean that Management is no longer a single department? That's it?" His gesture encompasses the marbled bits of gray.

Bouffant Head nods rapidly. "Isn't it brilliant, inspired, twirlational?" he sings while spinning.

"But why? How will it work?" asks Snarrow.

"Even better, we hope," answers Bouffant Head. "Go ahead, send a memo."

Snarrow begins to compose a mental message, and feels simultaneous reception to his thoughts. "It's instantaneous," he marvels. Bouffant Head sparkles.

* * *

Terry paced, picking up and setting down the telephone book on several passes. Coincidentally, his phone rang. Wrong number. He took a resolute breath, looked up Tull's number and dialed.

"I don't know if you remember me," he mumbled after a pause. "I was at Ricki's Halfway in October."

"Terry! Of course I remember. It's good to hear from you. How have you been?"

Terry exhaled and sat down. "I'm actually calling to ask if you'll see me. Professionally."

"What did you have in mind?" Tull asked.

"I don't know exactly. I guess I could go back out to Preston for a while. I did better when I got home, but things are getting really messed up again. I need some help dealing with it."

Tull took his time responding. "I actually don't spend a lot of time in Preston. I go there, as you did, for specific workshops. My practice is here in Auburn. But you know, Terry, I think you and I ought to talk about what you might be getting into before you sign up for therapy sessions. Would you like to meet when I'm up in the city?"

"Yeah, sure," Terry answered.

"Have you got time on Sunday afternoon?"

"I guess so."

Terry sat at his kitchen table and tried to implement Dolores' advice. After he'd spent the night tossing delirious on Cara's couch, she had suggested that he might attempt to write, paint, or in any way record whatever images he could recapture from his experience. She said he should try to reconstruct any memories of contact with whomever or whatever he had encountered. That maybe it would help him clarify his ideas about it all.

So far, each time he began to resurrect the remembered bits, all that he encountered was a rising haze of pressurized rage that blocked his vision. He stood, shoved over his chair and stormed outside.

A warm, full sensation abruptly spread from his chest throughout his throat and belly. Not unpleasant. Companionable even. With a groan he clapped his hands to either side of his head. "I swear," he said aloud. "I don't care if this is some kind of satanic haunting or divine revelation. I want out. Stop. Human, normal. That's all I'm asking. Please."

He meandered through the streets, crying freely.

* * *

Vormis glimmers close beside Bulista. The two are observing the interaction between Tull and Terry with considerable interest. "They look different!" Bulista exclaims. "What has happened to Terry's field?"

"He has changed archetypes...mostly. There is still some battling for dominance that goes on between the old and the new."

Bulista digests this. "I thought the archetypes were outside of our jurisdiction. How could they have changed?"

Vormis is startled by her question. Hasn't she been intimately involved in Mabel's sub rehab meetings?

"Terry's subpersonalities have shifted enough to allow resonance with a whole different set of conditions," he tells her. "He is becoming more unique relative to the mass human collective. A lot of former triggers no longer run him much." Vormis fixes Bulista with a bright beam of light. "You were working with Mabel in behavioral phenomena. Isn't the shift in sub reactivity a byproduct of that project?"

"Of course. Yes, I see." Bulista rearranges herself in an array of blush tones. "But I didn't realize that archetypal association could shift so tangibly. It is as if, by upgrading the persona's program, the lifestream got shuffled into a whole new species-specific program. Oh, that's right! And so, into a new archetypal self-association."

Vormis carefully regards her again. "That's right," he says. "It's exactly like when they change grades in school and get a new teacher. They only move on to the next grade level after mastering information and skills from the previous level. It's the change in

*the students that results in an association with a new teacher and
a new grade status. Archetypal equivalents, you could say."*

* * *

A thin rain fell, white-washing any trace of early spring
greening. Dolores shifted her shawl to cover her head. She was in
costume, playing Madam D to a small Healing Arts Expo crowd at
the fairgrounds outside of town. Chilled beyond humor, she left
her booth to find a hot drink. There weren't many options. Coffee
then. She sighed and stood in line.

"Hey, that's my cousin! Dolores! Hey, D!"

She noticed the two men at the edge of the food tent. One
was indeed her cousin, Brad. She had not seen him in years. The
other was taller and more strikingly dressed. They approached.

"I heard you were in, what was it, China or something?"
she asked Brad after they had hugged.

He laughed, "Mom still can't get it straight. Thailand for
about a year, but I've been back for almost six months now."

"You're not living at home?"

"No. I am in Auburn though, across town from the folks."
Brad turned to his friend. "Dolores, this is Greg Tully. From grade
school. You two probably met sometime out at the farm."

She shook hands with Greg Tully and smiled. "Well, if we
did, it would have been at least twenty or thirty years ago. Don't
be offended that I don't remember."

"Likewise," he offered. "Are you a performer?" he asked,
noting her dress.

"Some would say so. But I'm actually a psychic reader. I
do a booth at this fair every year, and it's always a miserably cold
day."

He laughed, and studied her appraisingly. "I'm interested

in your line of work. Are you done for the day, or can I still get a reading?"

"Just on break. Give me about twenty minutes."

They sat over coffee at a booth in a downtown café. Terry felt secure in Tull's company. "How does it work then? Will I come out to Auburn once a week or something?"

Tull smiled and contemplated Terry for a long time. "Why don't you catch me up on things first? You were out of your element and understandably upset at Ricki's. I was impressed at how you handled the situation. You didn't just make the best of circumstances; you took advantage of an opportunity and did some personal work. So, I've seen a bit of the stuff you're made of." He paused to leisurely sip his coffee before continuing. "Of course, I'd love to hear what your whole experience was like and how it affected your life, but I suspect that you've moved on." He looked up. "Am I right?"

Terry gave a slight shrug. "I guess so...the way I think about things is different from before the retreat. It's OK, that doesn't bother me. You had something to do with that."

Tull nodded and raised his cup, waiting for Terry to continue.

"But the thing that brought me to Ricki's in the first place is worse. I mean, I guess it's better in some ways. Physically, I'm better than I was. Not all better. But I need to see you because my mind is, um, not right. I know that. In a way I might need it to be this way so I can see things to paint, but I can't go on living with everything the way it is. I don't know what to do about that. The situation, I mean. I have a friend who's, uh, psychic." He held Tull's gaze carefully. "She says I paint things that she sees in my aura or something, and that I'm not crazy." He looked down at his hands, which had twisted his napkin into a corkscrew while he spoke.

"But, what it comes down to is I see and sometimes hear stuff that doesn't exist. Hearing is worse, because it affects my thinking. I'll get a thought, you know, hear a message that seems to come from someone else, only there's nobody there." He looked up at Tull. "That's what happens with those guys who end up killing people, right? They hear a voice that tells them their own grandmother is the devil, and they believe it. I don't want to end up like that. I don't know what to do," he finished softly.

Tull's silent presence was monumental. He finally asked, "What do the voices tell you, Terry?"

Terry smiled wryly. "It's actually just one, although he talks about 'us' as if he's part of a group. I don't know, it makes no sense." He fidgeted. "Something about they're rewiring me, and not to be afraid. Reassuring, huh?" His laugh was humorless.

"Have you asked who they are?" Tull wondered.

Terry fidgeted some more. "I usually get too angry and they disappear. Most of it is not very clear," he admitted.

"What do you get angry about?" Tull asked.

Terry shrugged. "I guess about being fucked with. My life wasn't too bad before all this shit started. Now someone's copping to fucking with my wires or programs or whatever the hell it is. I don't know what it all means. I just want it, they, or whatever it is, to leave me the hell alone so I can have a normal life."

"Normal." Tull smiled gently. "What does that mean?"

Terry regained his composure and returned the smile, silently acknowledging the setting in which they'd met.

"I wonder," asked Tull, "how you experience this thing,

besides feeling angry about the situation? Does it feel like there is anyone present, or is it just the voice that you hear?"

"No, everything changes inside. It's like a shift, like something opens into space. Have you ever been stoned? It's kind of like that."

"Do you ever feel afraid or threatened?"

Terry laughed. "Just about all the time. But when this thing happens, no, it's just the opposite. More like everything feels alright. In a way, that's what worries me, because if I only feel okay when this guy is directing me, I could be tricked into doing something that isn't right. Maybe it would be better for me to talk to a priest, but I haven't been to church after that priest sent me to Ricki's. Maybe that's part of the problem."

Tull's attention didn't waver, but he took a long time to respond. "Terry, I trust nature, just about more than anything else. That means I trust what the body tells me and what the feelings say. Nature can't lie or pretend."

He contemplated Terry's face. "I won't say that I know one way or the other that some demonic force is or isn't trying to wrest control of our minds. What I feel pretty certain of is that the fundamental, nature-based aspect of our being can tell the difference between benevolent and malevolent force. So long as an individual is fairly intact, that individual's body-consciousness can serve as a guide or determinant of what to trust."

He smiled. "My opinion, of course. I wasn't raised to revere the exorcist approach. I prefer to address and hear directly from any form of consciousness before deciding to banish or destroy it. Consciousness is, by definition, conscious. Which must mean that these so-called voices—whether they derive from some outside source or from within, as an aspect of the mind—

have some kind of purpose or agenda. Nine times out of ten, the purpose is benign, to protect us from being hurt or killed. If we can get them to talk about themselves, we can negotiate behavior with them."

Terry glanced up. "You think it's in my mind then?"

"I really don't know, Terry. And I don't know that it makes any difference. Consciousness is consciousness. I just think it's something you can explore without fear. And without giving up, or giving over your own authority. No one and nothing can make you do something against your will, unless you fail to affirm your will. You are clearly not psychotic, since it's evident that you are perfectly capable of objective self-witness."

Tull paused and laughed mildly. "Excuse the dissertation. What is your psychic friend's take on it all?"

Terry swirled the remaining coffee around his cup. "I don't know, I don't really believe in that stuff. I guess she wanted to do a reading one time."

Tull thrust his head back. "You mean you wouldn't let her look, and you called me instead?"

Terry wilted. "You think that stuff is for real?"

"What would it mean for you if I did? Or more importantly, what would it mean for you if it is for real?"

Terry responded immediately, "That it isn't just my mind. That they are messing with me, or God is punishing me. Or maybe it's Satan. I don't know."

"I think you do know. At least, I think there is a part of you that knows perfectly well what the truth is. The question is, are you willing to face the truth?"

Their eyes locked. "I think so," Terry said. "Will you help me?"

"Yeah, I will." Tull paused. "But I would like to get a psychic's take on it. I just met a good one who lives here in the city if your friend is not an option." He held Terry's gaze, brows lifted inquisitively.

Terry looked grim. "I think D might be mad at me or something. I don't want to upset her."

Tull waited for an explanation. Receiving none he asked, "D? Is your friend Madam D?"

"Yeah, you know her?"

"That's the woman I met at the fair. I was impressed."

Terry's expression, unreadable, intensified. He didn't otherwise respond.

"Terry, what's your connection with D? Is she an intimate friend?"

"That's the problem," Terry complained. "Everybody wants me to talk to Dolores, but I don't think there's anything to talk about besides this. If she's hurt because I don't see her enough, then I shouldn't see her at all because I'm too fucked up to be in any kind of relationship. I don't have the...I don't know, whatever it takes—time, space, stability—for it."

"I'll take that as a yes?"

Terry missed his point. "I don't have a problem with the way things are, but Cara—" He finally looked at Tull. "That's Dolores' best friend—she says I'm hurting D."

"What does D say?" asked Tull.

"I haven't seen her for a while."

Tull looked at his watch. "OK. Look, I don't know if therapy such as I can offer is even appropriate for you. I am interested in your situation, and I'm willing to help you sort things out if I can, but you'll have to confront this first on two fronts. You need to get the opinion of an expert on psychic phenomena as to the nature of the voices you hear and, for God's sake, you need to talk to your girlfriend and clarify your relationship."

"She's not my girlfriend."

Tull stood. "Call me after you've seen her."

* * *

"Who is that?" asks Snarrow, indicating an unfamiliar sub.

Mabel shakes her head. "That is the latest subdivision of the Helen/French guy merger. Calls himself Frank. He—or they—is/are still wrestling with self-identity.

What had formerly been the meeting room for sub rehab is now an amorphous cathedral of pastel light, through which freely flow the same assortment of colorful entities that stream through all of Methods division. Most of these are invisible to the subpersonalities.

Nevertheless, in context of the prevailing fluidity, Frank's rigid carriage has the effect of a jagged rock protruding from a river. "What is it you want, Frank?" Mabel asks.

"I want to die," he tells her.

"Hogwash!" Mabel retorts.

Frank's form diminishes as his whine crescendos. "I want to be...I want to matter. I want them to want me. Love me."

Mabel intervenes before he loses himself to a tantrum. "It is not about them, Frank. Helen, remember your source light. Can you?"

Frank falters before gradually beginning to stabilize and then to fade, revealing in his place the Helen/swordsman duo.

Snarrow turns to Mabel. "Has he—the swordsman part—made any progress at all in recovering his faith?"

Mabel shrugs. "It is difficult to assess his progress and

really, it will be impossible for him to progress unless Helen, Frank and any other subdivisions remain cohesive. At this point, it is essential for Terry to step in and work with his own subs directly. Until he does, we are in something of a holding pattern. From our end, we can continue to reinforce this group's ability to fill themselves with light and to realize they are safe and valued. Gradually, it ought to become their default behavioral pattern. Knowing to turn to source—that might be a kind of faith, might it not?"

"Such behavior requires some measure of faith," Snarrow agrees. "Would you say that he has regressed in this regard?"

Mabel emits golden rays of amusement. "I would say we have all been displaying some odd behavior," she says with a sweep of her arms, "since the latest big shift around here. Have you heard anything about it from Management?"

"Not yet, their operation has been down. But I think you are right. Whatever happened has affected us all, and that includes Management."

"Maybe CW knows what it is about," Mabel wonders.

Snarrow chuckles. "I don't think they had anything to do with it, but of course, they are enjoying the new scenery. It is unfortunate we have not yet found the secret to celebrating fear. That would help Frank and the rest, wouldn't it?"

"Yes, I am convinced that celebrating fear is key," Mabel agrees.

A sudden storm, like a meteor shower, illuminates Methods. Tiny fragments of light are converging and consolidating from seemingly everywhere.

Snarrow stares, open-mouthed. "It must be Management's

response to our memo."

Pryluck frowns. "It's like a jigsaw puzzle. We'll have to arrange the pieces."

They all study the distribution of the fragments.

"Look at this," Mabel announces. "It can have different meanings arranged different ways."

Snarrow sighs. "Alright. So what do we want it to mean?"

Bulista giggles.

"No, really," Snarrow insists. "Our question to Management pertained to the origin and significance of the lifestream Terry's restructuring. Let us assume this memo is our answer." His broad gesture takes in the swirling, multi-layered environment.

The Workers collaborate, designing various patterns from the bits of encoded light. Cara's guides, and soon several Creative Works reps join in, attracted by the raucous laughter that erupts over possible alternate meanings.

Two primary themes eventually surface. The first confirms the aptness of their meteor shower analogy. While it is outside the realm of expertise of all personnel, the best interpretation they can come up with is that near-space—their own solar system—has been affected by a collision of celestial bodies in far-space—another solar system within the same galaxy. The resultant disruption of heretofore stabilizing magnetic forces is apparently ubiquitous.

Interestingly, all potential arrangements of the message, except for one, concur that the apparent accident has opened the potential for wondrous change. "All is now possible," one translation states. "Everything now open," another reads. "Light abounds. All free," is Bulista's favorite.

The second theme that emerges, like a corollary to the first, has Creative Works hooting and preening before Methods *personnel. Every version, without exception, carries the directive to lighten up. "Joy above all," is the nearly unanimous choice of phrasing.*

Barwin, the technie, sums it all up in his memo log. "Choose. Create. Enjoy."

~ 32 ~

Terry phoned Cara. "I don't know how to talk to Dolores," he complained.

She was unsympathetic. "Hang up with me and redial. *Her* number. Now."

He stalled for another day. Bill called, saying to come in to work.

"I can't. There's something I gotta do." He sat on it one more day. Went to The Oyster. Got drunk. Thought about driving out to Preston to see Wanda and family. Didn't. Tapped into outrage. "Why should I be the one to say something? I'm fine with things the way they are, if she's got a problem she should call me." That conversation afforded him another two days.

What finally dried the quagmire was an invitation from Fran to attend baby Tracey's first birthday party. "Bring Dolores," she commanded.

"Shit," he swore.

Walking seaside, Terry reflected. "I don't want to bring Dolores. I would be nervous, and I don't want to be nervous around Tracey." The thought surprised him. He wondered why he would think that Dolores would make him nervous.

A thin ribbon of self-awareness wound itself around his mind. It manifested as sensation, like an internal tension from which he shrank. Scenes from Tull's self-identity groups at Ricki's flashed through his mind. "I feel insecure with D," he marveled. "Like I don't know who I am."

He called her.

Dolores was surprised to feel a warm receptivity toward Terry when he asked her to meet. He was definitive and, for once, upfront about his state of mind.

"I've been avoiding you," he told her. "I'm sorry. I guess we need to talk and I'm afraid because I suck at it, and I don't know if you would be willing to talk with me. I'd like to see you sometime if you wouldn't mind."

In person, he did not know where to start. His first tendency was to flirt. No. He checked himself and took her arm. "Let's go find a bench." They were in the park by the western pier, not far from her school.

"Turns out someone I know got a reading from you. At the fairgrounds. Tull. He's a shrink. Sometimes works at Ricki's. I met him when I was there."

She showed no sign of recognition, but he persisted. "He lives out in Auburn, but I thought he might work with me. You know, maybe help straighten me out."

Her face cleared and she asked, "Auburn...are you talking about Brad's friend, Greg Tully?" At the same time as Terry blurted, "Everyone calls you my girlfriend, and that kind of freaks me out."

"What?" she demanded as he answered, "Could be Tully.

I only ever knew him as Tull."

"Terry, what are you saying?" Dolores felt a cold thud in her gut, and was vaguely aware of Forwyn, pressed comfortingly against her side.

They cleared up the issue—hers—that he might be embarrassed to be associated with her. Next came deciphering the nature of his concern. It boiled down to, "I just can't be in a relationship."

"That's not what I thought we were doing," he said. "I mean I love what we do together." He smiled at her as their eyes met. "But I'm pretty messed up. I'm having a rough time with the way things are inside me, so I can't think about caring for someone else. People are telling me I should. And that I'm not treating you right or I should do more. I don't want to hurt you, but I don't think I have anything I can give you."

She gazed at him from within a floating sense of detachment. "Cara said something to you?" she asked.

"Tull did, too. He said he wouldn't even see me until after I clarified the relationship with my girlfriend."

Her brow furrowed. "How did he know about me unless you brought it up?

"We were talking about psychics. Turned out the one I knew and the one he met were the same. He said he was impressed by you. He guessed about our relationship. I didn't say you were my girlfriend."

"Thanks."

Her sarcasm was lost on him. "He also wants me to get your professional opinion about the stuff I see and everything. I guess he's deciding whether it's worth it for me to do therapy with him."

She felt her breath relax. The conversation seemed less and less to have anything to do with her. "So what do you want, Terry?"

His expression was unusually open, revealing both anguish and passion. "Dolores, more than anything I want to wake up in the morning and feel OK. Normal. I don't know if I'll ever have that again. In the meantime, I want to do whatever I need to do, if something can help me get there." He paused, but held her gaze. "I don't want to lose what we have, but I also don't want to keep you from being with someone who can love you if that's what you want."

She blushed, but he didn't let her deflect his purpose. "I would if I could, D. I'm sorry."

"Damn Cara! What did she tell you?"

"No, it's not her. I'm just not OK enough with who I am to love anybody."

For a third time, Dolores experienced the serene sense of being personally uninvolved with the conversation. "You love Cara, Terry."

"No. That's different. I'm more comfortable with her, but I don't feel about her the way I do about you." He smiled intimately.

She shook her head and shrugged. "Still, you love her," she insisted.

"*Is* love what you want then?" he asked.

"Oh, I don't know. No, not with you." They both smiled. "I'm not very comfortable with you, either. I think we're basically too different to be any closer than we are." She regained a bit of her habitual posture. "So don't buy into anybody's trip that you're doing me wrong. That's a crock of shit."

They relaxed against the bench, holding hands in silence

and letting their minds drift.

Dolores sat alone on a pile of cushions, reflecting. Incense burned, lights were low. Her attention slipped in and out of light trance, thereby including communion with Forwyn in her reverie. The question at hand was whether or not to accept Tull's request for her to be a part of Terry's treatment team. Tull was apparently fascinated by otherworldly phenomena and, she suspected, by her as well. His idea was for her to provide psychic development classes for both Terry and Tull, in conjunction with the more conventional counseling he could provide Terry. His offer of counseling services extended to Dolores as well if she were interested.

Without a doubt, she wanted no part of the therapy, and wondered too about both the wisdom and logistics of interpersonal dynamics within such a group. Although communication and behavior were presumably Tull's forte, she questioned his neutrality.

She also questioned her own feelings. Terry's relationship talk had upset her, after the fact. Of all things, to ask her if she wanted love. To apologize for not loving her! She felt ashamed, like some not-quite-right product. And his clumsy kindness made it worse.

She took a deep breath, letting the feelings wash through her as she leaned into Forwyn's presence. *"Let the truth come up,"* she heard. She did. The truth of Love, pervasive and self-evident, suffused her awareness, filled and surrounded her body. *"There is nowhere you can go, nothing you can do and not still be loved completely."*

She observed her mind's division between perspectives.

"Silly rabbit," she thought, remembering the line from her childhood, and addressing her self-rejecting self. It was actually a very good question. Did she want love on the level to which he referred? The day-to-day, need oriented attachment that people called love? An irritating shadow of her smaller self tried to answer yes. A host of bigger, tougher selves tumbled over themselves to deny it.

Forwyn laughed. "You don't need to be ashamed of your humanity, Dolores. No one else is judging, so give yourself a break. By the way, the delegation for your friend's evolution sends its regards and," he laughed again, "eagerly supports your participation in his training."

She bristled, but before she could retort he added, *"They're wondering if you could teach him to do what you do."*

"What is that?" she asked, curious despite her annoyance.

His luminous face smiled lovingly. "This. Conscious interaction with both guides and sub personas."

She felt a jolt through her mind-body. "As in Tull's proposal? With me introducing him to guidance and Tull digging out the subs? I don't understand, Forwyn. And I feel a little scared. This looks like a lot more manipulation, or outright control, of our lives than I thought you guys were allowed."

"No one will ever force you," he reassured gently. "Actually, they were all quite respectful and polite in their request. Your earlier complaint was well-heeded."

"But I still don't understand the point. Why don't they just communicate with me directly?"

He was gone, she knew, on reconnaissance. She waited.

"I am sorry, dear one. I can't get an answer for you. It is just not available."

"Well, did they infiltrate Tull's mind then? Is the whole idea for this therapy and psychic class the brainchild of Terry's own guides?"

Forwyn wavered and hesitated. "No, not really. There have been major changes occurring on our levels as well as on yours. Reality structures are dissolving at a rapidly increasing rate, and synchronicity is at an all-time high. It is all part of a collapse into Oneness. There is nothing to be afraid of. The change is only occurring on superficial—illusory—levels. You know the Unity has always, will always, be intact."

She wondered.

* * *

Snarrow calls a meeting. As personnel gather, he surveys the group. Fields are perceptibly more rarified these days. Even Millicent, who, as a matter of course clothes herself in the most intricate translucence, has gained still more lacy delicacy.

All who are in any way associated with the lifestream transfer project have been invited. Thus present are representatives from Creative Works, along with the Methods core team and several of Cara's guides. Even Forwyn has been permitted to look in on select, uncensored portions of the proceedings.

Snarrow opens the meeting. "About the living lifestream transfer, Terry. It seems that we are approaching a critical decision point." He nods in the direction of technie Barwin, whose field is fluctuating self-consciously in response to the attention.

Barwin makes an awkward show of shuffling his paper facsimiles. "Statistical probabilities show an encroachment of a traumatic event or events in relation to, and stemming from the lifestream's failure thus far to recognize his own subpersonalities."

Vormis asks, "Do you mean emotional trauma or some kind

of physical health crisis?

Barwin's field is an unusual shade of milky blue-gray. "We do not track that kind of detail. Until after the event, of course, when it becomes an historical factor."

Snarrow takes over. "The soul, in conjunction with Management, has agreed that this lifestream is at an impasse. His limited degree of conscious self-awareness is increasingly disproportionate to his current level of vibration. This puts a certain amount of strain on the system that will necessitate action. Anything that will precipitate some kind of equilibration."

"Which implies," suggests Mabel, "that the mind requires a shock to jolt it off its familiar course?"

All pause to regard Mabel curiously. Recently she and Bulista have both been exhibiting signs of losing touch with their own...what? Memory? Or intellect?

Pryluck, who is still associated with the project despite his ongoing training in Creative Works, blusters, "Naturally, Mabel. Hasn't that been the effect of the process from day one—a disorganizing jolt to the lifestream's mind? What must happen— which has not yet begun—is that his mind has to then turn within to begin to recognize it—or him—self. So far, Terry tries to look just about everywhere else."

Mabel's field flushes like sunset. "Yes, of course," she murmurs.

Conversation continues among smaller groups after the meeting disassembles. General consensus holds that a crisis is not yet inevitable. The timing of Tull's proposed three-way class/ therapy session is serendipitous, and appears to be the most creative and most likely means to further the interests of all involved.

Pryluck rallies for aggressive intervention, but even Diamond Hoops disagrees, flowering wide for emphasis. "The circumstance lacks nothing. The man, Tull, has proposed an ingenious format, utterly harmonious with our lifestream's destiny, which happens to align as well with the soul intentions of the other two participants. How can they refuse?"

"But," argues Pryluck, "if they do refuse, we lose our best opportunity. I'm just suggesting a gentle shove in the right direction."

To the amazement of all, Mabel expands to engulf Pryluck in a radiantly pink and loving embrace. "What, and ruin the fun of the wager? Let us give the lifestreams a chance to choose. If it does not work out, we can create an even more magnificent template."

* * *

Dolores hedged and brooded. Terry painted furiously, and finally disappeared for a week. He went to stay with Wanda and Jack in Preston. And brooded.

After two days, they put him to work on the woodpile. After four days, he took off for another two, equipped with fishing and camping gear. His last night in the woods was cold and clear. Snow had fallen throughout the afternoon, just enough to outline the world in a thin patina that sparkled by moon and starlight.

Terry stared into his low-burning fire. His chest ached deeply, but he was too weary to resist the sensation. "I give up," he said aloud. "If there *is* a God, please forgive me. I don't even know if it makes sense to pray anymore. Whoever is there, just tell me what You want from me. If this Vormis is for real, what am I supposed to do? Just direct me. I give up." Through smoke, he gazed at stars shining from between the frosted fir boughs, feeling empty and prepared to wait for a response.

Vormis and Snarrow stare at one another. "Is he addressing me, do you think?" Vormis wonders.

Snarrow smiles. "I don't think he knows. He is still confused by the religious program about the deity."

"Then, what should I tell him?"

Snarrow's laugh is an electric-hued sparkler. "You sound just like he does. Let him know we are with him, of course...and if you can, that we are not God. Nor are we the devil's spawn, for that matter."

* * *

It was all but inevitable. The three met at Dolores' office space. They agreed to a time-by-time assessment of the format. Terry would pay for therapy services. Tull would give half the fee to Dolores.

Dolores tuned the vibration of the space with incense and vocal tones. Tull held the energy of the space with his deep-rooted therapeutic presence. Terry took up space, fidgeting until Dolores began to outline the construct of a human being, referring to mind, emotion, and even spirit as distinct, interacting bodies analogous to the physical body. They did exercises to train perceptual awareness, in order to identify each of these bodies by its unique quality of sensation.

Each one left the meeting feeling invigorated. Each lingered outside the church with unspoken desires: Dolores for Terry, Tull for Dolores, Terry to go paint. The three parted with a commitment to meet at the same place and time the following week.

~ 33 ~

A desperately restless Fran implored, "Can't we try again? The last time Terry was over here, he was great with Tracey. He has a girlfriend and his painting thing now. Maybe he's over his problem."

Bill regarded Fran as if she was some kind of alien.

"What?" she demanded.

"Well, I'm not opposed to the idea of asking Terry to watch Tracey for a weekend, it's just I don't see him quite the same way as you do."

"Quite which way?"

"That he had some kind of problem and got over it. The guy I always knew as my brother? He's gone, Fran. He didn't get over nothing. He doesn't work for me no more. He doesn't drink at The Oyster no more. He doesn't sleep around with whoever he manages to pick up. And you're not gonna convince me that it's because of any girlfriend. Whatever is going on with him has changed him big time, and he ain't exactly making himself family around here. It's been, what, three weeks since we've even seen him?"

"Please, Bill? I need a break."

"That's fine, Honey. Yes, we'll find a way to go," Bill told her. "I'm just saying that I don't know Terry too good these days. And, you know, he—or someone—is gonna have to take charge of Gilli's Girl when I'm away."

"Bill, he can't fish if he's watching Tracey! Can't you just close down operation for a couple of days?"

"Of course, but someone has got to be responsible for the

boat in case of weather. That's all I'm saying. I don't know if we can trust him."

"Better him than Fred," she said under her breath.

The weather sucked, with no break in rain and clouds, going on eight days. Cara and her band were set up in the entryway of The Oyster's Pearl. Terry took a table near the bar and, for his first time, tuned out enough clamor to give the trio his full attention. They sounded good. He watched Cara move, allowing rhythm and sound to fill his head and he smiled, unaware of doing so.

Bill showed up minutes later. "Aren't you drinking?"

Terry turned to face his brother. "Hadn't yet."

"I'll go get us a couple of schooners."

Terry watched Bill push his way to, and then from, the bar.

"When'd they get the new barmaid?" Bill asked, setting down the beers.

Terry shrugged. "Didn't know they did. Is Suzanne gone then?"

Bill zeroed in on Terry's face. "Don't you come in here at all anymore?"

"Not much, I guess," Terry answered through a sip of beer. "I'm glad you got me out though. Cara's pretty good, don't you think? I never really watched them before." He was unconsciously bobbing his shoulders.

Focusing on the trio, Bill shook his head as a faint smile touched his mouth. "So, that's Cara? You and she...?"

Terry's face closed. "Cara? No. She's Dolores' friend. Great girl. Really good person. So what'd you call me for?"

Bill's bark, "A friendly visit?" yielded an inert glare. "I do have something to ask," he relented. "But you know, it's true we haven't hung out in a long time. I never see you these days."

Terry nodded. "Yeah, I know. How's business?"

Bill drank quietly for some moments. "Fish are still swimming into the nets. But it ain't the same." He shrugged. "Guess I miss you out there."

They both stared at the table.

"Yeah." Terry finally broke the silence. "Would you, uh, ever think about maybe taking a couple of days off to go camping? We haven't done that in forever."

Bill grimaced. "Well, that's kind of the same question I called you about. Only it's Fran who's on me again about taking some time off with her. She wants to know if you'll babysit. But by God, you're right. You and I should plan a trip."

Terry shook his head. "Fran never got her getaway weekend. I bet she blames me for that. You think she'd let you and me go off camping without her?"

"Well, if you come through for her this time..."

"Right. That'll bring my score up to zero, and we'll have a clean slate?"

They both grinned.

"I want you to meet Cara," Terry told Bill when the band went on break. He half stood, waving to catch her attention.

It was with her inner rather than outer vision that Dolores detected the electric simmer in Terry's field. The closest image she could compare to it was a multi-colored sparkler. Only the sparks and crackles were so minute they appeared sub-atomic.

Methods, to the casual observer, has all but disappeared.

A pastel crescent of stratus-like opacity is the only visible vestige of the electrical stew that has temporarily consumed Mabel, Bulista, and the congregation of Terry's subpersonalities.

Most of the remaining lightworkers are engaged in various forms of revelry. Snarrow and the field guide Percy Barnett take Vormis in tow. "Come on, you'll love this," Percy tells him. "Remember snow? This is like a cross between snow sledding and body surfing."

"But what is it? What's happening?" wonders Vormis.

"Cosmic weather," Snarrow ventures. "The cloud-like patterns form when lights of various frequencies come together and, for some odd reason, stratify."

"What is going on in there?" Vormis asks, indicating the central morass of popping electricity.

"No idea at all," answers Percy.

After the weather finally clears, Mabel and Bulista are the last to re-emerge. Both are more luminous than ever, and neither has the slightest inkling about their roles thus far in the subpersonality rehab program.

Snarrow is concerned. He approaches Bouffant Head in Creative Works. In truth, Creative Works is now so well integrated throughout Methods as to render the distinction meaningless. Still, Snarrow prefers to maintain some sense of classification within his mind.

For once, Bouffant Head is willing to communicate on Snarrow's level. "It is odd, isn't it?" he agrees. "It looks as if the dissolution process that is to re-form the lifestream's persona is having a backwash effect on us. Bulista and Mabel are getting the main brunt of it."

After a pause, he resumes his customary manner. "And

you will agree they are becoming more and more ravishing."

"More ravishing, but less and less effective," Snarrow *laments.*

Bouffant Head flashes bright, then dim, several times before vanishing.

* * *

The brilliance of starlight was unprecedented in Cara's memory. She found an old, still-functioning payphone near the beach and called Terry. No response. No surprise, but his damn answering machine did not pick up either. She decided to leave a message on his cell, in case he ever checked it, but to her amazement, he answered.

"Come down to the beach!" she insisted.

"I can't. I'm babysitting my brother's kid."

"Bundle her up and bring her along."

"Uh, Tracey's bedtime was 8:30. It's what, 1:20 now. Why don't you come over here?"

"For God's sake, Terry, if anyone has got to see this it's you. It's not like you might get another chance."

Consumed by guilt over the deed, he gently lifted the sleeping Tracey from her bed, wrapped her in extra blankets and packed her beside him in his truck. He drove right up to the sand.

The scene was spectacular. Terry left Tracey with Cara and approached the shoreline, mesmerized by contrast and clarity. A familiar longing to paint the scene before him—in this case, diamond starlight reflected on night-black water—coincided with a tinge of frustration at his inability to ever quite capture the essence of what he saw. His body trembled.

Cara, holding a still-sleeping Tracey, stepped up onto

a rock beside him. They stood shoulder-to-shoulder, inhaling beauty. When his reaction seemed to ebb, she nudged his arm and proffered Tracey. "Hey, uncle," she softly teased. "A working girl needs her sleep."

He turned to face her. "You played tonight?"

"Mm, hmm. Beach Bar Café."

"You busy tomorrow?"

Her grin mocked him. Reflected starlight crackled electric in her eyes. "What'd you have in mind, big-boy?"

Distracted, he ignored her response and continued to stare at the reflection in her eyes. "I've got to paint. This." His arm swept vaguely around him and came to rest with straight fingers pointed at her. "You know, or you wouldn't have called me. Would you watch Tracey for me? Please?"

She groaned. "Alright, look. I'll give you five hours, noon to five. That's all. But you don't get to run off to the studio and get lost in the process. You go pick up your supplies and then paint at your brother's house. I'm leaving at five whether you're done or not."

* * *

Mabel's and Bulista's memories have blessedly recovered, with few apparent glitches. Mabel visits with Cara's guide, Millicent, over tea in her very authentically manufactured café setting.

"What do you think of the teapot?" Millicent asks. "I considered a more Grecian look…" its shape and glaze change to illustrate her thought. "…but I love the Chinese color scheme."

"I agree, muses Mabel. "The Chinese is lovely."

"Mabel," Millicent asks. "What is the status of your lifestream's transfer? Does he recognize your team and his

subpersonalities yet?"

Mabel titters. "He is not quite sub-conscious, but his own mind has begun to pull him in that direction. I think it will not be long now."

"And has your function altered in any way?"

Mabel's field shuffles like a deck of colors. "You know, I have not yet shared this with Snarrow, but I think our function is changing a lot. And I think that it is happening in conjunction with the shifts in configuration that have been taking place here."

Millicent glows. "That is what I imagined would occur. How do you experience the change?"

Mabel again destabilizes in a brief rose-hued drizzle before she leans in close. "I believe our roles as guides can no longer be fulfilled in the same old manner. In my case, I see my work with subs becoming more the setting of templates instead of the mediation process it used to be."

Millicent nods vigorously. "The old mode is obsolete, isn't it? I have seen it coming. Templating makes so much more sense."

"Oh, yes, and it is much more fun," effuses Mabel.

* * *

Tull suspected that the key to Terry's process would lie in his ability first to recognize, and then to learn to tolerate a wider range of his own feelings. Prior experience had taught him that they might best accomplish this by circumventing the conscious mind and bringing Terry straight into his body.

Flat on his back, Terry focused as per instruction, on his breathing. From time to time, Tull requested that the breaths extend deeper or fuller.

After observing for a while, Dolores spoke up. "This area." She touched her own right hip while nodding toward Terry's. "It's not charging as he breathes. The breath is bypassing around it."

Tull gently placed a hand on Terry's hip in the region that Dolores indicated, and suggested, "Try bringing your attention to this spot under my hand. Keep breathing."

As soon as he became fully aware of the hip, Terry's muscles tensed. His attention wandered and the rhythm of his breath faltered. A similar sequence recurred several times while Tull gently and patiently encouraged him to stay with and explore the sensation.

And then, with the suddenness of a recoiled spring, Terry's body curled into fetal position.

Lightworkers hover with open interest. "Can we partici-pate?" Bulista wonders.

Chuckling, Mabel suggests, "Let us try holding our focus on that foul, dark spot he is trying so hard to avoid."

While holding Terry in a cocoon of subdued amber light, Vormis splits his attention. "Do you want me to beam in and light up the area?" he asks his co-Workers.

"No, please, no," urges Mabel. "Let us just put our focus there. Set the template. We shall watch it for him and see if his attention follows.

Within minutes, Terry was sobbing oceans of bottomless grief.

Tull's voice slipped through the waves, "Any idea what this is about?"

Terry shook his head without changing position or uncovering his face, which remained buried in his hands.

"Stay with the feeling in your hip, Ter. Explore around in there. What do you notice?"

Terry shook his head again, clearly not grasping Tull's

instruction.

"Allow your observing mind to have eyes, ears, a nose. Take a look. Is there a color where you are?"

"It's dark. Black."

"Black. Great. Check out the blackness. How does it feel? Does it have texture? How hot or cold is it?

"Like nothing. Smooth, maybe. No temperature."

"What do you hear?"

Terry began to make a soft whooshing sound, followed by a gentle thumping sound with his tongue.

Questions and answers continued, with Terry entering deeper and deeper into his experience. When Tull finally asked, "So what is the sadness about?" Terry's tears resumed.

"Not fair," he managed to choke. "Couldn't stay."

Ultimately, it turned out that the great angst had to do with Terry's essential reluctance to undergo human incarnation. Tull and Dolores exchanged a startled glance.

~ 34 ~

Session after session revolved around Terry's previously unconscious resistance to life on Earth.

"It is interesting that he is so stuck on this point," Snarrow ponders.

Pryluck is flippant. "Oh, he's just sulking. It's the babe taken from the teat thing. He thinks he has been cut off from his source and supply of nourishment. Don't they all go through a bit of the same when they lose consciousness at birth?"

"Yes, Pryluck, but this lifestream is peculiarly stubborn on that point. I wonder how long it has been since he has budged on the issue."

They turn to the technies for historical data. It is impressive. The strand of consciousness they can trace to Terry's current identity program, continuing through time and contained within a multitude of lifestream formats, has never accepted the conditions of human birth.

"He is totally fused with archetypal mind patterns," marvels Mabel. "He totally believes in separation and loss."

"Well, they all do, that is a given," Snarrow asserts. "But this one has never glimpsed the truth of it in any of his prior formatting, which is unusual. More often, there are at least some cracks in the belief constructs, which allow light to shine through. This one has refused to allow the cracking to occur...ever."

"No wonder he's exhausted," murmurs Bulista.

"No wonder he is enraged about Vormis getting through," sighs Mabel.

Vormis perks up. "How is that?"

"The anger load in this lifestream is exceptionally high over the issue of apparent separation from unity that the lifestreams must undergo in order to experience incarnation," Snarrow answers. "His soul is actively engaged in the human workshop, but he has refused to cooperate, or to forgive the fact that he was recruited, despite his greater will's opinion in the matter."

"But why is he pissed at me?" asks Vormis.

They all laugh.

"The reality that he is not, and never was, cut off from Love both comforts and enrages him. It exposes his whole resistance

campaign as a mistake, see, a grand waste of energy."

* * *

Gradually, bit-by-bit, through sessions with Tull and Dolores, Terry was coming to the same realization. The grief that was unleashed seemed infinite and it swamped him for weeks. Dolores came to dread the therapy sessions, and considered skipping them.

Tull had a different take on it. "He is doing some great work," he told her one evening after Terry had left. "What makes you so uncomfortable? Is it strong emotion?"

"Fuck you, Tull, don't try to therapize me. Terry is becoming like a helpless baby. He was always moody, and I've seen him despondent a few times, but never like this. How can it possibly do him any good to break down this way?"

Tull wrinkled his chin. "It must be painful to work with your lover in this way."

She didn't answer, so he went on. "My sense about you was that you weren't holding any idealized illusions about Terry. Did I misread your feelings?"

Her body fought an upwelling of hatred toward Tull. "What is that supposed to mean?" was all she could manage.

"Dolores, Terry is breaking through, not breaking down. He is finally connecting with the place that has been robbing him of life force. Now, he discovers that maybe there is another choice of how to go about life. You, especially, ought to recognize and support the dissolution of someone's defensive illusions. Isn't that what your work is about, too?"

"No, I don't think it is," she answered.

"Then what is the point to it?"

"I'm just a goddamn medium, Tull. A message relay

system. I 'deliver de letter' is all."

"Then what's the deal with your psychic development classes? Why bother?"

"People want to learn how to connect to the Source and get acquainted with their guides."

He smiled. "And why do you suppose that is?"

"People feel alone. Maybe they sense that there's more to existence than what they've already experienced. Some people have memories of other-side contact from childhood. They're curious. What's your reason?" she challenged.

He beamed. "All of the above. Together with the same longing for home that apparently drives Terry." His voice thickened. "Dolores, I don't think what he's feeling is just personal to him. And if you would let yourself touch your own core feelings, under the anger you feel toward me, you'd be bawling too. It's the human condition, and we're all walking around like helpless babies. It isn't just your lover."

He tried, but couldn't stop himself from adding, "It isn't fair to expect him to maintain some he-man façade just to appease your own sense of helplessness."

She grinned triumphantly. "Where did your non-attachment go, Herr Doktor? What's that all about?"

With a grimace, Tull raised his hands in surrender and finally laughed.

The mail brought bills, of course, together with assorted ads and fliers. Among them was a bulletin soliciting funds for a church relief mission in Somalia, spearheaded by Father Sulleran. Terry cursed and flung the offending paper across the counter, then snatched it up and venomously mashed it between his hands before tossing it to the coffee grounds and rotting banana peels in the kitchen trash.

He cursed again and slammed the door on his way out, bought a six-pack, proceeded to the park and set to work on the beer. It wasn't easy getting it all down. His body was much more sensitive these days. With grim determination bordering on spite, he noted the boundary of his tolerance and pushed beyond it.

Terry's foul disposition took him into a foul little corner bar. The one female in the place must have been as far along as he. He ordered whiskeys for them both. Their knees touched, he ran his hand up her thigh. "Let's get out of here," he told her.

On the sidewalk, she had trouble figuring out which direction to take to get to her apartment. "I'll help you," he said. At the door, she turned to leave him. He grabbed her by the shoulders. "I want to fuck," he insisted, and directed her inside.

That was Wednesday. When he got home on Friday, there were two messages on the answering machine. The first was from Tull, questioning his failure to show up for an appointment. The other, from Emilio Garcia, informed him of an upcoming studio show, in which Terry was invited to enter a painting.

Terry listened, turned off the phone and went to bed for two more days. He dreamed beautiful scenes of sparkling blue water, through which he entered worlds of lucent shimmer and the rhythmic roll of balmy oceans, where he rested in the hand and heart of the mother of the world. Her voice surrounded him in song, and eased his burning nerves.

He awoke in tears, with a heart that felt exquisitely sad and broken.

* * *

"This is just not going to do," Mabel objects.

Snarrow agrees. "I am out of ideas. He has dug himself into a pretty deep hole. With any other lifestream, we could just give him space and time—a lifetime if that is what he chooses—to be with the experience. But with him...if we simply allow him the space to be as he is, does that essentially constitute termination of the project?"

"Oh, Snarrow," Mabel urges. We can not just cut him loose after setting his whole destabilization into motion. The original condition for the project specified no psychosis or lapse in consciousness. He is within bounds of both requisites. His personal will must come into play at some point. Maybe now is the time."

"I don't know. If his path is to lead through joy and celebration of life, he or we are on the wrong track. And he still is not recognizing his subpersonalities."

"No, he is not. And I am convinced that is the crux of the matter, but it is no longer a question of potential. At this point, he is perfectly capable on every level. It is simply a question of his willingness to accept his own role and contribution relative to his experience. The catch is that there are apparently one or more subpersonalities at the root of his resistance to recognizing them. It is a conundrum."

"Oh, I like that. It makes it all sound more promising."

Mabel notices that Snarrow's field is beginning to resemble mosaic tile. "Cracked," she marvels to herself.

* * *

Together, Dolores and Cara knocked at Terry's door. "Did you try his cell?" Cara asked. "He answered it one time I called."

"You spoke to him? When?" Dolores asked.

"No, not recently. But his answering machine was turned

off that time too."

"I think he is in there," Dolores said, banging again at the door.

They heard a sound from inside. His voice? Both women called to him.

"Not now," came a reply, distinct this time.

"Terry, we're coming in," Dolores warned.

Their eyes met. "Do you think we should?" Cara asked. "What if he's...engaged...?"

Dolores scowled. "The pig. Let him squirm if he is." She removed his hidden key and opened the door.

Ooh, not good. The apartment smelled unhealthy. Garbage had not been removed. Dolores hesitated just inside the door, visibly regretting having gotten this far.

Cara headed straight for Terry's room, where she found him sullen, disheveled and unwashed. She sat beside him and took his hand. "Terry, you stink. It's about time you decide to either let people support you or else stop messing with their lives. A lot of people care about you, and you treat them like crap when you refuse to communicate. It's enough already!"

She gave him a light kiss on the forehead and left the room, taking Dolores with her to the street.

* * *

"Template? Hell, let's stage a drama." Bouffant Head raises a pair of simulated arms and, baton in hand, gestures before an unseen orchestra.

Mabel glides near. "Another sub psychodrama?"

The CW rep shakes his head. "Even better. Introducing... The Soma." He stops conducting and lowers his baton. "Create a window. Let the subs be present. There is more than one way to en-tr-train the masses," he winks.

  Barriers dissolve between dimensions. Some subperson-
alities watch as from a distant amphitheater, while others filter
freely through Terry's sleeping body. Bouffant Head conjures a top
hat and bullhorn. "We now present…The Dream of Fornix Brayne!
Co-starring…Harold Harte!"

  Multicolored floodlights illuminate a parting curtain that
reveals Fornix Brayne reclining on a couch. "I dreamed a dream
of black and white. The worlds divided. Yes and no were born. I
dreamed I was rejected by the other side, no matter which I repre-
sented. I suffered without end." Fornix Brayne looks up with large,
tragic eyes. "I want no part of what you have to tell me."

  Harold Harte aligns his pudgy mass more directly in front
of Fornix Brayne. "The truth," he insists. "I'm telling you the truth.
You've suffered over a mistake." He laughs. "A bad dream. That's
all."

  "Insanity," moans Fornix. "I have plunged myself into
insanity." His stare burns into Harte. "There is no way out."

  Harold contemplates Brayne's mournful eyes. "Insanity,"
he repeats to himself. "Look," he tells him. "You woke up in a bad
mood. Give yourself some time to finish waking, get up, move
around. I'll be back in a few."

  Fornix Brayne shouts, "I told you I am not *going to get up!*
So just leave and forget about coming back."

  Harold sighs and presses a fleshy hand on Brayne's
shoulder. "You know I can't do that, man. Why not tell me the
whole of it?"

  Fornix relaxes his coiled posture. "I don't know, Harte. Just
talking to you pulls me away from myself." He shakes his head. "I
don't think it's a good idea."

Harold sits close, his upper arm barely touching Fornix's. "Naturally, man. You know you can't maintain the separation. It takes too much energy, for one thing. So why do you insist on this?"

Brayne fixes Harte with a laser gaze and tells him, "It's my dream. I have to finish, to see it through."

"Through to what is what I want to know," says Harte. "There can be no end to it, no resolution." His voice softens. "Your only choice will be to just pull yourself out of it, Fornix. Sooner or later."

Harold Harte leaves to make a phone call. "Back soon," he tells Fornix.

"Yeah, I'm with him. Tried talking. I just don't know how to get through. He's miserable, I'm frustrated. I don't see how we can possibly function this way." Harte pauses. "I mean, he's not considering the bigger picture, is he?"

The Voice on the other end of the line is calm. "This is not something you'll convince him of. He isn't wrong, you know."

Harold Harte remains silent.

"OK. Here," the Voice resumes. "Bottom line. If you want to keep communications open, you will have to hear him out. Find out why he doesn't want to hear your truth. Learn what it is about that truth that upsets him. This isn't about you versus him or any such rubbish, so go back in there with an open mind, Harte."

The room is dark, shades drawn. Fornix Brayne has not budged from his position on the couch. Harold Harte shuts the door behind him. "Hey," he says softly. He can feel Brayne listening despite his feigning sleep.

"Maybe I was a little pushy. Overzealous, or something like that. I'd like to try again. Maybe I don't understand where you're

coming from, man. Tell me about duality."

"Duality," Fornix repeats. "I dreamed a dream of black and white." He uncovers his face and again stares hard at Harold. "There is no place for you there. You try and follow me in, I won't be able to do my part. You'd just wreck the place, Harte. You've got to let go."

"What do you mean I would wreck it? How?"

"Your truth and duality can't coexist in the same space. And me? I would lose myself in your truth." His eyes are desperate. "You can't do this to me, Harte, it's not fair."

Harold does not speak. He nods several times with his lower lip protruding.

"Okay," he eventually says. "I guess this isn't about making sense. So, is what you're proposing then a split? To what extent do you intend to take it?"

"I don't know, Harte." Brayne hangs his head. "I made a commitment, an agreement."

Harte jumps up. "You what? When? What did you agree to?"

"To forget. Everything. I agreed to dream, to enter the reality of the dream. To lose myself in it."

"But why would anyone ask that of you?" Harte trembles and perspires.

"I don't know." Brayne's eyes brim with tears. "I couldn't do anything else. I pledged fealty ages ago. I have to cooperate with whatever design is laid out before me."

Harte begins to pace. "Bear with me a minute, Brayne," he pleads. "I admit I don't get the point. I'll give you my blessing..." He paces faster. "But let me show you what I see." He waits, and receiving no veto from Brayne, he projects his perspective.

The realm of material substance appears before them. Together, they observe themselves in Brayne's vaulted chamber, which opens outward onto a forest landscape, vibrant with trees and boulders. A river ambles bluely through it.

Bit by bit, the light changes to reveal a web-like matrix. Slender columns in electric blue provide anchorage from the central core of every tree into the earth's own heart, which swells and pulses like a glowing sun. Beneath the surface, and connecting each tree to the next in a spiral of fellowship, run root-like runners of that same blue essence.

The river and rocks, too, glow with vibrant emanations extending ocean-to-ocean, upward and outward, humming the tune of galaxies and weaving the manifest world into a single, lacy organism. Brayne and Harte are part of it, irrevocably linked and rooted, flowing with the cerulean current that injects the nourishment of love into every breath.

Fornix Brayne breaks the vision. "I know!" he shouts. "You haven't listened. There's a rule I must obey. Truth can't follow into where I'm going."

"Fornix, Fornix, I do hear you, man. You'll sleep, you'll dream. Now hear me. Your sleep will be supported, rocked and held. You'll think you have been cut loose, I get it. But you can ride the nightmare to its farthest reaches and you know what? You'll fall into our arms. You'll cry out in anguish in your sleep, you'll scrape the lowest bottom, and you'll still feel our web.

"You'll do this and resist it time and time again—dream, forget, return, remember. But one time, Fornix Brayne, you'll decide you've had enough. And then? Then the rules are gonna change. Go ahead, make the call and ask. Phone's just outside your door."

Flooded with the sense of peace despite himself, Fornix

flattens out against the couch. "You've got to be kidding. We don't talk that way."

"Well, why the hell not, Brayne? That's what I'm saying. You received your orders third hand, eons ago. It's about time you reported back for an update is what I say. No wonder you feel like you're out there on your own," Harold adds under his breath.

Fornix comes to attention. "Harte. Harold, friend. Listen. My host is waking up. I've got to go back."

Harold expands fleshily and extends a hand. Their gazes hold as they shake. "Yeah. Well. Guess we'll see you, then."

~ 35 ~

The day of contrition arrived. Terry returned Emilio's call and agreed to enter a painting in the studio show. He then called Cara to once again acknowledge her help and support. To Dolores and Tull, he offered apologies that barely concealed his eagerness for another meeting. "I had a completely weird dream," he told Dolores.

"You told me you never remember your dreams," she said.

"I know it, that's what makes it weirder. I forgot a lot of it, but I wrote down what I could...like you told me."

"Was it another encounter like you had that night at Cara's?"

"No, this is something else. I have no idea what it means."

In Dolores' office that evening, Tull's response was bemused. "Brayne and Harte?"

Terry looked surprised. "I didn't think of it that way before. Do you think it means I have something wrong with my brain?"

His anxiety struck both Tull and Dolores as hilarious. Tull recovered first. "I think we should try regressing you back into the dream. You can fill in the memory gaps and get a chance to consciously experience your reactions to it." He studied Terry's written account of the dream. "Have you ever taken a class in anatomy?"

Terry shook his head no.

"What intrigues me," Tull continued, "is the name, Fornix. Calling the Harte guy Harold I can understand. But you've gone and named your Brayne character after the fornix. That's an actual part of the midbrain." Neither Terry nor Dolores seemed impressed by the supposed significance.

Terry was responsive to regression, and was able to almost completely reconstruct the dream.

"Who do you think the Voice is?" Dolores wanted to know.

Terry shrugged.

Tull agreed it mattered. "You find out who Brayne and Harte receive their orders from, and you've got the source you're looking for. Any idea, Terry?"

"I just figured it was maybe symbolic of God or something."

Tull nodded. "Yeah, so how do you suppose we might find that telephone?"

In a moment of inspiration, Dolores interrupted, "Ter, imagine the feeling you get when images change for you. How does the change feel in your body? No, just feel it. Identify it. OK, there you are." She observed Terry's energy field as it opened to display a bluish network, similar to the one that Harte had revealed to Brayne in Terry's dream.

"OK. Stay anchored in the rooting channels, the ones that go down. And then, follow the stellar channels up and out. But don't lose the anchor. You need to keep extending downward at the same time as you open upward. It's like how you'd see a plant grow in a time-lapse photo, both shooting up and rooting down. Now, ask inside to find the Voice from your dream."

"Clever girl," Dolores heard Forwyn affirm within her mind.

Terry appeared to have entered an in-between state—between wakefulness and sleep, between imagination and form.

"It's guarded," he said.

"What is?"

"Guard soldier. Can't pass."

Tull took over. "Would you ask if I might speak with the guard?"

With eyes closed, Terry dipped his chin in a barely perceptible nod. "He's listening."

Tull introduced himself to the soldier in Terry's reverie. The guy had seemingly been at his post forever since his comrades had departed. He had become fatigued beyond belief, his body numb and frozen. Tull inquired as to what he was protecting.

"Door," a brittle sounding voice rasped.

"Which door is that?" Tull asked.

"Secret. Hide."

"What are you hiding?"

Terry shook his head, no. "He's guarding the most... sacred...place." His tears flowed freely.

Tull and Dolores gave Terry a moment with his experience before continuing to question him. "What is in the most sacred place?"

Terry opened his eyes. "It's like the truth—the deepest truth that he can't let anyone know, or violate."

Tull remained cool. "What is it like in there, where the truth lives?"

To Dolores' surprise, Terry answered without hesitation. "Green. Lush. Waterfalls, pools, rocks. There are other people. Helpers."

Tull waited. Terry was plainly in no need of additional prompting. "They are inviting him to go in and rest, but he won't leave his post."

"He...you mean, the guard?"

Terry nodded. "Now they've put him into a warm pool." He chuckled. "His armor is frozen on. He's got to soak it off first. Garrison's upset."

"Who?"

"The garrison that sent him. The door's unguarded now. The room is getting real bright, like sunlight is streaming in from the floor."

"Terry, do you suppose there might be some value in opening that space? Could you maybe access the truth without violating it?"

"Needs protection."

"Can your guard continue to protect it in the way he has been?"

"No. No, wait. Different. Someone else is in there talking to the garrison."

It was Chaz, who, upon Mabel's encouragement was exuberantly describing how he had learned to hold light as a more effective protection than aggression. He moreover offered to join forces with, and even help to retrain the frozen guard, along with

the rest of the garrison, once the guard had thawed and recovered.
A sense of peaceful accord prevailed for the time being.

Terry turned to Dolores. "So where is all this shit coming from? Am I seeing and talking with guides?"

Dolores smiled, noting both a swelling sense of tenderness and her resistance to it. "No," she answered. "Not guides, more like...I don't know, the mind?" She addressed Tull. "This is your area, right?"

Tull reflected. "I'm not sure what the mind encompasses. The way I understand this process is that everybody's personality is more like a composite of many facets than it is a single entity. Each facet holds its own viewpoint and serves its own function, like personalities within the personality. They can be all different ages and, unless for some reason someone bothers to pay attention, they are usually unaware of the other facets. It's not much different than a collection of people living in the same neighborhood, all so wrapped up in their own lives that they don't get to know or even notice the neighbors.

"The average person walks around unconsciously ruled by these personality fragments. Now and then, something will trigger a fragment to behave in its own particular defense pattern." He smiled at Terry. "The way your sentry has been doing. When we become aware of these fragments and engage them in interaction, then they can all start to work together as a community, and our behavior becomes freer and more consciously directed." He shrugged. "I believe it's an avenue to personal power."

Methods swirls with relief and joy. "I like this guy," Mabel gushes. "He has facilitated the opening that we could not."

Snarrow's gaze encompasses the shimmer of Creative Works' presence. "Well, here's to our multidimensional community."

* * *

The studio show was part of a citywide open-studio day, an annual event held the week before Easter. Participating studios opened their doors to the public, transforming each work space into a gallery for the day. Emilio encouraged his students to display their work, and gain experience in details such as price setting and interfacing with potential buyers.

Terry contributed a painting, but shied away both from the marketing process and from the event itself. He left town to go fishing.

Occasional patches of snow clung to shadows under ledges and on north facing slopes. A steamy haze lifted as the alpine sun rose higher. Terry bouldered over granite outcroppings, descending to the stream. Its water ran strong and deep with snow melt. On the bank, where sunlight filtered freely through the trees, Terry observed delicate arches of yet-to-unfurl leaf shoots and fresh new fiddleheads pushing through the forest floor.

He studied the water's surface, looking for bugs. He listened for birdsong, assessing by the presence of particular species, which insects might be a current food source for fish and fowl. He noticed molt casings on a rock and decided to try a March brown fly.

The arc of the fishing line drew his eye mid-cast, and soon became more interesting than the task at hand. Terry pulled a sketchpad from his pack. *Lightworkers cluster about his shoulders to peer at the emerging image. Water, of course, with swirling patterns of light and shadow. Rocks...*

Pryluck nudges Vormis. "Would you look at that? He sees

the energy lines."

Excitement undulates throughout Methods. "I wonder if he recalls the image from the Harold Harte dream or if he actually sees what he is drawing?" asks Mabel.

They watch Terry's portrayal of intersecting lines of energy beneath and between river stones, until the picture becomes a dual portrayal of his solid world overlain by one of subtle unity.

"He sees it," states Vormis with certainty.

"Alright," declares Snarrow. "We were given a project to reconfigure this lifestream mid-stream as it were. So where are we in the process?"

He allows the question to sift among the congregated Workers. "Stage one is clearly behind us—most outdated programming has been stripped and deleted. New formatting has been, for the most part, accepted. Conscious awareness of both guidance systems and subpersonality input is in early stages of integration." He turns to Mabel. "How do you propose we proceed from here?"

Technie Barwin arrives in a flash, waving a trailing document. He appears to hop from side to side, apparently excited, but reticent to speak without invitation.

Snarrow asks, "What have you got, Barwin?"

"It looks like orders, I think, or maybe suggestions. He holds up the image for perusal. Vormis and Mabel press closer.

Mabel exclaims, "It is another puzzle from Management."

Snarrow grumbles, "I don't think this is intended to be a puzzle. They are simply not retaining any semblance of linearity."

"Poor Snarrow," Mabel teases.

They gather around the seemingly scrambled transmission,

offering ideas for how the words, thoughts and images can be pieced together to form an intelligible message. One by one, other lightworkers congregate, alighting like birds at a feeder. The scene turns lively with their chatter.

"Add another dimension," someone offers. Doing so reshapes the message into holographic form.

"Set it in motion," someone else calls out. The images began to spin, and various scenes emerge like 3-D movie clips.

Snarrow looks to Mabel. "What might we make of it?" he wonders.

"Possibilities?" she suggests. "Maybe they are showing us various potentials, possible choices or realities in the lifestream's path."

Vormis nudges Snarrow. "Hey, look, you're in this one." They watch a while longer.

Snarrow poses the question, "Can we identify any common element, consistent from scene to scene?"

Bulista speaks up. "I think it's what varies that is most significant."

The others wait for her to elaborate.

"Watch the relationships. Roles and configurations shift from image to image."

"Mmm, they do," Mabel agrees. "I think this memo might be more of a question than an order: How will we restructure relationships with the lifestream, inside and out?"

Snarrow pulses vigorously. "Our relationships? Are you referring to Millicent's question about how our roles will change?"

Mabel considers. "I suppose so. That, along with the restructuring of the lifestream's mental body. His awareness of subpersonalities. His sub-consciousness. It will all have to lead to new ways of processing and perceiving incoming stimuli."

"Look," Snarrow points. "This hologram shows variable relationships between his mental and emotional bodies."

"I like the ones over here." Bulista indicates a series of circular and spiral images that resemble constellations of stars in assorted size and brightness.

Congruity permeates the group. "Isn't that the way it is?" murmurs Mabel. "All of us are like related strings of variable astral consciousness. Wouldn't it be nice to manifest this version?" She indicates a jeweled circlet of radiant points.

* * *

Terry's toes ached. Just the latest, he presumed, in the fleeting bodily malfunctions he was obliged to live with. He walked to a downed tree and sat. His eyes rested on his sore feet. "What now? Am I going to have to hobble the whole way back to the truck?"

An effervescent almost-thought—more like the bubble of a sense impression—arose, ridiculous but irresistible. He concentrated on his toes and asked them what's up. They didn't answer, but Terry did have the feeling that a conscious presence listened. "Toes?" he asked.

An image formed in his mind, not of toes, but of a timid pair of eyes that shyly responded to his attention. "What, are you my toes?" he addressed the image.

A slight nod.

"Well then, how come you're hurting?"

The image retreated.

"Damn!" Terry complained. "Don't do that. Tell me something."

The eyes reappeared, and from somewhere—somehow

connected to the image—came the thought, "Water."

"Water," he repeated.

Another nod.

"What about water?" he demanded, but the moment had already passed.

"Water. Shit. Water." He resumed his walk, laughing aloud at the absurdity of his experience.

On the way into town, he stopped for gas. With a twenty in hand, already extended to the cashier, he had a revelation. "Hang on a minute," he told her, and walked to the cooler to grab a bottle of Poland Spring. An upwelling of giddiness made him add, "For my toes," as he handed over the money.

A message waited on the answering machine from Emilio, urging prompt response. He checked the clock. 10:45 p.m. "What the fuck," he thought, and returned the call.

"Terry, there you are! No, no problem, I'm up. Listen, Mr. Artiste, your *Moon-Man* sold. No, no shit. We got $160 for it. Not bad for a recent "Color and Form" graduate. But that's not what I called about."

Terry waited in a strange mix of wonder and calm. Emilio went on, "There's this lady who runs the Blue Turnip gallery downtown. She goes to open studios, kind of like a talent scout will go to plays and concerts—a good reason why you should learn to brave these events. Anyway, she wants to see more of your work, meet you and all. I'm going to give you her number. You need to call her."

High octane flowed through his body. Forget sleep. He wanted to talk. Surprisingly, he thought of Jim, his cross-dressing friend out East. West Virginia or Arkansas or wherever.

Either way, it would be even later out there.

Cara would be out on a job. He considered waking Dolores and decided against it. The Oyster then.

There was a mediocre blues duo covering uninspiring standards. Not much of a crowd. He sat on a stool at the bar, next to the same hard-drinking regular who had once lauded his disenchantment with Suzanne.

The man was deep in his beers in his customary posture: his head fallen forward, with his rheumy gaze on nothing tangible. "Good for you," he mumbled, cackling seemingly to himself. "Haa, ha, good for you." The sot raised his head to look squarely in Terry's direction.

Never imagining the comment might to apply to him, Terry ignored the old man until a sinuous, yellow-spotted talon of a hand suddenly grasped his arm.

"You show them. Show the whole goddamn world the way it is," the codger rasped. He apparently did not expect a reply, but resumed his nod.

Neither blues nor beer could touch Terry's restlessness. He drained his mug and stood, pausing first to contemplate the oracular drunkard at his side, who now showed no sign of consciousness. After a moment's hesitation, Terry placed a firm hand on the man's shoulder and took his leave.

* * *

Gradually, the flavor of their meetings turned more companionable. Over tea, Tull had questions for Dolores. "Do you think," he asked, "there is a distinction between higher mind and so-called guidance?"

"What?" she replied, biding time to decide whether or not to defend her sense of reality. That he noticed her reluctance showed only in an unformed smile behind his eyes.

"I'm just wondering about the source. When we receive information, how do we know whether it comes from some aspect of self—either higher awareness or even subconscious mind—or if it's actually a message from a distinct other entity?"

Dolores shook her head, expression rich in her eyebrows and cheeks. "How the hell should I know?"

Terry witnessed their interaction with a child's silence, unwilling to involve himself, but clearly interested.

Tull persisted. "How do *you* tell?"

Dolores released a deep breath. "I ask them, if that's what I want to know."

Tull smiled, Terry waited, and Dolores mined the unspoken question in the air between them.

"Alright, if you're suggesting that subpersonalities and spirit guides are essentially different levels of a person's own mind...I mean, you're heading toward that mind-fuck that everything we experience is within our own mind, and we're all one person."

She and Tull both smiled. "Well?" he persisted.

"I don't know that it matters, Tull."

"What do you believe?" he asked. "What do your guides tell you?"

"That things just aren't so defined. Realities adjust as we shift from one dimensional perspective to another. So I guess I believe all of it, that I am certainly a distinct individual relative to you two clods, but that we *are* of the same originating source. And if you're getting personal, then yes, I do experience the sense of unity from time to time...like an indivisibility of all life. You know that's what I do this for.

"But it doesn't change the day-to-day experience of one's separate, individual identity and it doesn't lessen pain or make each moment any easier." Her emotional charge loitered like a fourth member of their group.

"I think it does," Tull said. "Not that the pain lessens or that events change, but that the awareness of a greater whole makes it easier to endure the fragmented experience of life on Earth."

Dolores shrugged. "You still need to eat your bowl of rice."

"Sorry?"

"Some Indian guy said that everyone comes into life with a portion of the collective human residue—like a bowl of grain—and that even after you attain personal liberation you still bear your share; you have to eat what you were served in your bowl."

Terry fidgeted. "Anyone want to go for a beer?"

~ 36 ~

The thick, balding man who unlocked the door wore shiny shoes and unpleasant cologne that twisted Terry's stomach. "I'm looking for a Mrs. Thorpe," Terry told the gentleman. "She said to come by after ten."

"I will let her know you are here. Please have a seat."

Terry remained standing, and perfunctorily checked out the paintings on the gallery walls. None stirred more than his mild interest. He felt ill at ease in the room's spotless formality.

"Good morning. I'm Leticia Thorpe."

Terry turned to the throaty voice. He guessed her age as mid-sixties. Fussy looking, he thought. Moneyed. She wore glasses with a thin brass chain that hung unused beneath her chin. Her scent was old lady, though thank God, subtler than the man's. Terry forced his body to shake hands and return the greeting. His natural impulse would have had him out the door.

Mrs. Thorpe conducted him to her office, a small room behind the gallery space. "Please, sit. Make yourself at home." Her welcome included a toothy exhibit of enormous wide-spaced incisors.

Terry's right foot bounced compulsively, as if the leg would walk out on its own if not duly restrained.

"May I see your portfolio?" she asked. "Emilio tells me you are quite prolific."

With an inarticulate grunt, he proffered a large, gray folder that contained photos of his paintings. When she failed to take it, he finally looked up at her face. She was examining him with evident curiosity.

"Emilio tells me you're a fisherman."

He nodded.

"You have developed an eye for water," she observed, glancing at the first few images. "Tell me about these," she commanded, holding up a couple of sketched attempts to capture Vormis' face in a stream.

He blushed and shook his head. "I, uh, I don't know. I just try to paint what I see. Or...imagine." Again, he averted his eyes from her face.

"Terry," she asked. "Are you nervous about being here?"

"Nah."

Her silent pause effectively recaptured his attention.

"What, then?" she demanded.

Panic rose in his gut, as was evidenced by the increased vigor of his right foot's beat. "I don't know. I guess I'm not used to any of this. Look..." He stood. "Maybe I ought to go. Thanks for looking at my stuff."

Her laugh was a frightening, chaotic discord. "Mr. Gillis. Sit down. I am not going to bite." He shuddered at the image thus evoked of her oversized chompers.

"Your work shows talent, what we call vision. If you have an interest in eventually showing and selling your paintings— which no one will ever force you to do, believe me," she laughed again, and he cringed—"I can help you. I make it a practice to promote developing artists." She handed him her card. "Keep painting. Come show me what you have got from time to time. When you come up with a saleable piece, I'll hang it up front for you."

She stood and extended her hand with a smile. "Call me when you're ready."

* * *

Snarrow is brooding. Or that's how Mabel interprets his recent pale green predilection.

"The longer we work with this lifestream's transfer, the more I come to resemble him," he complains.

Mabel laughs. "What now?" His attractive flash reminds Mabel of lightning.

"Don't you find it discouraging that we do our part—we boost him, strip him, configure and reconfigure—and those aspects outside our jurisdiction keep trying to recreate the past?"

She studies him for a long time. "There is something you are telling me here. I wonder if it is the part about the lifestream or about you?"

He sighs. "Mabel, I am not getting the point of the project. Out of the blue we are given a task that stretches our resources to the utmost, and that changes our own format and structure. We are asked to get creative. To break barriers. And we do. Our little Frankenstein survives the laboratory, but its indwelling human soul turns out to be reactionary. Left to his own initiative, Terry would revert to an earlier program in an instant."

Snarrow focuses intently on Mabel. "I do not perceive any of this joy and celebration that we are incessantly exhorted to cultivate. And," he adds, "the creativity bit? I'm out of ideas. Dry. Mabel, you work with subpersonalities. Do you not experience the futility of this whole task?"

"You have taken on a share of their mentation," she marvels, sweetening the air. "Snarrow, dear, is that necessary?"

He shakes his head. "I am not sure that I can help it. I think it might be part of the process. Most unpleasant."

Mabel's field dims. "Snarrow, that does not sound right. You are resonating with a lower vibration, and retaining it. That is how the lifestreams make themselves sick."

"I know it, Mabel. The whole experience is unaccountably peculiar."

The two lightworkers share a sudden blaze of insight. "Creative Works?" Mabel asks at the same moment as Snarrow exclaims, "They wouldn't!"

* * *

Snarrow's state has quickly become the focal point of office talk. "It's downright odd is what it is," is Pryluck's opinion.

Creative Works denies having had a hand in it, although Diamond Hoops is highly amused. "How can you tell he is any different now than he ever has been?"

"Oh, really," Mabel clucks.

Millicent makes an incandescent appearance. *"Maybe each of us responds to influxes of rarified vibration in our own unique manner. Perhaps what we are witnessing in Snarrow is an exaggeration of a predisposition."*

Mabel isn't so sure. *"Well then, do you suppose that Bulista and I are predisposed to memory lapses?"*

This strikes Diamond Hoops as hilarious. His cartwheel creates a spray of sparks.

"No, I suppose not," replies Millicent, *"although the ongoing transformation has obviously affected you. As is the case with all of us. On the whole I find it quite flattering."*

Vormis hovers at the edge of the group. *"You know,"* he offers, *"Snarrow is exhibiting signs of sympathetic resonance. It's a human trait. And one that is not uncommon during the early, denser, phases of field guide training. We lower our vibration to match and blend with that of our lifestream, and then pull them up with us to a higher level. We sometimes call it the drowning swimmer rescue."*

Blank stares meet Vormis' comment. Mabel insists, *"Vormis, Snarrow is not a field guide. He has never been human. How, never mind why, could he possibly penetrate the field, or even come vibrationally close enough to get stuck in this lifestream's patterning?"*

Snarrow himself interrupts his co-Workers' speculations. *"I would like to call a strategy meeting,"* he announces. *"Alright,"* he concedes upon noting the retracted fields of his co-Workers. *"I need to call a strategy meeting. Look, I am not oblivious to my current situation. I will need you all to work with me, to help me through this process. I think it is all about collaboration, now more than ever."*

*   *   *

Cara awoke with the residue of a dream dominating her mind. She could not recall any details, but a flavor remained, like the aftertaste of a nondescript meal, heavy on the garlic. Something about the dream demanded expression. She spent the morning with her flute, trying to capture the dream's essence.

Later, she agreed to meet with Terry. He apparently had some kind of news he wanted to share. They ambled, following their most common route past the zoo and ultimately down toward the beach.

Near the top of the hill, they passed a yard where a large pine tree had been recently felled. Cara bent to inhale the fresh cut scent and touch her tongue to a drop of resin that still oozed from a wounded branch. Straightening again, her eyes rested on the broad vista that overlooked the bay.

"This is it!" she gasped. "I dreamed this place. I was standing on this stump enjoying the view." She closed her eyes, remembering. "But it wasn't you with me, I don't think. D was there, and someone else." She held the rest of her remembrance to herself, but remained pensive.

Terry was full of his own untold story. He bristled with annoyance at her withdrawn attention.

Nearing the beach, she stopped and touched his arm. "You wanted to talk about something, didn't you?" Her blue gaze was intense and, as always, mesmerizing.

He shrugged, and nodded with a tentative half-smile.

"God," she said. "It's just I had this dream. A mind-blowing dream."

He thought her stare might burn a trail through his brain. Suddenly she laughed. "I think you might get it."

* * *

Millicent beckons Mabel. Agleam, she invites her friend to observe the dreaming lifestream. "You once asked me what it means to celebrate fear," she says. "Look at this."

Cara stood on a slightly elevated structure, thoroughly enjoying both the expansive view and the sensation of height. The vista from this perch encompassed a multidimensional existence. Two other women—*Mabel thinks she recognizes one as Dolores*—stood nearby.

Desiring to share her experience with her friends, Cara opened her mind toward them. As if in loving assistance, first one woman and then the other gently directed Cara's attention to places in her own being where fear resided.

Cara was casually aware of the fear, but in the sole context that it belonged to a rather insignificant bit of human mind-stuff, bound by a narrow set of beliefs and conditions. She observed fear's coexistence with other aspects of herself that were fully supported and connected on so grand a scale that all was clearly in order. All OK. Nothing to do. Ecstatic joy was the only option.

Cara wanted to share the revelation with her friends. But, with a dreamer's uncanny vision she observed each woman's essence and knew there was nothing to say. Each would be able to perceive no more than the slice of self that shows up limited and flawed.

"We all see different scenery," she realized just before she woke.

As if by telepathy, Jim was back on the scene. Terry

answered his call, thrilled by the coincidence. "Hey, Jim, I almost called you the other night!"

Once again, the glory of Terry's news was pre-empted. "Mira's gone," Jim told him.

"Gone? What do you mean?"

"She went back to her wife."

At first, struck by Jim's dejected tone, Terry failed to note the peculiarity of the statement. When he caught it, his feelings reeled. Amusement over Jim's phrasing collided with the inherent meaning of his words. Twisted gender definition elicited a corresponding twist in Terry's gut, not unlike his predominant state of anxiety during his stay at Ricki's Halfway. He said nothing while he waited out the impulse to laugh, to curse, to hang up.

Eventually he managed, "Does that mean she is, uh, reversing the reversal?"

"She never went through with the surgery. She stopped the hormones a few months back and went into therapy. Her therapist thought she had unfinished business with her family. I'm pretty messed up over things." Jim's voice faded.

Terry had no idea what to say. "Remember Tull, from Ricki's?" he finally asked. "I've seen him a few times."

"You have? No kidding. Well. How've you been?"

Meeting as planned on the street outside Terry's apartment, Cara and Dolores groaned. "No, Terry. If you want to take us to dinner, The Oyster's Pearl won't cut it. How about we all pitch in and go somewhere..." Their eyes met and they giggled, "...where the food is edible. Non-toxic." More giggles.

At this dinner, Terry intended to finally announce and celebrate his first sale of a painting. The three of them, along with

Tull, ended up at the downtown café where Cara had first met Terry's friends, Jim and Mira.

"Have you heard from those two?" Cara asked.

Tull was stunned upon hearing Terry's recent news of Jim. "Are you talking about Jim and Mira from Ricki's?" Tull asked. "They got together? And visited here?"

"That's right, of course you know them too," Cara reflected.

"I didn't realize Jim had it in him," mused Tull. "The whole business must have really messed with his head. Good man," he added.

"What about you, Tull?" Terry mumbled.

Tull smiled. "Me? Am I a good man?"

"Do you have it in you or what? How come you work with the guys at Ricki's?"

Tull's smile broadened. "Ha! You've been dying to ask that for a long time. Alright, I go to Ricki's because they ask me to... and pay me to. I was friends with the guy who founded the place. As to my sexual preference, I've explored possibilities, like Mira and Jim were apparently doing, but I'm primarily hetero."

Terry's forehead creased. "What the fuck does primarily hetero mean?"

"It means that for some of us, divisions and definitions are less rigid than they are for others," he said gently.

Tull studied Terry's face for a long time before he ventured, "Why do you suppose you've become, and remained, close to the fringe characters that you have? You didn't just escape from Ricki's when you learned what it was. You made lasting friends with some pretty off-center kind of guys. And when you wanted counseling you called me, of all the myriad therapists available."

Terry's face darkened. "What are you implying?"

Dolores fiddled with her fork.

"Get this straight," Tull said. "I am not suggesting anything about your manhood, I'm not your father and I don't give a hoot which way you swing. But I am curious about the company you choose to keep—that's a compliment, ladies—in light of the image you prefer to project."

Cara took Tull's and Dolores' hands, and spoke brightly. "I love the company Terry keeps. We're a fine, quirky bunch." She turned to Terry. "Tell us about your painting."

* * *

"But," Mabel asks, "is celebrating fear really just putting it in its proper perspective?"

Millicent glimmers. "I don't know. My lifestream's dream simply brought to mind your question. It's funny. Fear is so minor a concern for her and such a major one for yours."

"Yes," agrees Mabel. "It is a fortuitous combination." The two link arms and allow their rainbow edges to merge companionably. "May the lifestreams figure it out for themselves."

"Has your work with the lifestream continued to undergo revision?" Millicent wonders.

"Naturally," Mabel affirms. "He has begun to run a bit more independently. With him self-coordinating now in several areas, direct intervention on our parts is less essential, and we are beginning to revert to a more natural, supportive role. It is a relief after relying on emergency measures for so long."

Millicent murmurs, "That's interesting. I would have thought that things would change more dramatically."

"Of course," adds Mabel, "a swing toward normal simply addresses your question of how we work with him. Really, every aspect of our realities has changed since the project began, and

is continuing to do so. In that sense, I would say the divisions between him and all of us are breaking down. Poor Snarrow seems, bizarrely, to be caught in the middle of that process."

"Poor Snarrow," Millicent chuckles. "Do you think he might transmigrate down to become a field guide? Or even do a turn as a lifestream?"

Mabel sputters, "But it is not possible for us to take on form! At least it never was before."

* * *

Cara would not be contained. She was delighted at Terry's description of Mrs. Leticia Thorpe and immediately begged to meet her.

Terry stared, exasperated. "Here I am trying to tell you about my traumatic encounter with a grotesque old monster and you act like she's some kind of cuddly bunny." He grinned. "You should've seen her teeth. I felt like Little Red Riding Hood."

Cara pretended to pout. "You see? It's not fair. You meet all these fascinating people." Dropping the tease, she grew contemplative. "You know, Tull has a point. It's like you're surrounded by more color or something than most people."

Dolores, silent up until now, had nevertheless been intently focused on some spot near, not on, Terry's face. "This woman is important, Terry. Get over your resistance. You need her input as a stepping stone into your future."

Her gaze relaxed and she faced him with a half-smile. "So don't be a narrow-minded dodo."

~ 37 ~

The natural result of Terry's extended unemployment finally came to pass. By May, he had run out of money. It was back on Gilli's Girl by day, and painting in the studio by night. Therapy was on hold, at least through the summer.

At first, Bill had mixed feelings about the situation. He noticed changes. Terry moved more slowly than he used to, and seemed more responsive to his surroundings, attending to details he would have previously overlooked. He'd pause in his work to listen to the wind, examine the texture of a fish's fin, and of course, watch the water. It challenged Bill's patience to adjust his work style to Terry's current rhythm.

After some mutual initial caution, and with concessions on both their parts, the two settled into a new pattern together. Over time, the dance became increasingly harmonious.

"Thirty seven years ago, man. Mom's belly was about to burst. We're getting close," Bill said.

Terry laughed. "No way you remember Mom's belly."

"I sure do. She was scary. Shit, they carted me off and abandoned me at Aunt Edna's that night. All they told me was the baby's coming. That would be you."

"Bullshit. You were only three years old."

"Three and a half. Memory is funny, isn't it? What's the first thing you remember?"

"Geez, I have no idea."

"By the way, Fran wants to have a party for your birthday."

"Give me a break. What does she want to do that for?"

Bill grunted while straining at a net before answering. "I

don't know, probably an excuse to have a family do." He opened the squirming, flopping net onto the deck and grinned. "And she probably wants a chance to rub elbows with your girl."

Terry leaned against a crate, an idleness that compelled Bill to take a deep breath to calm his temper. "Who, Dolores? We're not really seeing each other anymore."

Bill gave him a sharp glance. "That's the first time I heard you admit you ever were seeing her."

Terry finally bent to sort the catch. "Well, it was never the kind of thing everybody wanted to make it into. We're friends I guess, but we haven't slept together in a while. It's probably better for her that way," he added with no detectable rancor or regret. "It'll make it easier for her to find a guy."

Bill set down the fish he had grabbed and examined his brother. "What, you don't qualify?"

Terry smiled at him. "Nah, I don't want to be nobody's guy."

Bill tossed the undersized rockfish overboard. "Confirmed bachelor, is it?"

"Yeah, whatever. Fran can invite Dolores if she wants to."

Both Dolores and Cara came to Fran's party, which turned out to be more of a family gathering. Fran's sister showed up with her family, as did the youngest Gillis brother, Fred, who was now out of work but otherwise untouched by his drug infraction. School age cousins played dolls with Tracey, starring Tracey in the role of living doll.

Before five o'clock, Terry proposed a move. "Let's go out on the Girl for sunset."

Fran and her sister protested. Too stinky and cold.

Dolores and Cara weren't keen on the idea either. Wrinkling her nose, Cara slid an arm around Terry's waist. "You guys go ahead. You're used to freezing your buns out at sea." She and Dolores each gave him a birthday kiss and left.

Fred was next to bow out. "Yeah, happy birthday, Ter. I'm gonna pass on the boat."

"You wuss," came the routine brotherly accusation.

"Looks like it's the two of us," Bill told Terry. "Take one of my sweaters. The girls have a point about the cold."

They sat at anchor in the harbor, savoring the last of sunset. With a grin, Bill dug out a small package Fran had tucked into his bag. "In your honor, bro," he said, unwrapping Chocolate Decadence and pulling out a small bottle of champagne.

Twilight faded to darkness, and stars began to emerge. The merest crescent of a moon appeared, resurrected for another month. Beyond the harbor, an occasional boat passed like a satellite along the horizon. Bill relaxed back onto the deck to stargaze.

Terry's attention remained on the water. "I've been hearing a motor. I think someone's out there."

"Mm," Bill conceded.

"Where are they? I don't see any lights, do you?" Puzzled, Terry tried to relax beside his brother. He could not. "I swear it's getting louder. It's got to be a boat." He got up and walked over to the rail.

"Holy shit!" Bill heard Terry's shout in near synchrony with a chorus of similar shouts from off port side. A beam-shaking thud followed, splintering the rail of Gilli's Girl and setting wave upon wave to wash over the deck. At port side, suddenly illuminated sidelights revealed the presence of a large pleasure boat. Curses, whimpers and "oh my God's" could be heard from inside the cruiser.

Bill was incensed. "What the fuck were you thinking, running with no lights? Get your asses out here, will you?"

A disheveled, red-haired man wearing only boxer shorts and a wool sweater staggered from the cabin. Clearly disoriented, he steadied himself against the doorframe. Through the open door, Bill could hear a woman's heavily slurred reprimands. An overwhelming gust of booze and cigarettes wafted outside.

They were blitzed. Bill was nearly mute with rage. "Where the hell is your captain?" he managed. Reflexively looking for support, he turned and realized he was alone on the boat.

"Terry!" he shouted. And again. No answer. He ran the length of the trawler, calling Terry's name as he completed a visual search.

"My God, he's not here. You, inside! We have a man overboard. Can you help?" No response. Bill saw that the man who had come out was now slumped on the deck, snoring.

Bill radioed for help before lowering himself into the inflatable dinghy. He circled the two boats, searching the waters with a flashlight and continuing to call out to Terry. Neither the cold nor the tight band that gripped his chest and throat, and strangled his cries, touched his awareness. Time stopped, telescoped down to a world bounded by the circumference of a flashlight beam.

At last, a Coast Guard cutter arrived, and searchlights joined their world to Bill's. The Coast Guard saw him first, floating face down, just the roundness of his sweater billowing above the surface.

* * *

Lightworkers congregate, filling and surrounding the ambulance in its race to the hospital. Pryluck pops into their circle. "That's that, then," he chirps. "I'll go ahead and snatch him."

"Pryluck, NO!"

Too late. Life support monitors flat-line. Methods Workers are all over Pryluck. Even Creative Works is displeased. "For heaven's sake, Pryluck, no way was that your call to make! You'll have to get us out of this...oh, hello, Terry."

* * *

From the black soundlessness of the void appears a star-like point of light. It expands, drawing Terry's dispassionate attention. As the light begins first to touch and then to engulf his sense of self, he feels the cares and concerns of life fall away, to be replaced by a wash of exquisite peace.

Further into the brilliance arises an ocean of love beyond all earthly experience. He steeps blissfully, all his senses ecstatically yielding to the experience. After a timeless eon, he becomes aware of images. People? No, some kind of luminous beings. More love emanates from them, pulsing through his already sated being. A familiar face appears, by now portrayed in countless paintings—familiar, and at long last wholly visible.

"Hello, Terry."

"Vormis."

* * *

One by one, Methods Workers embrace Terry with great tenderness. Pryluck, who has relinquished nearly all form as is requisite to his Creative Works training, reverts to his former Methods image so as to be visible to the lifestream.

"Hello, Terry, remember me? Um, ahem, you see, we

weren't supposed to let you body drop..." Pryluck feels his colleagues' mind-link pinch him hard. "Uh, my mistake, actually. So, listen, you've pulled through everything thus far and you've gotten it pretty much together...more or less...so what say you go back and pick up where you left off? The water was cold enough that you have some time yet. If you go soon, there'll be no brain damage."

Terry receives Pryluck's proposal with less than full comprehension. He does, however, understand the part about being asked to return to life in a drowned and hypothermic body. "You want me to leave?" he protests. "Why would anyone ever want to go back?"

Compassionate peach suffuses Methods. Mabel is at his side. "We know, Terry. It takes a special fortitude to go through the human experience. We cannot force you, but we hope it might afford you a different and more tolerable existence to know we are always with and behind you."

"Will I know that if I go back?"

Mabel faces the technies.

"I think his consciousness has attained the capacity to retain a significant portion of this encounter. Enough to matter, anyway," is Barwin's assessment.

Mabel twinkles at Terry. "It sounds like there is a pretty good chance, dear. Worst-case scenario is that, at the very least, you will know us in your dreams. But we have something for you to see before you make your decision."

Terry's perspective shifts. In place of Mabel and Methods headquarters, there wafts a group of delicately hued, buoyant beings. Some appear in forms that resemble children. One reminds Terry of a magnificent peacock, but translucent as a dragonfly's wing.

Millicent greets him warmly. "Terry. Hello." She extends her hands and he feels himself engulfed in effervescent joy. "We guide a friend of yours," she tells him. "Her lifework and yours have become intertwined, one for the other."

Terry becomes aware of an Earth-time bar where Cara is performing with her band mates and emanating, as Terry can now see, a radiant display of pink, gold and turquoise, not unlike the appearance of her guides. As he watches, he feels himself expand until he can scarcely tolerate his sense of intense appreciation.

"She has kept me alive!" he exclaims before realizing the irony. "How can I ever return even a fraction of what she has given me?"

At once, his field of vision shifts to encompass the cold, limp body he has recently departed. A very stressed and self-important EMT frantically fusses over the corpse. From Terry's current vantage point, the medic appears to be making romantic overtures to a dead fish. He marvels, "What a funny bunch humans are."

"Utterly true."

Terry hears Pryluck's reply, although he can no longer see him.

"You all furnish us with eons of entertainment." Pryluck hardly pauses. "Sorry, old man, but we've received clearance to give you the boot."

Mabel and Millicent move in close. Mabel places an affectionate hand on Terry's face. "It is due to your soul's concern for Cara," she tells him. "Remember us, and come visit sometimes."

"Right," adds Vormis. "Don't make yourself a stranger."

* * *

Bill was sure he detected movement. He bent closer and cried out, "He's having a convulsion!" At the same moment the medic noticed a jump on the heart monitor.

The EMT pivoted to attend to Terry and stared, arrested in mid-motion. "That is not a convulsion," he pronounced slowly. "I think he's laughing."

IV

Back from the Dead

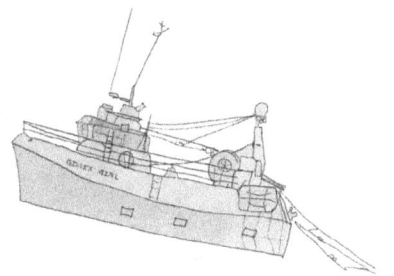

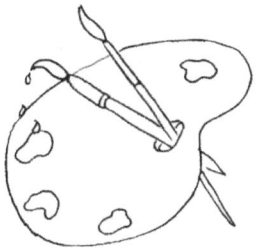

~ 38 ~

Fran arrived, breathless and shaken. Bill met her in the hallway. "They revived him on the way here. They're waiting for test results, but they think he'll be OK."

She collapsed into her husband's long embrace. "Are you alright?" she asked tearfully.

"I'm OK. Still a little shocked," he admitted. "And tired. Are you ready to go in and see him?"

"How bad is it?" she wondered.

"He's conscious, Fran. Fully alert, but kind of banged up. He looks pretty pale and bloated. There are some broken ribs and a dislocated shoulder. They're still checking for internal injuries. In a way, though, he acts like he's in better shape than we are."

Fran could see recognition in Terry's eyes as she entered the room. "Hello, Terry," she said, not sure whether she actually saw or imagined his smile. To her, his face appeared shockingly distorted. When she reached the bedside, however, an unmistakable grin transformed the doughy flesh.

"Sister-in-law." His voice was a raspy whisper. "How'd they get you in here alive?" he joked, alluding to her fear of and utter aversion to hospitals.

She took his hand, both laughing and crying. "Because of you," she told him. "I'll get you for that."

Bill pulled up a chair to sit beside her.

"Your fault," Terry croaked. "You gave me death by chocolate."

Horrified, Fran watched his body begin to shake, until she recognized the tremors as laughter. "God, Terry, how can you joke about that? Bill told me you were dead." She started to cry.

Bill pulled her onto his lap. "Shh, it's alright now," he murmured.

Terry watched them, the smile never leaving his swollen face. When Fran had quieted, he told her, "I was."

"What?" She asked.

"I was dead," he said and resumed his laughter.

Fran looked from Terry to Bill. Bill shrugged wearily.

"It was wonderful." Terry's laughter turned into weak sobs. Two days later, he asked to see Dolores.

Cara and Dolores had not heard the news of Terry's accident until Dolores received the summons to his bedside. The two friends were at the psychic institute sharing tea when Fran phoned.

"I'm sorry I didn't call sooner. I've been...it's been crazy..." Her voice trailed off until she managed to get control of herself. "Anyway, he and Bill are alright. It's a good thing we didn't all decide to go out with them that night. You didn't have some kind of premonition, did you?"

Dolores sighed. "No. What is his room number? I can go see him in the morning."

"Actually," Fran told her, "they're releasing him tomorrow. I should've said. He'll stay with Bill and me for a few days. Could you come to our house?"

"Sure, I'll come by."

Dolores turned to Cara. "Terry had a near-death the night of his party. A drowning." Her eyes welled up. "Fran wanted to know if I had a premonition."

Cara put an arm around her friend's shoulder. "D, don't. You're not supposed to be anything more than human." She paused and then asked, "Is Terry OK?"

The scene at Fran and Bill's house resembled a second birthday party, with people coming in, out and congregating. Terry held audience in the spare bedroom, graciously receiving visitors.

They gossiped about him around the kitchen table.

"He's different," Fran advised Dolores.

Her brother-in-law Fred snorted, "Always was different."

Fran slapped his arm. "Asshole. No, it's true. He's nicer."

Bill agreed with Fran. "He really is. It's like he's constantly stoned or something."

"Is he on painkillers?" Fred asked.

"No, he won't take anything." Bill turned to Dolores. "Come on. We'll kick the nephews out of there. He wants to see you alone."

She followed him up to Terry's bedroom. The door closed behind her. With a smile, Terry held out his left arm. The right one remained close at his side, although she noticed that hand, too, was extended in welcome.

"Dolores. Come here." He made space at the side of the bed where she sat beside him. He continued to grin at her.

Bill was right. Terry did appear stoned. There was a wide, drunken or maybe a hot quality to his smile. "How are you doing?" she asked him.

His smile intensified. He put his hand against her cheek. "Dolores. I was there." His voice broke as he declared, "I never knew how…blessed…you are."

She met his gaze with interest. "Where were you?"

He shook his head and shrugged. "Wherever. Maybe a wild dream. But I get it now, how being in life is so narrow and sad if you don't know or see, or here's the funny part—if you don't *believe* the rest of the picture. It's like there's some kind of conspiracy going on. We're surrounded by all this fantastic support all the time, but everyone—I think even a lot of the priests and them—is scared shitless thinking we're all on our own, that it's up to us to run the whole show. Everybody thinks so. Why is that?"

She rolled her eyes.

Terry took her hand. "Dolores, what happened to you? Did you die, too?"

It took a moment for her to register how he had arrived at the question. "No," she answered with a slight smile. "I was born weird."

His hand returned to her face. "I can't thank you enough for everything. You've been unbelievably patient with me. So kind." His eyes brimmed. "I think you're some kind of saint."

She took his hand between hers and shook her head. "Terry," she told him. "I'm like a postal employee, a letter carrier. I transmit information from one place to another." She dropped her gaze, holding onto his hand like a lifeline. "I've never had the kind of experience you had. I maybe have passing moments where I touch that higher vibe." She paused as if changing internal channels. "Those contacts comfort and sustain me. But to me, it has never been that all-encompassing, life-changing expansion kind of thing. I envy you that, Terry, but I can't quite take it in."

He gathered her to him as best he could, gingerly holding her on his left side and touching his lips to her forehead. They remained that way in silence until her breathing slowed and synchronized with his.

Terry stayed on at Bill and Fran's longer than anyone expected, and did not seem at all anxious to leave. Recalling his previous stay, Fran was incredulous. "I love having Terry around," she marveled. "Can you believe the difference between last summer and now?"

Bill grunted in agreement. "It is strange, isn't it? Almost like he's a different person. I mean he's got to be in pain, right? His ribs are broken. But you would never know that anything bothers him. I don't think I've ever seen him act so happy."

"Maybe he appreciates life more now because he came so close to dying," Fran speculated. "Like knowing the value of something you almost lose sort of thing."

"Who knows?" Bill got up to pour a glass of milk for Tracey. "He don't talk about it."

What Terry did do was play with Tracey—by the hour, and with uncharacteristic patience. And he appeared to genuinely enjoy it more than anything except his painting. Always strictly right-handed, Terry now had to use his left. A stack of discarded attempts piled up as his body learned a new sort of coordination. To the amazement of friends and family, he remained unbothered by the reeducation process and laughed frequently at the stilted, angular results of his efforts.

In time, the left-handed strokes became smoother and freer. The ribs and shoulder healed, and Terry continued to paint with his left hand.

* * *

Snarrow, Mabel and Bulista, together with the field guides, traverse a simulated prairie. "Don't you love the way these grasses bend and flow like water?" One of the older field guides holds a deep, abiding appreciation for Earth, which has led to his frequent indulgence in creating wilderness replicas, such as this one.

Vormis reclines, eyes closed, to relish the experience. "You've even captured the smell of it."

Snarrow and Mabel try their best to vicariously absorb and assimilate the field guides' familiarity with physical sensation.

Resonating strongly now with his human memories, the old guide slaps Snarrow on the back and says, "There's nothing like a good trauma to snap a lifestream to attention."

"I suppose," Snarrow tentatively agrees.

Ever since Terry's brush with death, and to everyone's relief, Snarrow seems to have almost wholly recovered his innate disposition.

"It is better if they can make changes more consciously, but when all else fails..."

"He is less concerned about his body now," notes Vormis.

"He is less concerned about everything," answers Snarrow. "But that will wear off. And then, some of his life focus will have to be taken up with the residuals."

"What residuals?" Vormis asks in concert with Bulista's question, "Why will it wear off?"

Snarrow looks from one to the other. "The residual healing process. His consciousness is not sufficiently aligned with the physical tissues as to facilitate rapid healing. He will have to go about it in accordance with the prevailing medical paradigm."

Vormis muses, "But with all the changes he has already undergone, why would he not be able to intuit his body's ability to heal at once?"

Mabel answers, "He has no template in place for that idea to shape itself around. We will initialize the process, but he will have to walk through the steps to learn the concept on a concrete basis."

She then turns to Bulista. "The euphoria will wear off because it always does. At first, lifestreams who come to us and then return to their lives walk around in love with the world. But gradually, they resume a resonance with their own dimensional environment. The longer they are able to maintain the heightened state, the more likely they are to retain memory of the experience, and to be functionally changed by it." With a gleam she adds, "We ought to make the most of his current lowered resistance."

* * *

Bill was having a harder time than was his brother in the aftermath of their accident. For one thing, Terry's injuries were physical and obvious, whereas Bill's was an insidious trauma. Constantly on edge, his sleep was haunted by images of lifting Terry's blue and lifeless face from the water. With no other focus or outlet for his nervous energy, Bill reported updates on the legal investigation that surrounded the incident, almost on a daily basis.

Terry listened with minimal interest.

"They're pressing charges against the boat owner now, to try to get someone to talk."

Terry looked up from his painting—an oil overlay of celestial light on a pristine seascape. "Why the owner? I thought it was a bare bones charter. The owner wasn't even on board."

"Right," answered Bill, "but they want to put pressure on everyone connected, to get someone who was on board to talk. Nobody admits to being on watch. Nobody will account for what was going on with the captain or mate and nobody admits to going below to party, with the fucking boat on automatic pilot. Coming into harbor, for Christ's sake! And the dumb-ass prosecutor can't even make up his mind what to charge them all with."

Terry laughed. "Helluva challenge to stick a manslaughter charge with the alleged victim living five miles away."

Bill smiled. "Yeah, he's probably wishing you'd have stayed dead and kept his life simple."

"Yeah," Terry said lightly. "Me too." He sighed and looked at Bill. "Hey, would you find out where Cara's playing this weekend? I need to see her."

"Why don't you just call her?" Bill asked.

"I can't. Help me out here, will you?"

Turned out, Cara was playing for a private party. Uninvited, Terry was obliged to wait until she was free. Which ended up being nearly two days later.

Fran received Cara in the kitchen and sent her up to the guest room, which had all but officially become Terry's personal studio. She stood just inside the door, taking in the array of paintings in various stages of completion.

Terry set down his brush and faced her.

With characteristic insight, she allowed him a moment of transition, watching his eyes eventually refocus on the here and now. Even so, she noted that his eyes were different from before the boating accident. Always arresting for their color, the green had acquired a layering of light that reminded her of sun-drenched tropical oceans. More remarkable was the calmness of his expression. The former anxious vulnerability was gone.

She hugged him carefully. "How are you feeling?"

"Great. Glad to see you." His glance searched her face. "I..." He laughed. "Shit, I don't know what to say. I need to tell you something."

She offered the crook of her arm. "Are you walking these days?"

"Yeah, OK. Let's walk."

They left the house and walked to the beach in silence. She took a tentative stab. "You've been painting. I haven't seen much of you since your party."

His response was an oddly intense, if not quite confused look. He steered her out onto the jetty. Waves broke, showering the two with icy spray. Footing was hazardous on the slick, algae-covered rocks. Cara smiled to herself. Terry was evidently unfazed by his near drowning.

They sat at the far end of the jetty, surrounded by the swirling waters. Terry closed his eyes and breathed deeply. He seemed to imbibe water and wind like a sea god, at ease in his domain. He spoke softly, his voice blending with the ocean's own. "I want to tell you about what happened to me that night."

Stillness engulfed them during a long period of silence before he eventually continued. "Dying was amazing. There's this incredible love—not like anything here—all the stuff that matters here, all the worry, just disappears. There's nothing like it." Terry's voice came in halting spurts, radioactively charged with emotion.

"A lot of it is like a dream. I can only remember pieces... some images." He waved his hand. "It's like a general impression without many details." He sat quietly again, with his head bent forward. When he resumed his narrative, Cara had to lean in closer to hear him.

"They wanted to send me back, but I had a choice. I wanted to stay." He began to sob. Her hand rested on his back, but she made no move to interrupt his momentum.

"It was you—something about you that they showed me, or maybe said—that brought me back. I don't remember." At last, he raised his head and attempted a smile. "It would probably help if I knew what I'm supposed to do with or about you, but I don't remember."

Her face held the crackling intensity it always did when she listened, but Cara felt something at her core contract at his words. She forced herself to stay focused. "Who are the 'they' you're talking about?"

He shook his head. "I don't know, really. They aren't people the way we are. But you know that face I keep seeing, the one I try to paint? He was there. Vormis. He's some kind of spirit guide or something. It's too much. I don't know what to do with it all."

She studied him. "You paint it, don't you?"

He laughed. "I try. Not even close. But yeah, it's coming. I can capture more of the other side when I use my left hand. Weird, huh? What I can't do yet is show, or even say what it's like to be in that love. Totally carefree. Other people should know about it. It would make it easier for them to be here.

"I mean, growing up I was taught all about Heaven and Hell." He fixed her with his gaze. "You know me, I should have gone straight to Hell when I died, right? But it's not that way." His face relaxed and his thoughts now flowed more freely. "I've wondered a lot about that, you know? Like maybe I *was* judged, and going to Hell was having to come back into my messed up body. But that's the thing. I can't remember exactly how it happened, but I do know that they didn't make me leave. It was somehow my choice, and the choice was based on something about you."

"Well," she said gently. "That's pretty heavy."

"Yeah, I guess so."

Despite the nervous tension in her belly, she grinned slyly. "I still don't want to have sex with you," she told him.

He laughed. "That's a relief."

~ 39 ~

National news somehow picked up the story, and the Gillis brothers' fight for anonymity was on. "Pain in the ass reporters," Bill grumbled, slamming the receiver back onto its base.

"How do they find us, anyway?" Terry asked. "It's the accident lawyers that really get to me. They're like sharks."

"I bet they're paying off someone at the hospital, probably a records clerk or something," Bill speculated.

"I'm thinking of leaving until it blows over, "Terry told him.

"Leave where? They'll find your apartment as easy as they found our house."

"No, I mean leave the city. I can go out to Preston for a while." Terry did not miss the flicker of panic in his brother's eyes.

"What about your physical therapy?" Bill protested.

"I can have Wanda massage my shoulder. It'd do a lot more good than those machines down at the hospital. All else they do in therapy is give me exercises, which I do at home anyway." He added casually, "Look, why don't you come out and visit for a day or two? We can fish, relax, get away from all the buzz."

Bill hesitated. "I don't know, Ter. You're going to need to testify at some point. I don't think you ought to just leave."

"Fuck 'em! They almost stole my life one time, I'm not handing it over to anyone now. If I have to be here, I'll run my own show." He softened his tone. "Bring Fran and Tracey. They'll love Wanda. She's like a country version of Cara."

Terry spent a month with Wanda and Jack. They put him to work. When his injuries limited his effectiveness in the yard and garden, they sent him to the kitchen. Fresh air and activity did him good. With their blessedly short attention spans that allowed Terry time to paint, Wanda and Jack's two young boys were the best kind of company.

Sporadically, Wanda stretched and kneaded his sore body. He told her about his near-death and how Cara was, in some way, responsible for his return.

Wanda slapped him—not too hard—mid effleurage. "You ran away again, didn't you?"

He raised his head from the table. "What do you mean?"

"You came back to life for some woman, and you're hanging out here. How come you're not with her?"

"Wanda, it's not that simple. It's not like we're together. I don't know what I'm supposed to do with her."

They both smiled. He rephrased. "She's an amazing

person. Really intuitive, strong, completely out of my league if I wanted be with her. But it isn't like that. And anyway, she's best friends with Dolores, the woman I was seeing all last year. They're more like sisters."

Wanda sat on the edge of the massage table, stretching Terry's right arm as she worked the contracted tissue beneath the shoulder blade. "You're telling me you came back to life for some chick you're not interested in?"

He sat up, moving away from her hands. "No! She means the world to me. A real lifeline. Cara is just about the only really sane person I know." He lay back down, but one hand found and pinched her hip through the sheet between them. "Not too sure about you," he mumbled.

She laughed. "Don't get fresh with me. I'll sic my big, strong husband on you."

"You better not. I'd whup his ass."

"Alright, Hercules, then how come you're hiding out? What are you afraid of?"

He was quiet for a long time. "I just don't know what it means. I would do whatever I'm supposed to do if I knew what that was."

"How do you expect to find out if you won't have anything to do with her?"

He didn't answer. She worked up his neck to the base of his skull. "You know, it might end up being a small thing, some isolated event. Maybe you'll be there at the exact moment a brick falls from a building and you push her out of the way or something."

He turned his head to give her a twisted smile.

"No, really," she insisted. "We never know how we impact

each others' lives. A lot of times we never even know who we have affected. Maybe you don't need to do anything different."

"What do you mean?" he asked.

"Maybe you already help her or affect her in whatever way you're supposed to. Maybe it doesn't need to be some grand task that you have to figure out."

After dinner, he told her, "I think you might be right. About Cara. I just wish I could remember what seemed important enough for me to agree to come back."

Wanda looked hard into his face. "Would you like to invite her out here?"

"Yeah, I would. I actually asked my brother and his wife, but they're too caught up in the investigation and all. Bill had a pretty bad scare. I think he's having trouble getting past it." Terry bent to put away the last pan. "I would like you to meet Dolores, too. Would you mind if they stayed in the cottage? I can pitch a tent for myself by the stream."

The timing appeared to be orchestrated in Heaven. Or perhaps, a manipulation by Creative Works. The dates Terry proposed for Dolores and Cara to visit in Preston coincided with a retreat at Ricki's, at which Tull was to facilitate.

Dolores had mixed feelings about accepting the invitation to Jack and Wanda's. She did not relish the idea of being away from home in a location where both Terry and Tull would be nearby. Compounding her discomfort was the fact that Tull had also asked her to visit him in Preston after the retreat at Ricki's ended.

Cara's initial reception to Terry's invitation was likewise lukewarm. In the absence of other intervening interests, she preferred city to country charms. And then, Evan showed up with a newspaper clipping about a new music venue just outside of Preston.

"I called these guys," he told Cara and their band mate, Boze. "This place will be bringing in nationally known bands. They're auditioning for opening acts. Let's go for it!"

Wanda and Jack prepared for the additional company by planning an open-fire barbeque. They sent Terry and the kids to collect firewood, and sat down to a bottle of wine. The car on the drive was almost to the house when Jack set down his glass with a long look at Wanda. He stood and held out to her a brown, muscular arm, which she took before stepping out to meet their newest guests.

Midway out of the backseat, Cara gave a slight gasp and froze. Dolores, who had not yet seen their hosts, followed Cara's gaze. The man who faced them was tall, with long brown hair worn loose, a strong, work-weathered body and humor-filled eyes. Dolores rested a hand on Cara's back before they both emerged from the car.

Introductions exchanged, Jack and Wanda regarded Cara. She smiled, regaining her poise, and addressed Jack, "For a minute I thought you were a ghost. You look so much like my... someone I was close to."

Dolores agreed. "You really do. Only Jeb would have been older now."

Terry and the two boys arrived, and chaos ensued.

* * *

"Just what are you doing?" Mabel demands, catching Pryluck alone with Vormis.

"Mabel, darling, relax. You're spewing like a squid."

*Vormis laughs, despite his fondness for Mabel. "It isn't him,"
he reassures her, gesturing toward Pryluck. "This convergence
at Wanda's happened in accordance with the lifestream's own
initiative."*

*"How can you be sure?" she insists. "It has the mark of CW
if you ask me."*

*"Which no one has done," Pryluck points out, his tone
neutral. "Why not simply accept and applaud the synchronicity?"*

*"Because I do not trust your meddling ways," she replies
sweetly. "Really, what could possibly be the point, bringing them
all together?"*

*Vormis marvels at Mabel's attachment to the lifestreams'
play of events. She seems to be exhibiting human attributes, like
Snarrow did during his recent spell. He flushes with compassion.
"Maybe the lifestream is attempting to integrate. Isn't that a major,
and necessary, goal of his transformation?"*

*Mabel seems to snap to a different attention. "Yes, of
course it is. Excuse me," she tells Pryluck. Her field reverts from
inky jet stream to its more customary gold and rosy tones. "I have
been feeling odd lately. Something is in some kind of flux. Have
you noticed it?"*

*Vormis has not. Unable to resist, Pryluck blends with
Mabel, shoulder-to-shoulder and suggests, "Maybe change of life,
dear?"*

She laughs. "You impertinent oaf!"

*He relents. "You could be reacting to another stellar
collision wave. Barwin has mentioned some kind of new pattern
they've detected."*

"And why do some of us appear to be affected and others

do not?" she wonders.

*Pryluck shrugs. "Different frequencies, different resonance?
Who knows?" He regards her with amused affection. "Might as
well enjoy the ride?"*

"Yes," she concedes. "We might as well."

* * *

From the standpoint of compatibility, the barbeque
was a success. The trio both entertained and rehearsed for the
following day's audition. They planned to stay that night and the
next morning, and then to hit the Quail's Tail Alehouse on their
way back to town.

For the moment, the group was a cacophony of percussion
and ecstatic dance, accentuated by pots and spoons, whistles,
shouts, barks and an utterly tone-deaf rooster's crow. The two
young boys savored their integral roles and begged to be taken
on tour.

Boze affirmed, "This group has reached new heights of
excellence with you guys on board, most definitely. The thing is,
we're playing at this place that serves liquor. That means no one
is allowed in unless you're of legal age. How old are you guys?"

Gregory frowned. "I'm almost eleven. He's seven." The
younger boy nodded solemnly.

"Listen, we're gonna have to wait a few years, but that
doesn't mean you should stop practicing. You've got to shout and
stomp and bang on pots and pans with all your spirit whenever
you can."

Wanda grabbed a handful of ice cubes and managed to
slip it under Boze's shirt. The boys banged and shouted with
spirit.

With subtle skill, Cara steered the group indoors after sunset, leaving Dolores and Terry alone to tend the remains of the fire. Jack, Boze and Evan departed for a game of darts at the local tavern.

Terry and Dolores steeped in fire-induced reflection. She felt the near-tangible current between them and sighed. "Terry," she said miserably, "I need to talk. And I don't want to."

"Mm?" he responded. "You don't have to say anything if you don't want to."

She felt a familiar wave of exasperation at his failure to grasp her intention. She drew a breath. "I do have to. What I meant was it's hard for me to talk about this."

"What is it?" he asked with a tenderness that made her cry.

"I've been hanging out more with Tull. Becoming friends. And I feel guilty or bad in some way because of your connection with him, or because of our connection or whatever." He could hear her smile as she continued, "I think he wants that relationship that you were so careful to warn me that you weren't interested in."

"How about you?" Terry asked.

Her voice broke. "I guess I like him. But I'm afraid you might feel hurt if I'm with him. And I still feel like going to bed with you. I think of you that way and it gets in the way of being with him, or anyone else."

He laughed softly and gathered her to him. "That's not such a bad feeling, is it?"

She laughed too, caught up in the numbing sensation as if in wads of cotton. "It's a problem, Terry. I need to be free."

"Yeah, you're right," he told her, mindlessly caressing the

back of her hand. "If that's what you need, I guess we could just be friends. Or not see each other. That would hurt, but I guess it might be easier. It's probably the best thing for us to do."

She leaned against his chest, allowing tears to flow and basking in the fullness of his presence.

"It's alright, D," he told her. "We'll do whatever you want."

"I want you to hold me," she murmured.

In the morning, they lingered in his sleeping bag and amiably agreed they might have a problem. "What do we do now?" he asked sheepishly.

She shook her head and sighed. "Nothing's changed. I still feel the same way about it. Maybe we just need to let things evolve."

His tone was unusually firm and serious. "Dolores, you and Tull are good for each other. I'll be OK with it." He added with a poignant smile, "I love you both, you know."

"I know."

* * *

"There." Pryluck brushes his hands together. "That's done, then."

"What is?" Bulista asks him.

"That chapter. Check out the change in the cords between those two. Whatever their behavior, from here on in, they have made the transition. Wrapped things up."

Vormis rolls his eyes in a fellow field guide's direction and addresses Pryluck. "You all don't begin to get what it's like to have a body."

* * *

With the kids in bed, Wanda gave Cara a warm smile. "Tea?" she proposed.

They shared a large couch, easy in each other's company. "Who was Jeb?" Wanda asked.

Cara met her gaze. "He and I were partners. We had a daughter, fun...a life together. Both of them died in a car crash."

Wanda listened with a still intensity, similar to Cara's own. "You said he looked like Jack?" she prompted.

Cara smiled softly. "Startlingly. You have good taste." After a pause she added, "Only Jeb would be near fifty by now if he had lived. Jack looks more like the age Jeb was when I knew him."

"That must feel strange," Wanda offered.

"It was a shock at first, but not for long. I don't usually think about them much."

Wanda regarded her with interest. "Has there been anyone else since?"

Cara smiled. "Just for fun. It was horribly painful at the time—for a long time—but it's all good now. My life would have been totally different if I had done the mother and family thing. At the time, I didn't want anything other than that. But the way it turned out made me become independent, or whole, in a way I wouldn't have had to until much later in life, if ever. I like my freedom."

They sipped their tea. Cara surveyed the rustic, pillow-laden room. "Terry is quite taken with you all. I can see why." She smiled at Wanda. "You're generous to welcome all of us, too."

"The more the merrier. The way I understand it, it's you he's taken with."

"Yeah, it's kind of odd," Cara mused.

Wanda again felt drawn to the open clarity of Cara's eyes. Their effect was like the restfulness of gazing at a summer sky.

"Terry has an interesting life," Cara observed. "I really liked Terry's friends from Ricki's," she added. "How did you end up working there?"

Wanda looked surprised. "Terry's friends? He introduced you to guys from Ricki's?"

Cara nodded.

"Were they in drag?"

Cara nodded again, solemnly, with latent amusement lighting her eyes. Wanda stared for a moment before they both burst out laughing.

"He probably wouldn't have," Cara told her, "but D and I ran into them in a restaurant. He handled it pretty well."

Wanda was clearly impressed. "He can be incredibly resilient, don't you think?"

Cara agreed. "Yeah, he even did death and resurrection with a lot of grace."

Wanda studied Cara's nonchalance before asking, "Did Terry tell you what made him come back?"

Cara nodded once more, with her chin puckered and brows contracted. "He told you, huh? I hope he doesn't make it into some kind of big deal, you know?"

Wanda spoke gently. "For him, it was the biggest kind of deal. He really wants to do right by his life's purpose and not blow it."

"Yeah, I know." Cara sighed. "But we never do get it right or wrong and anyway, even if we did, how could anyone ever really know that? It's so much easier to just get on with the living and not worry about it all."

~ 40 ~

Bill paced and ranted. "Goddamn dinosaur. He is impossible to reach. Who anymore doesn't have email, for Christ's sake? And check phone messages? Forget that. God forbid he should turn the damn thing on."

He caught sight of Tracey's open-faced stare, and checked his tirade. That he was high-strung since the accident had not escaped his notice.

Fran rinsed the sink, thankful that the disposal's choking fit could drown out Bill's invective. "Maybe they don't get a good signal out in Preston," she suggested.

Bill stopped pacing to consider the possibility. "Well, they've got a land line at the house. Shit, I wish he would just call and check in. Isn't that what any normal person would do?"

Fran lifted Tracey to free her from her high chair. She knew enough to let Bill's snit run its course without a lot of interference.

Terry called later that evening. "I got Bill's messages," he told Fran. "Good news, eh?"

Fran smirked over the receiver, mouthing to Bill, "Terry."

He grabbed the receiver. "Ter, we heard from the owner of the boat. Looks like the guy has had nothing to do, at all, with overseeing his own fucking boat. He's some multi-millionaire who spends most of his time in Brussels or someplace. The captain on board was supposed to be managing charters for the owner, but he pretty much did his own thing for like the last four years. I guess it got completely out of hand. Of course, he's fired.

They're prosecuting him, but the owner has apparently decided to assume full responsibility for damages to the Girl and you. Us actually. He called and wants to come out and meet with you. Us actually, but he wants to talk to you in person."

"Yeah, alright."

"Alright what? When can you get here?"

Terry could not resist needling. "I don't know, when do you think I ought to be there?"

"Shithead! Get your ass here NOW."

Terry laughed. "See you tomorrow night, Bill. Give Tracey my love."

"I'm a God-fearing man," boat-owner Franklin Tudds told them, fixing wide, hazel eyes on Terry's face. "When I heard about what happened to you, I searched my soul and did a lot of praying. I sought counsel from my clergy."

"I thought you were in jail," Bill muttered.

Mr. Tudds faced Bill. "Yes, I was in jail. My incarceration turned out to be a blessing. It brought me back into the fold. I'm sincerely grateful on my own account, but I deeply regret the suffering of your family." He turned once again to Terry, extending his arm for a handshake.

Terry smiled sheepishly, offering his own right hand on an arm that barely reached halfway in front of his body.

Franklin Tudds noticed Terry's limitation and blushed. "I'm sorry I can't give you back the soundness of your limb. That is in God's hands. But I can compensate you for your trauma and loss of wages, and am prepared to offer a lump sum of $1.5 million.

"I am also prepared to pay all expenses related to the

repair of your trawler and," here he faced Bill, "for you and your family's anguish, I would like to extend an additional $500,000. My lawyer has submitted a draft to this effect to your lawyer. I wanted to meet informally, in person, to ask your forgiveness for my negligence."

Terry beamed, unmistakably amused, but gracious. "You have our blessings, Mr. Tudds."

Mr. Tudds visibly relaxed, if a bit too much. Emotion-logged, he was on the verge of gushing gratitude, but Terry was already conducting him to the door.

Back inside, Bill stared at Terry. "Fuck me! He's giving us millions and he thanks us."

"Humans!" Terry laughed.

"What, you don't qualify?"

Terry shook his head, still chuckling. "That's the whole point. I used to think just like him."

Because no legal proceedings had precipitated Franklin Tudds' endowment, they could not technically call it a settlement. In his newfound and still lingering euphoria, Terry customarily referred to it as grace. Upon occasion though, he considered both the windfall and the blissful experience of death itself to be his just due—payback that Vormis and the gang owed him for the ordeal they had put him through.

"Do you think he'll ever get over his anger?" Bulista wonders.

"Why not ask him?" suggests Mabel. "We really ought to be in closer contact while we have the chance."

"And what chance is that?" asks Vormis.

"Vormis, he is as barrier-free as he can get. It is still up to

us to train him to consciously receive and work with us. Anyway, it is what he wants."

"Should we try during dreamtime?"

"No, let us go for conscious contact. The technies said there is a good probability for him to retain it."

"While he paints?"

Diamond Hoops interjects, "Darling, you've just got to be bold and jump right into his daily moments. You were once human. You know the expression, 'grab him by the balls.'"

Bulista looks quizzically at Mabel, who responds with a dismissive shake of her head.

* * *

They take advantage of his heightened sense of pleasure, as Terry nests in the jetty rocks appreciating sea and sky.

"Why not open space between dimensions and project our dimension onto his?" suggests Snarrow. "His brain has the capacity to make sense of the image, now that he has seen us."

What Terry experienced was an abrupt onslaught of light, and a rush of inner warmth that catapulted him out of body into an astral realm.

Vormis is disappointed. "He fragmented."

"So? We shall visit where he is," insists Mabel.

Tentatively and one by one, each manifests their most recognizable form in front of Terry's astral body. He expands to enjoy an exquisite sense of fullness that accompanies the encounter.

Vormis attempts a greeting. "Long time, no see. Don't make yourself a stranger," he reminds him.

Terry's mind receives the thought, which his astral body engulfs like an amoeba ingesting its prey.

The lightworkers maintain a space of golden, rarefied vibration, while Terry blissfully floats, feeding on the light.

"Darling," announces Diamond Hoops in a rare Creative Worker-to-lifestream encounter, "it's time you learned to bring this into your body. Healing TIME!"

Terry heard/felt a crude thud as he reentered waking consciousness. His body gradually reoriented to solid Earth sensations. His mind was somewhat slower to catch up. In the interim before it did, time and space were seemingly suspended in vacuum-like silence, while Terry's senses simultaneously registered the physical world. With satisfied ease, the body sighed.

The sun shone for almost three days running. Parks filled, pasty skin emerged and beaches received the first of the season's pilgrims. Terry sulked in a morass of depression. He missed Dolores, now that she and Tull were exploring time together. Cara, too, was often busy and unavailable. He hadn't been in touch with, or interested in his cronies from The Oyster's Pearl in months. He supposed he was lonely.

Infinitely more disturbing to him was that he could not paint. Since his first Color and Form class, Terry had never before hit a dry spell. Frustrated and uninspired, he felt disconnected from whatever source had once fueled his passion.

When he failed to stop by to play with Tracey for the second consecutive week, Fran insisted there might be something wrong.

"Give him a call if you need to." Bill's absent-minded response emerged from the cabinet beneath the kitchen sink, where he wrestled with a leaking pipe.

"You're not even listening," she complained.

Bill's torso and then his head slid into view. "For Christ's sake, Fran, what's the problem? If you're worried about Terry, you know how to pick up the phone."

She glared at him. "Right, and you expect that he'll answer? Won't you just go over there for me?"

Wrists and hands appeared from the cabinet and Bill sat up. "Look, you go on over if you want. I don't notice anything unusual. He was just here, I don't know, not that long ago. Since when are we supposed to be some kind of close-knit family?"

Fran took a breath and sighed. "Something isn't right," she insisted. "He was so much better lately. And besides, he's your brother. You should take an interest."

Bill smiled despite his exasperation. "You sound like my mother." He got up and put an arm around her. "Why does this matter so much to you?"

She reflected for a moment. "I'm afraid that whatever was wrong with him before the accident might be happening again. And," she bit her lip and reluctantly added, "I like having him around to help with Tracey. She does too."

Bill led her to a chair. "I don't think you should count on him being here, hon. I know you need a break sometimes, but Terry is just an uncle. He's always going to have his own life, girlfriends, his painting and all. You can't depend on him."

She looked sad, but did not answer.

"Listen," he told her, "how about I try this weekend to find out what he's up to?"

Depressed in the outer world, Terry's inner world was rich with dreams and sensation. Flickers of the light realm penetrated his gloom, but never quite emerged with sufficient clarity for him to transpose into any defined visual images. His sense of loss was, at times, overwhelming. One time, he had a hazy glimpse of Vormis. He almost heard his voice, and intuited some kind of encouraging pep talk that bore the lightworkers' energetic stamp, but fell just shy of crystallizing in his mind.

"Fuck this," he eventually told himself, and walked to Madam D's psychic institute. He did not go in, but left a note folded in the door. "I need an appointment. Is that OK? –TG," the message read.

~ 41 ~

Their gathering ignites the ethers in a kaleidoscope of color, sound and texture. Someone projects the image of a grandstand to metaphorically contain the meeting. Waves of amusement set lights a swirl. The atmosphere could have been a carnival at night, attended by every guidance team who has thus far, no matter how insignificantly, cooperated in the lifestream transfer project.

Management sparkles ubiquitously, for once recognizable not as gray particulate scatter, but as a penetratingly golden brilliance. Its messages are broadcast with precision throughout the assemblage of lightworkers. Among those lightworkers, communication is simple and direct. Most in attendance have dispensed with all pretext of humanoid speech, in favor of instantaneous transmissions of light. Whenever necessary, Mabel elucidates subtler points for the intern, Bulista.

In essence, the lightworkers agree to minimize the impact of their presence. They will remain strictly in the background, observing and nothing more. Dolores' safety is of their utmost concern, as all prepare for the momentous event.

Nevertheless, the effect of the lightworkers' collective presence presented a startling and overwhelming blast, from which Dolores reeled. "My God," she whispered, recoiling and squeezing already-closed eyes. Realizing Terry's vulnerability in relation to her behavior, she tried to control the reaction. "Excuse me for a minute, Terry," she managed.

While continuing to shutter her inner vision, she mentally requested Forwyn's counsel. "What's happening?" she asked. "Is this why his guides have kept him shielded from me?"

Forwyn's compassion is warm and soft within the electric buzz that threatens to fry her circuits. "Let it all keep moving right through you, Dolores. Do not get involved, or grab hold of anything. There are many present is all, but none to fear. Your friend's guides will choose a spokesperson that may speak directly through you if you permit it. We will anchor you, and ground the high frequency. Your body will not be harmed."

She struggled to maintain her focus.

"You can do this," Forwyn reassures her. "Hold fast to your own center and allow the rest to unfold. You do have a couple of choices: First, you do not have to go through with this."

Dolores was astute enough to receive his non-articulated addendum, *"Though all the heavens await this moment."* She glowered as his affectionate laugh reverberated through her mind.

"It's true," he tells her. "You can do what a doctor or a lawyer does when personal interest intervenes in a case. Recuse yourself. Bow out."

"No," she answered. "I've always been curious about

what's up with Terry, and I still am. But how could I possibly have known before now why my access to his higher consciousness was always barred?" She sighed. "I guess I was rude about it. Please excuse my arrogance."

A boisterous jumble of benevolence, from both Terry's and her own guides, engulfs and blasts her with a "not to worry" sort of message.

Once he's seen that she has recovered, Forwyn proceeds. "Your second choice is whether you will be present or absent during the reading."

Dolores' only response was a puzzled silence.

He clarifies, "You can check out, and the spokesperson will animate your body for the duration. Or you can share your body. If you choose the latter, you will be asked to sit back and simply observe, along with all the guides and lightworkers present. We have all been barred from direct participation, with the exception of your client's personal guidance team. You will be held to the same standard of behavior."

"I'm not about to check out!" she told him.

"Naturally, you wouldn't. Alright, stay close to me, and please try not to resist the process."

She sighed again.

Terry was fidgeting. Lacking any prior experience with psychic reading, he assumed that Dolores' long silence and inattention was normal, albeit boring.

Now, she opened her eyes. "Ter, your guides are going to talk directly to you through me. I don't usually do it this way, so..." Her sentence fizzled.

"OK." His voice reflected his disappointment that the reading was to be no more than the usual encounters, rife with reassurances and empty invitations to stay in touch.

Dolores closed her eyes. In seconds, her focus seemed to reach deep inside herself.

"Hello, Terry." The now familiar voice emanated strangely from Dolores' lips.

"Vormis."

"Terry, we welcome you. We are all here with you, now as always, but only one voice will speak with you—no, not me—unless you specifically ask to address someone in particular. We are one. Be blessed."

Terry felt confused already. "How do I know whether I should ask for someone in particular?"

There was a pause, during which Dolores' face went from animated to Sphinx-like in appearance. *"Ease your mind,"* she tells him.

Dolores' voice has become softly liquid. "Terry, to begin we would like to point out the fortitude and flexibility shown by yourself during recent life changes. These are qualities you would do well to affirm and continue to develop throughout the life journey, for indeed, they are among your soul's priorities. You are blessed with many fine attributes and potentials. Additionally, you have available to you a hundred fold more support than most people ever receive, to guide and sustain your life journey. To recognize and give thanks on a regular basis would best serve your current path."

Terry felt a corner of his mind go numb. "Excuse me," he began. "I don't really understand what you're saying."

"Open your heart," comes the response.

Before he could answer that he did not understand the meaning of that either, he felt a shift inside his body. Something like relaxation, or something like a buzz. There was a definite expansion. More comfort.

"Like so," continues the voice. *"Notice this sensation and learn to recreate it at will. From this place and this sensation, you may contact us directly. All is accessible and all is well. You may now proceed with your questions."*

"I wanted to ask why everything shut down lately. I can't find Vormis and I can't paint. I also don't understand why I had to come back to all this." He shook his head, voice faltering as he added, "It feels unfair that I couldn't stay."

In the moment of silence that followed his comment, Terry recalled the last time he had uttered the exact same words. It was during one of his therapy sessions with Tull and Dolores, when he had sought the source of his essential sadness, and discovered resistance to his own birth.

"Yes." The spokesperson answers his thought. *"It is always the same until all learning has been extracted from an experience."*

"What am I supposed to learn?" Terry asked.

Compassion cloaks a light chuckle. "That is what you are working to discover, is it not? We will point out first that much of what you feel is a shared byproduct of your human existence, and is not really personal at all. By the same token, your sense of separateness from our realm is illusory, and exists merely in the mind-programs of your species. Your goal here and now is to break down the illusion and to remember the truth. Yes, it is that same deepest truth that you hold within your 'most sacred place.'"

Again, incomprehension mingled with a triggered memory from the work with Tull. "How did I get so far removed from you that I can't see or hear you anymore?" Terry asked.

"We are with you."

"But why is it so hard to find you anymore?"

"Not hard, it is simply a question of where your attention is focused."

"I don't want to lose my connection with you."

"You can practice staying connected with you. That is what this is about."

"Will I be able to paint again?"

"You have lost nothing, and nothing has changed. It is simply a matter of practice. Reconnecting and refocusing is much like exercising the muscles of your body. Give it sufficient rest, build strength over time and in joy. Always in play. You get too serious about your life, you know, like a grim mission. Enjoy the falling as well as the floating."

"Enjoy the falling!" he challenged.

"Remember the repetition of learning in childhood, and the fun you had in the process? Think of when you learned to catch a ball, or to fish. Even learning to paint carries this vibration for you. It is play, and the falls are a part of the process."

"I don't get the point of being here. You're saying I can learn to reconnect with you, but I feel like I was exiled. Why couldn't I stay dead?"

There was a momentary pause while Terry's lightworkers conferred. A weighing of what he was able and ready to hear. A decision. "This feeling of exile stems from divided will. You made the choice. Are you aware of this?"

"I...kind of...I guess. But why? I can't remember. It was something about Cara."

"Yes."

"What about her? I don't remember what I'm supposed to do."

"Your decision was made from love, Terry. Love is the highest and greatest motivation. In witnessing this other one, Cara, you felt appreciation and recognition of her essential being. You felt gratitude. There is great virtue in such a bond."

"But what am I supposed to do about it?" he persisted.

Dolores' face smiled. *"Nothing at all to do. Relax the mind. You owe nothing to anyone."*

Terry blustered, "What do you mean? Are you saying that just because I love someone I'm not allowed to die? That's not true. It happens all the time."

"Naturally it does. Love does not end with the body's demise any more than you do. You are allowed to die if that is what you want, Terry. You, like all of your kind, are free to choose. The catch is that most people only know a tiny fraction of themselves. To have what you want, you need to know what you want, to know yourself in totality.

"As to your choice in regard to the beloved, you have simply chosen more time to practice the experience of love for another simultaneously flesh-bound being. A most noble and worthwhile endeavor we might add, and, among the most challenging. True love requires that a soul cultivate all manner of virtues."

"So what, are we supposed to be like married, or some kind of couple?"

The voice, through Dolores, laughs heartily. "Heavens!" Then laughs some more.

Terry colored, inexplicably embarrassed. "What?" he demanded.

"Sorry, we sometimes forget the scope of the human mind." Dolores cleared her throat and composed herself.

"It is not necessary to change or impose definition upon the

relationship. Love requires many things, but asks for no particular format or behavior. What it does require is acceptance of all things. You can see how this can become a lifelong goal toward which one may strive."

Terry stewed in silence.

Eventually the spokesperson continues. "Your heart, and thus the will, is divided. Another aspect of yourself yearns to dwell within the Greater Love for which you and all humanity pine. You merely intuited a glimpse of this Love upon the so-called death threshold. You will find that same Love, reflected and contained in the very life you resist. You will not at this time grasp our meaning, but if you undertake the practices we have thus far outlined, you may begin to gain a sense of this."

"Uh, which practices?"

"First, the practice of connecting with your own self. In addition, you may practice acceptance, which asks you to release others from judgments and expectations. This leads you to experience the purest love available on Earth, which is a true reflection of the Love you seek."

Terry barely noticed tears on his face. He felt neither better nor worse than he had at the outset. It was more as if something hard inside himself had somehow broken apart. He could no longer hold intact whatever the thing was, and he felt himself relinquish the effort.

The voice resumes, settling into him like a balm of kindness. "You have done extremely well. There is no reason to fear a cessation of such success. Take heart in your journey. All is well."

"Well?" Millicent joins Mabel and Snarrow. "How would you say it went?"

Their three fields blend harmoniously. Snarrow chuckles, "So much for our participation."

"Was that Management all the way?" Millicent asks.

Mabel agrees, "Pretty much."

"They didn't do too badly, although I can't imagine that your lifestream was able to make much sense of it all. Or was he?" Millicent wonders.

"No, not much, but he is holding up well."

Snarrow points out, "He has become far more proficient at not resisting the unfamiliar."

Mabel agrees. "His greatest strides continue to be in the area of acceptance."

Millicent laughs. "For a lifestream of his ilk it is quite amazing. He might be beginning to rival mine in that department."

They share a resonant glow, thinking of Cara's open nature. The trio of lightworkers link arms, and Millicent addresses Snarrow. "Can you answer my question yet, about the effect the transfer project is having on your role with the lifestream?"

Snarrow disengages his arm and remains stationary for some time. "Yes," he finally concludes. "We are becoming mirror images. As above, so below, as they say."

Millicent sparkles rapturously. "I suppose that is all we ever have been."

~ 42 ~

Terry smiled with satisfaction. He cleaned the brush,

wiped his hands and took a beer from the fridge. Partway out the door, he hesitated before backtracking to dial the phone. "Cara, I want to show you something. Are you free?"

He met her on the street below his apartment, and led the way up to his kitchen. A large and commanding painting was propped on an easel, greeting all who entered the room. The silent scrutiny she gave it was softened by an equal measure of wonder. "Terry, it's beautiful!"

"It's you," he told her.

She tilted her head, half-smiling the question.

"It's how I saw you when I was dead." It took a moment for the strangeness of his statement to register before he clarified, "I couldn't remember for the longest time, but I've been learning to open my senses." He smiled broadly. "And I finally saw the scene again. You were dancing with your band, only all these colors surrounded you. They're the same colors as your guides. I met them then, too. I don't see you like this now, with my regular eyesight, but I think that what I've painted is your energy field. At least, to me, you feel like these colors."

She put an arm around his waist and they gazed together at the painting.

He told her, "I have an appointment downtown. You can come. Do you still want to meet Mrs. Leticia Thorpe?"

She perked up. "The gallery owner with the teeth?"

"The same."

"Terry, I feel so honored," she grinned.

"You are," he told her.

* * *

A festive mood permeates Interdimensional Soul Works, Inc. Workers from all divisions parade holographic projections of their most colorful and eccentric designs, in honor of Pryluck's admission into the ranks of Creative Works. Technically speaking, he will be Pryluck no longer, individual neither in name nor form. Nevertheless, everyone expects they'll be seeing him around, perpetuating the façade of form that Bouffant Head and Diamond Hoops have initiated in fun.

A new intern's arrival disrupts the costume party. Snarrow and Mabel assume their more customary appearances to greet the novice. "You have come at an auspicious moment," Mabel flutters. "One leaves, another steps in to take his place. All in balance." She swirls with satisfaction.

Bulista materializes at Mabel's side, gesturing in the direction of an approaching haze. Like a storm front, its advance obscures the horizon. The cloud comes to rest directly above Snarrow before it bursts, showering him with a fine dusting of iridescent confetti.

Snarrow groans, and Methods Workers pause to observe his evident agitation. "A message from Management," he sighs, extending his field for their view. "You all had better have a look."

Glossary of some terms at
Interdimensional Soul Works, Inc. (ISWI)

Body drop: death.

Creative Works Unit: a department within Interdimensional Soul Works, Inc. CW lightworkers are formless and not restricted to—or by—individual identity, although they often enjoy creating holographic "self" images and characters for their own amusement.

Field guide: departmental jargon for a spirit guide who, at some time previously, has experienced life on Earth in a human body. Field guides can interact directly with human beings (aka lightstreams) via the human energy field, or aura.

Frequency: vibrational rate, as in the electromagnetic spectrum of light or sound.

Guide: (aka lightworker, aka spirit guide): an employee of Interdimensional Soul Works, Inc tasked with overseeing and managing the life expressions of individual human souls. Guides manifest as bodies of light on a subtler plane than that of physical form.

Human transfer: the assignment given to Methods Division Workers at Interdimensional Soul Works, Inc. to reprogram a human being's personality while he retains his body and remains conscious.

Interdimensional Soul Works, Inc. (ISWI): a fictional organization of spirit guides who design, oversee and manage the life expressions of individual human souls.

Lightworker *(in context this book): same as guide, aka spirit guide.*

Lifestream*: (in context of this book, and from an ISWI spirit guide's perspective): a human being during its time on Earth while inhabiting a body.*

Methods Division*: a department within Interdimensional Soul Works, Inc. Methods is responsible for designing and executing programs that run individual human lives, aka lifestreams.*

Person transfer*: aka human transfer.*

Ray projection*: the manifestation into human form of an individual soul, i.e. a human being.*

Soul collective*: a group of individual human souls that share a common larger soul.*

Spirit guide*: aka guide, aka lightworker.*

Sub-personalities*: aspects of an individual's psyche that underlie and influence human perception and behavior.*

Techno-conductor (aka technie)*: programmers at Interdimensional Soul Works, Inc.*

About the Authors

Mooslie Wiggins works within the Creative Works Unit of Interdimensional Soul Works, Inc. Being part of a group mind whose members are without physical form or personal identity, Mooslie is assisted by LJ Swanson, who does have a body, teaches others about bodies, and has previously published several works of short fiction.

LuviaJane Swanson has recently relocated to Asheville, NC, where she has achieved marginal success in adjusting to winter after residing for more than a decade in Puerto Rico and the Virgin Islands. She likes trees and rivers, and sometimes she writes stories.